She lives in Somerset with Richard and their two small and very much adored children, Harriet and George.

Jane Welch's web site address is: *www.janewelch.com*

BY JANE WELCH

The Runespell Trilogy

The Runes of War
The Lost Runes
The Runes of Sorcery

The Book of Önd

The Lament of Abalone
The Bard of Castaguard
The Lord of Necrönd

The Book of Man

Dawn of a Dark Age

Voyager

JANE WELCH

The Broken Chalice

Volume Two of
The Book of Man

HarperCollins*Publishers*

Voyager
An Imprint of HarperCollins*Publishers*
77–85 Fulham Palace Road,
Hammersmith, London W6 8JB

www.voyager-books.com

A Paperback Original 2002
3 5 7 9 8 6 4

Copyright © Jane Welch 2002

The Author asserts the moral right to
be identified as the author of this work

A catalogue record for this book
is available from the British Library

ISBN 0 00 711250 5

Set in Goudy by Palimpsest Book Production Limited,
Polmont, Stirlingshire

Printed and bound in Great Britain by
Clays Ltd, St Ives plc

For Richard, Harriet and George
with all my love.

A huge thank you to a great friend, Captain George Mills of the Lord Nelson (*Jubilee Sailing Trust*) for his invaluable help and guidance on all matters of tall ships and the sea.

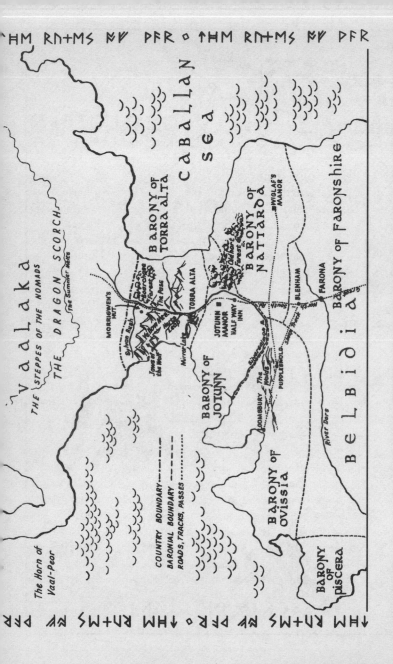

Prologue

She was tired. Every breath that rasped through her body was a painful effort, the cool evening air sharp in her lungs. Her muscles screamed out in protest at their labour.

The deep red glow of the sun shining on her right flank became the centre of her focus and she climbed higher, valiantly thrashing the thin air with her wings in a determined effort to catch the last of the day's heat. Once the sun set, she knew her last reserves of energy would be quickly drained by the chill. And there was nowhere to land. Below her stretched a blue carpet interwoven with silky golden threads where the evening sun kissed the sea.

Her brood flapped feebly behind her, calling to her desperately for help. The two strongest tried to soar upwards to her altitude but, though they were young and she was ancient and withered with grief, they lacked her strength.

'Feeble wretches!' she hissed at them resentfully.

'Mother! Mother! Save us,' one of her sons cried, his red and golden scales becoming a dark crimson in the twilight.

Since there was nothing she could do to help, she didn't bother to answer him but concentrated her thoughts on keeping her wings beating regularly, maximizing the glide between stokes to conserve what little energy she had left.

'Mother! Great Queen!' A feeble cry came from below as one of her daughters glided down on trembling wings, her legs spread wide as she skimmed the water and finally plunged into the waves.

The queen was too exhausted to feel any deep loss. Her

great golden son was dead and, since that loss, no other bereavement touched her steely hearts. Her daughter would drown in time or, too weak to defend herself, would perhaps be eaten by sharks.

She glided on, the sea below now darkening as it fell into the shadow of night. Then she saw it; a fishing boat, its lanterns blinking as it rocked in the waves. And beyond that was the dense black outline of land. She flinched as another of her young crashed into the sea but she had hope now that, perhaps, he might swim to the shore before the sharks shredded him. Easing her wing-beats, she gradually lost height, aiming for a single tall peak that rose up from the island now appearing on the horizon. It was a distinctive isle, tall and rocky amongst the smooth flat lines of its smaller sisters dotted about.

She had succeeded in making the long journey. The sight gave her strength enough to call to her remaining brood and urge them on. Compared to her majestic mass they were small and feeble, but a part of her still loved them for being hers.

'No!' she roared at her smallest daughter, who aimed for the fishing boat, gliding down on wings that could flap no more. But there was nothing she could do as the young dragon crashed onto the deck, became entangled in the sails and capsized the boat. Her daughter's tail thrashed feebly but her body was pinned under the boat and she would drown in moments. But the queen could not think of that. She had to reach land; she had to succeed. She had been promised a means to resurrect her precious son and nothing would stop her.

Crashing into the shingle of the beach, she laid, her two hearts pounding wildly until what was left of her brood landed heavily beside her. One thumped against her side, knocking the breath from her body. Lifting her aching wing to cover the young dragon, she sought to offer her warmth. Huddled together, they lay there all night, shivering pathetically. By morning, two more had died from cold and exhaustion.

The great queen angrily shoved their corpses aside and attempted to stagger to her feet, which sagged beneath her. They needed food and lots of it.

The slanting rays of the morning sun crept across the beach and slid over her body, easing the cold-induced cramp. She was dangerously cold and suspected that all the lesser dragons would be dead by nightfall if they didn't feast. The long, strenuous migration had taken its toll.

Even the heat of midday in this gloriously hot climate was not enough to revive her and bring her to her feet. She needed food. Her young were whimpering beside her, pressed up against her belly. There was nothing she could do for them. They might well die, but their sacrifice would be worth it so long as Silas fulfilled his promise.

It was evening before he arrived. She could smell him; smell his excitement and the fearful sweat from more of his hideous kind surrounding him. With him, too, were bitter-tasting hobs. She recognized at once the shorter-limbed Gobel amongst their number.

'Great Queen, I have never seen you so weak and pathetic before,' he gloated in the hob's ugly barking tongue.

The Queen produced a gurgle in her throat before spitting out the alien sounds. 'Another word like that, wretched go-between, and you die where you stand.' She twitched her barbed tail to demonstrate that she meant business. 'We need food,' she snarled.

'Silas thought as much. He has brought an offering.' The hob waved his long-fingered hand at the huddle of humans behind him. All were manacled to a lengthy chain.

Using her wings as extra support, the magnificent she-dragon pushed herself up onto her faltering legs. She staggered forward, her tongue flickering out to taste the sweet smell of human. The mouth-watering scent revived her and gave her renewed vigour.

'Unchain them!' the golden dragon commanded and Gobel barked the order to the hobs standing guard over the snivelling band of captives. 'I want them to scream and squirm! I want to see their miserable attempts to try and flee me! I want the air to ring with their screams!'

Three of her sons were already on their feet and the pack spread out to corner the humans against the cliffs at the head of the beach.

The hobs released the first human, a young man who did not run but stood over a female, spreading his arms wide in a futile effort to defend her as she, too, was released from her manacles. The great queen scurried forward, her lumbering size beguiling, disguising her sudden burst of speed. A claw sprang forward and pinned the human, the talon piercing his pelvis. In the same fluid manoeuvre, the dragon snapped at the female, who was just beginning to break into a run. While the man bellowed in protest, the golden queen tossed the woman's flimsy body up into the air and caught it, closing her mouth only partially. The girl still wriggled and screamed in her mouth before she slowly closed her jaws, inching her great incisors deeper into flesh and finally puncturing the heart. The man screamed hysterically and she relished his anguish.

'Your kind killed my son! Killed the only golden dragon to have been born in centuries,' she bellowed, though she knew the man would not understand her roar.

At last, she tired of his screams. Raising her other fore-claw, she raked it across his chest, ripping open the ribcage before tearing out his heart and lungs in one easy movement.

Soon the queen and her surviving brood purred contentedly as they chewed on the bones. The queen's long tongue curled in and scooped out brains to leave clean empty skulls. Belching loudly, she watched Silas approach and wondered what kind of a man could stand by and watch his own kind scream, shriek and snivel as they were torn apart by dragons.

Chapter 1

The earthy scent filling the blackness of the tunnel gave way to a strong aroma of horse. Dust and grit sprinkled down from the low roof as something thumped and kicked ahead, the dull thudding echoed back to them along the underground passage. Rollo shook his head to free himself of the dirt.

For a moment, he forgot the others. The sense of their racing hearts and laboured breaths, as they struggled to control their apprehension at being deep underground, receded. He found the experience curiously comforting, much as if he were crawling into a warm bed and pulling the covers over his head. The smell of horse lured him on. It was inexplicably tantalizing; the aroma of fear mingling with the juicy smell of plump horse flooded his mouth with saliva and he surged forward.

His father caught his arm. 'Rollo, be careful! Stay behind me.'

His father's touch sent a cold shudder through his body and the youth was suddenly aware of himself and the situation. 'The dark,' he murmured. 'It was as if I were dreaming.' Shaken for a moment, he let Caspar move on ahead until his cousins caught up and nudged him forward.

'Come on, Rollo, we don't want to be tripping over you,' Guthrey's voice taunted.

Rollo sniffed and marched on. The sound of stamping and kicking was now much louder.

'There must be a horse trapped in the tunnel ahead.' Quinn stated the obvious, his voice strained. 'I thought it might be hobs.' He laughed nervously.

'It must be Sorrel. But Arathane would never leave his horse! Something's happened to him.' Baron Caspar's voice echoed in the tight confines of the earthy tunnel.

Together, the Baron and the four youths stumbled and felt their way forward until Caspar suddenly leapt back, treading on his son's toes. 'Stay back, Rollo; I just touched her rump. An animal of that weight will have a nasty kick on her, so be careful.' He still sounded calm and in control but, ever since they had left behind the last threads of day-light, Rollo could just detect the unease edging his father's calm tones.

'What is it? Why is she here?' Quinn's young voice was anxious as he called out from the rear of the party.

'Uncle, tell us what's going on!' Guthrey's voice demanded more insistently.

'I can't see a thing!' the young woodsman, Gart, complained for the tenth time.

Baron Caspar took a deep breath. 'Sorrel is wedged in the tunnel ahead. Arathane!' he bellowed out and then fell silent. Rather than penetrating the confined emptiness of a tunnel ahead, his echo bounced straight back at them and all knew at once that the way was blocked. They listened vainly for any answering cry but all that was audible were the frantic stamps from the horse's rear hooves.

'What do we do?' Quinn's voice wavered. 'Sir, we must go back for the women. I can't leave my mother up there unprotected.'

Their voices rang abnormally loud in the blackness, the air thick and humid with the scent of horse.

'I can only imagine that Arathane is trapped on the other side of his horse. The roof must have come down on the animal,' Caspar said with steely control. 'I'm not leaving Arathane trapped down here in this labyrinth of tunnels. Who knows what other manner of creature beyond hobs and ravenshrikes Silas kept down here beneath the arena? Guthrey, Quinn, Rollo, get back out to the surface. Quinn

6

is right; you have to go back to protect Isolde, Brid and little Leaf. Gart, you stay with me.'

While Guthrey and Quinn turned and raced away, eager to protect their mother and the rest of the women, Rollo pressed his back against the soft earth of the tunnel wall. Why would his father order Gart, a mere stranger, to remain with him? Did he think his son incapable or was he trying to protect him from a further collapse of the roof? Either way he would not have it. He would play his part.

'I'm staying with you, Father.'

'The first thing a Torra Altan should learn is obedience,' Caspar told him stiffly.

Rollo shrugged, a rather futile gesture in the dark. Still he was gratified when his father changed the order.

'Gart, go with Quinn and Guthrey to the surface. Rollo, you go with them.'

'But Father . . .'

'No argument. These tunnels are not shored up; they could come tumbling down at any minute. Go back with them.'

Rollo did not reply; nor did he obey. He knew Caspar was not able to make him go and he wasn't about to crawl away from danger. It didn't occur to him that his father was right and that the tunnels could collapse at any moment. He simply refused to retreat like a coward.

'Don't stay for my sake,' Caspar told him more softly. 'If you want to prove your love for me, do it by returning to the surface so that I know you will be safe.'

Rollo snorted. 'I'm not staying here for you,' he said cruelly. 'I'm just not running away like a coward.'

Caspar only grunted in response, leaving Rollo to regret the harshness of his tone as his father began to talk in soothing tones to the horse's rump. 'We need another way round,' he said after a minute. 'I can't get past her.'

'What do you suppose happened?' Rollo asked, breathing deeply. There was a rumble through the earth as he spoke

7

and dribbles of fine earth fell like the sand of an hourglass from overhead.

'The tunnel must have closed in and Arathane must have gone on ahead. I'm amazed that he left her; when I first met him a couple of days ago he was completely obsessed by his horse.'

'You're one to talk!' Rollo chided him. 'The way you go on about Cracker . . .'

'I know I feel strongly about Cracker but I've had that war-horse from a colt and he's carried me safely through many battles. And, by the way, he had better be safe and sound with Baron Oxgard.'

'I told you he was, didn't I?' Rollo said in the most hurt tone he could muster to try and stave off yet another scolding. 'I left him at Baron Oxgard's northern castle and he was as right as rain. How can you even begin to think Arathane is obsessed by his horse when you go on the way you do?'

Caspar grunted by way of refutation. 'Sorrel could be his queen, the way he behaved. And now he's left her.'

'Or perhaps the hobs got him,' Rollo suggested.

'All the more reason to find him,' Caspar replied.

There was silence for a moment and in the pitch black of the tunnel Rollo wondered what was going on. He could hear grunts as his father struggled to dig earth away from the horse with one of the rusted hob swords they had taken from the arena above. Clearly, the animal was held too tightly in the tunnel to kick out and hurt them, so Rollo joined his father and did what he could to scrabble at the earth on the opposite side of the horse. It was hard work and it seemed like an age before Gart returned.

'The Lady Brid says you're all to come out at once; it's not safe,' Gart dutifully passed on the order.

'Kindly tell the lady that I cannot leave a friend down here to the mercy of the hobs,' Caspar said calmly. 'There's a good lad, head back on up to the surface. It won't be long now before we dig this horse out.'

'But . . .' Gart mumbled, clearly uncertain as to how to react to conflicting orders.

'Arathane!' Caspar called again but only his muffled echo came back at them. 'Listen, Gart, we're not coming out. Why don't you find a torch and bring us some water?'

'Sir!' the youth replied smartly, evidently pleased to be of service.

They worked in the dark, side by side, for what seemed like an hour but was probably only a matter of minutes before Gart returned, his eager faced swathed in the glow of a burning torch.

'Good lad.' Caspar put down the rusted hob sword and reached out for the water.

Rollo blinked at him. The Baron was unrecognizable; his teeth and the whites of his eyes, glowing dimly pink in the torchlight, were set within a face black with grime. His hair was clogged with earth that also clung to his clothes. Trickles of sweat had turned the soil to a slurry around the edge of his hairline.

Rollo, too, took a swig from the canister and turned to look at the obstacle ahead. The rump of the horse was just visible, packed tightly in earth. Caspar was right; there was no point them all being down here, waiting to be smothered beneath the earth. A moment of trepidation filled Rollo's heart as he imagined the slow gruelling death of suffocation.

'It's hopeless,' he panted. 'We can't dig her out like this.'

'We have to,' Caspar told him. 'Arathane will be on the other side. Arathane would never abandon his horse. He can't . . .'

Rollo grunted, not really interested in the where's and whyfore's of the matter, only that they were trapped in this stuffy tunnel that might cave in at any moment. Should they be risking so much just for the vain hope of rescuing one stupid horse and a man they barely knew?

'What did this man, Arathane, think he was doing charging

a great war horse into these tunnels?' the petulant youth complained to his father.

'He was after Silas,' Caspar grunted as he worked the blade around the horse's rump. 'He wasn't about to sit down and watch the vile man escape.'

As he dug around the horse's hindquarters, a chunk of earth slid away from her back and she suddenly had freedom to do more than stamp. Bucking, she lashed out, catching Caspar on the knee. Rollo flung himself back and only managed to avoid being kicked by the barest of margins.

Swearing and rubbing furiously at his knee, Caspar pushed himself up and looked straight to his son. 'Rollo, are you hurt? I'm an idiot; I should have seen that coming. The poor girl can't see us and she's probably terrified that we're some hob that's about to eat her – rump first.'

'Now what do we do?' Rollo asked, his voice barbed, and he glared at his father for his thoughtlessness.

'Rollo! This is not my fault,' Caspar began to protest in exasperated tones but then paused and looked at him in despair. 'You go back up to the surface. This kicking is only going to make it worse.'

'I've told you, I'm not leaving you. Do you want the world to think I'm a coward?'

'No one thinks you're a coward.'

No, Rollo thought. But nor will anyone believe that it was I who saved everyone from Silas and the dragon. All they would remember was how the strange knight Arathane and Baron Caspar had charged into the midst of the hobs to rescue Brid and Guthrey. The fighting had been so intense and the chaos so violent they would have been too confused to notice that it was his cry that had controlled the dragon. His voice had rung out with that same note of command his late mother had used to control the great bears of his homeland. He drew a deep breath and squared his bony, adolescent shoulders.

Did it really matter that no one had noticed, that no one would believe he had such a power? Watching his father struggle with a loop of rope as he tried to slip it under the horse's hooves, Rollo decided Caspar had never noticed anything good he had done in his life, so what difference would it make now? He was used to it, wasn't he? For a moment Rollo managed to coax himself into feeling better, but in his heart he knew he wanted recognition. As a result of his affliction, all his life he had only ever won sympathy or scorn from his fellows. Wasn't he entitled to the slightest admiration or praise for his bravery?

'Got it!' Caspar exclaimed, snapping tight the noose that hobbled the horse's back legs. The end of the rope was stuffed into Rollo's hands. 'Hold that tight,' the Baron ordered, 'while I try and loosen the soil.' Although hobbled, the great war-horse could still kick a little, but was slowly soothed by Caspar's firm, soothing strokes to her flank. At last, she ceased to attempt to kick and seemed a lot calmer, though Rollo could see thick runs of foamy sweat breaking through her hide and she continued to tremble violently. The animal would soon be exhausted.

Caspar returned to loosening the soil around Sorrel's flanks but it was a laborious process. At long last, he cleared the rear portion of the saddle and stopped to take a drink. Brushing the clods of mud from Sorrel's sleek coat, he revealed old wounds on her rump where it looked as if a vicious hob had sunk its pointed teeth into her flesh. With firm hands, he continued to stroke her flanks, to reassure the animal that they were not about to eat her.

'Spar!' A young female voice echoed down from the entrance to the tunnel behind them. 'Spar, where are you? Come out.'

'Leaf, what are you doing here? I told you to stay with Brid,' Caspar chastised the approaching girl.

'I couldn't,' she replied with remarkable composure for one so young.

Rollo flashed the girl a quick look. She was about the same age as his sister, Imogen, whom his father had left in Artor to take up the reins of command after the tragic death of their mother. He scowled. It hadn't taken Caspar long to find another girl upon whom he could lavish his affections and find even more opportunity to ignore his son.

'I've come to tell you that you must return to the surface. Brid says we must leave at once. Isolde is ill and you have been down here an hour. Sooner or later these tunnels will collapse.'

'All the more reason for you to get out of here.' Caspar grunted. 'Arathane saved us. He risked everything to help us and I'm not leaving him trapped down here.'

The little girl shouldered her way alongside Rollo and looked up at him quizzically.

'You are not what I imagined,' she said bluntly, and the youth was taken back. She looked to be no more than eleven but the way she drew in breath and looked so steadily at him and his father astonished him.

'Cut the saddle loose. If you pull that off you'll probably be able to get her free,' Leaf told Caspar. 'Her hide will slip more easily through the earth and she may well be able to slither free once the obstacle of the saddle is removed.'

The Baron looked at her and smiled wearily. 'Now, why didn't I think of that?' Pushing his hand into the compacted earth under her belly, he tunnelled a small hole big enough for his arm. His face twisting with the effort of delicately feeling his way, Caspar pushed his shoulder a little deeper and then gave a grunt of satisfaction. 'There, that's the girth done!'

Now able to reach up around the horse's back, he worked the saddle back and forth until he was able to twist it sideways and drag it free. Loose earth poured over the sides of the horse and they all worked frantically to clear it back and out of the way.

Using his knife, Caspar freed the hobbles around the horse's rear hooves before leaping backwards, allowing the great chestnut mare to complete the work herself. With her hind legs tucked beneath her, she squatted down on her haunches and used the power in her massive hindquarters to heave herself backwards, wriggling and kicking, until she suddenly stumbled back. Yells, grunts and the clash of metal suddenly echoed around them.

Rollo blinked in the dust, unsure of what was happening as the horse squashed him against the tunnel wall. He couldn't see his father but he could hear angry shouts.

'Back the horse out. Make some room for them,' the young girl was yelling in his ear above the other raucous sounds that so confused him.

'How?' Rollo spluttered, trying to clear the loose earth from his mouth and shove the struggling horse off him. Someone was going to get kicked by those hooves any second, he thought to himself.

'Do something!' the girl was yelling at him. 'Back her out.'

'I'm trying,' he yelled in frustration as he wormed his hand forward and, with fortune working for him for once, managed to get a hand to the reins and gain control of the horse. Luckily, the animal appeared to be well-trained and instantly responded, backing up calmly. It was only then that Rollo saw what was frightening Leaf. There was Arathane and he was in desperate trouble.

Two dwarves swung their double-bladed axes at him and he was struggling to block their heavy blows. The man was near exhaustion as he staggered and stumbled under the impact. Baron Caspar kicked his way past the horse to leap forward into the tunnel and stand by Arathane against the broad, powerfully built dwarves.

'Send Leaf out of here and back the horse up,' Caspar yelled over his shoulder as he blocked an axe blow aimed at his chest. 'Move it, lad. Now!'

Impressed by his father's skill at withstanding the solid power of the dwarf, Rollo immediately obeyed. Poor Arathane, he thought. The man must have been fighting like that for at least an hour.

13

'Leaf, you heard; get moving now,' Rollo growled at the young girl. Unable to turn the horse in the tight space, Rollo painstakingly backed her up. All the while, he cast over his shoulder in fear for his father as the sound of metal on metal rang through the earth. The mare squealed in alarm, reluctant to obey as the dwarves concentrated their attack on Arathane, who was breathing hard, his movements becoming jerky and laboured.

'Get behind me!' Caspar shouted at the big warrior.

'You can't hold them alone,' Arathane protested.

'I can and I will. Give me space! Another minute and you won't be able to fight at all.'

To Rollo's amazement, the huge knight obeyed and stumbled backwards, feeling his way through the broken tunnel. Blood streamed into his eyes from a cut on his forehead and Rollo guessed he could barely see as, arms outstretched, he made for the horse. Caspar roared in fierce defiance as he braced himself against the full onslaught of the dwarves. There was no room for him to swing his long blade but he had time to stab forward at one dwarf, pricking him in the belly. Retracting the blade, he twisted it downward and smashed the pommel of the sword into the dwarf's face. The wounded dwarf fell against his comrade, giving Caspar enough time to take a leap back through the soft earth to where the horse had been trapped.

'Strike the roof,' Leaf yelled at him, snatching the smouldering torch from Gart's hands and holding it high.

Caspar took another step back and, rather than lunging at the dwarf who had shaken off his injured fellow, heeded Leaf's words. The dwarf had but one moment to strike at Caspar's vulnerable body. The Baron twisted away as best he could while still set upon his task. The tumbling earth smothered the dwarf's axe, softening the blow, and Caspar staggered back, watching blankly as the curtain of earth cascaded down, blocking the way.

'It won't take them long to break through,' Caspar grunted. 'Come on, quick! Let's get out of here.'

14

Arathane skilfully backed his horse up and the rest followed as fast as they could. Rollo glanced anxiously at his father, who stuffed his sword into the boy's hand so that he could cradle his left arm to his body. Rollo was impressed that he had made no cry of pain when, clearly, the dwarf's blade had connected with flesh. The tunnel widened and Arathane was able to turn Sorrel. After handing Rollo the torch, he threw Leaf up into the saddle and soon they were able to make much faster progress.

'We'll be safe in the open,' Arathane told them between panted breaths. 'There was only two of them and, even if they find another way out, they won't follow us out into the open of the arena. Dwarves like to fight in bands and they are never foolhardy.'

'Save your breath, then, and run,' Caspar ordered hoarsely.

Rollo blinked as they burst out into the sunlight. Only then did he see how grey his father was. Dropping the torch, he held out his hand and pulled Caspar up the tiered steps of the amphitheatre, barely noticing the crisp bodies that had been incinerated by the great golden dragon earlier that day. Nearing the top of the steps, he paused to look round just as the dwarves staggered out from one of the many tunnels set in the arena wall. They, too, blinked in the daylight and stumbled to a halt. Doubled-over to catch their breath, they looked up at the sorry band of humans but made no attempt to follow. Arathane nodded in grim satisfaction before helping Caspar onto his horse so that he might sit behind Leaf.

As they staggered up the remaining steps circling the arena, the warrior ordered Rollo to gather any discarded weapons before leading them down the steep embankment towards the grassy plain that spread between them and a choppy sea.

Rollo panted from the weight of iron he now carried as they progressed at a steady jog, hurrying across the open ground to a small cluster of holly trees whose leaves rustled in the breeze. Rollo continued to glance over his shoulder but was relieved to see that no one followed. As they jogged after Arathane and his mare, Quinn and Guthrey burst out from the bushes, brandishing swords that they soon lowered.

'Uncle Spar, you're hurt,' the taller youth exclaimed as he saw Rollo's father.

'It's nothing, Quinn,' Caspar assured him as he sagged out of the saddle. 'Help get Leaf down,' he ordered the two youths. As he stepped away from the horse, he suddenly swayed and staggered, wincing and clutching his arm to him. The shorter of the two youths stepped smartly forward to catch him and Caspar nodded his thanks. 'Thank you, Guthrey. I trust all is well with your mother.'

'Yes, sir,' Guthrey replied with military sharpness, reminding Rollo that his two cousins were born and bred to a warrior's caste. 'But Isolde . . .'

'Quickly then,' Caspar ordered.

They pushed their way into the thicket and Rollo was immediately alarmed at what he saw: sitting cross-legged, Brid was gravely hunched over an inert girl lying on her side; her head flopped into Brid's lap.

Caspar sank down onto his knees and looked from Brid to the limp girl in her arms. 'What's happened?' he croaked. 'Isolde was fine when I went after Arathane.'

Rollo was amazed to see tears rolling down Brid's cheeks. Her long brown hair streaked with tresses of red was matted to her wet cheeks and she wiped them away, drawing in a breath that shuddered with sobs. She coughed to gain some composure. 'She cut herself with a rusted hob blade. She wanted to draw blood from her arm and so contaminate the potion within the Chalice to ruin the spell but she used a rusted hob blade. I fear that poison has entered her blood through the wound. She is very ill.'

Brid lifted Isolde's hand and Rollo blinked at it in revulsion. A long jagged scar marked her forearm where the girl had bravely slit the skin and let precious drops trickle into the Chalice. Rather than looking red and raw, the scar oozed a greenish brown liquid and the skin was blackened as if it had been charred. Isolde also appeared to be running a high fever; her skin was blotched with bright pink patches.

'Oh, Isolde,' Caspar murmured, stroking her forehead. 'Brid, she's so hot!' he exclaimed in alarm. The girl looked exhausted and was beginning to tremble.

'We're not in very good shape,' Arathane said heavily, 'and we're not safe here. We must head towards the sea where at least we can protect our backs. Then we can see about getting this young girl fit. And the salt water will do your arm some good, I have no doubt, Spar.' He raised a thin smile but then his face fell again, his mouth clenching in grim defeat. 'I let him get away. I was so close, so very close, and he escaped me.'

'He can do no more harm,' Caspar said brightly. 'The Chalice was broken.'

'Can't he?' Arathane asked sourly. 'Never underestimate Silas. We need him dead. I need him dead,' he added emphatically.

All looked at him a moment before Caspar broke the uncertain silence. 'Rollo, let's have a look at those weapons. What have you got?'

The youth had long since let them drop to the floor. He bent down and laid them out to display an array of daggers, a belt with a dozen knives in it and two short swords. 'A hob sword,' he pointed out, 'and –'

'Of little use,' Guthrey said scathingly. 'The other looks like a short dwarf blade, though. I'll have that!'

'I found it!' Rollo protested.

'Don't bicker!' Caspar growled. 'Your own sword is a perfect fit for you, Rollo. Quinn has the master blade crafted by the dwarves and endowed with immense strength. He found it on the field of battle and so it is rightfully his. That leaves Guthrey with the greatest need. You don't need the dwarf blade but you and Gart could do with a dagger each in your belt. And hand me that belt of throwing knives.' He looked at the dozen slender knives pocketed into a sturdy

17

belt, which was missing its buckle. 'Very nice!' the Baron exclaimed in satisfaction. 'It won't take much to fix the belt.'

His newly acquired dagger at his side, Rollo wandered to the rear of the party. He was ordered to watch their backs while Arathane, mounted on his horse and with Isolde in his arms, took the lead and the two half brothers, Guthrey and Quinn, shouldered their mother, Brid. Caspar limped quietly along beside Brid, all the while looking anxiously towards Isolde and constantly asking Brid how the girl fared.

Rollo scowled at his father and the rest of the party, seeing how all had something to say to one another yet no one paid him the slightest heed. He grunted in disgust at the state of affairs. No one had mentioned how he had saved them all with his magnificent song of command that had cowed the dragon. No one had talked in hushed whispers of his power; they had all dismissed it as an anomaly, a freakish stunt that had, by chance, caught the dragon's ear. He chewed at his lip, watching resentfully as Caspar fussed over Isolde.

Staring from the salt-crusted plain towards the shore, where crisp thistles stood stiff against an early spring breeze, Rollo sucked in the moist air and looked longingly eastwards towards the country of his birth that was further than an ocean away on the other side of the world. For a moment, it was almost possible to believe that, thousands of miles away, his mother was still at home, sitting in her cool marble palace, waiting for him to return. The youth blinked back the tears, realizing that, only a year after her death, he could not fully recall her face. He knew she was beautiful, with dark, almost black hair cropped short against her tanned face, but, though he screwed up his eyes in concentration, he could not reproduce the image of her face in his mind's eye nor recall her voice. All he could do was remember her smell, that faint sweet smell, which imbued him with a deep sense of belonging. But she was gone – gone forever, and only his sister remained in Artor, sitting on its splendid throne as the rightful queen.

Rollo, Prince of Artor, only son of the deceased Ursula,

Revered Queen of Artor, lowered his gaze and stared at the Belbidian soil at his feet. It was so alien to him, yet clearly pleased his father. He missed his homeland; he missed his mother. He looked up and glared at Quinn and Guthrey as they marched beside their mother. How he loathed them for having a mother when he had lost his.

Brid continually reached out to pat her sons' hands and worriedly looked up at both youths, who were much taller than the small priestess. Rollo felt excluded. He didn't even know what to say to his own father. The Baron was clearly injured but was stoically refusing to admit to this since all his concerns seemed to be focused on Isolde, who was being cradled in Arathane's arms as he rode ahead. The Baron obviously considered Isolde to be very important. Rollo knew that, like Brid, she was one of the three high priestesses. Along with his grandmother, Keridwen, they were the mortal embodiment of the Great Mother, as the Maiden, the Mother and the Crone. Their unity channelled great power, to be used for the betterment of all, but Rollo believed his father had more personal reasons for caring about the Maiden's well-being.

He could well see Brid and Keridwen as worthy of holding such lofty positions. Brid commanded immediate respect and had great skill at helping and soothing others. Keridwen, his beautiful grandmother, had been left behind in the castle of Torra Alta helping his father's uncle, Hal, to command the fortress. He held her in even higher respect than Brid. But Isolde was frail and self-apologetic. Her mysterious eyes, which were green shot with flecks of bright gold, regarded all warily as if they had accused her of some terrible crime.

Rollo fell into brooding about how Hal had appeared so unimpressed by his father's return and so reluctant to hand back the reins of command after fifteen years. How dare he feel he owned the place! Rollo glared at Guthrey, Hal's son, as if his father's sins equally belonged to the black-haired youth. Quinn he exonerated from the crime. Who Quinn's father was, Rollo had not yet learned, but at least it was not Hal, whom he had hated on first sight. Stamping along moodily, he became suspicious that there were eyes on his back. He wondered whether the dwarves were in pursuit or if a number of hobs had escaped the dragon's wrath and were now stalking them, waiting for an opportunity. He twisted round to see but could see nothing untoward and so he shrugged away his concerns, glad that the sea breeze was already stirring his hair. He welcomed the change.

It wasn't long before they had crossed the plain, which was bordered to their left by a rocky escarpment. Now they picked their way across rolling dunes, the sand abrading their legs and stinging their eyes as the occasional gust of wind whipped the fine grains up into dancing sand-devils. The dunes led to a wide beach beaten smooth by the assault of rolling waves. The beach headed a narrow bay that probed deep inland. To the right lay grassy down-lands but to the left rose stony cliffs of an abrupt ridge that stretched out as a peninsula into the sea.

Rollo breathed in deeply, the smell of the sea refreshed and calmed. His head was pounding and he only now realized how exhausted and worried he had been.

'Rollo, get some wood,' his father ordered. 'Scour the tide-line for driftwood and let's get a fire going. Quinn, you had better go and find water. Guthrey, help Rollo,' Caspar ordered.

Rollo didn't want any help and he certainly didn't want to be with Guthrey. The youth was very dark with almost blue black hair and bronzed skin in contrast to his own auburn hair and freckled sun-reddened skin that he had inherited from his father. Beyond their quarrel, he had barely spoken to Guthrey. Their first quarrel had been dramatically cut short when a ravenshrike had snatched Guthrey just after Rollo had tried to kill him. After that, they had not spoken beyond the few brief words they had exchanged in the arena when he had saved Guthrey from the dragon. It was an awkward

20

silence that therefore accompanied them as they trudged up the beach.

Rollo had spent much time with Guthrey's elder brother, Quinn, who, not being of Hal's blood, was much more congenial. Although Guthrey was, like himself, only just thirteen, he was very similar to his father in the way he was impossibly arrogant and overbearing.

After long minutes had passed and Rollo could no longer bear the silence, he snapped at Guthrey. 'Listen, I'm sorry. I didn't really want to hurt you and you cannot believe how awful I felt when you were stolen away by that monstrous ravenshrike.'

'Not as awful as I felt,' Guthrey assured him haughtily. 'It hurt! And don't forget I was hauled all the way here and stuffed into one of these dungeons, listening to the screams, the endless screams as the wretched hobs tortured men to death. In the dark, I was left wondering when it would be my turn. You couldn't have felt one jot as bad as I did. I doubt you could even imagine it.'

'No, no, I can't imagine,' Rollo admitted, deciding that Guthrey had good reason to feel vexed about it all. 'But that wasn't my fault.'

'No, it wasn't your fault,' Guthrey told him gruffly. 'No, that was down to the hobs and the dwarves and that treacherous man, Silas. You came back for me. I'm not angry with you and I've already told you I'm sorry for attacking you. That, however, doesn't mean that I welcome you and your father, cousin,' he said bitterly. 'Your father abandoned us fifteen years ago, leaving my father to run the castle of Torra Alta just when the dragons and the hobs poured in from all sides to attack us. I don't see how he has any right to come back here after so long and just claim it for his own.'

'Don't you think we have more important things to worry about for the moment?' Rollo snarled, flinging down the driftwood he had so far collected. 'And who says I want any part of your rotten, stinking barony? It wasn't my idea

21

to come here and, believe me, the first opportunity I get to go home to Artor, I'll take.'

'Go home? Go home to what? Go home to be your sister's little pet?' Guthrey sneered cruelly as he bundled bleached and split driftwood into his arms. 'How can a prince return to his country knowing that his younger sister is queen of the land? You would feel like a fool.'

'She's my sister and I love her. I would do everything I could to help her in her difficult task,' Rollo said nobly, though he knew in his heart that Guthrey was right. It would be very hard indeed to be subordinate to Imogen. Though she did indeed have the mystical power inherited from their mother to control the great bears of Artor, she was still just his little sister.

Rollo regathered his driftwood and sauntered moodily back to the others, only to be met by his father's stiff frown.

'Where have you been? Can't you see she's in trouble?'

Rollo didn't reply but looked back at his father resentfully. Was it any wonder that, already, his father was more concerned about Isolde than he was about him? Rollo stared at the young priestess, wondering what to say. Guthrey had already set off after Arathane and Quinn in search of food, leaving him to stand by, helplessly watching as Brid did her best to cleanse Isolde's ugly wound.

'What's the matter with her?' he finally asked since no one had offered a full explanation. The girl was sweating profusely and looked sickly green. Brid was busily stirring a potion and muttering prayers while Caspar fretted without helping at all. At last, the Baron slumped down, still cradling his arm, and stared glumly at Isolde.

'I remember, Isolde, how I was left to care for you after your poor mother died.'

'I know,' the girl croaked. 'I remember too.'

'You couldn't,' he said in some surprise and then turned to Brid. 'She's delirious.'

'I don't think so,' Brid said wearily. 'Just in a lot of pain.'

She looked at Caspar. 'It is one thing to be in pain oneself but altogether a deeper torment to watch a loved one suffer.'

Caspar nodded and to Rollo's humiliation looked at him with those blue sorrowful eyes and sighed.

'Well, I'm sorry that I've been such a disappointment to you,' Rollo snapped angrily.

'But I didn't mean that at all!' Caspar protested.

'Yes, you did. You were thinking of my fits and how they have brought shame on us and how I am less of a person because of them. I can see it in your eyes every time you look at me. Well, I don't want your sympathy.'

'But I –' Caspar began to protest but Brid caught his arm.

'Leave him be. None of your mutterings will make him feel better. He's blaming you for something that isn't your fault. No amount of reassurance will help.'

'Yes, but –'

Brid fixed the Baron firmly in the eye. 'Now just sit back down, Spar. Stop thinking about everyone else and take care of yourself for a change. I've seen you guarding your arm. I can't do anything more for Isolde until the potion has brewed, so let me have a look at you.'

Caspar reluctantly obeyed and Rollo looked at him piteously. It was so typical that his supposed high and mighty father was already taking orders from a woman. His look turned to one of disgust and his father caught his gaze, held it for a shocked, bewildered minute before the more usual sad and haunted look filled his face. Rollo turned away.

He studied the debris washed up by a past spring tide at his feet and it was a minute before he looked up again and surreptitiously eyed his father. Brid was peeling back the Baron's shirt; Rollo gasped in shock at the sight of the deep purple gash to his upper arm. The skin was gaping and the muscle had been slashed; Rollo could just glimpse white bone beneath. Suddenly, he was angry with himself for behaving in such a boorish manner. How could he have spoken like that when Caspar was so badly hurt? Still, he comforted himself with the thought that, all the same, his father should have said something. It had been foolish of him to make everyone think he was unharmed when, clearly, the dwarf's axe had done serious damage.

Brid also seemed annoyed with him. 'Well, for a start, Spar, you won't be able to use your arm at all until the muscle has knitted together again, and I'm sure it's going to be painful for weeks.'

'I didn't need you to tell me that,' the Baron grunted.

Brid offered him some poppy juice from a vial. 'That'll do you some good and you'll need it while I clean up the wound.'

Caspar made a face.

'Is there a bone in your body that you haven't dislocated or broken?' the priestess asked as she cut away what was left of his shirt. Rollo's stomach turned as he looked at the pulp of flesh and the curve of glistening white. Brid sought patiently through a leather pouch that she kept tied to her waist for various materials and implements.

'Now hold still,' she warned Caspar sternly.

With a fine pair of bone tweezers, she probed the wound, extracting pieces of thread, dirt and grit that had become trapped in the congealed blood. She then doused it in water and took a needle and thread to make deep stitches before closing the wound. The poppy juice was clearly having the required effect on the Baron because he was lolling back, barely wincing at this treatment.

'Well, you're not going to be a lot of use to us in the immediate future,' Brid complained.

Between Isolde's gash and Caspar's wound, Rollo didn't know where to look and stared glumly down at the cracked leather of his boots.

'At least be grateful, lad, that we haven't been eaten by hobs, which could so easily have been the case,' Caspar said flippantly, which was just the sort of irritating remark Rollo expected from his father.

He scowled at the Baron, not feeling in the least bit grateful for anything right now.

Falling into a broody silence, he listened to Brid and Caspar muttering over what possible illness or infection now beset Isolde. With extraordinary composure, Leaf insisted on helping. She was given the task of crushing seeds between two pebbles so that Brid could make a potion for Isolde; it was a task that she performed with painstaking care.

'We need honey really,' Brid explained, 'for both Isolde and Spar. It's the best thing to draw out impurities and we particularly need that for Isolde.' Everyone's eyes were automatically drawn to the child's arm: the suppurating wound oozed dark green pus.

'Will you have to cut it off?' Rollo asked callously. He liked Isolde and her quiet ways but he was hurting inside and, somehow, it made him feel better if he could make others feel uncomfortable.

'Of course not,' Brid retorted harshly and fixed him with her piercing green eyes. She rose, marched up to him and looked him fiercely in the face. 'I don't know what gives you the right to feel sorry for yourself; we've all suffered here. If you want to feel better, start thinking about others. It is the best way to heal the soul.'

'Oh, I am sure that you, a privilege high priestess –' Rollo began but his words stopped in his throat as he caught sight of Quinn leaping through the dunes, hotly followed by Arathane, who looked clumsy compared to the youth's long-legged grace.

'Run for it!' Quinn was shouting.

'Go! Go now! Head for the sea!' Arathane bellowed.

Chapter 2

The stinging cold of the winter sea cramped Rollo's muscles. He did not like water at the best of times but the waves crashing about his chest and the fierce undertow that threatened to drag him down and wash him into deep waters filled him with terror. He was not a poor swimmer but never before had he been so aware of the immense power of the sea. Nevertheless, with the hobs at their back there had been no choice.

In a wild attempt to escape the gang now hollering and barking on the shore, they had plunged into the icy waters and were now wading chest-deep in the waves. Isolde had screamed in frenzied panic but she was unable to resist Arathane as he dragged her into the sea. The tide was in; water swept right up to the cliffs of the steep-sided headland and they hoped to round the promontory whose tall cliffs were unscalable from the cove they had just fled. Both Brid and Arathane were certain that hobs would not follow them into the water and so this course of action was the only route left to them.

To Rollo's right, the murky green of the sea stretched into the horizon. To his left, white foam hissed at the base of the cliffs as another wave beat its head against the rock and disintegrated into a million white droplets that gradually subsided to join the foam. Again and again, like the pulse of the earth, the water washed in and out, a relentless battering ram against the stoical rocks.

His foot slipped on ribbons of seaweed and, for a second, he was dragged under, salt water stinging his eyes as he blinked in the sandy flow and struggled to regain his footing. A hand yanked him upwards.

'Steady there, lad.' It was Arathane who held him. 'Here, Gart, get a grip on this boy before we lose him.'

Normally Rollo would have been humiliated by this but, right now, he was too frightened and too miserably cold to care. Grimly, he clung to Gart's sodden sleeve, his fingers white in the cold of the sea. It was only after they rounded the fierce waters of the headland, where the roar of the sea pounded their ears so that they could barely hear one another shout, that he had enough thought left for the others. On entering quieter waters, he looked around at his wave-lashed comrades. If he had found it hard then how had the injured and the weaker ones managed to fight their way around the headland? With the waves now urging him forward into the cove ahead, he sought sight of his father and with relief saw Caspar's red hair. When they had sprinted for the sea, he had not thought of himself but only of the women. He was in the middle of the party. His hand was fiercely gripping Brid, who was clearly too short to stand in the water. They only managed to progress because she was being towed along by the Baron. Quinn and Guthrey struggled with Leaf between them whose cries of fear were being drowned by the thrashing waves and the echoing boom as they beat the cliff walls.

Standing head and shoulders above Caspar, Arathane still held Isolde in his arms as he was the only one now capable of bearing the girl. The chestnut mare was making her own way, half-swimming and half-leaping through the waters, obediently following her master, who constantly looked round for her. Rollo admired the man's strength and his imposing figure, and hoped that he might grow up to be like this warrior and not like his lean-limbed father. Guthrey had been right; Caspar had abandoned his duty to Torra Alta and, as a result, was forcibly yoked to the same burden of shame.

Another large wave washed over his head but, thankfully, this one swept him further inland. His feet touched down on solid rock and he was able to stand above the waves. The others were close by, shouting in panic to one another, and Rollo realized that, whilst he had been under water, something terrible had happened. They were shouting for Leaf.

'She was pulled out of my hand!' Quinn was yelling. 'There was nothing I could do!'

Rollo turned and, like everyone else, desperately searched the sea for a glimpse of Leaf's small white face.

'The undertow has her! Leaf! Leaf!' Caspar was shouting in despair.

'There! I see her!' Brid yelled, pointing to a spot near where a cormorant plunged into the water.

Rollo caught a glimpse of a thrashing arm. He didn't think. He knew his father was badly wounded and that Arathane was clinging to Isolde and was too encumbered by armour to swim. The thought of proving that he was better than Quinn and Guthrey drove him to it. He saw both half-brothers hesitate a second, heard Gart yell that he could not swim and, without another thought, dived forward, beating the waves with all his might as he kicked out to sea.

His action must have goaded Guthrey because he was almost immediately aware of the youth just behind his shoulder as he struck out for deep water. Suddenly the current snatched him and he was swept out at a terrifying rate. The cormorant dived again, though he was no longer sure where Leaf was. It was so hard to judge distances over the tossing waters of the sea. Guthrey lurched away to the right and Rollo presumed he had seen her. He plunged after him and, a moment later, he caught up with the youth, who was now swimming in hasty circles as he searched frantically.

If Guthrey couldn't see the girl, there was only one way she had gone. Rollo took a deep breath and dived, his legs kicking hard as he struggled to swim down into the murky gloom. He could barely see for the seaweed that was being dragged back and forth by the current. His ears hurt with the pressure but he knew he had to find her.

He kicked down even more, his lungs bursting with the effort until he feared he would not have enough breath left to swim up again and reach the surface. Then he spotted her another six feet below him. She was still sinking, bubbles dribbling from her mouth. The sight fed his strength and determination. He kicked again, squeezing his eyes tight shut in effort. His hand hooked into cloth and he turned upwards, hoping that he was dragging Leaf up by her dress. The surface seemed a mile away. He didn't know whether he could do it. In fact, he became sure that he wouldn't. He had to breathe. How could he stop himself opening his mouth and sucking in salt water? Any second now the sea would fill his lungs and claim him.

Feeling weak and disoriented, he was aware of the light from the surface above him only as a hazy glow. He thought he was still kicking his legs but he was no longer sure. Leaf was so heavy, dragging him down.

Dimly, he was aware that she was being pulled from him. Suddenly, he was lighter and the feeble flaps of his legs now drove him upwards. Even then, it seemed an age before he glided up to the top and the air screamed into his lungs. Below the surface, the world had been muffled and still but, on top of the waves, the sudden violent noise panicked him. Cramping cold bit into his brain. He felt so exhausted and afraid, and no longer had the will to swim through these icy waters.

It was then that he felt the first snagging jab of pain through his brain and the flash of white that shot across his vision. He had been deprived of oxygen for too long; a fit was inevitable. First, his hands went into spasms and then his back arched and the water swilled into his mouth. Spluttering and choking, he did his best to fight off the attack but, even though he was aware of the water washing over his face, he could not stop his body from jerking rigid.

Salt water stripped the lining from his nostrils and the back of his throat. With staring eyes, he watched his world dim. Slowly, inexorably, he sank back into the quiet of the smothering sea. Time slowed. The world and its pain receded. Then, at last, a hand plunged down and yanked him to the surface. Though he was now blinking in the light, somehow, he still couldn't draw breath. Looking into Guthrey's face, he saw that he was struggling with one arm also about Leaf. He was shouting but Rollo couldn't hear a word. Guthrey then whipped his head away to look back towards the shore and slowly Rollo's hearing returned to him.

'Help! For pity's sake, help me! I can't do this alone!' Guthrey yelled back towards the shore.

Rollo was too exhausted to panic as Guthrey's grip lessened around his collar and he felt himself sliding away but relief came when another hand held him firmly. Soon he was being buffeted by waves as he was tugged back towards the shore.

'Can't you do something to help?' Quinn spluttered at him. 'Kick your legs, Rollo. Come on, you've got to help me.'

Rollo breathed hard, straining his neck to keep his mouth free of the sea. For every lungful of breath he took in he spat out a cupful of liquid, but he had gathered his composure and the air brought him strength. Though half-drowned, he knew he had to swim. Dragging his dead weight Quinn didn't have the strength to swim in against the current, and he knew he had to make an effort to stop them being swept out again.

Shoving Quinn off, he struck out for the shore, his eyes focused on the beach. He had swum out much further than he had thought and was able to see both sides of the sheer-sided headland. He could not make out any of the others in the water though he was gratefully aware that Quinn swam alongside to help him if need be. Now he could see his father, chest-deep in the waves, shouting and waving his good arm frantically. The others were on the beach except for Arathane, who was on Sorrel and urging his horse out into the sea to meet them.

Cries to his left made him glance that way and he paused in his feeble strokes. He could still see back around the headland around which they had fled and, as a wave lifted him up, he caught a glimpse of their pursuers. Standing on the beach were a dozen yelling hobs accompanied by three bellowing dwarves, all savagely brandishing swords or axes. They all hesitated at the water's edge; obviously none were keen swimmers. As he drew level with the headland, the waves and the current at last worked with him, easing him up the beach towards Arathane and his mare. Gripping her saddle, he allowed himself to be hauled back up the beach. He was the last ashore but had no time to gather his breath as the others were already running inland.

Arathane, however, urged him forward while he turned his horse and stood his ground. He lifted a quarter-size crossbow, which he aimed towards the headland, covering Rollo's back as he staggered up the beach. But, fortunately, there was still no sign of the hobs as he reached the dunes at the back of the beach. Arathane charged after him and supported him under his arm to help him along until they caught up with the others.

'We can't rest,' Caspar announced, giving Rollo no more than the briefest nod.

Rollo looked at him darkly. Were those the only words his father had for him after he had so very nearly drowned?

Caspar ignored his look. 'My guess is that, since they haven't come after us yet, the hobs will work their way inland to where the cliffs on the ridge between us become less of an obstacle. Then they'll cross over the ridge and come after us.' He waved up at the escarpment separating them from the grassy plain that had led them to the sea. 'Or does anyone think they will eventually brave the sea – the taller ones at any rate?' the Baron panted, supporting his right arm as he ran.

'Hobs hate salt water,' Brid told him, 'so I doubt it. Their skin is thin and cracked along their spines so they absorb the salt too easily. It makes them very ill after a while.'

Caspar nodded. 'In that case, we head on along the beach and try to find a boat. Then we can put out to sea and run along the Nattardan coast until we find a safe place to land.'

31

'I lost my precious sword in the sea!' Quinn announced glumly. 'It was when I was struggling to help Rollo.'

'The least of our worries, Quinn,' his mother told him with a smile. 'We are all safe and, if all we have lost is a sword, I think we've been lucky.'

It was near three miles before they found anything remotely resembling a boat. Rollo's skin chafed from his wet clothes and the salt sticking to his skin; the experience was physically gruelling and, for the hundredth time that day, he wished he were home in Artor. Arathane and Quinn remained at the rear of the party, both keeping an eye out for hobs. At first they saw none, but after they had struggled for about two miles Arathane warned them he could see a couple in the distance.

Caspar had optimistically insisted that this area of coastline belonging to the Barony of Nattarda was spangled with hamlets and so they should have found a boat much sooner. Instead, they had passed through two deserted villages where the boats had been broken up on the rocks and there was no sign of a single person anywhere.

'It's strange,' Caspar mused. 'As soon as Arathane and I reached Nattarda it was as if life had never changed, as if the dragons and the darker creatures had never returned to our sunny land. But here, approaching Jotunn, the coast has been ravaged like the rest of Belbidia.'

Rollo wasn't interested. He was exhausted and still coughing up water; his head was spinning and he didn't know how much longer he could keep going. It was deeply frustrating being able to see but not reach the larger sailing vessels riding the deeper waters of the Caballan Sea, which stretched eastwards. Without the discovery of a smaller vessel on the shoreline, the beckoning sanctuary of the huge merchant vessels was of no use to them at all.

'Hob!' Arathane warned. 'Up there to the left.'

All turned and scanned the hillside. For a fleeting moment, the hob was visible before it went to ground.

'There must be more,' Brid said quietly, 'but obviously not enough yet to give them confidence to attack.'

'Keep moving!' Caspar urged.

They staggered on as fast as they could, spirits low. They were beginning to snap and grumble at one another, blaming each other for their discomfort and choice of plan. But at last, they found a well-trodden path leading down to a stony beach backed by caves at the foot of a crumbling cliff. From out of the cave disgorged an underground river, its roar competing with the breaking waves that lashed the shore.

Arathane boldly approached the dim cave and then halted. 'Well, what have we here?' he asked the shadows. 'I thought we would find no more than a coracle and that Sorrel and I would be making our own way, but this looks ideal.' He was about to step forward and examine his find more closely when he held up his hand to halt the others behind him.

Rollo stared and blinked and at last made out the outline of two men, striding forward to stand protectively before a coveted rowing boat. Two others stood up from where they had been resting. Deeply tanned from their life on the seas, they were thick set, distinctively dressed in striped trousers, and fearless looking. At their broad belts hung shining cutlasses.

With his horse by his side, Arathane stood feet astride, hands on hips, and looked the two men up and down disdainfully. Without making any attempt at a polite introduction he demanded, 'Your boat, pirates, or you die.'

'Ha, ha! You fair-skinned landlubber, do you think we're handing over our vessel just 'cos you're a yelling at us?' One man spat out the weed he had been chewing and then drew his cutlass, twitching it threateningly in his hand.

Rollo sank to the ground in exhaustion and watched almost with disinterest.

'No, not because I'm yelling at you but because I'm going to kill you if you resist. This is your last chance to surrender,' Arathane snarled.

Rollo blinked at the knight, impressed by his stance, and

even more impressed by his action. When the pirates refused to back down, Arathane, true to his word, gave no more warning before raising his loaded crossbow and firing into the belly of the first man.

Rollo gasped, astounded that he had done such a thing. The next sailor was at least quick-witted enough to fly at Arathane before he had a chance to reload the crossbow. With his left arm, however, the knight snatched his mace from his saddle and swung it up at the man's chin, splitting open his jaw and sending him sprawling to the ground. He did not so much as whimper but lay still, face down in the lapping waves. There was a splash from the far side of the boat as the two remaining men dived into the water and made a swim for it.

Arathane nodded at his companions. 'It seems all arguments as to ownership of the boat have been satisfactorily resolved.'

'How could he?' Quinn gasped. 'He didn't have to kill them. They were Belbidians!'

'We didn't have any time for the luxury of negotiation.' Caspar sided with the big knight, which greatly surprised Rollo. 'Now, Quinn, clamber aboard and see if there isn't some form of planking or gangway you can lower onto the rock here. Most of us aren't up to climbing today.'

Quinn smartly obeyed and a few moments later shoved a broad plank over the bulwark and let it slap down onto the stone ledge.

'My Lady,' Arathane graciously waved Brid forward and she mutely obeyed, like the rest of them too exhausted by their trials to make any comment.

The horse was as little trouble to coax on board as the people and it was only moments later that Arathane had the youths seated at the oars. The boat was heavy and Rollo was exhausted but there was no choice. They could not defend themselves in their present condition from a mob of hobs and they had to get into deep water.

Surprisingly, it was a dwarf that made it down to the shore

first but, as the boat ground and bounced down the shallow river and then smacked into the breaking waves of the sea, he was quickly out of range from Arathane's crossbow. 'Heave!' the knight shouted as the boat sloughed sideways and the waves buffeted her sturdy hull. 'Heave!'

Once the boat was beyond the breakers it became much easier. Rollo was paired with Gart while Quinn and Guthrey pulled together and Arathane took the helm, steering them through the swirling brown beds of seaweed and out into the turquoise above the speckled cream of the sandbanks.

Rollo looked back at the line of hobs cackling and barking on the shoreline. Already they were squabbling with the dwarves, but he didn't care; for the time being he was safe. Arathane steered them along the coast until they spied a wide bay and the youths rowed inland, the effort of heaving on the oars driving them to silence. At last, they dropped anchor and Rollo sunk his head between his legs and thought he would faint. It was a few more minutes before he was aware of his father, who now sat at his side, looking pale. The man was sucking in breath through his teeth; clearly, his injury pained him.

'What now?' Guthrey asked at length, and it was very apparent that he was addressing the question to Arathane rather than the Baron. Rollo resented how quickly his father had relinquished his authority.

Arathane sagged down onto a thwart and rested his chin on his hands as they gripped the tiller. 'Obviously, we need food, water and shelter. We have some severely injured in our number, and Silas has got away.' He shook his head at the sorry state of affairs. 'And I so nearly had him. As soon as I have seen all you good folk to safety, I shall go after him. There will be no peace until he is brought down.'

'Who is he?' Caspar asked, all the while looking at Brid who was tending to Leaf and Isolde. Both were wrapped in sacking cloth and sail bags that they had found on board. Their wet clothes had been hung out across the empty thwarts in an attempt to dry them in the breeze.

'Silas the sage, he calls himself,' Arathane growled bitterly. 'Once a very fine and learned man indeed, greatly respected for his intellect and wit. We thought his genius would help us. He brought us hope, but people change and the world cares nothing of it.'

Brid snapped her head up at this. 'The world cares. The Great Mother weeps from her very soul for her children, however foolish we might be, just as we weep for our own young ones.' She looked towards Guthrey and Quinn, who both appeared oblivious to her sombre words. Quinn was rooting around under a sheet of canvas and suddenly his triumphant face rose up into the sunlight.

'Well, we shan't go hungry. Look what I've found here!' He held up a large, round, waxy black object. 'It's a cheese coated in black wax. Those pirates were stealing cheese! Isn't that the most ridiculous thing you've ever heard in your life? I've heard of pirates risking all for gold, but cheese . . . Really!'

'In these times, food is worth far more than gold,' Caspar said heavily, his breathing laboured. The muscles around his injury were beginning to stiffen uncomfortably. 'Now, let's waste less time philosophizing and get it divided up. See to the women first; they have suffered the most and are not as strong.'

'Speak for yourself,' Brid snapped. 'I have indeed suffered – suffered, as none of you could know, since I lost my child – but I am not weak.'

While Arathane began slicing up the cheese and handing pieces to the others, Guthrey lifted another cheese up from a hold under his bench. He thumped it down next to Caspar before clambering over the thwarts with a third to give to his mother. He grinned at her broadly. 'I know it's not your favourite, a bit like me, but it'll do you good.'

'Oh, Guthrey!' she chided him.

Rollo was so hungry he could barely taste the cheese. It

crumbled as he unconsciously squeezed it hard in his anxious fists. After several minutes gorging himself, he realized that he was much more nervous than he had thought. He worried about the poor little girl that had nearly drowned and was somewhat annoyed that his father praised Guthrey for the entire rescue. Not only had the Baron loudly applauded Guthrey for saving Leaf but also had thanked him for saving his son. Rollo scowled, knowing that the truth was Guthrey would never have managed it if he hadn't pulled Leaf up from the bottom of the sea first. No one was praising him for that though.

But now, though Leaf was cold and very tired, he could see she was going to recover and he couldn't quite understand why he still felt so fretful. Slowly, the seriousness of Isolde's condition dawned on him. He wondered why she was so ill from such a small cut.

'Well done, Guthrey! You saved us all,' Arathane said cheerfully as the youth returned to rummaging under the seats and jubilantly held aloft two flagons. 'Get them unstoppered, lad. We could all do with a drink of that.'

The flagons were passed round and Rollo was pleasantly surprised to find the first held water but, even better, the second was filled with a strong-tasting red wine to warm his stomach. He wiped his mouth and passed it on to his father, who raised it in a stiff and tired motion to his mouth. All the while, the Baron's eyes were focused on the stern of the boat where Brid was stooped over Leaf and Isolde.

It was only after Arathane had finished pouring water into a canvas sheet so that Sorrel could drink and sat down beside the Baron that Caspar's attention drew away from the women. While his father and the knight fell into a deep discussion about what should be done now, Rollo clambered over the thwarts to the stern of the boat and peered over Brid's shoulder.

'How are they?' he asked, trying to sound curious rather than too concerned. He didn't want to be seen caring for anyone. He didn't even want to admit that he did to himself.

'Leaf is shocked and frightened.'

'I'm not!' the girl protested. She was sitting up, shivering in the canvas wrappings, a piece of cheese crushed in her hand. She had nibbled at it but clearly was not in the mood to eat. 'I am not frightened; I am angry.'

'We saved you, didn't we?' Rollo protested.

'That's not the point,' the girl spluttered. 'It was a foolish thing to go crashing into the sea like that and now we're stranded on this boat with hobs sitting on the coastline, watching us. I'm angry with myself that I ever considered leaving the Haven. I'm even angrier that I threw in my lot with half-witted humans.'

'We're not half-witted,' Rollo protested, hurt by the suggestion and very surprised that she had said it.

Leaf sighed. Despite her teeth chattering away, she managed a faint, nervous smile. 'I didn't mean it. I know you can't help it,' she murmured and looked sadly around the company.

Rollo tried to view them all through her eyes. Bedraggled and stranded on board this boat with nothing more than cheese to sustain them, they were indeed a sorry lot. Brid looked deeply perplexed and only gnawed at her cheese absent-mindedly as she stroked Isolde's hair.

'She needs strength. Her power, her vitality is slowly leaking out of her,' the priestess told them grimly.

All were deeply concerned by this news, none more so than Quinn who knelt by Isolde and gripped her good arm. 'Don't worry, Issy; Brid will soon have you mended.' He stared glumly at her injury. A deep gash ran half the length of her lower arm. The wound was open and filled with grey-green pus. The surrounding skin had a disturbing green hue.

Rollo was watching Brid and could see from the nervous smile that flickered across her face and the way her worried frown never once eased that something was seriously wrong. Clearly, Brid didn't know how to fix Isolde.

The hobs on the beach shrieked and screamed for two hours or more and there was nothing they could do but bring up the anchor and drift along the coast, waiting to come by chance across a safe harbour.

Caspar kept a very thorough watch on the water, wearily scanning the depths for any enterprising sea serpent that may be sniffing along the coast. Quinn, Guthrey, Gart and Rollo rowed, their tired eyes watching Brid as she sang into the growing fog that rolled down from the hills to their west. Her voice was extraordinarily soft and melodious, the notes in accord with the tranquil sea and the mysterious mist. Soothed and lulled by her song, Rollo hoped it would help Isolde. Though his back and arms ached from heaving at the oars that rolled rhythmically in their creaking rowlocks, Brid's voice gave him ease and peace. He began to feel a sense of remoteness from the shore and the troubles that existed for them all on land. Rocked in the gentle waves, it was as if he were a baby in his mother's arms. Nothing mattered; here he was safe and time meant nothing.

But when Brid fell finally silent, her voice tapering off in weariness, he felt deeply sad and lonely. It was as if he had returned to the time just after his mother's death and that deep sense of bewilderment and loss gripped his soul. At the time the only thing that had made him feel better had been to light a fire and stare deeply into the heart of the dancing flames; the fire spoke to him; the fire beckoned him. He closed his eyes and tried to imagine such a fire and saw only the memory of the blasting heat from the dragon's maw as it swept through the ranks of hobs, shrivelling them where they stood. A flicker returned to his face and he smiled. He did indeed feel better. He had proved his ability to control a dragon, if only for the briefest moment.

Again, he wondered why none of the others had spoken of it. At first, he had thought that they had been too concerned for their safety as they ran from the hobs. Then they had been too worried for Leaf and Isolde. But now they were arguing as to what had happened to that wretched man Silas. None had spoken a word expressing their amazement over how he had mastered the dragon. Could it be that, in all the chaos and the fighting, they had not noticed or had already forgotten? Or perhaps it had been his own imagination and the dragon had been conjured from a wild, savage dream that he had too often experienced whilst suffering one of his fits?

'We must put into shore,' Brid broke the silence. 'Isolde is very cold. We need to get dry and warm and my potions are not purifying her wound. I need to prepare essential oils, which will be far more potent. I need fire. She is very sick indeed.'

Her words were like an ice wind cutting across them. Despite the gash to his arm, Caspar leapt across the boat and sagged down beside the poor wounded girl. 'Put to shore now,' he demanded. 'If she needs fire, we must build one.'

Arathane nodded at this. 'And I must go after Silas.'

'You can't leave us,' Rollo protested. 'We need your help.'

'Many people need my help. I am grateful to you all, naturally, as you risked your lives to get me and Sorrel out of the ground, but I can be no more than grateful; I have to go after Silas.'

'But why? Surely he can do no great harm now that the Chalice is broken,' the Baron queried.

Arathane looked at Caspar and sniffed. 'I have my reasons. Silas and I go back a very long way but, if you had not noticed, Silas seems to have befriended many dwarves, some wearing the bright red tunics of the Secret Guild of the Free Alchemists.'

All looked at him blankly. Arathane stared back at the white, worried faces, all exhausted with cold and the strain of the recent battle as well as their worry for the two girls.

'The Chalice may have mystical powers but it is still made of gold. It might take the dwarves a year to figure out how to fix it but, be assured, in the end they will. Moreover, Silas has wrung nearly all he needed to know from Brid about how to make the artefact work for him. His abilities to reproduce weapons as deadly as the one Quinn lost will be very effective. I have to stop him.'

Caspar was quietly nodding. 'I didn't realize. I thought we had succeeded. You are right. You must go after Silas and it is imperative that you succeed in stopping him this time. So large a task in the hands of one man is too precarious but I regret my priority now is to look after Isolde. However, one way or another we must all get to shore.'

'We can't! Look at the hobs!' Guthrey said curtly. 'We'd be eaten alive before we set foot on dry land.'

'The red cliffs of Jotunn!' Brid suddenly announced. 'They are surely only a little way north of here. The griffins are thick along the coast there and a family of red dragons lives in the cliff tops, presumably enjoying the camouflage offered by the iron-rich rocks.'

'What about it?' Caspar asked dubiously.

'There will be no hobs there; the dragons will keep them away. We would be able to land.'

'Mother,' Guthrey said with some irritation and not the slightest tone of respect that should have been due to her rank and status. 'The dragons will care little if it's hobs or men they slaughter for their supper. In fact, I have no doubt that they would prefer a crisply toasted morsel of human flesh.'

'Well, I would prefer our chances against a couple of red dragons than a host of hobs. These are not like the hugely powerful golden dragon that haunts the Yellow Mountains of Torra Alta.'

'I wouldn't sniff at any dragon if I were you.' Arathane's steady voice drowned out all other discourse on the matter. 'We cannot sit here and wait for a sea serpent to spear the bottom of the boat. We can't sit here and allow this poor girl to die.' He nodded at Isolde. 'We can't sit here and allow Silas time to repair the Chalice and do who knows what other damage besides. He is set on an evil path and he must be stopped.'

'How do you know of his intentions?' Guthrey asked suspiciously. 'What exactly do you know of this man?'

Arathane raised his square chin; the wind lifted his ragged long hair off his shoulders, the spray dampening the white horns of his helmet. He, at last, took the helmet off and all could see the balding top of his head, caused not so much by age but by a heavy gash to his scalp, the wound so deep that the hair would not grow. Rollo looked at it in revulsion. The man smoothed back his hair, his fingers avoiding the bald area as if the wrinkled purple skin was tender to the touch.

'It looks like someone's had a good go at scalping you,' Rollo commented without consideration for the man's feelings.

Arathane slowly turned his head and stared coldly at Rollo. 'It does, doesn't it, Rollo?'

The horse whickered and stamped her foot in a disgruntled manner and Rollo now felt uncomfortable that he had displeased this man. The others had not so rudely pointed out the man's wounds and he regretted his over-eager mouth. They continued north along the coast, still debating their best course of action. As dark fell, they dropped anchor and took it in turns to keep a lookout or to sleep. They awoke early as Brid, increasingly fretful for Isolde's safety, urged them to action.

'She's sleepy with cold and I can barely wake her. We must do something.'

All looked glumly towards the shore, only to see the dark specks of hobs scrambling about the cliffs and beaches. Stiff with cold, Rollo and the three other youths stoically returned to their oars. They rowed on for most of the day until, at last, they spied the red mountains Brid had described. They looked warm and welcoming in the mellow glow of the late afternoon light.

'Well? Do we risk the dragons?' Guthrey asked.

Arathane nodded. 'We go ashore. At least there's no sign of hobs – at present.'

Much to Rollo's surprise and to his mild gratification, Brid actually looked to Caspar to see whether he would confirm the order.

'We go ashore,' the Baron agreed, his voice heavy and weary.

Gart and Rollo were already dipping their oars into the water whereas Quinn and Guthrey still looked to the high priestess for confirmation.

'Mother?' Guthrey queried.

'Inland!' she told them with some frustration. 'You should obey your uncle without question. He is lord of Torra Alta.'

Guthrey shrugged and dipped his oar into the water, straightening out the boat and compensating for Gart's over-eager strokes. They were soon cutting through the choppy shallows towards the high, reddish-brown cliffs of eastern Jotunn.

The sandy yellow bottom deep below them darkened as they entered the seaweed beds. Tendrils of swilling black hair drifted back and forth in the flow and tug of the waves. Rollo's oar kept becoming entangled in the heavy weeds and the boat became sluggish in the water. The black murk made him feel deeply uncomfortable since any creature might be lurking, unseen, just bellow the surface. A splash far out to sea and the sight of a huge tail thrashing the water made his heart miss a beat and, instinctively of one accord, all four youths pulled hard as they hurried towards the shore.

Thankfully, they speeded up as they pulled out of the seaweed-choked reaches. Rollo craned his head to peer over the side of the boat and could see the seabed not far below. It was formed from a smooth pavement of rock that led them inshore towards the foot of the cliffs.

'Steady,' Caspar shouted from the prow. 'Arathane, steer to your right. There's a ridge of rock rising on our left and we don't want to go aground here.'

Rollo snatched a moment to lean over the side again and noted the dark deep fissures slicing into the pavement. In other places these fissures cut right through the rock to show golden ribbons of sand running beneath. Something deep down in the depths flicked through his vision but all he caught sight of was a thin pointed tail. A moment later, a bubble broke the surface and then he was distracted by the sight of dead crabs, lying limply in the foam, being washed back and forth by the waves.

Rollo put his back into heaving on the oars, determined that he and Gart would match Quinn and Guthrey in their efforts to propel the boat. Close into shore the water was calmer, and they were making steady progress. All the while, Caspar carefully directed their coarse to avoid any rocks lurking just beneath the surface. Rollo was just beginning to feel very much happier at the prospect of landing when the boat suddenly reeled violently as something moving at great speed thumped into the port side of the hull. Water splashed into the boat, drenching Rollo's thighs and swirling about his feet, chilling his toes as it seeped in through the holes in his worn boots. It was a moment before he could gather himself and grip his oar.

'Pull hard!' Caspar was shouting. 'Arathane! To the starboard! Hard, hard to starboard!'

Rollo accidentally bit his tongue as, again, the boat shuddered and jarred, sending them tumbling this way and that. He crashed onto his back, his oar leaping from his hand. By the horrible scraping sound and the way the boat reared up on the left, Rollo knew they had ridden up onto a rock and were now stuck fast.

Guthrey was already standing and using his oar to try and push them back off the rock.

'Quinn, get up here and help,' he ordered his elder brother.

Rollo staggered up onto his feet only to see that his oar had jumped from its rowlock and was drifting away on the tide. He scrambled back to reach the next one and watched in alarm as a silvery, snake-like head rose from the water, gripped the oar and snapped the wood cleanly in two before it disappeared again.

'Get us off the rocks!' Arathane was shouting as he, too, clambered over the thwarts and reached for an oar with which to push them off the rock.

Rollo felt confused and panicked as everyone shouted urgent commands and yet nothing was being achieved. Disorientated by the noise and by being flung on his back, he sat for a second on the drenched thwart, watching the water sloshing at the bottom of the boat. A second later, he was up on his feet, his mouth gaping in panic and drawing in deep fearful breaths as the planks by his side had split from the impact of something ramming against the underside of the boat. It took him only another second to get to his senses, pick up an oar and join his companions. They were doing their very best to shove the boat off the rocks as, time and time again, they were rammed. The boat reeled and the timbers screamed and screeched from the impact.

With one last shove, the boat suddenly came free with such speed that Rollo nearly found himself in the water just as another snake-like head reared out from the waves. It gripped the blade of his oar and he was alarmed at the force with which it yanked and jerked at the wood. He flung the broken oar into the water and then struggled to get another spare into position. Once seated, he pulled with all his might, the tendons on his neck rigid and his face red with the effort. Repeatedly, they were buffeted from either side and water was beginning to trickle in through the battered hull. Rollo hoped that Arathane had chosen a good route to shore; they certainly couldn't get there fast enough.

'What vile thing is it?' Caspar demanded though none answered him.

'Just find us a channel that takes us as far into shore as possible,' Arathane told him. 'In these circumstances I'm going to be most happy if I don't get my boots wet even up to the ankle.'

The boat ground to a halt ten feet from the shore and they all sat motionless for a moment, listening intently, waiting to hear another rushing sound as the creatures sped through the water to deliver more ominous thuds. But the only sound was the lapping of the waves on the stony bench of the beach.

Arathane was already standing by his horse, looking about as if deciding what was the best thing to do. Rollo prayed that whatever manner of thing had attacked them couldn't find its way into such shallow water. By their expressions, the others were surely thinking much the same thing while also glancing helplessly at Isolde's prone body. Leaf fearfully wrung her hands and Caspar made a brave attempt to square his shoulders but still stared glumly at the waters.

To Rollo's amazement, it was Leaf who spoke out. 'We can't just sit here. Obviously Arathane is going to have to carry Isolde since he is the most able. That leaves Spar to lead the horse out since he is in no fit state to use a sword and fight if need be. The four boys will have to run fast and, hopefully, keep any attack at bay. Brid should go up on the horse where she shall be safest. I shall just have to do my best to run.'

'Do you think it's safe?' Guthrey queried.

Leaf shook her head. 'Although they haven't attacked, I think we can safely assume that they can reach the shallow waters,' she concluded.

All looked at her blankly.

'We've only been skimming over the rocks as it is and they have had no trouble squeezing out from between the narrowest of fissures. They may be powerful but they are certainly slender enough to hunt along the shoreline.'

Rollo braced himself. He stood on the prow of the ship, taking Arathane's right while Guthrey flanked his left. His eyes searched the water and he saw nothing, yet his imagination turned the very foam into savage, writhing creatures.

'On three,' Arathane commanded.

Rollo and Guthrey nodded.

'One . . . two . . . three!'

Chapter 3

Rollo was at a disadvantage. He was right-handed yet it was his left side that was exposed. The shore was no more than ten yards away but, the second he plunged into the thigh-deep water, a distinctive arrow-shaped ripple darted towards him.

'Keep running, boy,' Arathane was shouting at him. Though encumbered with Isolde, the big warrior was making powerful strides through the water.

Rollo tried to run but his foot twisted on a loose rock. Down on one knee, he was immediately a couple of yards behind Guthrey and Arathane.

'Rollo!' Caspar shouted from behind him. 'Look out!'

Rollo tried to raise himself fast enough but he was scrabbling hopelessly in the water.

'To your left,' his father warned as Rollo thrashed, managing to slash back and forth with his blade but failing to get any clear view of what attacked. But the sea was suddenly red as his sword dug into flesh and a long silvery body about ten feet long floated to the surface.

He could hear the sound of splashing behind him. 'Get up and run, Rollo,' Caspar urged as he bounded through the water towards him, dragging the horse behind him. Brid sat tall on the mare, clinging to Leaf in her arms, who squealed fearfully.

The boy managed to take only one pace before something bit his ankle. He had time to gasp in air before he was pulled under and dragged rapidly along the smooth, stony platform of the seabed. He came to the surface twice and snatched air, only to be dragged down again. Already, he had lost his sword and had nothing with which to hack at the thing holding his ankle.

He stuck fast. The creature was trying to pull him down into one of the narrow fissures but his leg had jammed. The silvery creature was tugging hard at his foot and Rollo half hoped and half feared that his foot would soon be severed. Though he did not want to lose his foot, it seemed it might be the only way he would survive.

Though growing rapidly weaker and faint from lack of air, the intense fear of death was still with him. Panicking, he did his best to struggle and his arms feebly clawed at the water. A strange screaming sound filled his ears and in his panicked, confused mind he could only assume that it came from the vile slithering monsters that lurked at the root of this fissure. He wanted to scream back but only a faint stream of bubbles escaped from his mouth.

Through a haze of black, he saw shapes moving about him in the water. Something was dragging at his arms and he thought he would be pulled in two. A sharp pain stabbed through his ankle and then, with a rush, he was free and being hauled up to the surface.

He could not take in what was happening, only that he was being held under his arms and dragged through the shallows and up onto the beach where he was laid down. A second later, Brid was thumping his chest and he could see her shouting at him though he could not hear her words.

Sound returned with a sudden explosion. Caspar was shouting to the others to form a circle and stand guard; the horse was shrieking fearfully; the sound of swords slashing through the air and clattering against rock were mixed with cries of fear and grunts of effort.

'Whose bloody idea was it to land here?' Guthrey was demanding in anger.

It was only then that Rollo knew he was going to be all right. He coughed up water and a slither of seaweed that had been sucked down into his throat. A second later, he was able to breathe more freely.

'We've got to get across the shingle and up onto the cliffs and the marram grasses,' Leaf was shouting from Sorrel's back. 'They won't be able to follow us there.' It was only then that Rollo realized that they were still under attack from the silvery creatures. Despite his weakened state and the fact that he could still barely breathe, he desperately struggled to get to his feet. His father took him under one arm and Quinn took the other.

'What the hell are they?' Rollo gasped.

'They're only eels,' Caspar said calmly, supporting his son as Rollo attempted to put his weight down on his left foot. Pain screamed through his ankle and he looked down to see blood oozing out through a number of puncture holes in the leather of his boots. He looked wildly about him. Everyone was standing in a tight knot about him, even Isolde, who stood in a trance-like state as Brid struggled to aid her. The others used swords or simply hurled pebbles at the silvery snake-like creatures that flipped, wriggled and squirmed towards them from all quarters through the stones. Some even came straight out of the shingle itself, like worms rising from the soil, as they pushed aside the rocks.

'We move as one unit,' Caspar ordered. 'Keep a sharp look out.'

They crabbed across the shingle, heading for a shoulder of rock that dipped towards the beach. Rollo was barely aware of the pain in his ankle as he picked up pebbles and flung them viciously at the red, screaming mouths with their needle sharp teeth.

Quinn gave out a yell of pain. Guthrey was instantly beside him and, with one swift slash of his knife, dispatched the ten-foot-long creature that had embedded its pointed teeth into his half-brother's calf.

It took at least another five minutes to reach the head of the beach. Guthrey scrambled up onto the ledge of rocks that rose above the shingle and helped the others up behind him. Even Sorrel, with Leaf clinging to her back, eyes squeezed shut against her fear, managed to haul herself up. Caspar led her, taking a careful route over the rocks and up onto coarse blue-grey seagrass that whispered in the stiff offshore breeze. None took their eyes off the ground as they picked their way and wound back and forth, up through sandy rocks, until they all found themselves on the dusty grassland.

Up here, there appeared to be no sign of the silvery sea-creatures and, within minutes, the company staggered to a halt. Rollo sagged to the ground and Leaf slid from Sorrel's back, shaking with fear, big tears rolling down her cheeks. Eventually, she fled to Brid and clung to her, burying her head against the woman's bosom. Rollo wished he could do the same and that he, too, could find solace with the high priestess. But Brid was too preoccupied with Leaf and Isolde to help anyone else and so, after a moment of checking the ground about them, it was Caspar who knelt by his son's side. He gave Rollo a brief smile.

'There's nothing else dry to wrap you in for the moment but you can at least have my cloak.'

Rollo was too exhausted even to nod in response.

Moving awkwardly because of his wounded arm, Caspar bent down towards his son's ankle. 'We'll have to get this boot off,' he said softly.

Rollo nodded cautiously, aware that he felt somewhat sick. He dreaded seeing what mess had been made of his flesh.

Caspar raised his head and called out gently to Arathane. 'I can't do this alone. Can you help?'

The man nodded but, before kneeling, sent Gart and Guthrey off to scour the layout of the land and discover somewhere safe for the night. The two hurried away, leaving Quinn behind to grimace at his own leg though the lanky youth waited patiently for his turn to be attended to.

Arathane slit Rollo's boot down through the leather over his calf and foot so that he could more easily slide it off without hurting the boy further. Rollo looked in revulsion at the ragged tears and deep puncture wounds where the creature's teeth had locked around his ankle. Alongside that was a long straight slice, the flesh peeling back from the neater wound.

Caspar made a face at it. 'I couldn't get to the wretched eel. I was trying to stab at its head but it was impossible to do without cutting you. I thought I was going to have to cut your leg off.'

Feeling intensely queasy at the thought, Rollo closed his eyes and sank back. His father moved across to Brid to ask for advice on dressing the wound but she complained that her herbs were all spoilt or lost in the salt water.

'The best you can do for now,' she said calmly, 'is to bandage it firmly. Once we have a fire going, I can purify my needle in the flames and stitch up the tears in the skin.' The priestess then looked at her older son. 'I don't think your wound is as bad but you'll need the same treatment.' She smiled at Quinn warmly and squeezed his hand, offering her sympathy.

'What were those creatures?' he asked.

'Eels, of course,' his mother replied.

'Eels. I've caught eels in the Silversalmon and they're about eight inches long. Those were huge and could move on the land.'

'Eels can live for some hours on land,' Brid told him.

'In better days, it would make fine sport to come down to these beaches and hunt the eels – lively villains that they are!' Caspar suggested, making light conversation. 'But I would not choose to approach from the sea nor to stalk them without dogs to draw them off.'

'You would lose a fair few dogs to the eels,' Rollo groaned, thinking the idea preposterous. He for one would be a lot happier if he never saw an eel again, nor would he ever walk confidently on any beach again since he would always be fearful of what might lurk beneath each stone.

Guthrey returned after about a quarter of an hour and nodded north along the cliffs. 'There's a hermit's cave that way. And the hermit is in. There's a good fire and he seems harmless enough.'

Brid looked at her son with disdain. 'Never make the mistake of thinking anyone is harmless,' she scolded.

It seemed to Rollo to be a very long walk to the hermit's cave. Their relief to be free from the hobs and the eels was somewhat tapered by the sight of a black silhouette lancing across a smoky evening sky. Huge wingtips and a barbed tail stretched out from a lean body. A long thin neck thrust forward, revealing the distinctive outline of a dragon. As it twisted and the rays of the sun flashed off its back, a glint of red filled its outline. For a full moment, the company stood still and stared, wondering, fearing that the flying monster might turn towards them but, instead, it made inland. The relief was tangible.

Since his foot so pained him, Rollo rode Sorrel and supported Isolde in his arms. He was disconcerted to feel the chill on her skin and yet could see she was sticky with sweat. He looked down at her face and was alarmed to see that, though her expression was stiff with pain, she had lapsed back into a stupor. Unable to witness her pain any longer, he lifted his head to study the way forward. A sandy track along the edge of the cliff-top dipped down into a fold in the rocks where it turned into a stony path. They picked their way along it towards the hermit's cave where they were greeted by the sweet smell of wood-smoke.

The man within did indeed seem harmless and Rollo was very much inclined to agree with Guthrey's opinion. The older generation was, after all, ridiculously over-cautious. The middle-aged man dressed in a heavy wool gown welcomed them in with a rather begrudging grunt and looked out beyond them, his eyes flitting across the skies to check for danger.

'Come in,' he said hoarsely and then coughed to clear his throat. His tone was strained as if speaking were alien to him. 'Sit down by the fire.' He offered them some warm water and a bowl of boiled seaweed, which he had evidently just prepared for himself.

Rollo looked at the meagre offering in disgust and wondered whether they were all meant to share it. 'I am not hungry,' he said in a surly manner.

'Please excuse my son,' Caspar hastily interjected. 'He has suffered a nasty wound and is not himself.'

The man nodded and he studied each of them in turn, his quick eye flitting over the shabby clothes and accumulated wounds. 'Well, it makes no odds to me whether you accept my fare; there's more than enough for my needs and I shall not go hungry. Nothing to do but eat here,' he said after a brief pause, but then fell back to his silent study of them.

Caspar coughed insistently as if to remind him of their presence.

'But where are my manners?' the man said more brightly after a moment's pause. 'I've been on my own too long and have forgotten what it's like to have company. What am I doing offering you this? I only thought to have a bit of seaweed myself by way of variety but you're probably not accustomed to the stuff. It's an acquired taste. It's lucky for you that I caught the very best seafood only this morning. I must get the frying pan out!' He prattled on harmlessly enough but Rollo thought his gabbled words were too much of a contrast to the way the man still eyed them with such quiet consideration.

Rollo's doubts, however, were forgotten when the hermit cheerfully sprang up and hurried out to a sack that was hanging from a tree near the cave's entrance. He dragged out a six-foot-long eel, which he swiftly beheaded, leaving the head for the grateful gulls, and Rollo felt queasy at the sight of the creatures that had nearly dragged him to a watery grave. Even though it was dead and lacked its head, he still felt nervous at the sight of the carcass. He felt better when it had been sliced into thin fillets and dropped into the sizzling fat of the hermit's frying pan.

Brid was busily searching through her herbs and tutting

over the sorry, damp mess. At last, she found her precious steel needle, which she held into the fire to singe the tip. 'Let's take a look at you, Rollo,' she said in such away that the boy felt it was more like a threat.

She looked sideways at the long gash to his ankle. 'Strange teeth, those eels had.' She glanced at Caspar. 'Couldn't you have been more careful with your son?'

Caspar gave her a half smile. 'As I said, I was afraid that I might actually have to cut his foot off.'

Rollo was deeply affronted by the light-hearted manner his father used. 'Well, I'm glad you think it's funny that I nearly drowned twice in one day.'

'I never said that.' Caspar looked offended and distressed by the accusation but was soon distracted by the high priestess.

'Do not trouble yourself with explanations, Spar. The boy will think what he will.'

'Ow!' Rollo protested as Brid began to stitch his torn skin back together.

'You're a strong lad. My boys would not protest at this and nor should you,' Brid scolded him.

'You are their mother; no doubt you show them more kindness than you show me,' Rollo accused her.

Brid only gave him a firm dismissive smile and refrained from entering into any argument. As soon as the gash was neatly stitched, she wrapped seaweed about the wound and told him to eat eel whether he liked it or not. Without giving him any more sympathy, since she was apparently satisfied that he would mend, the priestess turned her attention to Quinn's calf before returning to Isolde.

'I had thought that the sea water might draw out some of the impurities. I have never seen a wound go bad in quite the same way and I have seen far more than my fair share of wounds in my lifetime,' the priestess mused. She began stirring the embers of the fire with a long knife taken from her belt but her movements were far from absent-minded. Rollo realized with shock that she intended to apply the scorching heat to Isolde's arm.

'Hold her down, Arathane, in case she wakes,' Brid told the warrior, who looked at Isolde and raised his eyebrows.

'She looks too frail to suffer such treatment. Are you sure it's wise?' he queried.

'Look at her arm,' Brid told him angrily. 'You tell me whether you have ever seen someone survive such a wound. We must do what we can, otherwise . . .'

Arathane nodded and, with a cold hard look stiffening his face, leant over the girl and pressed his hands down on her wrists. The second Brid touched the smouldering stick to Isolde's skin, the young girl was awake and screaming wildly. Rollo felt his stomach tighten and he forgot his own pain for the moment. Though Isolde writhed and shrieked, Brid continued her torture until she had dabbed the glowing blade over every inch of the eight-inch-long scar.

Leaf looked on in horror. 'You are barbarians,' she accused once Brid stopped.

Isolde rolled up into a ball, sobbing, but it was only a matter of minutes before she had sunk back into her stupor.

'What now? What more can we do for her?' Caspar anxiously asked Brid but she pushed him aside and walked to the cave entrance, breathing deeply and clutching at her stomach as if her deed had deeply sickened her. When she turned back there were tears in her eyes and she would not speak. Deliberately avoiding anyone's gaze, she went to the back of the cave where she curled up in her cloak.

Caspar sat soothing Isolde's matted hair. Though Rollo felt sorry for the girl, he was angered that his father did not so much as look at him.

'Poor Isolde,' the Baron soothed. 'Sleep now, sleep. Do not worry; Brid is here and she will soon cure you.'

To Rollo's surprise, Leaf snorted sceptically at this remark. 'Do you think so?' she murmured just loud enough to be audible.

Caspar snapped his head round. 'Yes, of course! There is no one as skilled as Brid at healing. If a man is strong enough to live more than an hour after his injury is inflicted, Brid will cure him.'

Leaf looked doubtful. 'Poor Isolde,' she murmured softly.

'Brid will heal her!' Caspar emphatically repeated, though his hand was atremble and his wide eyes beheld Isolde fearfully.

'I hope so,' Leaf sighed but there was no note of confidence in the girl's voice and her lack of conviction in Brid's ability to save Isolde rubbed off on Rollo.

He stared at the grotesque area of skin on Isolde's arm. A green tinge was spreading out from the open wound that still oozed a thick, very dark green pus. The surrounding skin looked strangely dry and shrivelled and had puckered into tiny wrinkles. He sniffed. It was also beginning to smell.

'Surely it's gone bad. I don't understand why Brid hasn't cut the arm off if it's bad,' Rollo complained, deeply aggrieved for Isolde. He had known her only a short time but he liked her undemanding manner and she had been kind to him.

'Nor do I,' Arathane commented. 'Surely it's gangrenous. One swift clean stroke with a sword –'

'I have never seen gangrene so I am not fit to judge, but clearly Brid doesn't believe it is, otherwise I'm sure she would have severed the arm straight away. Other than that, some hob infection may have entered her body through the wound. She's feverish and weak and she will only be weakened further if we butcher her arm unnecessarily,' Leaf explained authoritatively.

While Caspar paced, flexing his fingers in anguish, Brid gathered herself together and soon returned to hold Isolde's hand.

'We must get her back to Keridwen as quickly as possible. Once we are home where the herbarium is full of herbs gathered from across two continents, we shall be able to help her.' The priestess bit her lip and, with a shaking hand, pushed back her tangled hair from her face before bending down to examine the wound again. It was now bubbly where it had been charred by the burning iron. Beyond the gash, which

56

Brid had attempted to cauterize, the faint greenish tinge had spread out and upwards towards the elbow, staining Isolde's pale skin.

'What do we do now?'

'Get back to Torra Alta as fast as possible,' Brid said without hesitation.

'It's a long way, and from here the going is very difficult and dangerous,' the hermit reminded them. 'She will suffer terribly and all for nothing because she will never last that long even if you do get past the red dragons and the hobs. It would be a kindness to let her rest here where you can ease her pain as much as possible until the end. If I were you –'

His words were throttled from him by Guthrey who flung himself across the cave floor at the stranger. It was then that Rollo first realized the youth's depth of passion for the girl. Guthrey, however, was halted in his attack by a blade suddenly pricking his neck. Extraordinarily, the harmless-looking hermit had anticipated the assault and, from somewhere within his grubby and torn habit, had snatched out a small knife, which he jabbed at his assailant's neck. Already his other hand was on the boy's hair and was pulling him back. Slowly, the pair rose to their feet.

'A mighty fine way to treat your host, I must say,' the hermit said casually, though he didn't remove the knife.

'Sir, sit down. The boy meant no harm,' Caspar said calmly though his eyes lost their pained look and regained an air of alertness.

'Meant no harm? His fingers were on my throat.'

'Please, let me answer for the boy.' Caspar rose and slowly approached, his good arm stretched forward in a conciliatory gesture. 'He has been through a lot lately and the girl is like a sister to him.'

'We have all been through a lot lately,' the hermit said with a sigh, shoving Guthrey back against the wall. Arathane caught the youth and held him tight, preventing him from flying at the hermit again. Since Guthrey continued to snarl and snap, it was quite plain that he had no intention of becoming peaceable.

'I was merely pointing out that it was a very cruel thing to increase the girl's suffering so,' the hermit explained, his eyes all the while on Guthrey.

Rollo was inclined to agree and yet he could not bear the alternative of not doing everything they could to save her. Quinn had gone quite white and Caspar and Brid had become unnaturally quiet, their eyes flitting between the diseased priestess and each other as if desperately seeking an answer.

'There has to be something we can do,' Quinn croaked and Rollo realized just how much these Torra Altans loved the quiet young priestess.

Brid tried to speak but the words would not come. She hastily wiped her eyes and then began to fidget with her hair, which hung in tangled knots from her head. She coughed and a thin voice managed to squeeze through her throat. 'I am inclined to think that our friend here,' she nodded towards the hermit, 'is right. The travelling may well be making her worse.'

Caspar bit his lip pensively. 'She is very sick. If we don't get her home, she may well die. Sixteen years ago her mother made me promise I would look after her daughter and I shall not go back on that oath. Sadly, she may suffer but, while she is still alive, there is hope. Somehow, we must get her home to Keridwen. Between you and Keridwen, you will find a cure, Brid.'

'We could head due north along the coast and then west through the Yellow Mountains towards Torra Alta; that is surely the safest route,' Brid said, brightening.

'You won't get anywhere near the Yellow Mountains, not any more,' the hermit assured her. 'Not without a trained army all about you.'

'We have to; it's Isolde's only chance,' Caspar said grimly.

The man dismissively tossed his head. 'Well, it's nothing to me what you do, but you won't get through. The hobs are encamped all along the southern edge of the Yellow Mountains and have spread towards the castle of Torra Alta itself. They have broken the country in two and severed Belbidia's land-link to the rest of the countries of the Caballan Sea; it's impossible to reach Torra Alta.'

After a moment's heavy silence, Caspar grimly nodded. 'I see. And what of Baron Oxgard?'

'You think I know everything here, hiding out in my cave?' the man grumbled. He sniffed and then rubbed at his nose, eyeing the Torra Altans. He sighed as if resigning himself to giving the truth. 'I've heard it both from men of Jotunn and Nattarda, who fled from one foe or another past my beach. It's common knowledge that he retreated from his northern castle the minute the hobs concentrated their numbers on Torra Alta's border.'

Caspar nodded gratefully for the news. 'I don't blame him. Let's hope he took Cracker with him and didn't leave my horse on the borders to be eaten by hobs.' The Baron laughed nervously and Rollo sensed how anxious his father was to see his old stallion again. These last few weeks must have been the longest that they had ever been separated.

'We must leave as soon as it's light,' Brid began. 'What on earth has enticed the hobs north towards Torra Alta, I wonder.'

'Food,' the strange man replied succinctly.

Rollo listened to the words being banded back and forth between the adults and went to sit by Isolde. All the noisy argument was confusing and he felt giddy and weak. He took steady, deep breaths. In all his childhood, he had suffered a fit maybe only once a season but, since his mother's death and the subsequent times of strife that had been thrust upon him, the seizures of his mind had threatened to grip him almost every week. He forced himself to nibble at the eel meat in the hope that it might strengthen him.

Quinn looked at him in disgust. 'How can you eat when Isolde is so ill?'

'I thought you Torra Altans always ate rather than being cowed by your emotions. I thought you were meant to be oh-so-very-tough-and-determined. It won't make her feel more pain or put her in any more danger if I eat,' Rollo snarled though, indeed, the food did feel as if it were choking him as he drew it down his tight throat. Rubbing his temples, which throbbed painfully, he tried to think of soothing thoughts that might still his whirring mind. Closing his eyes he imagined the sweet smell of his mother's hair. He would never forget that scent and Isolde always reminded him of it since, like his mother had, she washed her hair in lavender water.

It distressed him that he could no longer clearly recall his mother's face and so, hurriedly, he pushed that thought from his mind and tried to think of something that might better steady his thoughts. Remembering his beautiful colt, Chieftain, he imagined he was racing across an open plain. Then, fancifully, he pictured himself to be like Arathane, a powerful and respected knight, a knight that could slay monsters and drive back armies. Perhaps he had even slain dragons. The thoughts delved deeper into his fantasy world but, rather than picturing slaying a dragon, he revelled more in the invincible feeling of being able to control the beast. I shall be a great dragon-lord, he thought to himself, remembering how the golden monster had clutched him while spewing its torrent of flame over the enemy. He had felt like a king; invincible, respected and adored by his subjects.

The memory of the dragon became more vivid. He recalled the purring hum that had filled the dragon's throat momentarily before she belched fire and, strangely, it seemed a deeply soothing sound. He looked up and was aware that he felt very much calmer and more controlled now, his mind eased and pleasantly numbed.

'If Brid cannot help her, what makes you think that Keridwen will?' Leaf quietly asked Caspar, while she sat with Rollo's boot in her lap, doing her best to repair it with coarse stitches.

'She is older and wiser,' the Baron replied.

Brid nodded. 'There is very little in this world that Keridwen does not understand.'

'Keridwen is a woman? An ordinary, human female?' Leaf asked.

Caspar nodded. 'Of course. She is my mother.'

'Oh,' Leaf said blandly but in tone that might have been construed as somewhat dismissive.

'We have to do everything we can to help Isolde,' Caspar said with irritation towards the precocious child. 'Do you have a better plan?'

'I do, indeed. Keridwen may be wise but she will not be as wise as the learned scholars in my realm. Father was once considered the sagest of their number and, if his mind could be brought to lucidity for just a moment, he would, I'm sure, have an answer.'

'I'm sorry, Leaf, but I met your father; he is completely mad,' Caspar bluntly pointed out.

Leaf stared back at him defiantly. 'I know! Don't you think I know? He may have lost his wits, but there is still so much knowledge within his head, and in his time he would have known a hundred times more than Keridwen may ever hope to learn.' Leaf sighed heavily, her eyes glazing as if she were looking inward on an image of her own lands. 'Besides, we are a people who write everything down. If he has no words of wisdom, I shall find a book on the matter. Books always provide answers,' Leaf said confidently.

'You know nothing of Keridwen,' Brid bristled.

'I know that she is human and so can never reach the intellect of one of the great scholars from the hidden realm,' Leaf argued without any of the emotional show Brid displayed.

'If your people are so infallible then why have they not solved their own dilemmas?' Guthrey demanded. 'You told us that you are all infected with some irreversible mind-rotting disease.'

'Don't be so harsh,' Brid scolded her son.

Leaf shrugged. 'I have no wish to argue; I am merely presenting the facts as I see them.'

Eyeing them warily, the hermit attempted to offer them all more eel though none would take it.

Guthrey opened his pack. 'I still have a round of cheese from the boat,' he said brightly.

Quinn and Gart both nodded enthusiastically and even Rollo thought he would have some. He was sorry there was no more wine to go with it and contented himself with water.

Brid bathed Isolde's wound once more and then, after she had made her as comfortable as possible, saw to all the various other wounds gathered by the company. As the priestess applied her skills, Guthrey sat beside Isolde, moaning self-piteously that his life was over if the girl couldn't be healed.

Brid attended to Caspar's arm last. 'You should have complained more,' she scolded him. 'It's opened up again.'

Caspar gave Brid a smile that Rollo thought was all too comfortable, too intimate. He noted that Guthrey had also caught the look. Though Caspar had said or done nothing inappropriate, Rollo was quite sure that he and Guthrey had read the Baron's emotions correctly.

'It is very lucky that he has you here, Mother,' Guthrey remarked tersely. 'Though, naturally, Uncle Spar, you would rather she were safe in Torra Alta with her husband.' He fixed Caspar hard in the eye. 'My father will be overjoyed to hear that his beloved wife is safe and well,' he said pointedly.

Caspar nodded. 'I have no doubt,' he said smoothly, studying Guthrey curiously. No hint of ruffled emotions troubled his face nor did a wash of red colour rise up Caspar's neck to imply guilt. Rollo grunted uncomfortably to himself. It was not right that Caspar should look at another woman so soon after his mother's death, and even less decent that he should look to his uncle's wife, yet it seemed he was not even aware of his own heart.

Brid cut away Caspar's shirt and washed the wound in

salt water, which the hermit had drawn from the sea. Very tenderly, she strapped his arm up so the weight of it was borne from a sling about his neck to ease the pain a little. Arathane, too, seemed to notice the tenderness between the two and sighed deeply as if the thought had drawn up a deep pain from within his soul. He took the helmet from his head and smoothed the long strands of hair back over his battered skull. 'We are a sad, sorry lot,' he said heavily with self-mockery in his tone. 'More than half of us are wounded and we have nothing more than a hermit's cave for shelter.'

'Who said I was a hermit?' the man objected with some amusement at the idea. 'I stand watch for Baron Oxgard, minding his east coast. He fears that Wiglaf might seize his opportunity in these times of distress and spill over the much-disputed border. I am no hermit: I am Sergeant Aisholt at your service.'

'But you look like a hermit,' Guthrey rudely pointed out.

The man shrugged. 'Indeed I may. I took on the habits of the old man that lived here. He showed me how to catch the eels and where the fresh water supplies were so that I would not have to go up to the lakes where the dragons lurk. And we did very well until he fell foul of one of those pirates.' He paused and looked at them sideways for an amused second, a half smile lifting the corners of his mouth. 'I took the two youngsters here for pirates at first. Then this young lad,' he nudged his head towards Guthrey, 'blurted that he was in the company of the Baron of Torra Alta. It seemed so unlikely a story that I had to see you ragamuffins for myself and discover who you really are.'

Caspar raised an amused eyebrow at this remark but said nothing more. 'Well, soldier –'

'Sergeant Aisholt,' the man interrupted, correcting him.

'Sergeant Aisholt, then. We need to get to Baron Oxgard's ourselves but would be grateful if you would let us remain here the night to rest. I trust that would not be too much of an imposition,' Caspar said politely without confirming his identity.

The sergeant thought for a moment and then nodded. 'I see no harm in it and, in fact, whoever you are, I'm glad of the company. I just hope the young lass is strong enough to travel come morning.'

Chapter 4

Rollo was the first to wake and grimaced as he sniffed the stale air. The cave stank with the smell of yesterday's fried eel. The oil seemed to have stuck to everything, forming little golden beads of sweat on every exposed surface. His throat was painfully dry and raw; no doubt from swallowing too much seawater, and his ankle throbbed. He rolled over, thinking that the last thing he wanted was to get up.

Guthrey and Quinn began to stir so he twisted round to face away from them and saw that Isolde was no longer lying down but was a humped shape sitting beneath her cloak. In his concern for the girl, he immediately forgot his own troubles. Sitting up slightly, he warily observed Quinn and Guthrey, who both looked at the frail Isolde as if they owned her. He had understood from the beginning that Quinn was very fond of Isolde and that they shared a very close bond – like brother and sister, he told himself. But he had not been prepared for Guthrey to claim the girl as well. Although he vaguely remembered Hal saying that Isolde caused trouble between the two youths, he had never considered the matter before. Now he could see that it was indeed true. Yet it was preposterous to think of Isolde and Guthrey together; she was sensitive and gentle whereas he was brash and demanding. Guthrey would bring her only misery, he decided. All too soon her quiet, apologetic ways would lose their appeal and the over-bold youth would tire of her company and seek more entertaining sport elsewhere.

As the frail young priestess emerged from her cloak, Rollo

stared at her, secretly hoping for a glimpse of naked flesh. Although the priestess was a full three years older, he considered himself to be very mature for his age and didn't worry for one second that she might be beyond his reach. However, his look of eager anticipation soon soured. At first, as she lifted her hand and the folds of the cloak fell away from her arm, he thought it was a trick of the firelight, but then she twisted it in a beam from the morning sun and he could see that his eyes had not deceived him. The unsightly discoloration around the wound to her lower arm had spread upwards so that even the skin of her upper arm was now a repugnant green. The girl was holding her damaged limb up to the light, twisting it back and forth and examining it in disbelief. Suddenly she gave out a pained cry of fear and revulsion.

'My hand! My hand! What has happened? Brid, help me! What has happened to me?'

The noise of her scream rang back and forth in the cave.

Immediately Guthrey was on his feet and managed to crack his head on the low ceiling. With more prudence, the others rose with care. Arathane and Sergeant Aisholt both sprang to the entrance to the cave to see if there was any threat from without. Quinn and Guthrey shrank back from Isolde in alarm and fear as they stared at her hand. Leaf surveyed the young priestess with an unreadable expression whereas Caspar looked horrified and deeply pained for the girl. Brid was the only one who reacted positively towards Isolde, opening up her arms to embrace the stricken girl, trying to offer comfort.

Rollo thought he would be sick. It wasn't the sight of the withered and mutated limb that so repulsed him but the thought of what was going through Isolde's mind. She had fought so hard to help them all and been so brave; she did not deserve this. He loathed Guthrey for the way he stared at the girl's arm, pointing in horror. He hated Quinn for his look of shock and alarm. He hated his father for looking so piteously at the girl.

Isolde did not need it pointed out that her wounded limb

was so horrifying, nor did she need to learn that she was to be pitied. Rollo understood that look. Painfully, he remembered how, every time he had been gripped by a fit, his father had looked at him with that same expression of pained despair. It stripped all respect.

Rollo, however, did admire Brid for the way she so warmly clasped Isolde and gripped the mutated hand as if to tell her she was not afraid of the diseased tissue. So often, he had wished that there was someone around to do that for him. He may not have a withered, mutated limb but he felt as if his he were like that inside.

'Isolde, you have to stop screaming,' Brid told her firmly. 'You will draw all manner of predators to us. Take a steady, deep breath and remember who you are.'

But Isolde continued to sob and tremble as if possessed by a demon, shoving Brid away and refusing all attempts to comfort her. Eventually, Brid let her be and sat back. Raising her eyes, she wearily looked to the sergeant.

'Sergeant Aisholt, some food for us all, if you please. Food will calm everyone.'

The man did not respond since he was still staring at Isolde in revulsion.

'Aisholt!' Brid ordered harshly, at last gaining the man's attention. He snapped his gaze away from Isolde and hastened out of the cave in search of food.

Rollo was so shocked and appalled at what had happened to Isolde that he could think of nothing else. The poor girl was sobbing more quietly now and, remarkably, it was only minutes before she steadied herself, pulled her cloak around her and shrank back against the wall. Rollo was deeply impressed that she possessed such strength of character though no longer surprised by it. He had watched her in action as she had bravely struggled against hobs in her attempt to retrieve the Chalice.

Aisholt soon returned with more eels.

'I'm not hungry,' Guthrey snarled, and Rollo similarly turned up his nose though he was loath to take a similar line to his cousin.

Quinn, however, behaved himself and congenially offered to help prepare the meat. All the while he was slicing up the eels, the lanky Torra Altan youth cast sorrowful looks towards Isolde though he could not quite disguise his revulsion at the sight of her grotesque limb.

'Don't worry, Isolde,' Caspar said with forced brightness. 'We'll soon get you to the safety of Baron Oxgard's home and from there we can get help for you, whether it's from Leaf's people or from Keridwen. You'll feel much better when we're there.' He nodded encouragingly and turned to Aisholt. 'So, sergeant, which way must we go to reach your master's house?' he asked.

Aisholt looked him up and down suspiciously. 'Well, now look here, feeding you and offering you shelter is one thing, but leading you to the noble Baron, that's another. Do you think I would lead a bunch of strangers to him? It was only that you youngsters were hurt by the eels that I took pity on you. By rights, I should never have invited you in and fed you. I must be getting soft in my old age.'

'That would not have been very neighbourly of you; besides, Baron Oxgard is our friend and it will not go well with you when we tell him that you refused to help us,' the Baron warned.

'I have no proof and, as I see it, you are equally likely to be in league with that fat toad Baron Wiglaf,' he said, expressing the dislike the people of Jotunn and Nattarda held for each other. 'None of his men are going starving in these times of distress. Have you noted that? They're all still fat and round like their cheese, and it's mighty peculiar that you are carrying one of his cheeses, at that.'

'Only one that we took from a pirate hoard that, by all accounts, had been stolen from Wiglaf.' Caspar shrugged. 'It makes no odds. We shall manage very well without you,' he said confidently.

Aisholt, in turn, shrugged uncertainly and continued to cast suspicious looks at his guests and sigh with heavy indecision.

Although her arm looked much worse, the general state of Isolde's fitness appeared to be much stronger that morning. Brid carefully rebandaged her arm and, though Arathane repeatedly asserted that the limb must be gangrenous and should be severed to save the girl's life, Brid was convinced that the limb was not dying.

'It must simply be an infection from the hob iron that has weakened her. It is not gangrene but an infection, a sepsis.'

'But most of the poison is surely in the limb, otherwise it wouldn't look so diseased. Cut the limb off and she will be freed from the source of the infection,' Arathane insisted.

Brid stood up, opened her mouth as if about to shout at him, but then clenched her teeth, closed her eyes and took a deep breath. 'Never,' she said tersely, fixing her piercing green eyes on the warrior, 'argue with me. Isolde is my ward. She has suffered enough and does not need to lose the limb. She is far stronger than you think, and without undergoing the shock of an amputation she will have a better chance. She will fight the infection. I believe in her! I have always believed in her and she will prove me right!'

Rollo wondered whether Brid was acting for Isolde's welfare or if she was stubbornly refusing to admit she was wrong.

Arathane raised his arms in surrender. 'Far from it for me to interfere. I just think you are wrong.'

Brid shrugged. 'I can bear your criticism without a thought.' She turned to Isolde. 'You will feel better soon, dear. I simply need to get inland so that we can find new herbs and good food to help you regain your strength and resist the infection. We must head straight for Oxgard where we can get food, horses and enough protection to enable us to get through to Torra Alta.'

'First we have to find him,' Caspar pointed out.

Brid nodded and began scratching a hasty diagram into the dust on the cave floor. 'The hobs have moved north towards

Torra Alta and that means they are probably thinner on the ground in the occupied territories of the middle shires. Oxgard will not have stayed in his northern castle on the Torra Altan border. He fled the hobs once and he'll do it again and, to my mind, he has two options. He could either head to one of his forts on his Nattardan border or head home to his central seat. He may well be further from hobs out towards Nattarda but my guess he will feel uncomfortable so close to Wiglaf. Baron Wiglaf still seems to be very strong in his own lands.' Brid stopped to draw breath and Leaf raised an eyebrow at her words. 'Since the two baronies are enemies and not allies,' Brid continued, 'Oxgard will be wary of succumbing to Wiglaf or one of his lesser lords. I think it's clear that he will have fled home to his manor and the old ruin of a castle alongside.'

Caspar nodded at this.

'You are indeed spies.' Sergeant Aisholt was already barring the door, his sword raised. 'None of you will leave this cave alive.'

'Are you really going to slaughter these injured men and children?' Brid asked. 'I am deeply impressed by your bravery. Stand aside, Aisholt. We are who we say we are and wish your master no harm. His sister, Cybillia, is one of my dearest friends. I delivered her last two children.'

Aisholt began to look back and forth between the company. Caspar displayed his left hand and the signet ring bearing the crest of Torra Alta.

The man nodded uncertainly. 'Very well. Very well. There is an honest look about you, but what of him?' He nodded his head at Arathane. 'He's sat there too quietly, throughout.'

Rollo nodded at this and, indeed, soon all the company had turned with curious eyes on the man who now looked older than his imposing figure first implied. Though he was heavily muscled and clearly strong, his hair was greying and his eyes tired and lined with deep grooves of worry. Rollo had no doubt that a great burden of either guilt or responsibility weighed heavily on the man's shoulders.

'I am of no consequence,' Arathane dismissed himself. 'I have travelled afar, seeking out the wretched man-devil who's stirring up country after country into turmoil, setting brother against brother in his evil intent to gain more and more for himself. I have but one quest and that is to stop him. I shall not seek sanctuary at Oxgard's court. I go only to seek Silas.'

'But you can't leave us,' Leaf protested. 'Look at us! How shall we cope? Quinn and Guthrey are little more than boys. Gart wouldn't know one end of a sword from another. Spar's shoulder is severely damaged. Whether Rollo can walk or not I don't know. Isolde's is very sick indeed and Brid is only a woman.'

'Well, that leaves you to look after them all, doesn't it, Leaf?' Arathane said without too much concern on the matter. 'I do indeed feel very sorry for you and I am extremely grateful for what you have done for me and my horse. Nevertheless, Silas got away and Sorrel and I have to go after him.'

'You can't take the horse!' Leaf protested.

'I have to,' Arathane told them all. 'There is no choice in the matter. No doubt you will come across horses on your travels.'

Caspar looked at the man long and hard and Rollo was convinced that his father should have been able to say something to change Arathane's mind, but the Baron gave up all too easily.

'We wish you luck, sir. All our thoughts and prayers are with you. Let us hope you find this Silas and run him through – several times!'

'Have no fear,' Arathane told him. 'I shall see that it is done. It has to be.'

As soon as his horse was saddled, the mysterious warrior left. A subdued lull fell over the company and Rollo sensed that the sudden sense of vulnerability gripping him was also plaguing the others.

But the air of gloom soon lifted when Isolde, with her arm tightly bandaged, rose up and demanded food. Although croaky, she seemed very much happier that morning and every-one's spirits were raised as a result. She was also ravenously hungry and ate a whole pound of cheese, though, curiously she would not touch the eel.

'Now we are ready,' Caspar declared. His arm was supported by a sling and Brid had repeatedly warned him to guard it well for fear of the wound opening up again. 'Thank you, kind Aisholt, for your hospitality.'

The sergeant pouted at them uncertainly, then grabbed a satchel and slung it over his shoulder. 'I'm coming with you. They were meant to send me relief months ago and I think it's beyond the call of duty to remain out here beneath the eye of the dragons and feeding only off eels and seaweed for this long. There's been the odd messenger, but no one to fill my place. Since you seem to be completely clear about Oxgard's whereabouts, though I only learned of these developments a couple of days ago, I may as well come with you. I can't have the Baron think I actually sent you to him.' He looked hastily round the cave for anything of value he may have forgotten but, evidently, there was nothing since he turned his back on them and nodded inland. 'Besides,' he grinned broadly, 'I long ago decided you are whom you claim.' He bowed respectfully towards Caspar and Brid. 'Your emotions are raw to the bone yet you've been true to your story. I am at your service. I can't have Baron Oxgard thinking that I didn't do my best to help you. Onward, fair company!'

Without Arathane's horse all were forced to walk, and Rollo was ashamed to see that he, more than any of the others, held them up since the stitches to his ankle were sore and the leg slightly swollen. Even Isolde was able to march on at a pace, with Leaf skipping and hopping alongside. It seemed so incongruous that the unusual girl from the hidden realm, who was so serious and forthright in conversation, was now behaving like a normal child. At every turn in the path she fell on a new flower with great curiosity and ardent excitement. But this image of childish enthusiasm was soon shattered when she loudly named each plant and recounted its medicinal uses for all to hear.

'I am impressed,' Brid said warmly. 'Now, do something more useful and gather me some of each.'

Leaf smiled back, clearly glad to be of service.

Aisholt led the way, one eye always turned up towards the reddish peak that overlooked the bay.

'This is the worst part,' he informed them. 'After we've worked our way to the top of the cliffs, there's about half a mile of open downs to cross. Beyond that there's a shallow river, which is so densely lined with trees that the dragons won't be able to get anywhere near us once we are under their cover.'

Rollo looked south, his eye following the path that had taken Arathane from them. 'How dare he leave us? He had no right to leave us.'

Brid snorted at him. 'Rollo, you are a ridiculous child,' she said with some amusement that made Guthrey laugh and Quinn groan with embarrassment.

'Ma, please don't,' her elder son begged.

The priestess winked at Quinn. 'I'm sorry I shame you so,' she said with light-hearted frivolity that Rollo found most inappropriate and quite incongruous from the woman. He had seen her as completely humourless, a troubled mother too careworn for laughs, and yet now she smiled at every flower that Leaf brought and continually laughed and teased her boys.

Rollo hung back more and more from the rest of the group, muttering to himself that these Torra Altans had no sentiment. His father soon noted that he was lagging behind and fell back to join him. For a moment, Rollo was pleased, glad that his father sought his company, but was quickly disappointed when Caspar remained silent. The Baron glanced at him once or twice, his mouth opening as if to speak, but found no words.

Am I such a stranger? Rollo thought resentfully. It was only after a few minutes that he became aware of how pale Caspar looked and that he winced a little with each footfall. Rollo knew he should say something to show his sympathy but he couldn't bring himself to do it. Far off, the hush of a cool, overcast morning was broken by an eagle-like screech followed by a cry of pain that was quickly silenced. The hairs on his back stood on end and he found himself involuntarily pressing closer to Caspar. Though he tried to persuade himself that this move was a gallant act to protect his injured father, he knew deep in his heart that he sought the Baron's comfort and strength.

'Was that a dragon?' Leaf squeaked, fleeing to Brid's side.

The priestess nodded.

'It's all right, though,' Aisholt called out reassuringly. 'It's on the other side of the valley and it will be a while before it kills again this morning.' He seemed quite confident and Rollo had no reason to distrust the man's experience. Still, it was a great relief to come off the open down, where they were like helpless rabbits exposed to the eye of a hawk, and scurry down the steep sides of the valley where the tufted grass had slipped and rippled to form terraces. Soon they edged their way into a thick wood where the winter had nipped back the vegetation and they were able to pass into the dankness surrounding the banks of a dark stream.

Fish flitted in the waters, young brown trout nestling in the pools and lurking behind the smooth boulders, waiting for their food to be washed towards them. The mud squelched around Rollo's boots. He was already tired with the effort of keeping up with the others and he wondered how Brid managed to stay so easily abreast of the uninjured youths and men at the front of the party. He did not expect such a small woman in her middle years to have such stamina. But more remarkable still was Isolde, who had been so ill and weak over the last two days. She still looked sickly green and her eyes were dulled and pained, but she strode on faster than she had ever done before. Rollo guessed she was being driven by a need to get home, a need so strong that it overrode her physical frailties.

A small cold hand slipped into his and gripped tight. He

turned and looked down into Leaf's enigmatic eyes. Her teeth were chattering and she was pale with exhaustion.

'I can't keep up,' she said matter-of-factly. 'How far do we have to walk?'

'With luck, we shall pick up enough horses and men at Baron Oxgard's so that we can get through to Torra Alta.'

'It doesn't seem likely,' Leaf gloomily commented. 'I should think he's doing all he can to protect his own people.'

Rollo felt his heart sinking. They would probably have been better off sitting on the beach, waiting for the eels to devour them.

The dried winter ferns disintegrated into powder as they brushed past. Crisp strands of ivy dragged at Rollo's hair, which was becoming uncomfortably long. He wanted a bath. At home, where the climate was pleasantly warm, he would bathe as often as once a day, and he hated being this dirty and cold. And more than anything he wanted a new pair of boots. He was sick of having his toes pinched and feeling the water seep through the cracks in the old leather.

As they moved further inland, the vegetation grew progressively thicker, and for a while it slowed Aisholt, Guthrey and Gart considerably as they were forced to huck their way through the densely interlocking strands of vegetation. Elder branches grew up entangled in thick ropes of bramble, which were dried and brown but nevertheless thorny. As the others pushed forward, the brambles sprang back and lashed at Rollo's face and arms. Other briar fronds, which scrambled along the ground, reached up and grabbed his calves so that, as he moved his legs forward, he was snared, the thorns tearing through his breeches and scratching his skin.

Leaf was finding it far harder going than he was. He had forgotten her in his own struggles and it was with regret that he turned to see her slumped to the ground.

'Come on, Leaf, get up,' he coaxed her.

Her eyes red with tears, she looked at him and just waved him angrily away.

'Oh, get up, Leaf,' he repeated with some irritation. 'You can't just sit there.'

'I can and I will! I can't go on,' she countered.

Much irritated that he had to backtrack, Rollo stamped back to her. 'Now look what you've forced me to do,' he grumbled, yanking her up harshly. Although he did feel some sympathy for her, he was annoyed that he was left to look after her. Besides, if he were too nice, she would probably give up entirely and he would be forced to carry her.

'Pull your sleeves down over your hands,' he advised. 'And it's best to go through the worst patches of bramble backwards.'

Leaf, however, was clearly not at all used to such rough conditions and looked helplessly at the tangle of thorns about her. 'But there's going to be hobs and probably Holly's people down here hidden in this wretched undergrowth.'

'Yes, and there are dragons out in the open. We just have to trust Aisholt.'

'I should never have come. I should have stayed at home.'

'Well, some of us had no choice,' Rollo grumbled, finding it very hard to work his own way through the brambles, let alone pull Leaf along too.

'Are you two coming?' Caspar called from ahead.

'No, we're sitting here having a picnic and enjoying the scenery,' Rollo snapped back.

'Ow! Stop!' Leaf whimpered. 'Don't keep pulling me. I'm all tangled up.'

For the tenth time, Rollo pulled the brambles off her legs and then sucked at his fingers where the skin had been torn. 'Pick your feet up more,' he growled at her.

A little distance ahead the others had halted, resting while they waited for them. But, the moment they caught up, the others moved on again. Small relief came as they now entered an area where the brambles were not so thick and must have been eaten back by deer or foraging hogs.

A slippery bank took them down towards the stream again

and they splashed along through the shallows where, at least, they were no longer being ripped to pieces by brambles. The relief, however, was soon forgotten as Rollo quickly found himself peeved by the cold water seeping into his boots.

They climbed steadily, thick, close vegetation to either side overshadowing the stream that was like a black mirror at their feet. Rollo was fully aware of his hunger by this stage and hoped that it wouldn't be long before they sat down to rest and grab a bite to eat. Just a little way ahead looked to be an ideal spot to rest. He could see that two streams flowed down into the one they were following and at the confluence there was a pleasant grassy bank. Isolde was now lagging a little behind the leaders of the group though she seemed not so much tired but intent on the water, which rippled around her bare calves. Brid was nagging at her to keep moving but Isolde snapped up her head and flashed her a look. Rollo couldn't decide if it was one of resentment at being chivvied along or one of confusion.

But Isolde appeared to quickly forget Brid and flicked her gaze back to stare at the stream. Very slowly, she stooped over, looking closer and closer into the water and then, with a movement as fast as a kingfisher, her hand plunged into the stream and she snatched up a wriggling brown trout.

Rollo stared in amazement.

Isolde's mouth was open and her lips peeled back; she looked for all the world as if she were about to bite the fish's head off. Then the tension in her jaw slackened and she stared at the fish in disbelief. As her grip eased, the thing slithered from her hand, dropped back into the water and flitted away into the shadows.

'Issy!' Quinn exclaimed. 'What are you doing?' The youth hastily splashed towards her but then halted and took a step back, his face shocked and the look of revulsion raw and undisguised for a moment before he managed to recover himself.

Isolde glared at him, her lip suddenly atremble. She recoiled from Quinn. Clutching her clothes about her body, she drew them in tightly as if attempting to hide in them. 'Quinn, I . . . I –' she stammered.

Rollo moved forward and took her arm. 'Do you feel suddenly worse?' he asked kindly, pleased that for once he could say and do the right thing when others failed.

'I was hungry,' Isolde said in some confusion. 'I don't know what overcame me. I could smell the fresh fish in the water and I was hungry . . .'

'Keep close beside me,' Brid snapped at the girl. 'Just think harder about what you are doing.'

Rollo was angered to have Isolde pulled out of his hand and annoyed on Isolde's behalf that she was being treated with such disdain. Why adults were always so difficult, he couldn't imagine. Even his mother would have been rough or cross with him if he had been dawdling and behaving strangely. It was just so like an adult not to try and understand a youngster's difficulties but to scold them immediately instead.

'We'll stop and eat as soon as we can,' Brid announced with steely calmness. 'Aisholt, when can we halt?'

The man glanced up at the ribbon of sky above their heads and then looked back at them with despair. 'This is not good country to be in. We should keep on moving as fast as possible until we are beyond the red dragons' territory.'

'When will that be?' Brid demanded.

'Two hours, more likely three at the pace we are going.'

'Then we stop and eat now. It's a shame you didn't hold onto that fish, Isolde,' she chided. Though her words were harsh, Rollo could see that her face was taut with anxiety over the girl.

They dragged themselves up the bank and onto the grass where the two streams met. Perched on lichen-covered logs, they nibbled at the morsels distributed by Quinn.

'Cheese,' Rollo said in dissatisfaction.

'You don't have to eat it,' Quinn snapped back, peeling off the black wax which protected the creamy yellow cheese within. 'There are plenty of us that are hungry.'

'No, I'll eat it,' Rollo said, unruffled, before taking a hungry bite. He did actually like cheese but it was always his wont to complain and he didn't really know how to behave otherwise.

As he broke off and nibbled at small hunks of the pressed and matured curd, which was quickly satisfying to the point of being slightly nauseating, he watched the others about him. Aisholt was impatient and appeared eager to get going again, as was Guthrey who looked only to his mother. Rollo guessed he was worried for her. Quinn was eyeing Isolde with distress and appeared both concerned and revolted as his eye continually ran down to the arm that she held rather stiffly beneath her cloak. Rollo wondered how the poor girl must feel and was so lost in thought that he nearly broke his tooth when he bit on something hard in the cheese. Spluttering, he spat the foreign object into his hand and looked at it.

Covered in a slime of half-chewed cheese was what appeared to be a coin. He looked at the rest of his hunk and saw, buried within the cheese, a folded piece of paper.

Since everyone was now sympathetically asking Caspar about his shoulder, there was no one watching him as Rollo unwrapped the note. As always, the Baron was doing his best to appear noble and brave, dismissing his injury as nothing, which Rollo found very irritating. He looked down at the greasy piece of paper in his hands and read: 'Shipment at next full moon is bound for Withyman's Pond on the schooner *Whitewater*. With it will be the payment. I trust it will provide you with a new ship after the last disaster and here, for now, is a token of my commitment.'

Thinking the note meaningless, he was about to pocket the coin and toss the scrap of paper away, but Leaf stayed his hand. 'Let me look at it,' she demanded, 'and the coin too.'

Not wanting to argue, Rollo handed it over.

'Now, why would anyone be hiding money in a cheese?' the girl asked, her curiosity obviously aroused.

Everyone turned and looked at her as she held up the find.

'What is it?' Caspar asked.

'It's a Belbidian crown.' She looked at it thoughtfully, her head tilting to one side as she examined the dull piece of metal. 'Well, not quite plain. It has three scour marks on one edge. They are very faint but they're still there. And there's a note with it.' Leaf read out the note.

'It's meaningless,' Guthrey dismissed the note without thought, and Rollo was glad that at least someone concurred with his opinion. 'Here, let me see the coin.'

Leaf dutifully handed it over.

'No doubt it's meaningful to someone, but clearly meaningless to us,' Aisholt also dismissed the note. 'Now, we should be moving on.' He looked at the two rivers. 'The route to the left is the gentler, quicker climb though it's slightly more exposed as it rises into the hills. The route to the right cuts through a gorge where the vegetation is very thick, which will give us cover, but the going is extremely tough.'

After much debate, all were agreed that in their present battered condition they would take the easier route. Reluctantly, the party followed Aisholt back into the water and the left-hand stream where they splashed along through the dank shadows, all ears still listening for any sound from the red dragons. Once again, Rollo lagged at the rear, watching his companions. Isolde brushed aside Quinn's attempts to talk and stumbled on, head down and shoulders drooped, indicating that she did not want to talk to anyone. Guthrey was keen to march alongside his mother while Quinn and Gart stepped up the pace to march with Aisholt, who had taken the lead. Leaf, who had handed the note to Caspar, was unusually quiet, no longer delighted by the marsh marigolds and winter brackens, all of which she had been able to identify without hesitation. Rollo found this remarkable, especially since she claimed to have never seen over half of them before now.

'I suppose a cheese is as good a container as any to transfer messages. It does seem odd though,' Caspar mused, looking to Leaf for a response. But none came and so he continued,

'Why was the message not simply handed from messenger to messenger in the normal way?'

'For secrecy's sake,' Leaf told him. 'At least that's my best guess. It's easy to trace a messenger to his master. Cheeses rarely give away secrets.'

'Hmm,' Caspar mused, having trouble piecing it all together. 'But a cheese? It's so cumbersome, clumsy and messy.'

'Yes, but you can conceal a lot of money in a cheese. Also, it's the commodity the pirates were stealing,' Leaf reasoned, her tone now a little frustrated at having to explain. 'Food is very much at a premium in such difficult times. Certainly, there must be an unfortunate and unwitting middleman in all this, someone who is buying the cheese from the cheese makers and then trying to sell it on. This cheese merchant is then raided by pirates who take the cheeses. I suspect a lot of money is changing hands.'

'Cheese pirates!' Caspar laughed at the idea. 'So someone makes the cheese in the first place, sells it on and then has it stolen back? He could sell the same number of products a number of times like that.'

Leaf laughed and looked at him sideways. 'No, no, that's not the idea at all! It's not on any large scale but simply a method of passing on messages. The cheeses bearing messages are sold legitimately to genuine traders.' She paused momentarily. 'Then the unfortunate traders are no doubt slaughtered and the message passes from its originator to its intended recipient without anyone ever being able to see them communicating.'

'I don't see there's enough proof for that at all.' Caspar looked at her sceptically. 'It could be anyone.'

Leaf laughed that smugly amused laugh that always made Rollo feel uncomfortable. Being near her gave him none of the comfortable, safe feeling that Isolde imbued in him.

'Don't you remember? The cheeses were all perfectly smooth and round. We had to break open the black wax that sealed them. No one had stuffed anything into them after they were made. No, the cheeses had been moulded about the message.'

'Yes, but it takes ages for the cheeses to mature,' Caspar reasoned.

'Well, there you have it! Someone has been hatching this plan for a very long time,' Leaf said triumphantly.

'Well, it seems to me that all we have to do is to stay away from this Withyman's Pond and we'll be fine,' Rollo said dismissively. He didn't like Leaf monopolizing his father's time. It wasn't that he actually wanted to talk to Caspar himself, it was just that he was suspicious of the girl stealing away his affections. Caspar had always preferred his sister and clearly doted on Isolde. It wouldn't take this clever girl long to win an equally secure place in Caspar's heart.

Baffled by the whole message conundrum, Caspar laughed. 'I think we should think ourselves lucky that the pirates were stealing cheese and not money. At least we can eat the cheese.'

As they splashed on, Rollo noticed they were climbing, working their way upstream until the flow became a mere trickle with fewer trees growing on either side. A pain throbbed in his temples and he slowed for a moment, blinking. The light threading through the trees must have been too much for his eyes since flashes sprang through his vision. Suddenly, he felt furiously angry and confused at the same time and he had no idea where this rogue emotion had sprung from. The hairs on the back of his neck bristled and his muscles twitched. Laughter from Quinn rippled through his mind and he was again furious at such frivolity at a time like this.

'At a time like what?' he queried his thoughts out loud.

'What's the matter?' Caspar asked. 'You're all jumpy.'

'I don't know,' Rollo replied snappily and bumped into Isolde who had stopped in her tracks just in front of him. She was sniffing the air, her nostrils flaring as if she were a horse.

Brid slid her hand into Isolde's. 'Come on, child, you stay with me.'

'I thought I heard something,' she muttered.

Rollo became increasingly nervous as the trees thinned, yet

he could not explain why until he heard a heavy thud and felt the ground shake as if something huge had fallen out of the sky.

Aisholt swung round and hefted his spear onto his shoulders.

'Run!' he snarled at the company. 'Run and hide yourselves back in the thick of the woods! Get back to the point where the waters meet.'

Chapter 5

Rollo didn't run. He was too angry.

Caspar tugged at his arm, urging him to hurry, but Rollo pushed him off. 'Give me space to use my sword,' he growled.

'Just get back with the others.' Caspar yanked him hard with his good hand.

'You're injured. You'll be good for nothing,' Rollo defied him.

'I'm better with my right hand alone than you are with two and I will be for a good many years to come.'

'Just both of you hurry!' Brid shouted.

Leaf was crying and Gart was tugging her along. Poor little mite, Rollo thought whilst staggering after his father, who was muttering about his idiocy.

'Thirteen years old and he thinks he can fight a tiger with his bare hands.'

'Who ever said anything about tigers?' Rollo snapped back. His eyes searched the trees that were gradually thickening around them again but he could hear the snuffling and snorts not too far away and the heavy footfalls as some large beast stalked alongside, tracking their scent. Aisholt had led them back some distance along the path before they finally returned to the grassy bank and the confluence of the two streams. Choosing the right-hand stream this time, they resumed their ascent. Through the trees, Rollo occasionally glimpsed a dark body running very fast on powerful hind legs, its smaller arms curled up out of the way as it ran.

'We'll make it,' Aisholt called back optimistically. 'Where

the ground rises the river cuts through a gorge. The vegetation is very thick there and so, if we climb up through the watercourse itself, we should be fine. Beyond that is the enclosure and we shall be safe.'

'Can't we hurry a bit more?' Isolde chafed.

'Some of us can't run as fast as you,' Guthrey grumbled, looking her up and down in bafflement, his chest heaving as he sucked in breath.

'What enclosure?' Leaf asked but didn't bother to listen for a reply. 'I can't keep going,' she whimpered.

'You have to,' Caspar gently ordered her.

Rollo looked towards the dark shape on the far side of the trees; it was now standing, waiting eerily. Something forced him to turn his head and peer deeper into the gloom of the shadows; he knew that on the other side of the strip of trees there was another monster though he could not see it yet. He stumbled on, eyes flitting left and right, aware that his own breathing was becoming increasingly loud.

'We should stop,' he called to his father.

'Nonsense,' Caspar replied. 'The faster we get on to the refuge Aisholt's been telling us about, the better, before any more beasts scent us.'

'Red dragon,' Rollo warned. 'There's a red dragon!'

He had not truly seen its shape or hue since its body was camouflaged by tree trunks and the umber light sapped all colour but, somehow, he was convinced that it was such a creature. He found a snarl growing in his throat and took several breaths to calm himself before trotting on. They could not move fast for the terrain and Leaf was not as quick on her feet and too heavy to carry any distance so they were reduced to her pace. The tension had forced Rollo to overcome his injury, and he was frustrated by this slowness. The moment he had sensed the dragon, he had forgotten about the pain in his ankle and found renewed vigour.

His heart throbbed in his throat. At last, he had actually seen it! The creature was there, on their right, a shadowy shape stamping along beside them. A head snaked in and a roar swept through the trees. Leaf clapped her hands over her ears and flung herself to the ground. The rest stood stiffly and stared as little jets of red flame spurted towards them.

'Don't worry,' Brid said kindly but firmly to Leaf. 'The red dragons are not nearly so big or fierce as the golden dragon and their fire will not reach us here.'

'Maybe not as fierce but there's two of them,' Quinn pointed out.

'More than two,' Rollo corrected.

All turned and looked at him as if he were making things up in order to draw attention to himself. Guthrey snorted disdainfully.

'You shouldn't say things if you have no proof,' Quinn told him quite sternly.

Rollo paid them no heed but marched on. What was it to him what they thought anyway? It made no odds. He knew there were more dragons and, just because he couldn't say why, didn't mean he was wrong. It was typical that everyone doubted his judgement, he thought, ploughing on angrily through the stream. He no longer cared that he was marching towards danger; his only thought now was to prove to Guthrey and Quinn that he was right.

Intent on his purpose, he marched on as the woods thinned, putting some distance between himself and the others, who stayed together in a tight knot.

The roar came out of nowhere, the crisp needles on the pine trees shrivelling up as the heat in the breath ignited them. The skin on Rollo's face smarted from the sudden blast of scorching air. He stiffened and braced himself. Ahead of him was dense vegetation but it took him only a moment to realize it was only thorny bramble bushes that separated him from the monster lying in wait for them. Brambles were very hard for a human to pass through but they were no deterrent to a dragon. The thick stems of trees presented an obstacle but brambles would simply be trampled down.

He drew his small sword, aware that his hand was trembling as he held it up before him, his eyes aching as he stared into the unmoving tangle of barbed fronds. Even though he was expecting it, he still leapt back in alarm, his heart in his throat as the red snout stabbed through the undergrowth. Small, half-closed eyes, slitted against the thorns, focused on him. A thin flickering tongue unwound from a deep black throat, stabbing out to taste his scent, palpating the air right before him.

His mouth dry and his heart thumping, he stared at the fluttering tongue for a split second, then, as the disembodied face spat further forward out of the undergrowth, he thrust up his knife and stabbed. His blade jabbed against the dragon's scales and it felt as if he struck plates of steel. For the barest second, he stared at the scaled monster and it stared back, the eyes blinking at him.

His mind raced. What should he do? He tried to stumble back but brambles were quickly wrapped around his ankles and he tripped. Stumbling to the ground, he put his hand back to save himself. The red dragon drew back just fractionally, tensing its muscles, coiling in its energy, preparing to strike.

Rollo did the only thing he could and gave out the same ululating cry he had used to distract the golden dragon. The creature's mouth opened wider and gave back an ear-splitting roar. Rollo pressed himself back into the undergrowth and was now totally entangled and unable to move. A giant claw with its talons curled into a fist pushed through the brambles. The claw spread wide no more than a yard from Rollo's feet. He kept up his cry though panic rang through the notes.

Desperately, he sought to reproduce the cry his mother had used to control the bears, the cry that had won his sister the right to inherit the crown. The cry had worked on the golden dragon, proving that he had an even greater power than his sister and was not the worthless child he had so long believed. It would surely work now.

The notes rang from his throat, shrill and bestial. The dragon stood over him, a flicker of flame glowing in each blackened nostril. The jaws snapped open and the neck arched while, all the time, its eyes were fixed on Rollo's head. The creature hissed and then, with a sudden jerk, its head sprang forward, the long dagger-like teeth wide open, ready to snap closed about his neck. Rollo's cry of command failed him and became a scream of terror.

In a futile attempt to protect himself, he shielded his face with his arms and curled up into a ball, staring out between his fingers at his imminent fate as the dragon's snout darted towards him.

However, the jaws did not close about his torso. The giant head crashed to the ground, crushing his leg, the jaw shattering as the teeth were thumped closed by the impact. Rollo stared, his hands shaking, a pitiful whimper escaping from his throat. It took him a second to realize that his leg was pinned beneath the dragon's shattered head though he was still not aware of the pain.

A hand gripped his shoulder. 'All right, Rollo?' Caspar asked in a steady unruffled voice.

Rollo could do no more than turn towards him and hug his boot. Until he had arrived in this miserable country, it had been many years since he had looked to his father for comfort and security. He had long considered the man weak since he was overshadowed by his wife, but now all he could do was cling on.

Caspar gently peeled away his son's grip and heaved at the monstrous scaly head. Aisholt hurried to help him and, with some difficulty, they managed to drag it off the boy's leg. Rollo looked from the dead red dragon to his injured father. To slay a dragon was an art in itself but to do it with one arm in a sling and only a knife was indeed impressive. Certainly, it had impressed Quinn, Guthrey and Gart, who all stared on, open-mouthed, looking between the small, agile Baron and the massive monster. The handle of a short dagger stuck out from the monster's eye. The tip of the blade must have pierced its brain, felling it in an instant.

'Whenever did you learn such a skill?' Brid was enthusiastically impressed by Caspar's feat.

He was now clutching at his wounded arm, and clearly the exertion had pained him, but he managed to give Brid a warm smile back. 'I've been practising hard. An archer needs all his limbs and all the fingers of his right hand. You never know when some mishap might deprive me of them and I needed more than my swordsmanship to fall back on.'

'Interesting though this conversation might be,' Guthrey interrupted, 'we have to get to safety somehow. There's still more dragons behind us. Rollo might try and sing them to death again and we'll all be eaten.'

Rollo growled. It seemed that Guthrey had already forgotten how much he had done to save him from Silas and his minions in the arena and how his cry had controlled the magnificent golden dragon. Why the same cry had no command over the red dragons, he couldn't understand. Clearly, he did not possess the mighty power that, for a few glorious days, he had believed was his. Clearly, he was as useless as he had always been and, to his mind, there was nothing more useless than a prince without a kingdom.

Though his leg hurt, he pushed aside an offer of assistance from Quinn and pulled himself up again. The impact of the dragon's head had split open the wound on his ankle and he felt numb with bruising but at least nothing was broken.

'Take it easy,' Quinn kindly advised but Rollo was in no mood for his compassion.

'It's not me but Isolde who needs your sympathy,' he said harshly but found he needed to sit back down again to take the weight off his leg.

Quinn blinked at him and glanced anxiously at Isolde, his face tight with concern, but he did not move towards her and it was as if he were afraid to approach her diseased limb.

Rollo looked at him and sneered, 'I thought you two were close. I thought you shared a special bond.'

'I care! I care deeply about her,' Quinn objected. 'It's just . . .' The tall youth took a deep breath. 'What's the use? You can't possibly understand how I feel.' He turned and walked away.

After plucking out a number of hooked thorns that had embedded themselves in his skin, Rollo gingerly stood upright again, guarding his leg. He could barely put any weight on it. He sucked at his palm, which still had bramble thorns in it, and was feeling very sorry for himself. Only then did he note that the others were busily preparing themselves for action. Aisholt was up a tree, looking about and pointing vigorously, trying to catch Caspar's attention, who was in deep counsel with Guthrey and Quinn. Already, it seemed that everyone had forgotten that he had been in mortal danger and that a dragon had come within a yard of biting his head off.

'I can see two coming up behind,' Aisholt called from the treetop. 'But I can't see ahead. There may be more but that looks like our only route of escape. The only alternative is to wait here until dark approaches and hope that they will fly off to roost for the night. They need the heat of the day to help them climb up to their eyries in the peaks.'

'In that case, we should just crawl back into the thick of the trees and wait,' Brid advised.

'And then the ravenshrikes will appear and they may well be able to penetrate the cover of the trees,' Caspar argued. 'Not to mention what other night predators may be in these parts. The woods aren't going to stop taurs, a lequus, hobs or wolves.'

Brid bit her lip and paused in thought for a second. 'You are right. We shall have to press on and do our best to defend ourselves.'

Caspar then looked to the others, who nodded in agreement at this decision, and Rollo wondered how his father could ever be a leader if he always consulted everyone before deciding a course of action.

'Prepare yourselves,' the Baron commanded.

Aisholt slithered down the tree and alighted softly. 'We are very short of fit and armed men for such an adventure,' he commented brightly and without any hint that he was dismayed by the thought. Rollo was impressed to see that he did not seem at all scared but, rather, relished the idea of a battle. 'I have had nothing to hunt but eels and I'm quite tired of it. I would feel very much better if I could return to my overlord and say that I had slain a dragon or two.' He grinned.

His courage seemed to infect them all and even Isolde raised a smile though Leaf pressed close to Caspar. 'Are you sure this is the right thing to do?'

'Yes,' he nodded firmly. 'Can you think of a better plan?'

'We are so far deep into a plan that I thought was a bad idea right from the beginning that I don't think I have a right to an opinion on the matter,' she told him haughtily, but there was at last the wisp of a sense of humour developing in this strange, thoughtful child.

'First we cut staffs,' Caspar began organizing the company. 'We can each carry two. Guthrey, Quinn, Gart, sharpen the ends to turn them into spears.'

It turned out that Gart was the most adept at cutting handy-sized lengths of wood and infinitely quicker at whittling them into shape. Since the product he produced was far superior to that the others offered, they let him get on with it while Caspar turned to the dragon. He pushed his knife into the gum line and worked it back and forth, loosening the sharpest teeth along the length of the jaw.

'We can use these to give a good barb to a number of spears. Does anyone have any cord?'

All sorted through their clothing. Most had a pocket or purse bound with a leather cord and they soon discovered that these proved the most useful ties for securing the dragon's teeth to their staffs. After only a short while, all but Leaf were armed with one plain wooden spear and one tipped with a dragon's tooth. Rollo's was very glad to be given one such weapon.

'It's a great shame Arathane is no longer with us,' Brid mumbled. 'We could have done with his help.'

'He was intent on his own purpose. There was nothing we could do,' Caspar assured her. 'Let's have the women toward the centre. Aisholt, bring up the rear, and I shall take the fore. Rollo, you had better stand on my left to protect my injured side.'

The Baron smiled at his son and Rollo realized that he was being honoured with a favoured position. He gave it no more thought than that before standing stiffly and looking ahead into the thatch of brambles. His foot still pained him immensely but the thought of battle had stirred his spirit and he forced himself to overcome his injury. However, he was frustrated by the brambles. It didn't seem possible to move forward through the tangle of briars and they spent nearly all their energy hacking a path forward. Caspar soon changed the order of the company since it was impossible for him to hack effectively with his injury. He took up the rear while Aisholt and the youths took it in turns to cut a path, all the while wondering when they might be met by the snout of a dragon.

'I hope you have your knives ready again,' Brid commented to Caspar, who grunted in acknowledgement.

Rollo was already exhausted as the brambles that Guthrey peeled aside thwacked back at him. Others dangled down to twist at his hair and drag at his cheeks. Leaf's sobs were steadily growing louder as they made slower and slower progress.

'Let me have a go,' Isolde suggested, pushing Rollo roughly aside, taking his blade and proceeding to hack harder and faster than he had done. While everyone glanced at her in disbelief, she continued for about half an hour in which time all the others had swapped places several times beside her. Thanks to her efforts, they made steady progress. When at last they stopped, Quinn looked at her sideways.

'I don't know what medicine Brid gave you but she seems to have made you twice as good as new.' He laughed lightly but there was a hint of uncertainty in his voice, which, clearly, the girl read since she simply stared at him without raising even the hint of a smile.

'We must rest,' Brid told Caspar. 'We cannot go on like this for much longer.'

The moment she spoke, Leaf collapsed into a heap on the floor and wrapped herself tightly in her arms. 'This is madness, utter madness,' she whimpered into the earth.

Rollo sat back, took a deep breath and pressed at his tender ankle while Isolde and Gart peeled themselves back from the tunnel they were cutting through the coarse dry brambles. Gart had proved his worth and he was clearly pleased to receive the praise Caspar lavished on him.

'Well, lad, I am delighted that you came along after all. Your mother is no doubt preparing some curse with which to damn me for all eternity for allowing you to accompany us, but you have proved a true asset.'

'Thank you, sir,' Gart smartly responded and made an attempt at a salute though it was amusingly obvious that he had not the faintest idea how to perform one properly.

'Guthrey, the cheese. Distribute more supplies,' Caspar ordered and the youth dutifully obeyed.

Rollo was surprised by the discipline amongst the Torra Altans, noting how, since Brid had spoken to him on the matter, Guthrey now accepted Caspar's orders and responded smartly. Rollo considered that things would be very different if Hal had come to Artor and suddenly proclaimed himself overlord. He had no doubt that he would have been unable to obey him even if his mother's ghost had returned and begged him to. As the image of Hal's face sprang into his mind, he felt sick to his stomach. He could not understand how so fair a lady as Brid, with all her obvious accomplishments, could ever have married such an overbearingly smug and inconsiderate man. But he was given no more time to think about this puzzlement as Caspar was already on his feet, urging them on.

Everyone glanced anxiously from side to side, looking for

the two dragons that had been stalking them but, possibly, they had withdrawn, frustrated by the inability to reach their quarry. Certainly, there had been no sound or sight of them in quite a while.

'I think they've given up on us,' Guthrey decided, straightening up to try and look through the vegetation and rubbing at his right arm, which was stiff from hacking at the brambles.

'Dragons don't give up,' Rollo said stiffly.

'How would you know? Are you an expert on dragons? It seems not since your only thought is to try and sing them into surrender.' Guthrey's words dissolved into a splutter of laughter.

Rollo was furious at this humiliation and even more furious that his father did not come to his aid. It would have been so easy for Caspar to put Guthrey down with a well-chosen remark but it seemed he could not be bothered to do that; he was still looking about him, peering through the trees, his right hand always on the hilt of his throwing knife. Gradually, the brambles eased and they began dipping and winding between alder branches and scrambling through ivy. Gart was taking a rest from the lead and fell back alongside the little girl from the hidden realm, whom he saw as his duty to protect ever since Caspar had first bestowed him with the task.

'I don't suppose it's going to get any easier when we get to the enclosure Aisholt keeps telling us about,' Leaf said gloomily.

The young woodsman took her hand and towed her along. 'Now what makes you say that, young missy?'

'I should never have thrown my lot in with you. My grand-mother always warned me about humans and their rashness! I thought Spar would help me. In fact he promised! I thought Brid had a deeper understanding. But all that's happened is that we have just crashed from one disaster to another. This world beyond my haven is a very savage place indeed.'

Gart smiled at her and Rollo was very interested to hear his response. 'Indeed, Leaf, but the world is always wild and unpredictable and perhaps even cruel from the very moment we leave the cradle. But would you stay there for-ever?'

'I didn't mean –'

Gart didn't wait for her response but continued excitedly, 'My mother didn't want me to leave our retreat in the woods but I had to one day. What life was there for me with only my brothers and my sisters and my cousins for company and never a fair maid to marry, nor new friends to be made, nor, in fact, to ever see a wide open plain? Already, I have tasted the open sea, seen the sky stretching to the horizon and had a dragon slain before my very eyes. At home, it would be rare if I saw more than a squirrel, a fox and maybe a deer or two. I would spend my day gathering nuts, forever living in the gloom of the forest world. Look at me! I'm as white as betony flowers and all the rest of you are like nuts even though it's only just gone mid winter. And I wish it would snow. I have seen it falling high above my head onto the tree canopy but it never reaches the forest floor. I have never seen a field of white snow. Do you think we shall see snow soon?' he asked enthusiastically.

I hope not, Rollo thought. Snow was very rare in his home-land, which was blessed with a warm climate, and he had not seen snow for many years until he and Caspar had embarked on the terrible journey to reach his father's homeland. Then they had crossed over the frozen ice packs at the top of the world and the wind had whipped snow into their faces for an entire week until he thought his skin would be turned to leather. He did not relish the thought of seeing snow ever again.

Leaf, however, enthused about the idea. 'You are right, Gart; I have never seen snow either. Precipitation is filtered through the curtain shrouding the inner realm; rain is controlled and snow and hail never fall. I want to see if every crystalline structure is as unique as the books say. I want to see how it compacts in the hand.'

'You know a great deal about snow for someone who has never seen any,' Gart remarked.

'Ah, but I've read about it. Snow, rain, hail, ice; the

properties of water are among the first things we people learn about. Water is so important to us all. It is crucial to know as much as one can about water, earth and sunlight. There must be more written on those subjects than all the others put together.'

'Well, that's another thing I would like to do. Mother never taught me to read. She said there was no point and, besides, when our homestead was ransacked and we were forced to flee into the forest, she was unable to rescue any books. I would love to be able to read.'

Rollo's eyebrows rose as he wondered whether he had ever before met someone who couldn't read. Gart was not the only one experiencing new situations. It seemed extraordinary to him that someone should grow nearly to manhood and still be ignorant of his letters.

'I shall teach you, gladly,' Leaf offered, 'but only once I have found the answers I seek. I have to find someone who knows how to cure my people.'

'Won't the answers be written in the books that you have studied so carefully?' Gart asked.

Leaf laughed at him, though without mockery. 'No, I can't read it if no one has written it down. And no one can write about it unless they have knowledge of the subject. Since this phenomenon is new to us, there are no previous records or theories proposing a solution. It began only within the last decade, gradually at first but then more rapidly each year until all our wisest people have become dull and confused.'

'I am very sad for you,' Gart said with genuine sympathy.

Rollo, too, was sorry for the girl but could think of nothing appropriate to say.

'Don't worry,' Quinn said kindly. 'My mother and Keridwen will think of a solution as soon as we reach Torra Alta.'

'They may have too many other things on their mind,' Rollo said under his breath, looking at Isolde, who had used her fingers to scratch up some moss from a dead bough of wood and then began to chew it. He wondered if she hadn't lost some of her mind as well.

All were suddenly staring at Isolde in alarm. Catching their stares, she returned a dark look. Suddenly, she hissed and gurgled in her throat as if angry and frightened like a threatened wild cat protecting her young.

Brid put her hand on Isolde's arms. 'Cling to me, child,' she begged. 'Cling to me, Issy, and we will save you, but you must fight off this ailment. Fight hard. It won't be long now and we shall be at Aisholt's enclosure.'

Rollo hoped that the promised enclosure would bring them salvation.

'Do you know what I want to do?' Gart continued with his previous conversation. 'I want to follow this fine Baron Caspar or perhaps Aisholt's master and learn how to ride and bear arms and eventually become like that magnificent warrior Arathane. What a man, what a magnificent man! I would charge about the countryside, rescuing damsels in distress, who of course would be lavishly grateful.' He winked at Quinn, whom he clearly thought to be the only one of the youths old enough to appreciate his sentiments on this matter. However, Quinn only grinned sheepishly while he was met with guffaws from Guthrey, who continued to snort and snigger at the thought for the next minute.

'Stop it!' Brid snapped at her younger son. 'You do not rescue young ladies just with that aim in mind.'

Aisholt, however, also managed a grin and there seemed to be a conspiracy amongst all the men and boys that Gart was undoubtedly right in this matter.

'Anyhow,' the young woodsman continued, 'I would make my fortune galloping around the countryside, slaying dragons, beheading taurs and chasing away mammoths. All the barons would pay me handsomely for my services and, one day, I shall return home triumphantly to my mother and say, "Mother, I have made the world a safe place and found you a haven."' He grinned at all around and sighed, 'And she would be so pleased with me.'

'Probably not, since in the meanwhile you appear to have ravaged half the maidens in the country too,' Brid retorted though she was having trouble disguising her giggles.

'I have two sons and,' she glared at them both, 'don't think that I don't know or can't guess what goes on in their heads. But to think that my poor Brannella is going to grow up and fall in love with someone else's son, who will most probably be as equally shameful as my two, is more than I can bear.'

'Brannella will have every man in the country at her mercy,' Rollo remarked.

Brid grinned. 'In truth you are right. She is as beautiful as her father is handsome.' The priestess sighed and, for the first time, Rollo realized that she was clearly missing her husband as well as her much-adored daughter. He still found it impossible to think that this fine woman was married to Hal.

'I would very much like the honour of meeting your fair daughter, my lady,' Gart said graciously.

Brid laughed at the idea. 'My dear boy, she is only four. You would have to wait a very long time for her.'

The youth also began to laugh. 'In that case I shall be patient and in the meanwhile lavish my attentions on you, fair Leaf.'

'You seem too eager by half to lavish your attentions on just about anyone,' Leaf retorted grumpily, apparently bewildered as to why her human companions sought humour in every situation. 'And believe me I have no interest in a human. Fair and courageous though you might be, it would never work.'

'I am crestfallen,' Gart said with mock hurt and in no time all were chatting and laughing as they continued their difficult passage through the woods. His light-heartedness in the face of adversity was infectious to all but Leaf and he quickly put most of the company at ease.

'I thought noble folk were always stand-offish,' he ventured after a while.

'Listen, lad, it's not your place to go around making comments like that,' Aisholt told him stiffly and cast anxious glances towards Caspar, searching the Baron's face for any sign of disapproval.

The Baron, however, simply laughed at Gart's openness and slapped him on the back. 'You'll go far, lad. Perhaps you really will even slay a hundred dragons and break a thousand hearts.'

They rested once more just before the trees thinned again, giving way to more strength-sapping brambles. Rollo drank his fill of water, thirsty after the hard labour, and rubbed at his bruised leg, aware that no one had asked him whether it troubled him.

Gart, alongside Aisholt, took the fore for the first weary assault on the brambles. Rollo looked at his torn skin and wondered how many such scratches would finally prove to be the end of a man since they would near that point if this went on for much longer. He noted that his father looked fatigued and was nursing his injured arm and that Isolde kept looking at her bandages and pressing at the dressing. He noted, too, that Brid was also looking, one by one, at each member of the company. As their eyes met, she nodded at him, acknowledging his curiosity.

He blinked away, embarrassed to be caught, staring and watching like that. It was one of the things about having few friends and always being on the outside; rather than chatting away, forgetting about who he was, he would brood on how he was never absorbed into a group. Unaccepted, he spent much time watching them, wondering how strange everyone was and why they did not understand him.

Leaf caught his eye next and he wondered, too, why he did not understand her. Caspar had explained that she was not human but of another species of speaking peoples altogether. That was not at all a strange concept; he had met a great many different peoples since he had begun his travel across half the earth. At home there had been many of the people of Ash.

The women were fabulously beautiful, frivolous and joyful and their desires hot. Their men were huge brutish giants that were kind and lumbering when not roused to action but fearful and uncontrollably savage when the call of war provoked them. Rollo admired them and was grateful for their training in war-craft.

He had met hobs, the people of Blackthorn, who were the vilest of all creatures he had come across. He shuddered at the thought of them. And, of course, he had met the troublesome but very skilled dwarves. He had heard of the gnomes and the gentle people of Hazel as well as the belligerent Holly's people that all took great pains to avoid; but Leaf was none of these things. She referred to herself as one of the scholars from the hidden realm and he imagined that such a place must be paradise.

Still, he certainly did not understand her and so concluded that she, therefore, could not understand him. It was hard enough for a human girl to understand a youth and all the burdens, responsibilities and duties expected of him, so it was no wonder that she, a scholar, must find him such a mystery.

It was to Isolde, however, that his thoughts kept returning. He sensed in her a deep and growing loneliness. When they had first met only a few weeks ago, he had found her to be unnaturally shy and always self-apologetic, but now she was even more frightened and lonely. He knew she was wounded and that there was something very ugly about the wound. He was ashamedly aware of how it stirred revulsion in him and he could plainly see how it did the same thing to Quinn and Guthrey; no doubt that was the reason for her deepened sense of loneliness and distress. The three of them, Quinn, Guthrey and Isolde, had apparently been the closest of friends all their lives but now the two youths recoiled from her. The girl regularly looked up at the two Torra Altan youths but it was particularly to Quinn that her eyes were drawn. She stared long and hard at a point between his shoulder blades, only to look down dejectedly at the ground once more.

Rollo knew that he had barely said a kind word to anyone in his life and had very rarely considered another's feelings before his own, but it pained him to see Isolde hurt and he was ashamed of his own feelings of revulsion. Well, he would conquer them!

Quickening his step to stride alongside, he reached out a hand to take hers. She looked at him in astonishment for a second and Rollo thought he would shrivel up and die of embarrassment. Clearly, he had made a terrible mistake and Isolde wanted nothing of his friendship. But, after an agonizing moment, a faint smile broadened her mouth and she squeezed his fingers in response. Rollo felt a comforting warmth run through his veins.

For a moment or two his mind relished the feeling of being so close to Isolde, but he could not maintain that sense of enjoyment for long. All too soon his thoughts drifted back to his shame at being unable to halt the red dragon. To make matters worse, Guthrey and Quinn were constantly putting their heads together and giggling like school children while casting amused looks in his direction. He was certain that they were thinking only of how idiotic he had been, trying to control the dragon by singing to it. And they were right! The idea was preposterous. It had been the act of a fool. Rollo flagged at the thought, staring glumly at Guthrey's back as the youth wielded a long knife to hack at the relentless brambles.

Rollo squeezed Isolde's hand a little tighter and was somewhat annoyed when she suddenly yanked it away from him. Only a split second later, he realized that she did so to cover her mouth and silence a scream that she bit back into a miserable whimper. This time it was not one but two heads that appeared. Two long snouts coated in red shiny scales pushed through the undergrowth, one springing out before Quinn and the other before Gart. The movement had been swift; there had been no warning blast of flame or even a grunt, just a sudden and savage attack. Rollo's mouth fell open though he had the wherewithal to reach for his weapon, spread his legs wide and flex his arms

101

in readiness to hurl his spear; but it was all too late. His line was blocked by Quinn.

The dragon's head had darted forward, jaws wide ready to relish the taste of sweet, young human flesh. Quinn and Gart barely had time to raise their pitifully small knives and makeshift spears in a futile gesture of self-defence before they were within the dragon's striking distance.

But Caspar had already reacted with the speed and precision born of hundreds of hours of dedicated training, flinging a knife hard as the dragon opened its mouth. The blade had somersaulted through the air, through the open mouth and stabbed into the palate at the back of its mouth. The creature gave out a strangulated cry like a giant crow and, as blood squirted in spurts from its mouth, began to cough and bark in an effort to free itself of the steel.

But, injured as he was, Caspar only had the capability to throw one weapon at a time. Guthrey had hurled his spear but it had done no more than skim the second dragon's flank. Even Brid had hurled one, though it had fallen short, and Aisholt's spear simply snapped as it jarred against the dragon's scales. None of them possessed the skill or speed to do anything to deter the second dragon as it lunged at Gart. There had been no time for the youth to cry out even as the dragon's open mouth jabbed forward. A long barbed tongue sprang out and wrapped around the youth's neck before jerking him into its maw. The jaws crunched closed on his torso and bit clean through his upper body. Gart's legs and lower body fell away, half a lung and his liver spilling from the bottom half of his severed ribcage.

Rollo gaped in horror, too shocked to scream or even breathe. Leaf was screaming uncontrollably while a horrible howl sprang from Isolde. The others overcame their shock and hurled what weapons they could at both dragons but, in the end, it was still Caspar that defeated them. He was the only one that possessed sufficient accuracy and it took accuracy rather than strength to slay a dragon. A dragon's armour of scales was proof to common weapons and the only means of felling them with steel was to pierce one of their very few vulnerable spots.

Up until that moment Rollo had thought their most vulnerable spot was a soft area under the throat. In order for the beasts to draw in and control the air needed for the furnace within the belly, the skin at the throat could stretch and swell like a giant bladder. The need for elasticity meant that this area was not armoured with the shiny, shield-like plates that covered every other inch of a dragon's body. The other vulnerable spots, as Rollo now learnt, were the inside of the mouth and the eyes. Even with his right arm in a sling, Caspar had managed to find every one of these spots on both dragons to topple the monsters. One crashed down over the remains of Gart's body.

Rollo looked on with utter abhorrence at the sight of blood squirting and sputtering out of the lower half of the carcass. It was too much. He had seen people die before and, of late, seen a number of unspeakable atrocities, but never before had he been chatting merrily to someone one minute and the next moment seen them gruesomely slaughtered right before his eyes.

Quinn was blinking at the slain dragons before him, his hands clutched across his chest; as if not truly believing he was still alive. To Rollo's amazement, Brid moved calmly towards her eldest son and took his hand firmly. She did not burst into hysterical screams as a normal mother might but looked calmly round, checking over the others. 'Is everyone else safe?'

'How can you ask such a thing?' Guthrey croaked, his lips trembling as he pointed to the pool of sticky blood that had welled beneath Gart's broken body. 'Gart is dead! We were just talking to him! You heard him say how he was going to amount to something in life and I believed it. He was going to be my friend and now he is dead.'

'Do you think I haven't noticed?' Brid snapped angrily at her younger boy. 'Do you think I didn't see what went on right before my own eyes? But it is done; it is over and none of us can undo it.'

Rollo felt the tears springing to his eyes. 'Poor Gart! He had only just begun to live; he had only just stepped out into the world, disobeying his mother to seek adventure.'

'Well, it just goes to show that mothers are always right,' Brid snapped irritably. 'We've got no time for sentimentality. Aisholt, get ahead and see if there are any more dragons lurking on our path. Quinn, stiffen up and go with him. You were not eaten so stop quaking like a terrified kitten.'

Rollo thought to say in Quinn's defence that he didn't appear to be shaking at all and merely looked shocked, as anyone would have expected, but he didn't want to speak out. He was appalled himself and couldn't drag his horrified gaze from the remains of Gart's carcass. It wasn't fair! He should not be dead. It was all so sudden, so violent, so messy. Something as strong as life should not be snuffed out in the briefest of seconds. It made no sense.

Brid put her small hand on his shoulder and pulled him away from the sight. 'It is right to look on death and comprehend it. One should never deny it but acknowledge that death comes to us all. To deny it is to fear it, and you must not fear. He has not gone for good. It is not the end but the start of a journey that will lead him back to the Great Mother, once more to be embraced in utter bliss before rejoining us all on Earth again.'

Rollo thought she read his mind as her extraordinary vivid green eyes looked deep into his.

She smiled reassuringly at him. 'Life is too strong, too powerful to be gone in the merest snap of a second. It goes on through other dimensions unseen to us, and we should not grieve.'

'You would have grieved if it had been your son that was taken and not poor Gart,' Leaf sobbed almost in accusation. The girl's eyes were red raw with weeping and she was shaking from head to toe. Brid reached out, embracing the child, and pulled her to her body. Despite her fear-induced rage, Leaf softened in Brid's arms as the priestess stroked her hair.

'I know, Leaf, I know,' Brid soothed. 'I would have been distressed beyond words if either of my sons were taken from me because I would miss them so much. I love them deeply and a part of my heart would have been torn from me. I would not be human if I felt otherwise. But as the ravages of grief lessened to a sense of empty loss and despair, I would comfort myself with the thought that they were happy and would soon forget all their pain and loss.'

'Gart's mother won't,' Rollo said flatly. 'She will wait and wait, wondering when her son will come home, each year worse for her than the last.'

Brid looked at him thoughtfully. 'You are an odd child. Not many boys your age would have thought such a thing.'

'I lost my mother,' he said flatly as if that explained every-thing. He glared at his father's back. He had lost his mother, who was more important to him than anything, and he was left only with Caspar. He pointed an accusing finger. 'He should have saved them both. He should have saved Gart as well as Quinn.'

'The dragons were too quick and your father cannot use both his hands. Saving Quinn was remarkable enough,' Brid defended the Baron and then pressed Leaf's hand into Rollo's. 'Now, Rollo, look after her. We must move on.'

'Aren't we going to bury him?' Guthrey asked, his face white.

Brid shook her head. 'He deserves more and we shall soon build him a cairn, then send word and a token to his mother to show how we appreciated her son, but we can do no more. If we were to stop and bury him, we would all too soon need burying ourselves. The smell of blood will quickly draw the night predators.'

Rollo nodded in understanding, his heart heavy with sorrow. There had been nothing he could do and he had so wanted to save Gart. He had liked him. Yet again, someone he had valued had immediately been taken from him.

'The way ahead seems clear,' Aisholt called out to them. 'Any other dragons should have headed home by now, while there's still warmth in the air. I fear we need to make the enclosure before night and so must risk the open ground in order to make good speed.'

Dejectedly, they picked their way out of the trees and entered the long shadows on the edge of the snaking trail of woods where an evening sun had lit the sky in a wash of gold and scarlet. The young priestess was still looking behind her at the slain dragons lying in the dark swill of blood spilt from their own and Gart's bodies.

'Isolde, hurry!' Brid snapped at the girl.

Rollo gasped as the young priestess turned to face them. Long sticky drools of saliva hung from her trembling mouth.

Chapter 6

Lord Hal, uncle to the Baron of Torra Alta and warden of the solitary fortress, stood on the battlements crowning the new north tower and gazed through the winter mist, his eyes straining to pierce the greyness. The fingers on his right hand stung with cold and the stump at the end of his left arm ached.

It's as if I've lost my life bit by bit, he thought darkly. Glaring at the lumpy stump of his arm, he wished he could lose his hand a thousand times over to gain his family back. What was life worth without Brid and his two boys? What was all this castle and land worth? Why didn't he just let the vile hobs march in and take it all? There was no point in this. No point in anything.

A slender hand tugged at his cloak. 'Father, please. Father, come back inside. It's cold.'

'The cold won't kill me,' he grumbled and pushed the small child away without thinking, without caring for her feelings.

'But it will in the end,' the girl said quietly in infantile tones. 'Mother said so. She always said so when I wouldn't come in.'

Without registering her comments, Hal asked bitterly, 'Do you see them?' Regretting his tone, he picked his little daughter up and folded her into his cloak for warmth. Her hands were like slithers of ice. Her breath rising in plumes of smoke, Brannella's dark, alert eyes slitted as she followed her father's gaze and stared into the mist.

'No, Pa, I can't see anything. Only mist and mist and mist.

It's been nothing but mist for days.' She looked up at her father's stubbly chin. 'Keridwen is cross with you; she says you haven't eaten.'

'Let the old woman grumble,' Hal dismissed Keridwen's complaint, though Brannella seemed shocked at the idea of not heeding the high priestess. 'I am commander here and I say whether I eat breakfast or not,' he said stiffly before softening his tone. 'Are you sure you can't you see them?' he reiterated.

Brannella shook her head.

Hal hugged her tight and kissed the top of her head, her hair crisp from the frost. 'No, nor can I; but I can smell them and I can hear them.'

'Humph!' Brannella sounded sceptical. Although she was only very young, too young, he hoped, to fully understand the extent of the catastrophe that was befalling them, she had grown up since her mother was stolen away. She had always been considered bright and spending so much time with Keridwen seemed to have sharpened her wits even more.

'There should be no wind down there today.' He nodded at the blanketing mist. 'Up here there is always a little wind but down there the cold night air is trapped within the canyon, forming the mist, and so there must be no wind. Yet I can hear the moan of the wind; I can hear its sighs and groans welling up from below. It is them.'

'I can't,' Brannella said flatly. 'I can hear ravenshrikes.'

'At this hour?' Hal objected though his ears pricked, listening urgently for that terrifying shriek which would shred a night sky, a cry he had heard all too recently. He listened intently and, though he still heard nothing, his heart forgave him; somehow he was certain it was not the cry of a ravenshrike but guessed her younger ears had picked up an altogether different sound. The wagons were expected this morning. He had sent fifty men to help the Baron Oxgard of Ovissia get supplies to Torra Alta. The men had been ordered to move early in the morning before the great birds had warmed themselves enough to launch into the air. That wagon train would be right at the head of the pass now.

'You're just imagining it,' he tried to reassure Brannella. How could he share his fear that the screams he could not hear but which came ringing to her youthful ears were the cries of dying men.

Brannella shook her head. 'I'm not imagining anything.' She nodded to the southern mouth of the canyon marking the gateway to the rest of Belbidia. 'I can hear them, Father. I really can. I'm not wrong,' she told him confidently.

'You had better be,' he said under his breath, craning forwards in vain to see through the mist.

Brannella said nothing but clung on tight about his neck and was suddenly quiet. Hal also fell to brooding. Surely he should just abandon this castle, leave the men and strike out on his own into the wilderness so that he could protect his girl. All else was already lost. Perhaps it was wrong to stay here, stubbornly and forlornly hoping to salvage what little could be saved of the castle and its men. Looking about him at the battlements protecting the deep courtyard, he saw the soldiers moving silently in their heavy cloaks, swathed in the warm mist from their breaths. Already in the milky grey light they looked like ghosts. It wouldn't be long now before they were.

He was aware of the warmth from Brannella's little body against his skin and all he could think was of her lying cold and dead; the thought was unbearable. He squeezed his eyes shut, trying to be rid of the image and, for a moment, thought he could hear a strange, shrill cry on the breeze though it was too distant and faint to be clearly identifiable.

'I'm hungry,' Brannella complained.

Hal stared south down the canyon's length. 'Sergeant!' he shouted across to the next tower, his strong voice carrying easily in the still air. 'Watch the south. The slightest thing out of the ordinary, you raise the alarm instantly, you hear?'

But what could they do? he thought bitterly. The hobs were

so numerous and, though the harshness of the winter climate at this high altitude had played in his favour, there seemed to be no end of hob gangs hurrying to replace the ones they slaughtered.

Brannella wriggled out of his grasp and scrabbled down the steps before him, showing no ladylike decorum. She had always charged after her elder brothers without any thought for safety and now hurtled down the spiralling steps more like a goat than a girl. Hal sighed. He had long since given up imploring her to be careful. It still made his heart gasp when he saw her behave in this manner – there was no way that the small female body was designed for such physical activity – and he was terrified for her. He was slower nowadays on the stairs than he used to be in his youth. Of course he was heavier and the loss of his left hand meant that he could not support himself on the rope that spiralled down the curve of the stairwell. Still, it was a sobering thought to realize that, one day, his daughter would outstrip him in pace. At least, he hoped they would all live to see that day.

The mood in the refectory hall of the old keep was sombre. A porridge of millet was served to the men and there was much muttering amongst them about being treated no better than the horses.

'You're right there,' one of the men grumbled over his spoon. 'We're breakfast for those hobs and ravenshrikes just like the brood mares on the southern pastures were yesterday.'

Hal's eyebrows rose. He hadn't heard of this latest mishap; no one had reported it to him. But somehow he didn't care all that much; it seemed inevitable that disaster after disaster would befall them and he was numb to them all now. His distress over the fate of Torra Alta was entirely overshadowed by the profound grief over his family.

He had not eaten properly in days, nor did he want to eat now. It was only Keridwen's lancing gaze from the far side of the hall that persuaded him of his obligation to set a good example to the men. He threaded his way through the hall and took his place near the Crone, realizing at once that she was not quite her usual, composed self. He took a few mouthfuls of the gritty porridge, conscious of the men's eyes on him, their grumbling silenced as he ate.

'Well, if it's good enough for Lord Hal, it's more than good enough for the likes of us,' one of the younger men said brightly and a general air of approval stirred through the garrison before the normal mealtime chatter returned.

Once, such respect would have deeply pleased Hal; he had loved the adoration of the men. But now it meant nothing to him. He looked at the empty chairs to either side of him and, as he felt the tears welling up, he tucked his head down and concentrated on his food. Brannella had already climbed out of her chair to squeeze onto Keridwen's lap and was now hungrily finishing the woman's gruel.

'I don't suppose you ate half of that,' Hal chided the old woman.

'She needs it more than me,' Keridwen said matter-of-factly.

'What's wrong?' Hal asked, looking into the woman's eyes. The deep blue had frosted as if she were looking inward rather than outward.

'I can smell them,' she said very quietly. 'Their outlines shade the mirror; I see them in the water and on every polished surface, even on the blade of your sword. They are coming.'

Hal didn't need to ask whom. Unlike Keridwen, he had seen no vision of them but he had smelt them on the breeze.

'It'll be the wagon train,' the Crone said grimly.

'I know,' Hal confirmed regretfully. 'But what more can I do?'

'Nothing,' Keridwen solemnly replied as she soothed Branella's raven-black locks.

'We'll have beef tonight though, won't we, men?' One of the sergeants raised his cup of water tainted with the distinctive golden hue of the ground water.

'Do you want to tell them or should we wait until the messengers arrive?' Keridwen asked.

'Never, dear old woman, be the bringer of bad news. Delegation is everything at such times.' Hal even managed a half smile. Knowing already that disaster was on them and that there was nothing he could do, he felt remote and light-headed.

Of course he regretted his decision to send the men and took full responsibility for their fate. Supplies were low and it had been impossible to reach the western coast where ships sent by his friend Ceowulf should be anchored, waiting with a cargo of flour, apple, pigs and Caldean wine. Baron Ceowulf of Caldea, now martial lord of southern Belbidia, had sent messengers informing him that the ships were coming, but it had made no difference. The winter was particularly harsh and the mountain roads were impassable. Moreover, thick ice around the coast made landing the ships impossible. There was no hope of the supplies reaching him until the thaw began in the spring.

Nevertheless, a dwindling grain store had forced Hal to act and he had sent fifty men to his south to meet supply wagons promised by his good neighbour, Baron Oxgard of Jotunn. At first he had been against the idea, knowing how the hobs had been gathering in vast numbers along that border. Only one of the three messengers that Oxgard sent actually got through but Baron Oxgard had evidently been determined not to let his neighbour down. Both barons had agreed that if they sent a force large enough they could cut their way through the disorganized gangs of hobs. Hal knew now that it had been a mistake.

Men rose, ready to brace themselves against the elements and stand the first watch of the day. Shortly after, those that had stood guard on the battlements during the latter part of the night trooped in tired, hungry and shivering. With poor nutrition, they were not able to withstand the bitter cold of the early hours before dawn, always the very harshest part of the night when death's frosty kiss touched the land. Morale was low, a perfect reflection of Hal's own dismal spirit. He knew it was up to him to improve matters but did he truly care about the men? Did he truly care about Torra Alta without Brid, Guthrey and even Quinn for that matter? Torra Alta wasn't his anyway.

He had been left to command the place while Caspar, the rightful lord, marched freely about the world. He had returned for one day, Hal thought darkly, and just look at what disaster he and his son have brought on us all! His teeth ground together in anger. Hope seeped out of him like blood from a wounded warrior.

Keridwen stood up from her chair and rapped the table with a wooden board, demanding silence. She began to speak out in rousing tones but, continuing to brood, Hal was not listening.

Slowly it dawned on him that all eyes were on him and the echo of Keridwen's words ringing in his head finally touched his mind. She had demanded silence and then told the men that he would speak, thereby forcing him to do so. He stared back at them blankly for a moment and then, at last, his sense of duty overcame his reluctance. He rose slowly, pushing back his sleeves to ensure his hand and stump were clearly visible. He liked to speak with gestures, and that was no different since the loss of his hand. In fact, he took great pains never to hide the loss. To hide it was to admit that it lessened him as a man and he would never admit that.

'Men,' he sounded forth in his deep voice, trained to be smooth and assured. 'You fear the winter; you curse the cold as the chilblains nibble at the ends of your fingers and toes and the raw wind scrapes the skin from your faces.' He had noted that all the men who could had grown coarse beards to protect them from this fate. 'But winter is our friend. Her blanket protects us, and her icicle fingers grasp more tightly about the throats of the hobs than they do about ours. The hobs do not have skill with cloth or skin; they are used to

113

warmer climates and temperate conditions underground. The mountains are still ours because of the winter. Praise it, bless it; the cold is our ally.'

'And when spring comes?' a young voice called out from one of the lower tables. 'Shall we expect the hobs to come gushing in with the melt waters?'

Trust one of the youngsters to think of something negative in his words, Hal thought resentfully. Gone were the days when the men simply cheered at every word he said. His charisma had always buoyed them up before, but now he knew that his own heavy spirit was a burden to his men. He took a breath, ready to speak, but Keridwen must have sensed the vexation in his heart and feared that he would not speak well.

'Spring will bring new life and new beginnings. The Great Mother will provide for us at the rebirth of the year,' she began.

Hal wiped his mouth with the back of his hand. The men did not need religion now; they need military facts. He interrupted Keridwen. 'True, the fresh dry winds and the warming sun will ease the plight of the hobs. But, when the snows melt, the ships promised by our friend Baron Ceowulf will be able to put in to shore, bringing reinforcements and a plentiful supply of food.'

'The hobs eat their dead; *they* will not run out of food,' another youngster muttered bitterly.

Hal picked up a tankard and flung it onto the table. 'How dare you doubt me! How dare you answer back to me, lord and warden of this castle!' Before he knew it, he had leapt up and crossed three tables, kicking bowls aside, and had the man by the throat, pulling him up out of his bench. 'These are our lands and we shall keep the hobs out of them. So long as we are determined, we can do it; do you hear me? If I stand on the portcullis alone and fight them off five at a time, I shall. Never, as I breathe, will I let the vermin take our home.'

'You will never stand alone,' a steady voice reassured him,

tugging his hand from the spluttering youngster. 'Because I shall always stand with you.'

Hal raised his eyes that could barely see for the blur of anger. He looked into the wrinkled face of the old Captain, who had seen his family through many disasters before now, and smiled.

'And I!' another cried, and the battle-marked face of young Pip stood proudly before him. 'We are here, alive and free, only because our fathers before us laid down their lives willingly for us. And if we must do the same for our children, so we shall.'

Hal grinned at him, gratefully. He stood up tall and spoke out boldly to the men. 'We shall be heroes, men of legend. We few shall be remembered for all time as those who would never yield. It takes heart, men, to be like that, great heart and soul. And if there is one thing I know about all of you here, it is that you have heart. You are kings amongst men, and we shall prevail!'

The cheer that issued forth from the men did much to lift his spirits. The Captain gave him a quiet smile and Hal knew that now was his moment to exit before he ruined the impact. His elder brother, Baron Branwolf, who had held the barony before, had also possessed a sense of drama and had put it to best effect.

'Captain, they are yours,' he said grandly before sweeping from the room.

He badly wanted a drink. It had been his one solace since Brid had left, easing the pain, numbing the acuteness of his distress. Why couldn't he have been born a common soldier or a simple herdsman? Why couldn't he have turned his back on Torra Alta all those years ago when his nephew had thrust its care into his hands? Of course, he knew why. Though his nephew, Caspar was only three years his junior; Baron Branwolf had brought them both up as his sons and, as the elder of the two, Hal had always felt that Torra Alta was truly his. He had eagerly grasped the position of warden, unaware

115

of how it would prick him. Now, of course, he was the one on whom everyone depended; there was no luxury of escape for him, not even in the mellow tartness of strong Belbidian ale. He could not have more than his ration. Obligations and responsibilities cramped about him as if he had squeezed into plate armour built for a smaller man.

Striding out alone for the high North tower, he marched away from the keep without giving his daughter or the Crone a single word. He didn't need to tell Keridwen to look after Brannella; his daughter would never leave the woman's side unless the Crone sent her on an errand to him. It was as if Brannella feared that Keridwen, just like her mother, would disappear if she didn't keep her watchful eye on her. Throwing back his cloak so that the men could see him embrace the cold, he crossed the courtyard to the tower and climbed the spiralling staircase within. Breathing hard from the fast climb, he reached the top and leant against the battlements. The pink dawn light overlaid the mist, imbuing it with glorious, smoky-red colours. He estimated that it wouldn't be long now before the few miserable survivors came struggling up the canyon to bring him the tragic news of the fate of their men and the wagon train.

He knew it was coming yet still he hoped beyond hope that he was wrong. What was he to do now? He couldn't condemn his men to starvation here, and yet where could they go? Again, he wished he could abandon Torra Alta and steal away with Brannella. Sometimes he thought the only thing that stopped him was the hope, however forlorn, that Brid might return here.

Keridwen had told him a hundred times that Brid would have more sense than to try and get back to Torra Alta, which was now cut off, a lonely barren rock in a seething sea of hobs and ravenshrikes. She would protect the boys and find a place of safety, the Crone had assured him.

Hal shrugged. 'No, she would come back to me,' he said out loud, imagining that he was arguing with Keridwen.

'But how could she?' he heard the Crone's voice in his head.

'The hobs hold all the lands to the south. Not even the wagon train with its heavily armed escort could get through.'

His thoughts stopped abruptly as he watched a dark shape cut through the mist and come streaking up towards the root of the Tor. A trumpet blast sounded two short notes, announcing the rider's arrival. Hal wearily descended the tower in readiness to receive the news that he knew awaited him. Marching out into the courtyard, he had to wait only a few minutes before the soldier, whipping his exhausted horse about the neck, arrived at the barbican. The horse was smeared in foamy sweat and trembled on the cobbles, its hooves slipping out from under it. A groom rushed out to steady the animal's head.

'Well, at least there'll be horse meat on the table tonight,' one of the men said.

The messenger fell out of the saddle and was caught by two of the garrison.

'Speak up, man, before you collapse,' the Baron ordered with no sympathy in his voice.

Battered and bruised, with streaks of blood about his face, he had clearly been at the edge of the fighting. He was breathing with difficulty as if his ribs were broken. Hal felt saddened at the sight of him but was now immune to the shock that he might once have experienced.

'Hobs!' he gasped. 'Hobs in the early morning fell on us from all sides. There was no hope or help. None!' he moaned pitifully, panting in sharp, shallow breaths as he struggled for air. 'Twenty men died in an instant. Many hobs immediately fell to eating them and even took bites out of the horses while they were still alive and kicking. It was sickening.' He doubled over for a moment and clutched his sides, grimacing with pain. After a moment's pause he continued, 'About a dozen of us got away, running in all directions, but I was one of the few whose horse wasn't injured. I doubt . . .' he began and trailed off.

'Get the man some water,' Hal ordered.

There was no more he needed to hear from this man. The sea of faces around him became a blur as he realized they were all waiting on his word to give some explanation, some word of solace or reassurance. But what could he say? What was there to say about another fifty men dead and no promise of food?

'Back to your posts,' he ordered firmly. 'Lieutenant Piperol, take a dozen men, head down into the canyon and see if there are any more survivors you can help home. Captain, I wish to see you and the rest of your lieutenants in my upper hall. We must take counsel.' He pushed his way through the men who staggered back, dazed and bewildered. 'To your posts, men. I want another twenty to go out and forage for wood. Take the bullock carts. The smell of cow doesn't attract the hobs as much as the sweet smell of horse.'

'But sir!' voices implored about him. 'The wagon train! The men!'

'They are lost,' Hal said flatly. 'Nothing I can say will change that.'

The men had lost friends and family that day just as they had over previous weeks. He felt sorry for them but they had no more right to grieve than he had. His soul was devoid of any spare sympathy with which to salve their wounded hearts.

As he mounted the stairs to the upper keep, he knew that it was time for action. He was no good to Brid here and was gradually becoming less than an asset to the castle. It was no longer a time for delegation; action was needed and he would lead it.

Chapter 7

'Gatekeeper, open up.' Aisholt commanded sternly, easing the heavy sack from his back.

Rollo eyed the sack and licked his lips, eager for supper. After the last two days, he was heartily sick of eels and cheese and longed for something new. Roast peacock appealed greatly to him right now. After fleeing the woods and running across the open ground on their way to the enclosure, they had stumbled on an entire parade of peacocks. They had proved extremely stupid creatures and they had killed three in a matter of minutes. Rollo was looking forward to eating them.

'We are full for the night,' came back the gruff reply from the wooden tower above. 'Find your own shelter.'

'You must be new here, otherwise you would know my voice,' Aisholt called up with restraint. 'I am sorry, sir,' he turned to Caspar, 'but in rough times like this men lose their manners.'

'Don't you have a password?' the Baron asked.

Aisholt shrugged. 'We used to, of course, since it is the most obvious thing.'

Leaf interrupted, 'But enemies quickly learnt it and they were let in too easily. It is often better to question a man at length.'

'That girl is too sharp,' Aisholt observed.

'Gatekeeper, I am Aisholt in the service of Baron Oxgard. I have been lookout on the east coast, but I have in my company persons of some stature and I must take them to Baron Oxgard.'

'You all look like ragamuffins to me,' the bearded face shouted down from above, wafting a smoking torch.

'Hey, listen up!' Aisholt shouted back, becoming angry at this treatment. 'You open the gate to us. The previous gatekeeper was good man Robins and the one before that the excellent fellow Oxfeet. You I do not know, since I have been on the coast four months. We have travelled long and we have lost one to the red dragons. Now open up, gatekeeper, and let us in before we fall prey to the beasts of the night. We have brought good food for supper. We have three peacocks!'

'Ahha! If you have food you may enter, good man Aisholt. I hope you are whom you say because I have had word to look out for you. Baron Oxgard is eager to hear from you. It seems you have been remiss in sending in your reports.'

'I have sent them with the utmost punctuality; it must be the messengers who never fulfilled their errands,' Aisholt defended himself.

'In times like this, that is most likely,' the gatekeeper said congenially.

Rollo wondered when adults would give up using such phrases as 'in times like this'. Couldn't they see that the world had changed forever? It was impossible to turn back the clock to when they were safe and secure, growing old and fat in their comfortable homes.

He had been wondering about the enclosure Aisholt had told them about and was pleased to find that it appeared to be a small fortress built in the heart of dense woods. A stone tower topped by battlements stood above steel gates. A metal mesh covered the circular courtyard within, protecting them from any creature attempting to attack from above. Men with crossbows and light war engines stood crammed along the battlements, ready to repel assaults from any quarter.

'Come in, come in,' the gatekeeper welcomed them. 'You and your friends, Aisholt, may enter on the required fee. I need a crown per head.'

Aisholt raised an eyebrow. 'It becomes more expensive by the month, I see.'

'It costs our Baron Oxgard more and more to keep the enclosures open. If there are fools who wish to wander the outer lands for a whim or for some form of gain, they must pay the price. A crown a head or you must stay outside.'

'I do not carry that sort of money on me and we have brought three peacocks that will provide an excellent feast. Is that not worth our entry?' Aisholt asked.

The gatekeeper frowned. 'If we were to be paid in kind, we would be overrun with livestock and have no room for the souls that seek shelter here. However, presently we are short of supplies and I shall accept the peacocks as payment for three of you but I'll need a crown a head for the rest.'

Rollo wondered how much money this gatekeeper was making on top of his wage. It seemed that he could extort almost any amount he wanted out here and he doubted that Baron Oxgard received the full levy.

'Does your overlord know the amount you are charging?' Brid demanded coldly. 'I wonder at it because he is a generous man and has genuine concerns for his people.'

'He does indeed,' the gatekeeper replied smartly. 'Do you take me for a cheat?' he asked in an affronted manner.

'By no means,' Caspar said hastily and then hissed at Brid, 'Do you want to have a safe place to stay the night or not?'

She shrugged. 'It just isn't right to charge desperate folk so much. Think of the wretched homeless who must seek sanctuary here, forced to pay everything they have for one night of safety. And it would be their last night because, after paying the man here, they would have nothing left for another.'

'It is unlikely that he's charging more than Oxgard directed, as the Baron would soon hear of it,' Caspar argued.

'He may well be charging the correct amount but he may not be telling Oxgard the number that have stayed here,' Leaf said calmly. 'It wouldn't take much to say that twenty slept there

121

that night when in fact there were thirty and so keep the extra ten crowns.'

Caspar wrinkled up his nose. 'Indeed that is so.'

'Still,' Aisholt said, 'it takes a brave man to command one of these outposts. Do you have the money, sir?'

Caspar produced the four crowns without protest, allowing them to pass through the heavy gates into the courtyard that was tightly crammed with people. The gatekeeper had not been exaggerating when he claimed they were full. Looking about him, Rollo observed that the people around him were from all walks of life though most were merchants, still trying to pluck a living from one community to the next.

Exhausted by their long journey, he was content to fall asleep amongst their baggage while Aisholt and Guthrey presented their offerings, which were eagerly taken from them. The peacocks were roasted in the open courtyard beneath the mesh ceiling. Soon the two score or so that were crammed into the tight space were sitting down calmly, all watching in unnatural silence.

As tireless as ever, Brid was the last to sit. First, she carefully checked her sons over for wounds and gave them both a paste for their scratches. Then she attended to Caspar's arm before looking over the rest of them and finally coming to Isolde. The young priestess was breathing very quickly now and she kept putting her hand to her heart as if it pained her. The bright golden green colour of her eyes had dulled as they were bloodshot and sore and even her glorious strawberry blonde hair was beginning to look lifeless.

Rollo was glad there was no mirror. Although rather mousy and nervy, she had still been very beautiful at times, especially when unaware that he was watching her. But now her illness and her wounds made her hideous.

'It is time, my sweet,' Brid said tenderly. 'I must change the bandage.'

'Not here,' Isolde hissed, her eyes flitting around anxiously at all the company.

Rollo followed her gaze as she looked from stranger to stranger, her eye touching on either a club, sword or hatchet, one of which was gripped by every man present. Clearly, all feared to put down their weapons even here in the enclosure as they stared into the flames, waiting for the juices to run from the peacocks.

Rollo sat back, closed his eyes and quickly fell asleep. It was a while later that hunger roused him from his rest, the smell of roasted peacock wafting towards him and the aroma teasing his brain from his sleep. He sat up and yawned, his mouth dry and lips cracking a little.

Seeing that the youth had stirred, Aisholt brought him a plate.

'There is no need for you to wait on us,' Caspar said considerately to the soldier.

Aisholt smiled. 'You are kind sir, but, in truth, I was thinking of the welfare of all. Obviously, it's best if these fair ladies do not mingle with strangers and the youths are perhaps a little too inexperienced in life to go mixing with the rum lot that are taking refuge here. We don't want any fights.'

'You are wise, Aisholt,' Caspar agreed.

'You don't get to be a fully grown man nowadays without a little wisdom,' Aisholt replied with a smile.

Rollo scowled at his father, thinking him too familiar with the commoner. How could a man rule, how could he command even the simple tower of Torra Alta if he fraternized so freely with the men?

While Aisholt carried a large plate laden with meat for them all to share before going back for a pitcher of water, the gatekeeper was already yelling over the wall at some-one else.

'I said a crown a head; nothing less will do. We are full here and you must find shelter elsewhere.'

'There are hylups in the woods,' a terrified female voice returned. 'My sister and I have just fled our homes.'

'You should have made your homes stronger,' the man

123

retorted. 'Have you never heard the tale of the three little pigs?' He guffawed heartlessly at his own joke.

Caspar reached into his pockets and looked as if he were about to say something but Leaf stayed his hand.

'Do not do it, Spar,' she said, tears pricking at her eyes.

'I must. I cannot leave them out there to be torn to pieces when a simple coin will save them.'

'You mustn't do it,' Leaf insisted. 'If you offer to pay, all here will know that you can spare the money. And it is most likely that you carry very much more. Now looking at your fellow men here, I think it most unlikely that there is more than a handful that are law-fearing. Most would slit your throat while you slept for the chance to raid your pockets. That bunch there,' she nodded at a huddle of unshaven brutes clad in leather and armour, 'look like mercenaries to me.'

'You know, I think she's right,' Brid said though she continued to look towards the gates in anger and distress about the situation.

Reluctantly, Caspar sat back but was still champing his teeth in frustration at the exchange going on between the gatekeeper and what sounded like two young women outside.

'But good man, gatekeeper, our younger sister, mother and father were savaged by hylups. You must let us in.'

'I have heard nothing of hylups in these parts,' Aisholt murmured.

'No, indeed, but you have been away several months,' Leaf reminded him.

'Child, do you always have an answer for everything?' the man asked her.

The company of Torra Altans whispered intently amongst themselves, trying to blot out the argument between the gatekeeper and the female travellers outside the enclosure. Though their plight distressed his father and the others, Rollo was past caring. What did it matter if a few more died in this terrible country? It seemed to him that people were dying at every turn.

124

'But, Sir, we are just two young women lost and alone out here. You cannot turn your back on us. Not even the hardest of hearts could reject two maidens unable to defend themselves.'

Rollo instantly thought of Gart and how he had hoped to do more than his fair share of rescuing distressed maidens.

The gatekeeper grunted. 'Throw back your hoods and let me have a look at you so I can see whether you are who you claim.' There was a moment's pause. 'Indeed, two very fair maidens, if my eyes don't deceive me. Now, did I mention I was amenable to other forms of payment?'

The teeth clenched in Caspar's jaw and Aisholt's hand tensed around his weapon.

'I have a daughter of my own; she is in Baron Oxgard's service and I would hate to think that she might be treated like this by any of his men. We are an honourable people in Jotunn and this sort of thing is despicable,' the sergeant growled angrily.

'You are a noble man, Aisholt,' Brid told him. 'And I shall see to it that Baron Oxgard hears how highly I hold you in my esteem. But we can do nothing. If the girls are willing to buy their safety in this way, it is surely better that than being eaten in the forest.'

'The gatekeeper should let them in and protect them as is his duty. This is dishonourable!' Aisholt was not to be soothed.

'Many an honourable man has become dishonourable the moment he thinks he can get away with it,' Leaf announced.

'You do not know that! You have merely read such nonsense and just because something is written does not make it so,' Aisholt argued crossly.

'My people have recorded their observations over thousands of years, and therefore I think it is likely that it is so.' Leaf was unruffled.

'You cannot damn us all so simply.'

Leaf laughed. 'I did not say that *all* honourable men become

125

dishonourable, only that many may – if they think they can get away with it.'

'I think we are just about to see Leaf's theory tested,' Brid announced as the two young girls were ushered in through the steel gates and their cloaks were immediately tugged from their backs by two soldiers standing guard.

'You won't be needing them in here now, lasses, not with the heat from the fires,' one said, the firelight accentuating the leer on his face.

The two girls were pulled forward into the centre of the courtyard and they squealed in such a way that caused every man to turn their eyes to them. Rollo was surprised to see that the girls were much better dressed than he had expected. Their clothes were a light weave, bordered with lace and silk, and were barely substantial enough for the winter's night. Still squealing, they clutched themselves, and with wide eyes they twirled round and around in panic as the men tightened their circle about them.

Rollo could sense the sudden excitement. Four of the soldiers abandoned their posts on the battlements, climbing down ropes dangling from the battlements to alight in the open centre of the courtyard.

'You see!' Leaf exclaimed. 'Opportunity makes every one of you think evil thoughts. Are you not telling me that the desire to watch or even participate is not in your thoughts?' she accused Aisholt.

He coloured hotly. 'Indeed, it is not! I shall stop this!'

Caspar shook his head. 'No, let others do it.'

'But, sir, what if none other comes forward?'

'There will surely be others. I have faith that someone will help these girls.'

Brid snorted and Rollo was surprised that she had not marched out to stop the soldiers. In fact, it was a long minute before an old woman stood up and shouted at the men. 'You filthy brutes. Your duty is to defend these people, not abuse them.'

'Hey, old mother, perhaps you want to join the girls here? There are soldiers who've been out here months and would be happy of anything – even you,' one jeered.

The soldiers laughed, as did some of the travellers, though others stared on in horror.

'Aisholt is right; I have to stop this,' Caspar insisted, evidently already losing his faith in human nature.

Brid tugged him down. 'Save your temper, Spar. Those girls know exactly what they are doing. They will have fleeced half the men in this enclosure of three-quarters of their money by the time the evening is through. No one travels in winter dressed like that if they do not intend to use their natural assets.'

Caspar sat back and laughed at himself.

Aisholt finally relaxed. 'Still,' he grumbled, 'I am disappointed to be proved wrong.'

'You will not change human nature any more than the nature of any other people,' Leaf told him.

He smiled. 'No, it seems not.'

Rollo snorted; he was certain he would not have behaved so. He found no amusement in it at all though he saw Guthrey and Quinn's eyes bulge as they stared at the two girls, who were now twirling and spinning between four soldiers.

'Guthrey! Quinn!' Brid snapped. 'What you choose to enjoy in your own company is your own business, but you will show me the respect of turning your backs on such a scene and eating with the rest of us.'

'Mother, you do not own my eyes or my thoughts,' Guthrey calmly retorted, 'and, besides, I have seen you dance naked around the Beltane's fires with no thought for propriety.'

'With *all* thought for propriety,' Brid contradicted, though Rollo did not see how that was possible. 'Now do as you are told.'

Quinn reluctantly obeyed his mother, but Guthrey was clearly too tempted by the sight of the scantily clad maidens, who, little by little, were shedding layer upon layer of their lacy garments. In fact, he was so enjoying the spectacle that he seemed to have quite forgotten his hunger. Rollo grasped the opportunity to take more than his fair share and Leaf gave him a wink as if to say that she had noted his opportunism and that he had proved yet again her theory relating to man.

'So tell me, Leaf, are *your* people always honourable?' Caspar asked. 'Are there no times when you do the wrong thing for gain?'

She shrugged. 'I am sure we are not so very different from you and probably just as unaware of our failings. Like all other peoples, we are perhaps not as good at analysing ourselves as we are at observing others.'

Brid laughed delightedly at this and lent forward to kiss the girl's forehead. 'Oh, Leaf, you are a marvel,' she said, grinning broadly at the child. 'You shall grow to be the wisest and most respected of elders on our blessed Earth.'

'Sadly, not.' Leaf dropped her head and looked down at her small, neat feet. 'I shall grow mad slowly. Soon my thoughts will become blurred and milky and I shall remember less and perceive little. It will all be lost. The most of what makes me shall be gone and I shall be just a shell.'

Rollo was finding it hard to concentrate because the laughter of the soldiers was becoming more raucous as the two girls began teasing and taunting them. Soon, the soldiers began vying with each other for their attentions and, as Brid had predicted, it was only a matter of minutes before the girls were being plied with coins for the offer of an intimate embrace.

The old woman, who had done her best to stand up for them, now scowled in disgust and turned her back. 'I'm never going to offer to help another person again,' she declared, which produced a ripple of laughter from the people to either side. 'There's only one thing for it nowadays and that's to look out for oneself.' She stamped up with a plate to the table where the roast peacocks were being carved. 'I've paid a damned sight more than those whores have for their entry here and so I shall have more than their share of meat,' she demanded.

'That's what you think, old woman,' the soldier on cooking duty sneered, giving her no bigger ration than any other man, woman or child.

Rollo slept well that night and was disturbed only by Guthrey, who rose and slunk off to ply one of the two girls with yet more coins in an attempt to secure himself a pleasurable hour. Without raising his head, Rollo watched, wondering what the outcome might be. However, the young women had found themselves a quiet corner on the far side of the enclosure and he could see nothing. Frustrated, he waited for Guthrey's return, which he thought would be almost immediate, but to his surprise the young Torra Altan, who was no older than himself, was a very long time. He eventually came back, grinning from ear to ear.

Brid was awoken by his return and angrily snapped upright. Without any warning, she thwacked him hard across the head.

'It's all very well, Guthrey, but you should know better than to go showering your money about foolishly. And I thought you had none on you. Where did you get it?' Brid demanded.

'It was the crown from the cheese,' he said rubbing his head, his stupid grin still broad on his face. 'And it was well worth it.'

'Ooh yes, a crown for twenty seconds of enjoyment,' Quinn teased.

'You are no master yourself,' Guthrey sneered back.

Quinn looked as if he were searching for something sharp to say but then his eyes fell on Isolde and a pained expression clouded his eyes. He sunk back down dejectedly. 'No, perhaps you are right.'

The exchange woke Isolde from her deep sleep and she sat up suddenly, eyes wide, her whole body shaking. She appeared to have trouble breathing and was gasping in shallow breaths and pressing her shaking hand against her breast in an attempt to steady herself. 'Help,' she wheezed. 'I am lost.'

Somewhere deep in the forest a wolf howled its lonesome

wail as if echoing the girl's pain. Brid scooped her up in her arms and held her close.

'Do not worry, sweet child, we shall see you mended soon. Keridwen will know what to do.'

Wrapped tightly in Brid's arms, Isolde gradually relaxed and her breathing steadied.

Rollo slept for a few uncomfortable hours then, unable to sleep more, looked up at the starless night and wondered whether his grandmother in Torra Alta was safe and whether she knew where they were. The mysterious shapes of billowing black clouds rolled and stirred in the ink of the sky and he knew that a storm was coming. He only had to wait another half an hour to be proved right. As the murky light of dawn did its best to penetrate the clouds and crawl above the overhanging walls of the enclosure, rain thrashed down, making the fire hiss and smoke. Soon, the firm earth was awash and they slipped about in the mud.

'All out by dawn,' the gatekeeper shouted. 'That is the order. You get a loaf of bread each and you are on your way. We offer shelter for the night only.'

Caspar groaned and pulled his cloak tightly about him, his eyes running over his companions, counting up the number in their bedraggled company. 'Aisholt, are you ready to move?'

The soldier saluted. 'Yes, sir! And we are now but a day's march from Oxgard where we can at last offer you some proper comfort.'

'I do not seek comfort,' Caspar said heavily, 'only peace. We must help Isolde.'

As they turned out of the enclosure, Aisholt led them through the deep piles of beech leaves that carpeted the floor, the bare branches now offering very little relief from the rain. The large trees in this ancient wood of Jotunn offered them good protection from dragons and, since there was little grass, they were not at much risk from taur either. The biggest threat, Aisholt informed them, came from hobs and, sadly, opportunist robbers. In dribs and drabs, the other travellers leaked out of the enclosure and spread out to take their own routes, though a number followed behind the company of Torra Altans. It didn't take Rollo long to notice that the two young women who had entertained the soldiers the previous night were in the group behind.

Aisholt cheerily encouraged the Torra Altans, his step more sprightly than before and his grip on his spear more relaxed. 'I haven't seen my daughter in months,' the sergeant told Caspar. 'She's the fairest thing you ever saw and I want her to grow up to see a happier world.'

There was a snort of laughter behind them. Rollo turned to see that the two inappropriately dressed women had quickened their pace to join their company.

'A happier life! Better times!' one sneered. 'You should not think like that, old man, otherwise your life will be over before you know it. You should enjoy what pleasures there are to be had each and every day of your life. Smile whenever you have the chance, for, though life may be tough and hard, it is always more easily borne with a smile.'

'I see you are philosophers as well as trollops and cheats,' Aisholt said unkindly.

The taller girl, whose ginger hair now hung in wet ropes down her bare neck, dripping water onto her dress which was dark with rain and clinging hard to her firm figure, looked him in the eye. Her big eyes blinked rapidly in wounded pretence. 'Now come, sir, we did no harm. We gave fair pleasure and brought many smiles, is that not so?' She winked at Guthrey who puffed out his chest and grinned broadly back.

'Just like his father,' Caspar grumbled under his breath.

'Young ladies, you may think you do no harm but you do. To a father like me, you make me worry for my own daughter at home and you bring sadness to the women,' Aisholt rebuked them.

The girls shrugged as if this were meaningless. 'It seems to me that any one of them could do the same if they so chose.'

Brid looked at them. 'You celebrate nothing and you sully

the name of womanhood, but,' she said with a smile, 'I have to admit that I admire your spirit.'

'So do I,' Guthrey added and then giggled, rather ruining the effect of his newly procured image of manliness. Guthrey and Quinn continued to nudge each other and laugh smuttily as they went.

It had not taken long for the two young women to beg to join their company and ask for their protection as they travelled towards the heart of Jotunn. It even seemed to Rollo that his father was secretly amused by their company. Leaf appeared fascinated by them and studied them uncritically as they marched through the relatively easygoing territory.

'Well, were there hylups last night or was that just another ploy?' Aisholt asked, clearly finding it difficult to look the young women in the eye for fear that his gaze would slip downwards.

Both girls shrugged and smiled as if their answer was of no consequence.

Rollo was becoming increasingly aggravated by Guthrey and Quinn as they continued their lewd conversation. Guthrey's eyes were firmly planted on the buttocks of the dark-haired girl that swayed temptingly before him. She turned and gave him a quick wink and the two Torra Altan youths pretended to stagger for a couple of paces as if slain by this attention, which made the girls laugh. Rollo noted, however, that Isolde looked away in pained disgust.

'They are quite ridiculous,' Leaf commented in amazement.

Guthrey dropped back to be level with Rollo. 'Come, Rollo, cousin, do not tell me that you side with the women and Aisholt on these matters. Tell me that they tempt you too, or am I to believe you are not a man?'

'I think it is frivolous of you to behave in such a way at such a time. Can't you think of Isolde's feelings?' Rollo retorted haughtily. He saw no way that he could acquire attention from either of the women and so would save face by scorning them.

'Ha!' Guthrey goaded. 'If I spent my days worrying about what the last love thought of me, I would never find any sport and be old and dried up before I had feasted on my share of the fare. You are just afraid that they will laugh at you. Or is it that you don't know what to do?' he taunted.

Rollo scowled. He didn't want to be thought of as inadequate or any less of a man. Far from it, he could well see that the two females offered considerable satisfaction but he felt a fool in front of his father and Brid. Clenching his teeth, he tried to ignore Guthrey and looked away.

'You know what?' Guthrey said to Quinn. 'He knows he can't win them. I shall bet a crown that I can have my way with one of them without having to pay. Let us see who of the three of us will be the first to achieve it.'

'Guthrey, you know I'm not going to play that game with you.' Quinn laughed. 'I know you have no more crowns to bet but I suppose you've no need of one since I've been losing that sort of contest to you ever since you were ten. I may as well just turn out my pockets and hand you what I have right now.'

Guthrey shook back his glossy black hair and grinned, his white teeth flashing brilliantly. 'Well, it's hardly my fault that I'm the most dashing young chap around.'

'I'll take you up on your bet,' Rollo challenged impulsively, unable to bear the youth's smugness. 'Though I'll want paying when I win.'

Guthrey mocked him with a laugh. 'You? You have as much charm as a stable lad.'

'I should think there are a great many stable lads that have more charm than you,' Rollo smartly retorted.

'Ha!' Guthrey snorted. 'We'll just see how easily you make a fool of yourself, shall we?'

'There is little hope of that but I am looking forward to seeing you look even more ridiculous than you normally do,' Rollo said smoothly.

Rollo was aware that his father had glanced over his shoulder at him, his eyebrows raised. Brid elbowed Caspar in the ribs and

133

he smartly looked away. Rollo wondered what the priestess was saying to his father but decided that his most pressing business was to fulfil the challenge bestowed on him by Guthrey. Of course his father would not understand the importance of it all and would no doubt scold him for such ridiculous behaviour, but it mattered very much what Guthrey thought of him. His standing amongst all Torra Altans would depend on how he impressed Hal's son.

'To make it easier for you,' Guthrey suggested, 'I shall take the tall redhead, who is altogether the more forceful and attractive of the two. Are we all agreed that she will be the harder conquest?'

Rollo nodded at this. 'Conceivably she might be,' he said begrudgingly.

'Just to clarify the rules here, the one who wins is the one who persuades their allotted lady to kiss them fully and properly on the lips. Obviously, on the move as we are, nothing more is possible and it is well known that courtesans are loath to kiss,' he said authoritatively. 'Are we ready?'

Rollo again nodded.

After smiling smugly at Rollo, Guthrey marched forward. He scooped up some winter jasmine, which trailed through the trees at the side of the way, and Rollo thought that it was just his lot in life that his opponent had such luck and therefore the happy opportunity to offer something first. Although he had immediately thought of doing the same, he could not make such a gesture now as it would look lame and inept. Suddenly gripped by inadequacy, he watched as Guthrey effortlessly launched into a conversation with the very pretty, ginger-haired young woman, who fluttered her eyelids and flushed convincingly. All the while, her eyes looked the youth up and down, appraising him. Rollo wondered how well he would cope under such scrutiny. Guthrey, of course, appeared completely at ease under her critical stare.

'I trust I meet with your approval?' he said, bowing low. 'I am quite open to more detailed appraisal as soon as you wish.'

He raised his eyebrows suggestively and she tilted her head to one side as if not quite certain what to make of him. Then she burst out laughing.

Although Guthrey had not made the best of starts, Rollo decided that it was he who was fast on his way to losing a gold crown and one that he would have to ask his father for at that. The humiliation would be too great. There was nothing for it but to swallow his fears and get on with the task at hand.

He lengthened his stride to march alongside the dark-haired girl, who had dropped back to give her supposed sister a little privacy with Guthrey. Thankfully, his ankle only hurt a little now and he was able to force himself to walk without a limp. He had to add a little skip so that his footfall would match her rhythm but then found to his embarrassment that he had to put yet another skip in to get it right. She looked at him sideways and he suddenly could think of nothing to say and so looked down at his feet. He at once noticed the lamentable state of his boots and then could think of even less to say as he felt her eyes crawl all over him. Hastily, he glanced at her, gave her a sheepish grin and then looked away.

What was the matter with him? It wasn't as if he was inexperienced in the art of courting fair maidens. There had been little else to distract him at home in the year since his mother died. Whilst she had been alive, his interest in girls had not yet awakened and he had found them rather silly and dull. But soon after her death he had discovered much diversion in their company.

However, this girl was much older, in her late teens or perhaps even twenty, and was definitely very experienced in life. Already, she had the upper hand since he could not return her appraising look.

At last, he found the courage to speak. 'Your hair is very pretty,' he began, expecting her to thank him for the compliment; instead, she laughed.

'Is that the best you can do?' she teased him. 'I thought fine folk like yourselves were trained in the art of manners.'

Her eyes were twinkling and Rollo knew she was toying with him.

'Pray, tutor me then,' he said. 'What should a youth say to woo a fair lady?'

She laughed again at this. 'I am not for the winning but the buying. I thought that was fairly obvious after last night. What possible benefit would it be to me to befriend a youth half my age?'

'More than you might think,' Rollo retorted, now rather hurt by her behaviour. 'My father is a Baron. I have standing . . . wealth.'

'Indeed?' The girl looked at him a little more intently. 'But if I allow you to use me, none of that will come my way, will it? And who's to say your father's barony will still be intact by the time you get home? The hobs are on the move, you know.'

Rollo knew he was not experienced enough to judge but he thought that she was a little too educated for her profession. With such beauty and an obviously clear-thinking head, did she really need to resort to selling her body?

'So, young gentleman, what exactly is it you're after?' she asked into his floundering silence.

Rollo was lost. She had the upper hand whereas he could see Guthrey already pushing the red-haired girl's thick hair back off her shoulder and whispering into her ear. Rollo scowled and thought he must try harder. 'You were about to educate me in the art of winning a lady. Tell me how it is achieved.'

The girl tilted her head to one side and studied him again. This time her eyes were thoughtful and her smile less cruel. 'Actually, you know, I shouldn't have teased you about that because, really, there is no right or wrong way. People often talk about the right and the wrong things to say but, truly, it doesn't matter too much what you say so long as you can strike up a conversation somehow and are not rude. And it's not a bad idea to begin by asking for a name.'

'Oh!' Rollo said lamely. 'I am sorry. Dear Lady, I would be delighted if you would tell me your name.'

'That's more like it!' She smiled at him in amusement. 'Fanchon. I am Fanchon. You see, it matters very much more how you say something rather than what you say. Now, see your friend there? I don't know what he has said because Dominica is very hard to impress and yet she seems to be genuinely enjoying herself. I think you could not go wrong by taking a few hints from him.'

'But that's the whole point,' Rollo groaned. 'We had a bet. He said I would make a fool of myself within minutes and that he would be the first to win one of you.'

Fanchon looked at Guthrey's back, her eyes running up and down his body. 'That,' she pointed at Guthrey, 'is what it takes. Confidence. Women are attracted to confidence. But, there again, not too much confidence. It is not nice to be thought of as a forgone conclusion. I think your friend needs a lesson.' She nodded thoughtfully and then winked at Rollo. 'It's been hard lately. Very hard. The enclosures are brutal places and yet we must survive. I have had little fun in a long while and we thought that, since there are women in your party, joining your band might give us a little rest until we reach the next enclosure. We are travelling to our aunt's in the west and have a long way to go.'

Rollo looked at her. He knew this explanation wasn't quite true. He guessed that Dominica and Fanchon had judged them wealthy and therefore easier to fleece. He had seen how her eyes had appraised his father's rings and the amulet about Brid's neck. They were small clues but enough for someone whose livelihood depended on making such judgements.

'So how far did you have to go with me to achieve your bet?' Fanchon asked.

Rollo felt himself flush and cursed his freckled skin as the heat rose up his neck. 'Only a kiss, but a proper one,' he exclaimed.

Fanchon snorted again and then grinned from ear to ear. 'Well, you know, young lad, I feel sorry for you, and a kiss is but a kiss to me.' She halted in her tracks, pulled him towards her and wrapped her arms about him. 'Guthrey,' she called softly.

As the youth span round to see why she had hailed him, she plunged her tongue into Rollo's mouth and closed her lips about him, her mouth warm and wet. Rollo felt overwhelmingly close as her hair tumbled over him, her cool hands now on his neck, drawing him closer.

He opened his eyes to look over Fanchon's shoulder at Guthrey, who was purple with rage. The black-haired Torra Altan scowled at Rollo as Fanchon pushed him away and hurried to rejoin her friend. The two girls put their heads together and laughed. Rollo's mind was a happy, warm haze for a few minutes, his eyes glued to the back of Fanchon's gorgeous hair, his gaze sliding down the glossy dark tresses to rest on her swaying buttocks as she ambled ahead. He could barely hear Guthrey, who was snarling like a mastiff, until Quinn retrieved a coin from his pockets and handed it to his half-brother who, in turn, tossed it into Rollo's face. He caught it in a reflex action without even seeing it, pocketed it and grinned.

'I say you cheated. I demand a rematch.' Guthrey's eyes were black with anger.

Rollo laughed. 'No, Guthrey. I won fair and square and I'm quite content with that,' he said happily, certain that it would annoy Guthrey even more if he refused him the satisfaction of accepting a second challenge.

'I know you cheated,' Guthrey snapped sullenly.

'Oh, don't be so ridiculous, Guthrey,' Quinn laughed at him. 'Fair is fair. No one is more surprised than me as I've lost more girls to you than anyone else on this earth but, all the same, Rollo obviously has his own charm.'

Rollo was glad of the support. Since they had rescued Guthrey from Silas's clutches, Quinn had sought only his brother's company and so had barely paid him any attention. He had thought he had lost Quinn's friendship and so was pleased when he grinned at him. The Torra Altan's common sense and calmness balanced the turbulence in his mind and brought him some ease.

Isolde, however, seemed most displeased with him, and Rollo wondered why he cared so much. Isolde was hardly a catch and he would never have thought about kissing her.

A hand slipped into his and he looked down at Leaf.

'I would be careful if I were you,' she warned under her breath. 'I don't think you know what game you are playing; those women are not to be trusted.'

'How would you know? You are much too young to know about such things.' Rollo sniffed at her.

She smiled and let out a long, deep sigh, more as if she were his grandmother rather than a girl even younger than he was. 'Why do I have to explain everything to you? A huge number of people left the enclosure and those two could have chosen to leave with any of them. There were merchants, mercenaries, soldiers, farmers, townsfolk and no doubt a large number of villains. Those girls spoke with at least one man from each party last night and made themselves a pretty penny by the morning. When it was time to go, they didn't ask where everyone was bound; they merely selected us as the party they wished to travel with. Now why do you suppose that is?'

Rollo shrugged.

'They didn't say they wanted to reach Baron Oxgard, now did they? In fact, the story I heard was about trying to reach an old aunt who lived somewhere in the west. Remember? They could have left with anyone travelling in roughly this direction.'

Rollo nodded at this, suddenly looking at Leaf intently. 'You know, Leaf, you are right.'

The girl threw her eyes heavenward. 'Of course I am right! It doesn't take a genius to add two and two. Now listen; they certainly didn't choose us because we offered the best protection or even the best opportunity to earn money. If they wanted that they would have gone with that surly band of mercenaries who looked like they would have paid well for the services of those pair.'

'Perhaps they wanted a bit of a holiday?' Rollo suggested flippantly, still licking his lips and gazing at Fanchon, whom he found a hundred times more attractive now that he had sampled a taste of her. His body tingled all over.

'She's not interested in you,' Leaf told him sharply.

'How would you know?' Rollo asked, offended. She had kissed him; surely, she now felt something after being so close.

Leaf merely laughed but didn't trouble herself to make an explanation. 'Listen, Rollo, all that matters is that we weren't the obvious choice as the party to travel with and yet, when it was time to move out in the morning, they headed straight for us. So why do you think that was?'

Rollo shrugged. 'They liked the look of me?' he grinned, unable to guess at what Leaf was driving at.

'Of course,' she said sarcastically, 'but beyond that they must have learnt something about us.'

'From Guthrey?'

'Well, who else?' Leaf asked rhetorically. 'Of course Guthrey. He either said something or gave them something.'

'I don't think he gave them anything other than the obvious.'

'Hmm,' mumbled Leaf, clearly displeased by the lack of seriousness in his tone. 'He did; he gave them money. He gave them that crown from the cheese.'

Rollo nodded. 'Of course he did, Leaf, but that doesn't mean anything. Coins are all alike. A gold crown is a gold crown is a gold crown.'

'No, it had three scour lines on its rim; the coin was marked. Anyhow, something made them want to come with us,' Leaf said with certainty, her eyes following Dominica and Fanchon as they pushed past Isolde, taking great pains not to touch her, and hurried on ahead. The red-haired Dominica side-stepped straight towards Aisholt while the black-haired beauty, who had kissed Rollo, sidled up to Caspar, immediately all giggles and curls.

Rollo growled under his breath as he watched his father's involuntary beam at Fanchon.

Chapter 8

Crowded with trees, Oxgard's old mansion looked deserted in the evening light.

Rollo was tired; the last part of the journey seemed to be taking forever and he so needed to sleep. There had been nothing to take his mind off his father's deplorable behaviour on the journey as he flirted shamelessly with Fanchon. Rollo was very angry; his head throbbed and he wanted to rest.

Lights spun behind his eyes and he felt faintly sick. He had been pleased with his self-control of late and, despite very difficult circumstances, he had managed to keep an even temper and so control his fits. Even when Gart was killed and he had been forced to cope with the shock and guilt of surviving when so pleasant a youth had been torn asunder, he had kept his equilibrium. But the effort was taking its toll and he stamped along, pressing at his temples.

'What's the matter?' Leaf asked. She was the only one who bothered with him. Why, he could not tell, but she seemed to enjoy his company more than that of the others. Isolde was reluctant to talk to anyone and Quinn and Guthrey were so close and unapproachable that, since Gart's unfortunate demise, he was the obvious choice for Leaf, he supposed.

Rollo stared at his father's back. 'He's just making an idiot of himself; he has no right to talk to that woman like that.'

'Hasn't he?' Leaf queried. 'And it seems to me that, as men go, your father is no fool.'

Rollo snorted at such a preposterous idea. He'd seen his

father made a fool of all his life; he didn't expect anything to change now.

At last, they strode into the deep shadow cast by the old walls of a castle that blotted out the light from the moon. Attached to the castle was a manor house, unlit and apparently abandoned. The castle, however, was aglow with braziers smoking above the portcullis and along all the walls. It was a modest castle, solidly built on an old-fashioned square footprint. The corners were naturally a little decayed where the hobs had energetically worked at them in an attempt to undermine the structure but, at least for now, the castle seemed peaceful.

Aisholt presented himself to the watch, and a small gate alongside the portcullis was soon unbolted and they were ushered inside. The smell of wood smoke and sizzling fat teased Rollo's taste-buds unmercifully. He was thirsty too. That coupled with his weariness made it hard to concentrate. The noise confused him; the sudden presence of so many people toing and froing disturbed him.

'Why can't they be still?' he hissed to himself.

He found, yet again, a hand on his, only this time it wasn't Leaf's but Isolde's. 'I can't go in,' she gasped. 'I just can't.'

'We have to,' Rollo told her, finding no energy left for sympathy. 'We shall be safe here. Oxgard's men will be able to protect us.'

'But you don't realize! I can smell them, smell their bloodlust!' Isolde inexplicably exclaimed. 'I can't go in.' She was beginning to sob.

Too irritated to try persuasion, Rollo merely grabbed her wrist and pulled – only to be alarmed by the strength with which she pulled away. He turned and looked into her eyes, which were now red and raw with crying.

'They will kill me,' she mumbled, her lips trembling. 'But perhaps that is best after all.'

Rollo didn't know what to do and was relieved when Brid

pushed him aside and offered a hand to Isolde. 'Come, sweet child, you are safe with me.'

As if she were a very young child, Isolde dutifully obeyed. She followed after Brid, her feet pattering on the cold stone floor of the castle.

It was well lit inside and, to Rollo's amazement, he saw that the castle was far more dilapidated than he had expected. Plaster was peeling from the walls. Where it had fallen to the floor, great chunks had been kicked into heaps in the corners. Ivies had pushed their way in through the masonry and clung to the inner walls with their tiny suckers, inch by inch nibbling away at the mortar. Rough pillars of brick filled in windows that had collapsed, the elements having chewed away at the supporting lintels. It seemed that the castle had been left in a state of dereliction for a long while before being hastily resurrected for use. However, the doors that barred their way were solid and possibly brought here from another abode. They were oak and very heavy with ornate hinges wrought into marvellous swirling patterns to reinforce the timbers.

Aisholt gestured at the watch on duty to knock on the door and the man dutifully obeyed, producing a loud wrap with a stick. The sound of three great bars being lifted from the door echoed through the narrow corridor where they stood. The door shuddered and finally swung inwards, allowing a wash of warm air to be thrown out into the faces of the tired travellers.

Rollo blinked in the sudden firelight. The place stank of ale, drunken men and chewed bones. The men had clearly spent the last few hours since late afternoon relaxing in the halls, drinking their fill and squabbling over the food while packs of dogs growled over the scraps. A minstrel did his best to compete with the jeers and laughter from the men. Rollo sniffed again. There was a smell of vomit, he thought, and then corrected himself; no, it was simply sour milk and cheese. He squinted at the tables, finding that he automatically pressed up close against his father, uncertain in the strange environment. He felt enclosed, trapped. He couldn't help but imagine that all eyes were on him alone, though that was ludicrous. He was only one amongst many and, naturally, those at the fore, Brid, Aisholt and his father, were the ones of note and interest.

Baron Oxgard, Rollo remembered well from his brief visit to his northern castle only a short while ago. But since Baron Oxgard had kept him, Quinn and Isolde in his custody for their own safety and they had rebelliously escaped, he was not keen to meet the man's gaze. The heavily built Baron of Jotunn stood up and stared, frowning at the bedraggled party and then, slowly, a genuinely warm smiled spread across his face.

'Well, well, well, what have we here? My dear neighbour! Spar, welcome! Welcome! Welcome! Welcome! And timely too! I have your horse in my stable and I don't think the grooms can cope any longer.' Oxgard laughed heartily. 'It was a struggle and a half getting him here from my northern castle.'

Caspar returned the smile. 'It is very good to see you again, Oxgard. It has been a long time.'

The Baron of Jotunn grinned amiably and then looked at the rest of the bedraggled party. 'The lost are found, it seems. And all of you! That is a relief. And found by my own Sergeant Aisholt. It is good to see you, Aisholt. I had feared that you would not make it. Well, well, well, I don't know . . .' Baron Oxgard looked somewhat lost for words as he gazed upon the Torra Altans. 'You could not have come at a better time. This is an historic occasion. Three of Belbidia's mighty barons in the same room at one time. This could not have happened for over a decade.'

A sudden hush filled the hall, all eyes following Oxgard's gaze to alight upon Baron Caspar. Rollo realized that it was only then that the people gathered in the hall recognized his father.

'Please, please, join the merriment. Take seats!' Oxgard warmly offered his hospitality. 'More food! More ale!'

'It has been too long.' Caspar enthusiastically pressed forward to embrace the Baron of Jotunn, though he guarded his left arm, protecting his injury. He then turned towards the elderly man still seated at a large table. The man's ample folds of flesh filled and over-spilt the carved chair placed alongside the one Oxgard had vacated. He was very fat and white, his eyes yellow and slitted by his cheeks that pushed up into his lower lids.

Breathing heavily, the fat nobleman made an attempt to rise but then flicked his hands in a dismissive gesture. 'I am too old and fat to be doing with niceties,' he told Caspar. 'And though it's a long time since I've heard your name, it still seems to me you're too young to be a Baron. What are you doing wandering about Jotunn? Lost your barony already?' he asked cruelly.

Rollo coloured up, furiously wondering how his father could stand there and take such abuse. Oxgard looked uncertainly between his two eminent guests but then relaxed as Caspar laughed and extended his hand towards the Baron of Nattarda.

'Wiglaf, I do not blame you, old man, for being as sour as the milk from your cows in these days. Rubbing up so close to the hobs would turn anyone's nature – and enough to visit your oldest rival, I see. It must be the first time in two decades that the Baron of Jotunn and the Baron of Nattarda have shared the same table.'

Wiglaf tugged at his long grey beard, which Rollo was disgusted to see had dregs of beer and crumbs of cheese clinging to the tangles. He watched as Wiglaf's small piggy eyes, squeezed by the layers of lard, flitted through their company, studying them in such a way that made his flesh creep.

'I'm tired of these so-called pleasantries. Why don't you all just sit down and eat? Your arrival has ruined the minstrel's song,' Wiglaf chastized them.

'Do you have no manners at all?' Rollo could contain his anger no longer. 'Who are you to talk to us in that manner?'

Brid jabbed the youth hard in the ribs with a very sharp elbow. 'Forgive us, Lord Wiglaf, the youth has only been in the country a very short time and knows nothing of our ways,' she said smoothly.

'Fair lady, your presence excuses all.' Wiglaf politely bowed his head towards her. 'We are honoured to have one of such eminence before us. Now, please, be seated so that we may dine,' he added impatiently.

There was no further chance to speak as Isolde crashed to the floor in a sudden swoon. Her cloak fell back from her discoloured limb and suddenly the whole gathering fell silent.

'What manner of disease . . . ?' Wiglaf exploded in disgust.

Dominica screamed in horror while Brid hastily covered Isolde's bandaged arm.

'No disease but an injury. I must get her home to Torra Alta where Keridwen will help her.'

The men of Jotunn shrank back in horror, muttering about the many diseases that had swept through the land, spread by travellers and hobs alike. Stepping back from the Torra Altans, Oxgard glanced nervously at Isolde, whom Aisholt bore in his arms. 'A wound?' the friendly baron asked Brid again, evidently not reassured by her explanation. 'Are you sure? Shouldn't she see my physician to be certain?'

'It's a wound,' Brid repeated more emphatically.

'Then it must have gone bad,' Oxgard said sympathetically. 'Poor child, she looks so young. What a shame. It would be terrible to lose a limb at her age.'

Terrible, Rollo reiterated in his head, though he was really focusing on his disappointment that his companions had not seated themselves for the feast; it would have been churlish of him to gorge himself while the others were showing such concern for Isolde.

Brid nodded thoughtfully. 'Perhaps it would be wise to see your physician. He can also see to Rollo's ankle and more urgently to Spar's arm here as well. It keeps opening and probably needs cauterizing and restitching.'

Caspar grunted at this. 'I don't see the point of a physician, Oxgard. He won't be able to do more than Brid. You know that.'

'I know,' Oxgard replied in hushed tones, 'but my mother

won't be satisfied that it's not a disease unless I can say my own physician has examined the wound. You know how difficult Lady Helena can be.'

By dawdling at the back of the party, Rollo was surreptitiously able to grab a chicken leg before leaving the dining hall and following the others who were apparently determined to see Isolde examined before they eased their hunger. Just as he left, he noted that Fanchon and Dominica had already detached themselves from the Torra Altans and were making their acquaintance with Baron Wiglaf and his entourage.

While they waited for the physician, Caspar drew aside to speak to Baron Oxgard. 'What is Wiglaf doing here? He and your father never had a civil word to say to each other during their entire lives.'

'Though it galls me to say it, I need the old bastard,' Oxgard said with a sigh. 'As the hobs moved north, we were lucky to get away with our lives and return to our seat here. We abandoned the manor, of course, and did our best to secure the old castle. Wiglaf found his trade routes were being closed off to the ports and had learnt of my enclosures. He needed to sell his produce and I needed to buy much of it; our beef stocks have been halved by the waves of hobs but Nattarda has been fortunate enough to be far enough east and away from the worst of the troubles.'

Caspar nodded at this. 'I noticed.'

'Anyhow,' Oxgard continued, 'people can still manage to travel in some regions so long as they have somewhere safe to spend the night, and so I have built a network of small forts. These enclosures have been very costly in manpower but have been the only thing that has kept my barony together and the only thing that enabled us to head back here to the manor and old castle when the hobs came north.' He lowered his voice. 'They are closing tightly about your castle, Spar. Your uncle had already sent word that he was pressed and asked for supplies. I promised him all I could spare and sent wagons.' He sighed. 'Only two of my men returned, and in a very sorry state. They say the road north to Torra Alta is impassable.'

Caspar nodded solemnly. In a grave tone, he said, 'Thank you anyway, Oxgard, for doing what you could to help.'

Rollo felt sick. Hobs all over Torra Alta! The very thought of it made him want to retch. He wasn't sure why he felt so distressed because he was a tiny bit pleased that Hal might be having a hard time; after all, the man had got away exceedingly lightly compared to what they had all endured. Brid, to his amazement, didn't wilt under the news but drew in a deep breath and threw back her shoulder.

'Hal is strong. Keridwen is stronger still. The two of them will endure. They will look after Brannella.' It was only when she spoke her little girl's name that there was any hint of distress in her voice. She tossed back her head and clenched her jaw firmly before fixing her gaze on Isolde. 'First, we must see what we can do here.'

Blowing hard, a short plump man in a black gown arrived at the open door. He looked anxiously at Baron Oxgard. 'My lord, you summoned me. I hope nothing ails you.'

'No, no, not me!' Baron Oxgard hastily explained the situation and the physician bowed first towards Caspar and then towards Brid. 'My Lady, there is little chance that I will succeed where you have failed.'

'I seek any possible help,' Brid replied as she grimly peeled back the cloak covering Isolde's body.

'But I feel fine now,' Isolde protested, groaning. 'Please don't uncover me.'

'Why did you fall to the floor then?' Brid demanded.

Caspar was holding the girl's hand, his face taught, and Rollo was suddenly bored with the whole thing. So many of them had suffered over the last few years; why was Brid making such a fuss over Isolde?

'My opinion,' the physician offered after only a minute's appraisal of Isolde's mottled green arm, 'is that the wound is bad and we must cut the limb off.' He sniffed, his nose wrinkling. 'And it smells.'

'But it doesn't smell of gangrene,' Brid protested.

'But the foul flesh is spreading, eating up the skin and blackening it. There could not be a surer sign of necrotized flesh.'

Rollo was distracted from this conversation by Caspar rising abruptly. He took Oxgard's arm and dragged him to the window, the Torra Altan looking so small and light compared to the brawny Baron of Jotunn. The physician took the opportunity to examine the gash on Caspar's arm. Rollo was surprised and impressed to note how his father didn't flinch when a burning iron was pressed onto the skin to singe and close the wound. The physician continued to work, applying a paste of purified honey while the Baron talked in stiff tones.

'I still don't understand what you are doing with Wiglaf. I have been deep into Belbidia's countryside in search of my son. The land is swarming with savage beasts and everywhere I go there have been suggestions of underhand dealings originating from Nattarda.'

Oxgard laughed. 'Well, that would be nothing new. Wiglaf's always been a toad but he has no more power than the rest of us. He came practically begging for help. He's had so much trouble with pirates that he implored me to allow him to use our northern ports. He's supplied me with enough cheese to keep the enclosures open for another month without having to levy any fees.'

'A policy which your gatekeepers are ignoring, of course,' Caspar interjected.

'Of course. Wiglaf is not the only one suffering from corruption amongst his men. But how can I blame the gatekeepers? It is not an easy job and I do not envy them the task. Moreover, I can pay them no more than one of my stockmen used to be paid, which is scant recompense for their hardship.' He sighed. 'It's not just the beasts and the hobs that they have to contend with but also the criminals that prey on the innocent travellers. I've had two gatekeepers murdered in six months and I'm amazed that Aisholt made it back.'

'He's a fine sergeant,' Caspar commented.

'Indeed,' Oxgard agreed. 'I sent him to keep an eye out for the pirates that have so troubled Wiglaf but, even though my ports are just as accessible, it seems they are not interested in what little cargo I can ship out nowadays. Cheese is a lot easier to steal than livestock, which has a habit of running away or drowning all too easily.'

'Perhaps it was unwise to allow Wiglaf north into your ports then. The pirates might follow him.'

Oxgard's eyes widened at the thought. 'I must confess I had not thought of that.' He sighed and slumped down into a chair, his head dropping into his great hands.

After giving Brid the pot of honey and other supplies besides, the physician returned to examine Isolde.

Caspar's eyes turned from Oxgard to the frail girl lying on the couch. 'We must get north to Torra Alta. We have to get home and we have to get Isolde well.' He gazed at her sorrowfully and bit his lip.

Rollo's curiosity was stirred by the physician and Brid moving from Isolde's head to gather about her feet. Leaf was pointing something out and, soon, Caspar too tried to peer over Brid's shoulder to see what they had discovered.

'Mercy,' Brid murmured and sat down heavily into a chair.

Rollo still couldn't see what all the fuss was about and so moved to stand over Leaf and follow her gaze. He sucked in a sharp breath.

'Why hadn't I realized earlier?' Brid bemoaned her slow thinking. 'Why?'

Caspar put his arm around Brid. 'You have done your best. It has been a very hard struggle for survival and we had little time for clear thought.'

'What's wrong with her?' Quinn asked, his voice ringing with alarm while Guthrey began to gag.

Though he felt his stomach churn, Rollo felt no revulsion

151

towards Isolde herself, just a deep sympathy. He looked at the blood dripping from the scratches on her heel. That's how I feel inside, he thought.

Quinn's trembling hand reached out for his mother, seeking comfort. 'What's wrong with her, Mother? Why is her blood that colour?'

Rollo could not take his eyes from the grey, watery blood, glistening with specks of green, that oozed from Isolde's heel.

'What's wrong with me?' Isolde began to whimper.

Brid took a deep breath. 'You have scratches on your heels where you have walked through bracken and scraped yourself on twigs. They are no more than scratches and the skin is just a little pink and sore as one might expect. There is no blackening but . . .'

'But what?' Isolde demanded, her voice more of a snarl in her anxiety.

'The blood . . . ,' Brid said hesitantly. 'It isn't like the blood of any sepsis I have ever seen. It's thin and dark and has a strong aroma to it.'

Brid pressed either side of a cut to Isolde's heel and the thin dark liquid beaded up around the opening. A greenish liquid seeped out. Rollo snatched his gaze away, now revolted.

'I don't understand,' Isolde sobbed. 'Brid, tell me, am I dying?'

'No, Isolde, you are not dying.' Brid reached from a chair, which she dragged towards Isolde's head and slumped into it. Grasping the girl's hand, she said very softly, 'It is not an illness. Do you remember when you were struggling so bravely to contaminate the potion in the Chalice with your blood? You had already cut your arm and an injured hob was trying to stop you?'

Isolde nodded.

'The hob's blood must have already mingled with the potion when you plunged your cut hand into the Chalice,' Brid faltered as Isolde began to choke. The girl's face blackened with fear; a terrified scream stopped in her throat.

'I don't understand!' Quinn barked fearfully. 'Please someone explain. What is wrong with her?'

Brid was too busy trying to calm Isolde, who now writhed and clawed at her throat hysterically, and so it was Leaf who spoke.

'The essence of hob was within the Chalice and its essence was able to enter Isolde's bloodstream through the wound. She is turning into a hob,' she said heavily, her words falling from her mouth like the toll of a death knell.

A silence fell on the company as they stared at Isolde, who was being held down by Caspar, Aisholt and the plump physician. Stupefied by the revelation, Rollo was too shocked to absorb its import. He could only stare angrily as Quinn and Guthrey shrank back from Isolde. That was how people behaved towards him when he suffered one of his fits. That was how they saw him, as some kind of beast rather than one of their own. Just because he suffered fits didn't make him any less of a person and yet, in their eyes, clearly it did. He could see how Quinn and Guthrey, who had been Isolde's lifelong companions, now shrank away as if to touch her meant death. Pointedly, Rollo moved in closer and took her hand, looking deep into her eyes as if trying to find the real Isolde within.

'Issy, I am here,' he said. He didn't really know what to say; he just wanted to convey his emotions. He wanted her to know that he felt no different about her, that he was not afraid but merely sought to offer friendship and comfort. Isolde stared back at him, her eyes wild and afraid, but gradually they looked at him with recognition. Her writhing eased and she slumped back onto the couch, tears streaming down her face.

'Poor Rollo,' she murmured. 'Your suffering is great. I am with you in this tangled thorn woods; I can see you here amongst the nettles of my mind.'

'What does that mean?' Quinn croaked.

Rollo didn't bother to answer him, though Leaf whispered, 'It means that Isolde is finding herself in a place of torment and distress. She recognizes that Rollo has also suffered a similar emotional distress and so she is saying that they understand one another.'

'Oh,' Quinn said lamely. 'Issy and I used to have our own special place in the stones, but the dwarves took it from us. Took her onyx and my sunburst ruby and we have lost each other,' he whimpered.

'What are we going to do?' Caspar asked forlornly.

'What is the matter with her? What is the disease? Is it contagious?' Oxgard demanded anxiously, covering his mouth with his kerchief again.

No one answered him.

'I have never seen anything like this before!' the physician exclaimed, his eyes staring in horror at the back of Isolde's heel. Evidently he still had no understanding of what the Torra Altans were saying.

'Will someone answer me in plain speech?!' Oxgard bellowed into the intermingled mass of concerned questions and answers.

The physician looked at Oxgard helplessly. 'I do not know what it is.'

Brid stood up and silenced the man with a wave of her delicate hand. 'She is mutating,' the priestess said solemnly, 'mutating into a hob.'

A silence closed in on the gathering. No one spoke for a full minute. All that time, Rollo was thinking that, at the back of his mind, he had known. All Isolde's strange behaviour was now explained.

'Wouldn't it be kindness to . . . ?' Oxgard began, but one stabbing look from Brid immediately silenced him.

'Whatever happens, Isolde must live. Her lot in life is to perform a duty to the creatures and peoples of this earth. She is the Maiden, one of the Trinity, and she must live, whether as a hob or a woman. She has been injured by magic and so she will be cured by magic.'

Caspar was nodding slowly at this as if only just beginning to realize what was wrong with the girl. 'The Chalice, of course!

Why did you have to be so brave, Isolde? Why wasn't I there to stop you? Oh child, I have failed you.' He fell down on his knees alongside her. 'I promised your mother that I would protect you and I have failed her.'

All stared for a long time at Isolde, who withdrew into her cloak and even pushed Rollo away. Quinn marched to the wall and, in a sudden fit of fury, punched his fist into the plaster, which cracked and gave, leaving a crater. Clutching his fist, he came away red-faced but still wouldn't look at Isolde.

Brid was rapidly stroking Isolde's good hand whilst staring far into the distance, a tight frown creasing her forehead. Oxgard hastily excused himself, saying he must get back to his other guests. After that no one said anything, as if they were all waiting for Brid to come up with a solution. In the end, it was Isolde herself who broke the gloomy silence.

'Kill me,' she croaked. 'I cannot live like this. Kill me! Please, someone, save me from this torment.'

Brid's eyes leapt on the girl. 'You have responsibilities, child. You cannot escape so easily. You will fight this thing every inch of the way just as we all shall.'

Rollo was surprised at the brutality of the priestess's words and the lack of sympathy, but was impressed to note that Isolde appeared to pay heed to her words and lifted her chin.

'I suppose . . . ,' the girl croaked weakly. 'I suppose this is no worse than I deserve after all I have done.'

Ignoring these words, which Rollo did not understand anyway, Brid snapped her fingers. 'All of you, out of here. You all need rest and food. Rejoin the feast. Spar, see to it that these boys eat well tonight but do let them drink too much; we can't afford to have any more trouble on our hands.'

Caspar nodded at her and then waved Quinn, Guthrey and Rollo out of the room. Brid's two sons took no encouragement and fled, though Rollo was reluctant to leave Isolde. He sensed her fear and wished he could help. However, Brid glowered at him and he realized that he had no option but to leave. Leaf followed on quietly behind and then scurried past to put her hand in Caspar's, seeking his protection.

The Baron, however, fed her hand into Rollo's and murmured, 'Eat well. I'm just going to check on Cracker.'

Rollo nodded, surprised that his father had waited this long to be reunited with his beloved horse. When the youths returned to the table, Wiglaf was still eating greedily with no regard for the hard times that lay ahead. Rollo's dislike of the man only increased as he saw that Dominica was sitting on the Baron's knee, feeding him and giggling coquettishly. The moment they returned, she slid off, almost guiltily, he thought. Then, when Caspar finally returned, the dark-haired Fanchon immediately made a big show of finding him a seat and helping him into it.

Rollo was acutely embarrassed. How could his father allow himself to be waited on by a whore? All the world could see that this girl was blatantly using him, crawling first all over one baron and then another; it made Rollo feel sick. Couldn't Caspar just push the girl off? His feelings were only soothed when the tall redhead, Dominica, took a seat next to him, her eyelids fluttering. A half smile twitched on his face and soon the smile turned to a satisfied grin when he caught Guthrey's eye. The handsome Torra Altan hastily looked away, teeth clenched.

'Don't look at him,' Dominica said breathily. 'Look at me!'

Rollo let his gaze slide up and down the woman's pert body. The top laces of her bodice were beginning to loosen, her bulging breasts looking as if they might pop out at any second. 'How could I not look at you, sweet Dominica? You are more beautiful than . . . than . . .'

Leaf gave a loud snort right behind his ear, which did nothing to improve his confidence or help him to think of some pleasant compliment. Dominica, however, seemed unruffled.

'Thank you,' she said as if Rollo had completed his compliment with something meaningful. Edging her chair a little closer, she reached for a slither of juicy rare beef. Pinching it between finger and thumb, she lifted it towards his mouth. Parting his lips, he stretched out his tongue to receive the offering. Dominica giggled delightedly and pressed a little closer, her knee brushing against his.

'Is the girl well?' she asked breathily.

'What?' Rollo asked.

'Your friend, Isolde. Is she well?'

'No, not really,' Rollo said stiffly, annoyed that Dominica was not fully focused on him.

'That is sad,' Dominica continued, her pale green eyes twinkling at him. Rollo was deeply drawn to those eyes, which were made to look even bigger by a line of charcoal accentuating her lashes. 'Very sad for her.' She smiled, fluttering long eyelashes. 'But at least I won't have any competition for you.'

Rollo jerked his head back and looked alarmed by her forwardness. One part of him was deeply flattered and, of course, aroused by the prospect of her interest, but the other half was terrified. It was daunting enough to think that this older, worldly woman of dubious morals should be interested in him, but it was also much more unnerving to guess the reason why.

Guthrey had risen abruptly from their table, clearly put out that Dominica as well as Fanchon had ignored him in favour of Rollo. He no doubt sought to mend his reputation as Belbidia's most irresistible young man as he bowed towards one of the lower tables, where several ladies, from girls on the point of blossoming into womanhood to middle-aged matrons, were seated. Strutting confidently, he approached them and eased onto a bench, placing himself between the prettiest of them. Clearly, the youth was not in the least troubled by the fact that even the youngest of them looked to be at least four years older than him.

To Rollo, it was painfully obvious that all ladies, young and old, were vulnerable to Guthrey's brooding eyes and cheeky grin. He tried desperately not to think of it as he felt Dominica's warm breath on his cheeks and saw how her eyes lingered on his lips. All sensible thought was gone and his mind was filled with a fluttering of nonsense. He could suddenly hear nothing but the sound of his pounding heart and could see only Dominica's sweet smile and gorgeous eyes. There was a lushness and a comfort about her that he wanted.

He kept on staring, hoping that she would get closer, wanting to fall into her and become merged and immersed in her being. But this luscious, silent world of enthralment was suddenly shattered by a sharp dig in the ribs.

He looked round to see Leaf glaring at him. 'What are you doing?' she growled.

'It's none of your business,' he snapped back. 'Leave me alone.'

'There, there pet,' Dominica said to Leaf in the most belittling manner possible. 'You're not ready for him yet so you can just wait a few years and –'

Leaf didn't wait for her to finish. 'If you think I'm joining in a silly game of vying for this boy's attention, there's not an ounce of common sense in you. None of us has the luxury of time at this moment, and Rollo is wasting it. He's eaten enough and we must return to Brid; there are many decisions to be made.'

'Decisions?' Dominica sneered. 'What's a child like you got to do with decisions?' She laughed and at the same time moved away from Rollo and he suddenly felt cold and rejected.

Stiffly, he stamped angrily after Leaf, who had risen from the table to return to Isolde. She turned and looked at him disapprovingly. 'You're an idiot, an even bigger idiot than Guthrey.'

'Why?' Rollo demanded. 'You've just ruined everything.'

'Ha! Is that all you can think about? You think being with Dominica is important at a time like this? Are you really going to tell me that you've already forgotten about Isolde and all the troubles we face?'

'No, of course I haven't forgotten, but if I thought about that all the time I would go mad.'

158

Leaf sighed and muttered to herself. 'I had no idea that humans really were this stupid. No wonder the world is like it is. No wonder!'

'Oh, you're not so perfect,' Rollo muttered back. 'I'm sure you don't understand everything.'

'I do know that you don't fall head over heels for a girl who one minute is all over you and the next is all over a man three times your age the second you've left the room.'

'That's not true,' Rollo objected. 'She's still there,' he said, looking back as he worked his way around the tables at the edge of the dinning hall. But even as he spoke, he was proved wrong. Dominica had risen and was now sliding around the tables, weaving her way through ogling men and disapproving women to squeeze alongside Wiglaf. She batted her eyelashes at him and then pouted seductively over his shoulder at Oxgard.

'How did you know she would do that?' Rollo asked, feeling confused and offended.

'It hardly takes a genius,' Leaf commented wearily. 'Now, hurry up. We must find out what Caspar and Brid have decided to do.'

Letting himself be tugged along by Leaf, Rollo wondered whether he cared any more about what plans the adults had. None of their plans ever suited him and no one took him into consideration when they made a decision.

Leaf looked at him, studying his expression. 'This isn't about you,' she said stiffly. 'This is about everyone.'

Rollo wasn't at all sure that he was concerned about everyone.

Soon they reached the chamber where they had left Isolde. They pushed open the door to see Caspar still deep in conversation with Brid. Two dogs were pressed up close against her side, one an Ophidian terrier, so alike in looks to the dogs Rollo had seen at Torra Alta that he guessed it had been a gift from Hal to Oxgard. The dogs welcomed Brid as a long-lost friend. The priestess, however, paid them no heed. She was flushed in the face, her hand squeezing Isolde's shoulder.

'There is nothing for it; Baron Oxgard has made it quite plain that we cannot reach Torra Alta,' the priestess said heavily. 'He is prepared to give us every help he can, arming us, providing horses, rations and even these two dogs. But he insists that none of these things will enable us to get past the hobs. He has made many attempts to send help to Hal but, sadly, nearly all who have tried to get through have been slaughtered. It seems all the hobs in Belbidia are converging on Torra Alta's borders and the routes are impassable. It was mainly for that reason we had such an easy time reaching here. If we can't get to Keridwen then we have to go after Silas. We have to retrieve the Chalice. It's Isolde's only hope.'

'But it's broken,' Caspar protested. 'What good is it to us?'

'Broken but not destroyed,' Leaf interrupted as she and Rollo entered the room. 'A broken sword might still cut flesh; a broken cup may yet hold water. Besides, you have spoken of the dwarves you have seen in Silas's employ. As Arathane said, they will surely find a way to restore it to its full powers. After all, as you know, it has already been repaired once before.'

'How did you know?' Brid asked in surprise.

Leaf shrugged dismissively. 'Of course we have heard of this Chalice in our hidden realm and have long coveted it for our own ends. We had learnt that it had been recovered by the three high priestesses and also that it had been damaged; you must have found a way to mend it.'

Brid nodded, her face suddenly becoming flushed. 'That is true.' Her eyes lingered on Quinn and, though she mentioned nothing of him, Rollo guessed that he was somehow linked to this act. 'We did indeed mend it, but with gold from the great runesword that had torn through its fabric. Like the Chalice, the runesword was a gift from the Great Mother herself. The two were of the same metal and so the mend was pure and flawless. The two powerful artefacts of the Great Mother had worked together to create an altogether different magic. There are many ways in which the Chalice can be used, and Silas is seeking only one of those: the transference of the essential properties from one artefact to another.'

'Isolde is not an artefact,' Rollo said bitterly.

Brid nodded. 'No,' she said with a heavy sigh, 'she is not.'

Caspar looked pensive. 'Arathane has been after Silas for years and been unable to run him to ground. What makes you think we will fare any better? Wouldn't it be wiser to seek help elsewhere rather than plunging back into danger?' he argued.

Rollo sniffed. It was so like his father to seek the easier option.

Brid looked at him sideways. 'But what can we do? We can't stay here forever. We can't reach Torra Alta and, even if we could, I am now certain that even Keridwen and I shall be unable to cure her. We need the same magic that did the harm in the first place. We must go after Silas.'

Both adults turned and looked at Rollo and Leaf.

'Go and get a good sleep,' Caspar ordered. 'Tomorrow we are going after Silas.'

Rollo groaned. He knew his father wouldn't have considered his safety or well-being in the matter. Fatalistically, he resigned himself to more discomfort and hardship.

Leaf, however, lifted her head and looked up at Caspar. 'I do not hold with your argument.'

Rollo grinned. He found it wonderful that a child was able to speak out against adults.

'Nonsense,' Brid said stiffly, clearly somewhat taken aback at being challenged. Evidently, she didn't expect it from anyone save her own sons.

'It's madness,' Leaf continued. 'You're pinning all your hope on finding Silas, stealing the Chalice and finding a way to mend it so that you can reverse the process of mutation in Isolde.'

Brid nodded. 'What other option do I have? Don't you think I want to get home to my little girl? Don't you think that my heart cries out in misery every second I am apart from her? But this is not about our feelings. We have to do this; we have to stop Silas.'

'There is always more than one way to solve a problem,' Leaf assured her. 'If I put this difficulty to the scholars, their combined ingenuity would be enough to find an answer and save us from having to plunge straight back into danger.'

Brid shook her head. 'Leaf, it is not surprising that you want to go home. Your experience of life beyond the Haven has been traumatic to say the least. Of course you want to go home. But your people are suffering. The fact that they still have the logic and insight to solve this problem is seriously doubtful. Though this is a hard way, at least we know that, apart from helping Isolde, it is the best option we have to stop this man gaining in strength.'

'It's still too risky to pin all our hopes on one extremely difficult manoeuvre,' Leaf argued, unconvinced.

Brid looked at her thoughtfully and then sighed as if finally accepting the child's logic. 'What would you propose we do?'

'We split up. Some must go after Silas and the hope of retrieving and mending the Chalice. Others must return to my realm and seek advice from the wisest of the council. At least that way we have twice the opportunity of righting the situation.'

Chapter 9

For the first time in her life, Leaf began to wonder whether she hadn't been foolish. Up until this moment, she had always been certain of her thoughts and clear about her decisions; now she was afraid and bewildered.

'Leaf, stay close,' Caspar insisted, stretching back to grip her hand and tug her along the paved road. 'They're all about us.'

She did her best to trot on a little faster and was grateful that at least she was with Caspar. His arm was very much better now the wound had been cauterized and he had been able to forgo the sling. He was even hopeful that soon he would be capable of drawing the light bow Oxgard had bestowed on him, though the strength still eluded him at present. His strong grip about her wrist was all that kept her going. She knew she was lucky to be with just him rather than being dragged recklessly along behind the others into far worse perils than the ones she had already faced; it could so easily have been otherwise.

Much to her amazement, the humans had argued over what course of action they should take for hours with very little gain. What Leaf had found most intriguing was that human arguments consisted of repeating the same unbalanced argument time and time again in louder and louder voices until one side gave up. Just because someone repeated the same point more forcefully and more often didn't, of course, make them right, but these humans seemed unable to perceive that fact. Fortunately for her, the Baron and Brid had resolved their differences by deciding to split the company. Caspar had insisted on staying with her even though that meant parting company with his son. It had been universally decided that Rollo would only prove a hindrance if he accompanied his father. Caspar thought that his unpredictable manner might antagonize Leaf's people in their delicate state of mind.

'I promised I would help you,' the Baron had told her gravely.

Caspar was now looking at her with a curious mixture of restraint, impatience and sympathy. These humans had such muddled emotions, it was no wonder that they had trouble thinking clearly. Leaf sighed. But now she finally comprehended what it was to think in this confused manner.

For an instant, she had feared her confusion was due to the illness affecting the adult population of her people, the decrepitude of the brain, which had prematurely accelerated its development in her. After a moment's self-critical analysis, however, she decided that it was because she was afraid. How interesting, she thought to herself, trying to push all emotions from her mind. Obviously, she needed a sense of safety in order to think clearly. Was that why she had so adamantly insisted that she must return to the haven in order to seek a cure for Isolde?

She had known that Brid was right; of course, someone had to go after Silas. He had the Chalice and that was the obvious answer to Isolde's problems, and very likely the Chalice could also help her own people. Moreover, it had to be removed from Silas for fear of the terror that he might wreak with it. Yet, against that weight of argument, she had strung together a very plausible and convincing reason that it was better to look for two solutions in case one failed. On that basis, the company had split. They had taken little persuasion and Leaf realized that, already, they had grown accustomed to taking her advice.

She was ashamed. She knew the real reason she had argued hard for Caspar and herself to return to the inner realm was because she was a coward. She had wanted only to go back in time to that last second when she had stood on the soil of her lands, when she no longer shook with fear every time she drew breath. Even her fingers lacked the grip to hold on to Caspar any more. It was only because this extraordinary man held her so tightly and pulled her along with such tenacity that she was able to stagger behind him. In a continuous wave of self-reproach, she knew she should be intelligent enough to escape from whatever creatures were all about them, hidden in the undergrowth. There were no beings on earth more intelligent than a scholar from the hidden realm, and she should surely be able to master any difficulty. It was true that, because of the longevity of the wizards, they had acquired more knowledge and were wiser, but that didn't make them more intelligent; it was only her fear which stopped her from thinking with any perspicacity.

'Which way?' Caspar hissed at her as, again, something rustled in the undergrowth behind them. 'Come on, Leaf! We must move quickly.'

Through a haze of tears, she looked around her at the countryside. It hadn't taken them long to leave Oxgard's rebuilt castle. Though Leaf had felt much safer in the company of many, she could not argue that it was right to proceed to the hidden realm with more than a minimum number. If they were discovered, her mother, the High Lady Zophia, would immediately detain them as intruders, especially since Leaf had already so flagrantly defied her mother's orders. The fewer in the party, the easier it could be to move freely and find her father, who was surely the only one who would help her. After all, hadn't he once been the most acclaimed and applauded scholar of his time?

This course of action had also meant leaving Caspar's prized horse behind since the animal was so conspicuous. That was the one part of the plan that the Baron had been the most reluctant to go along with, and she was amazed to discover how deeply attached he was to the brute.

Leaf sighed. Once within the hidden realm, reaching her father wasn't going to be easy but, in all her panic and distress over this, she had forgotten that she would actually have to reach the edge of the Haven first. It meant braving the woodlands and open country again where all manner of savage beasts prowled.

She looked up at the position of the winter sun above the horizon and concluded they were a tenth of a degree too far west. 'East,' she murmured. 'We must veer just a little to the East.' Finding her bearings by the sun was something she could do automatically without even thinking, a task that was as easy for her as it was for a human to count the fingers on their hands. But she lacked confidence at the moment and so withdrew from her pocket a small dial, which she studied carefully and with relief saw that her judgement was affirmed.

'What's that?' Caspar asked.

'A compass,' she replied, but Caspar continued to look at her blankly. 'It's like a lodestone,' she explained succinctly. 'It confirms we have to head East.' She sighed and looked down at her hand helplessly and then across at the man. 'But that means we've got to go across there.' She nodded at the green hill that rose to their left. It was dotted with gorse spangled with bright yellow flowers.

Clinging to Caspar, she climbed above the dewy pastures of Jotunn and up onto the higher land where the grass was thinner and gorse had sprung up where the beef cattle had no longer grazed away the saplings. Approaching the top of the hill, the bushes became thicker and they were forced to squeeze between them. When Aisholt had led them up the ravine from the coast, she had thought she would die if ever she saw another bramble. But the gorse bushes were worse, far worse. The thorns were very much longer and sharper, and here, where they grew in tall clumps, they slashed at her arms and face.

Once at the top, however, the gorse thinned again and they

looked out across a completely different landscape. Blackened patches of scorched earth lay in pockets of frost-coated fields where the thin winter grass had been gnawed right down to the roots. Thin trails of smoke curled up from the burnt ground. Fully grown trees lay on their sides, either snapped off or uprooted where something powerful had ripped them from the ground. A criss-cross network of hedges that formed a grid over the landscape had been trampled by large feet and grubbed up by hungry jaws. The entire scene bore testament to the passage of some vast creatures that must have grazed their way along the hedges, gobbling them as it went. They were also, surely, creature with tusks, Leaf deduced as she noticed the occasional pair of parallel grooves that scarred the ground. Caspar was looking at the grooves with a frown on his face and seemed unable to discern what had caused the devastation to the vegetation.

Leaf sighed at him, finding that she now felt much braver seeing that she understood their new environment better than he did. 'Two things have happened here,' she explained. 'First a herd of voracious creatures has passed through here eating the vegetation, and after that a dragon has swept through and scorched the ground. And not so long ago, I see, since the ground is still smoking.'

They both looked glumly across the bare, frozen landscape before them.

'We'll be like rabbits out in the open,' Caspar said at length. 'You're certain your haven is on the far side?'

Leaf shook her head, pulling her coat up around her ears to keep her warm. There had been a sudden drop in temperature overnight and she wasn't used to the cold. 'No, it is right there in the middle.'

'Mmm,' Caspar said doubtfully.

Leaf glared at him indignantly. 'I know exactly where it is.' She looked up to the position of the pale sun in the heavens and then due north, her mind hastily whirring through the necessary calculations that allowed her to place herself. 'We've come thirteen and a half miles from Baron Oxgard's and we're approaching the second of five prongs that radiate out from our land. We shall hit the border in a little over twelve hundred paces.' She squinted into the distance. 'I estimate it to be near that cluster of domed trees, which, from this distance, I would guess are hawthorns.'

The Baron nodded, accepting her word without further question. 'How do we reach it without having to cross the open ground?' he asked, his eyes flitting behind him as the snuffling grew a little louder. 'It looks like a dragon has been busy here of late.'

Leaf pulled a face. 'We can't. We have no option but to cross,' she tried to say boldly, though her voice was now little more than a fearful squeak. Fixing her eyes on the gaps between the smoking patches of ground ahead, she consoled herself with the thought that she only had to cross that and then she would be within the safety of her inner realm, protected by the crystal curtain.

Their feet crunched on cinders as they picked their way round the patches of scorched earth, but that was not the only sound that dogged their footsteps. The snuffling and scratching behind them was growing louder. Leaf gave out a stifled scream as she glanced behind them to see a humped shape more than a foot long, excluding its tail, scurrying across their tracks.

'It's a rat, an enormous rat,' she whimpered.

Caspar squeezed her hand. 'Rats are frightened of the speaking races. You don't need to worry about them.'

Leaf looked at him uncertainly. 'If the rats are that big, there must be plenty to feed off. Whatever dragon has left these singed patches of earth has no doubt left behind plenty of carcasses for the scavengers to feed on.'

It wasn't long before they found the half-eaten, charred bodies of hobs, hazelines and cows lying in the ashes. Rats clustered around them like flies round a wound. Sickened by the sight of the heaving mass of rats, they hastened along and dropped down the slope. Leaf imagined that any moment now she would catch a shimmering glimpse of the curtain, but the way ahead appeared less clear than expected. The ground undulated softly and, as they picked their way through the clods of mud thrown up around the edges of the devastated hedgerow, she soon lost sight of her goal. Looking back at the hill behind her, she tried to make sure of her bearings.

Caspar, who was still gazing ahead, nudged her shoulder. 'Look at these dried-out mud pools,' he said, staring at the bowls of mud that showed the footprints of cattle and also something much larger. 'The animals have drunk the last drop from these dew ponds.'

Leaf agreed. 'And it's surprising to find them dry at this time of year, especially since the ground is still so damp after the rains.'

She bent down to examine an imprint that might have been a pig's trotter only it was enormous, so much bigger, in fact, that at first she had not recognized it at all. Though neat and round, it was more the size of a bear's footprint! Standing back, she looked at Caspar, her voice suddenly dry.

'I thought it was mammoths that had eaten the vegetation and ripped out the trees like that.' She cast her gaze around. 'I thought their tusks had gouged these deep grooves in the ground.' She tossed her head towards a pair of grooves that were deep enough to have been cut by a plough blade.

'Mammoth?' Caspar repeated. 'No, the grooves are not wide enough apart to have been caused by mammoths.'

Leaf heaved a sigh. 'Absolutely,' she said with impatience. 'These creatures are more the size of a very large ox.'

Caspar continued to stare at the unusual print while Leaf, without the slightest difficulty, recalled the exact page number of the catalogue of animals from which she had learnt the hoof that must have made such an impression. It was just a little under five years ago now. Once learnt she never forgot anything, and it had been a puzzlement to her to see how quickly these humans forgot detail. Some had an acceptable grasp of overall concepts but their eye for detail and their ability to recall it was minuscule.

'So what do you suppose they are?' Caspar asked with curiosity and not the least hint of fear, which Leaf found surprising because even a human couldn't fail to understand that this print had been caused by an animal of substantial proportions.

'Porcus Domesticus Ingentissimus,' she told him, looking at his face to see if that needed any explanation.

'A type of pig?' he asked uncertainly and then grinned at her. 'Leaf, you are teasing me.'

She shrugged. 'I have to confess that my nature does not permit me that frivolity,' she told him sternly, annoyed that he couldn't concentrate on the matter in hand.

He raised an eyebrow. 'Leaf, though I may not know this particular print, I am generally accepted as an accomplished tracker. These may well be cloven hooves but they are not made by pigs. There's a problem with the size.'

Leaf nodded impatiently. 'Giant domesticated pigs,' she told him, seeing in her mind's eye the sketch that had been entered in the catalogue. 'Normally, they are not found in this part of the world but live in the far north-east on the huge plains that even my people have not charted due to the sheer size of the land. The books say that, there, the trees grow three hundred foot tall and that the acorns are the size of apples.' She sniffed at the thought, thinking that this was unlikely and that the adventurous scholar who had catalogued the details for those in the hidden realm had misrepresented the facts. If an oak a hundred foot high could grow from an acorn the size of a fingernail, one three hundred foot tall need not be much bigger.

'So why on earth would these pigs have left their vast lands and travelled so many miles to where the pickings can only be miserable in comparison?' Caspar asked.

'That is not entirely clear without knowing what had driven their masters out.'

'Their masters?'

'I thought I had explained,' Leaf said impatiently.

'Not clearly enough, obviously. Please don't forget that I'm only a mere human who does not have the advantage of your vast intellect,' Caspar patronized her.

Leaf was taken aback. She had thought him mild-mannered and even-tempered and this was the first time he had been short with her. She blinked at him, her confidence waning. It was deceiving the way humans looked so similar to her own kind, it had lulled her into believing that she could understand them with ease, but clearly she could not.

'I'm sorry,' she apologized and immediately noted how the man's expression softened. Was it really as easy as that to win him back? 'What I was trying to say,' she explained, 'was that the pig is domesticated.'

'A giant *domesticated* pig,' Caspar's eyebrows rose in disbelief and Leaf immediately found it infuriating that he doubted her word. 'Domesticated by whom?'

'The great men of the northern ice plains.' She informed him. 'The great men of Haol-gar.'

'Leaf, I don't know where you are getting your information from but pigs can't thrive in the tundra. Even I know that.'

Leaf nodded. 'Of course, of course. Let me explain from the beginning,' she said patiently. 'Thousands of thousands of years ago these giants amongst the speaking races lived with the mammoths in the northern tundra on the other side of the world. Expert hunters, they thrived for many centuries and grew even taller and larger to survive in the cold. You see, the larger a creature's mass, the easier it is to conserve heat and survive in extreme cold.'

Caspar was nodding as if he understood her. 'A large pot of water stays hotter longer than a small thimbleful.'

Leaf nodded. 'Indeed! While the Haol-garen had an ample supply of food they were happy, but the mammoths developed a disease and their numbers thinned, forcing many of the Haol-garen to head south into the forests and steppes. Here they found their size an advantage since it helped them to defend themselves from the fierce numbers of Holly's people and enabled them to catch game easily. However, a Haol-garen needs a great deal of food. Fortunately, they had a deep enough understanding of the nature of the world to know that they must not eat everything in their path. It wasn't long before they sought out an ideal place at the edge of the woods where the forest pigs were the most healthy and grew to the best size. They tamed them and, with careful breeding, the pigs became bigger and bigger. It was then that a particular sow was born with a gigantic deformity, as happens with all creatures from time to time.'

Caspar nodded as if he had heard about such things.

'The Haol-garen worked very, very hard to keep this piglet alive though she killed her mother at birth and all the other piglets in her litter. Though her legs were so crushed from having little space in the womb and took a long time to straighten out, they carefully nurtured her until she grew to maturity. Only two of her litter were giants, but one was a boar, and that was enough from which to breed a race of giants.'

'Why didn't they keep with the smaller boar?' Caspar asked. 'It would have been so much easier.'

'Of course it would have been easier, but what they did was not as hard as it sounds since the whole process took hundreds of years. Perhaps it was just their natural desire for larger fare that motivated them. After all, you would soon get tired of eating squirrel or thrush because they seem all skin and bone and no flesh. The larger the animal, the larger the hunks of meat. You see, the Haol-garen were used to eating meat and they did not like to forage for green food as we more adaptable people can do. The giant pigs are excellent at converting the vegetation around them into meat. Pigs are very efficient at building up flesh.'

Caspar knelt down to look at the prints. 'These people didn't have their mammoths any more so they set about creating new ones.'

'Indeed, though they never reached quite such gigantic proportions,' Leaf confirmed, though she was now tired of this lengthy explanation. Something was very wrong and it was beginning to trouble her. 'But what they are doing here, I don't know. They shouldn't be here; the curtain should – unless I've got my calculations wrong.'

'Which is extremely unlikely?' Caspar prompted.

'Extremely,' she asserted. 'But something is wrong. Something has happened! Where is the curtain?' She plucked out her compass again and tapped it with an agitated finger. 'Along with the mercury particles, we send so many iron atoms into the atmosphere to form the curtain that the compass becomes confused and spins in the vicinity of the hidden realm. But look! It is still holding true.'

'Perhaps the curtain is still just a little further on,' Caspar said in that gentle, reassuring manner of his. He tried to coax her forward but Leaf dug her heels in.

'No, it has to be here, precisely here. It is not possible for me to make a mistake like that. The protective shield forms a precise shape with its centre at the pool of the inner scholars. It forms the traditional protective shape of a pentagram orientated so that one point is directed precisely at magnetic north.' She sighed and, again, looked up at the sun. In the blink of an eye, she calculated the number of minutes she was away from that point and therefore the distance to the edge of the pentagram. 'We are approaching on the arm that points roughly north-east.' She nodded at a cluster of small hawthorn trees surrounding one very ancient one, its trunk coarse and gnarled. 'That tree is on the very boundary.' Shaking off Caspar's hand, she skipped to the tree and marched about it. 'You see there's absolutely no sign of the Haven.' Her voice was strained and high though she was doing her very best to contain her fears. 'Something terrible has happened to them all.' Running back to Caspar, she clutched hold of his sleeve and tugged hard. 'Spar, something awful has happened. It's the only logical conclusion.'

He put a firm hand on her shoulder. 'Leaf, you must not jump to conclusions. There are a huge number of possibilities.'

She tried to stop her lips from trembling and clung on tight to him. He was right. She should have known he was right. It was quite illogical to jump to conclusions, but fear had prevented her from thinking clearly. 'You are right! Perhaps they have decided to reduce the size of the inner realm, thereby allowing the curtain to become more concentrated. I must have courage,' she told him. 'I wish I were as brave as you.'

Caspar laughed. 'Many think that bravery is the same as stupidity. We are all just running hither and thither, striving to survive.'

'But the act of striving is an act of bravery. You are endeavouring against the odds to make life better. It takes a brave and determined people to do such a thing. My own people hid. They were so afraid of the outside world that they shut it out as if it didn't exist.'

Caspar smiled and hugged her to him. 'There, Leaf, don't think less of your own kind. We humans find plenty of ways of hiding from the realities of life, whether it's in drink or song or by imagining them away. Believe me, if we could create a safe haven like you have done, then we would.'

'Are you trying to tell me you're not brave?' Leaf asked sceptically. 'Think of the dragons you slayed! Think how when you thought you had lost your son you struggled on and on to find him, battling against all those hobs! That took immense bravery. You never gave up until you found him.'

The man's face was suddenly crestfallen and Leaf wondered what she had said to unsettle him so.

'I lost my son long ago,' he murmured. Drawing a deep breath, he looked down at Leaf. 'My daughter understands me, you know. I left her behind on the other side of the world and she's no older than you. I just hope she is as brave as you are.'

'I'm not brave,' mumbled Leaf, wondering why this man

had such a strained relationship with his son. Why had he lost him so long ago? She thought about it and sighed to herself, fighting back tears. She had effectively lost her mother a couple of years ago when the dementia had stolen Zophia's brain to the extent that she was no longer herself. It tore at Leaf's heart just to think about it.

Holding tight to Caspar's hand, she stumbled on through cropped grass and, again, saw signs of the great Haol-garen all about them. There were even remains of a huge fire, the ashes still smouldering. Bones lay littered on the ground, gnawed and sucked at. Leaf looked at a huge thigh bone; bits of meat still clung to the shaft though the soft ends had been chewed away as if something had enjoyed sucking out the marrow fat.

Caspar followed her gaze. 'It's as big as an ox bone.'

'No, it's as big as a pig's bone,' Leaf corrected. 'Definitely a Porcus –'

'Domesticus Ingent-something-or-other,' Caspar concluded for her.

As they continued to follow the line of chewed hedgerow, Caspar suddenly halted and frowned at the wilted flowers beneath his feet. Summer blooms, which had no right to be out so early in the year, had wilted with the frost. Frowning, he studied them and then looked thoughtfully about.

'Leaf, it looks like we must, somehow, already be within your inner realm. These flowers would never have bloomed without the shelter of the crystal shield.'

Leaf nodded and gave him a wry smile. 'You didn't believe me before when I told you the border was at the hawthorns but, you see, the curtain really has gone. You said there were many explanations as to why the curtain was not there, but the only one you were thinking of was that I had got it wrong.'

'I didn't say that,' Caspar objected.

'You don't need to,' Leaf told him stiffly, wondering what they would do when they finally met one of these giant pigs. She was fully aware that pigs were omnivorous, which meant they would be happy to include a child of the scholars in their diet. 'The point is, however, that the curtain should have been where I said. These flowers had indeed blossomed early in the shelter and warmth provided by the curtain. The reason they have wilted is that the curtain has failed, allowing the frost in.'

The Baron looked at her but could think of no reassuring thing to say. 'In that case we had better hurry on.'

She nodded. Despite the fact that she knew the curtain had fallen and that, therefore, some disaster must have befallen the scholars of the hidden realm, Leaf felt a degree of confidence swell within her as her homeland unfolded before her. Copses stood on the top of rounded hills where the grass rippled in a soft breeze. The trees had lost their leaves in the sudden cold that had descended on them, but otherwise everything appeared to be as it should, even down to the sparkling streams winding along the valley floor.

Even though it was obvious something was wrong, a jaunt lightened her step and she hurried on faster, glad to be returning to the comfort of the scholars who would be able to help. She even wondered at her decision to leave at all. How could she possibly imagine that she could survive in the outside world? She was so caught up in her thoughts that it was a moment before she noticed a subtle change in Caspar beside her. He was tense. His hand slithered from Leaf's so that he could reach for his bow at his back. After knocking an arrow to the string, he tried to draw it but his injured arm still failed. The Baron cursed under his breath, slung the bow back over his back and snatched up one of the throwing knives at his belt.

'What's the matter?' Leaf squeaked.

The Baron grunted at her to keep quiet. Leaf could barely think for panicking. She had no instinct of danger herself but could tell from the way Caspar moved that he feared they were being stalked. She looked about her anxiously, shivers running up and down her spine.

'Just stay close,' Caspar hissed at her. 'And try not to leap about like a frightened deer; it attracts attention.'

Leaf scurried alongside, finding the man's hasty pace much harder to keep up with. Although highborn, she had become used to the tougher side of life since she had been hidden away in the village and worked on a cousin's farm. To prove herself to her cousins, who had at first mocked her for her smooth, soft hands, she had done more than her fair share, toiling until her nails were short and split, her hands roughened and her muscles hardened. All the same, she did not have the stamina of this lithe human with his quick hands and his quick eye.

She didn't even see the attack until it was all over. The first she knew of it was when she heard the whistle of the knife's flight as it spun through the air. There was no cry or squeal of pain but, as Leaf blinked and tried to focus in her confusion, she saw a beast lying on the ground, the knife piercing its skull between its eyes.

Her mind whirred. How had Caspar seen it, heard it, known it was there? She had seen nothing at all until the beast was slain. Caspar strode forward towards the beast. She didn't want to go near it but, at the same time, she was certainly not going to leave Caspar's side for a second. Without another thought, she raced after him and was glad when he halted a fewer paces back from the toothsome creature.

'Hylup magna,' she gasped.

'Is there nothing you don't know?' Caspar said too lightly for the situation, his eyes still flitting about him and his hand on a second knife.

'I didn't know it was there,' Leaf pointed out. 'But I do know that it's a flesh eater, a hybrid between a hyena and a wolf and that –'

'It hunts in packs?' Caspar guessed and looked to the child for confirmation.

Leaf nodded glumly. 'We should stay to the trees as much as we can. It's an animal of the open grassland.' She looked down at its heavy, bulbous head. Long teeth pushed out between dark black lips. A thick purple tongue had slid out and was now coated with earth, blood running down its tip to stain the ground. Its massively powerful forelegs and chest dwarfed its rear end, which made the animal look deformed and twisted.

'What do we do?' she croaked as Caspar retrieved his knife.

'We stay together and keep moving,' he told her firmly and winked at her. 'Don't worry, Leaf. I have plenty of knives.' With some difficulty, he retrieved the one embedded in the hylup's skull.

'Packs though,' she reminded him, wondering how they would possibly cope. Perhaps it would be better to be human and not have so many thoughts racing around one's head.

Tugging at her hand, Caspar led her to the edge of the woods. 'We'll run along the skirts of the trees as best we can,' he told her. 'That way we'll make good time but will still have the protection of the forest if need be.'

'I thought that once I was home it would be safer,' Leaf said glumly.

'I thought we were coming here to find answers, not to be safe,' Caspar leaped on her words.

'One of the scholars, my father even, will help us,' Leaf tearfully defended herself. 'But, I admit, I cannot think for the fear. I didn't know what to do other than to go home.'

Caspar winked at her. 'That is all perfectly normal. You would be mad not to be afraid.'

'But you are not afraid.'

Caspar laughed. 'Leaf, I was wrong when I said you knew everything. In fact, you barely know the first thing about humans; we are all afraid. All creatures are afraid; life is fearful because there is no life without death. Now come on! Stop thinking and start acting!'

They ran, Leaf feeling her lungs would burst and that her legs would drop off. She ran so hard she could hear nothing except her breath rasping in her lungs. Her arm socket hurt where she was continually being yanked forward by Caspar, who ran on with no thought for her discomfort. She could not see properly and found herself stumbling. Again and again, the man jerked her to her feet and dragged her on. He was saying something to her, urging her faster, but she could no longer hear; all she was aware of was her distressed breathing and the blood pounding in her ears. She could not do this any more. She just wanted to lie down and curl up into a tight ball, preferably somewhere warm.

Suddenly the Baron released his grip on her and she slumped to the ground in a feeble heap. After a moment, she lifted her head and saw that he was looking about anxiously, his knife held at the ready. Leaf tried to quiet her breathing and listen but she didn't have the strength to control herself; still her gasped breaths drowned out reasonable thought. Caspar was dragging her on again before she had time to get to her feet. With a grunt of effort, he finally picked her up and threw her over his good shoulder. They raced through trees that raked at her clothing as she bounced against the man's back. At last, she could hear what had alarmed the Baron as the sound of snorts, grunts and a low snarl reached her ears.

She was flung up onto a branch, her arm badly grazed and smarting, but somehow she managed to cling on. With enormous difficulty, since he could only use one arm properly, Caspar swung himself up, clambered over her and then reached down to heave her higher into the boughs. Leaf was doing her best to help but she didn't know how to climb trees. Her shirt snagged on a broken branch and began to tear. She kicked upward, trying her best to help herself, and it was then that her foot slipped.

Suddenly, she was dangling in mid air, Caspar's fingers clamped about her wrist. As she looked up at his determined face, she saw that he only managed to brace himself by wedging the shoulder of his injured arm against a stubby branch. Snarls from below jerked her gaze downwards. Arching her back, she jerked up her ankles as the hylup leapt for her, its teeth snapping shut less than a foot from her toes.

'Spar! Help!' she screamed, looking up helplessly into his eyes. 'Spar, do something.' She wriggled frantically and tried to fling her other hand up to reach his arm but she didn't have the strength or agility.

'Keep still,' he grunted at her through gritted teeth, 'otherwise I won't be able to help you, and you're only provoking the hylups more. Leaf, stop struggling.'

She couldn't respond to his instructions. She knew about hylups. Like most unnatural crossbreeds, they were far more vicious than either of the original species. They hunted in packs and killed more than they needed for their food. They were the weight of a small lion and had long curving teeth like a tiger. The males killed their own young if given a chance and the mothers would kill the young of even their own sister. They killed, not by suffocating their prey like a lion, but by tearing them apart, and usually starting at the belly, disembowelling them. She did not want to die!

'Leaf, listen to me.' Caspar's voice was strained and desperate and she could feel his grip loosening. Somehow, she had to do what he asked and trust him, though her instinct was merely to scream and struggle.

She willed herself to respond though the best she could do was to go limp. But that was enough to allow Caspar to haul himself back by pressing his shoulder into the stubby branch. In a few seconds he had her up beside him. Giddily, she clung to the fissured bark of the old tree, her vision swimming.

In seconds, Caspar had flung three throwing knives and two of the hylups lay dead at the base of the tree. Another slunk away, barking. Feeling sick with fear, Leaf slumped forward, breathing hard, wondering when this nightmare was going to be over. There were still more hylups approaching.

A snort broke through the snarls of the hylups, enticing her to look down. She blinked as dust flew up from the heels of a vast pig. Caspar was right; reading about something, learning all the facts about a creature down to the number of teeth and its normal blood temperature, did not prepare one for the reality of it. However well sketched, no likeness captured the ferocity of its soul and its determination to cling to life. Head down, it charged the hylups, which scattered from its path, the huge beast shaking the tree as it passed. One trotter caught the trailing hind-leg of a hylup and severed it clean off.

Leaf slumped forward onto the bough and, as she looked down in giddy terror, she spread her arms wide to close them firmly about the branch. From this position, she could see about another dozen hylups, creeping in from the edge of the plain, slinking forward undeterred by the bovine size of the hog. A huge sow and her litter of piglets were running hither and thither, incensing the drooling hylups, which were tearing after them. It was only a moment before one of the squealing piglets was caught and shredded limb from limb. Immediately, the hungry pack turned to seek more quarry.

She starred on dumbly, wondering how the hylups dared attack the huge boar, which was now bellowing with rage. But they had strength in numbers and were certainly not short of teeth. Several leapt at the pig's tail while others went for the throat, tearing at flesh and scrabbling with their claws. The hog swung round and around, lashing out with trotters and scrabbling at its own neck in an attempt to free itself from the vicious beasts.

The pig's long curving tusks scooped up several of the hylups, spearing some and tossing others into the air. Two fell with their backs broken and another had its stomach ripped open. A couple of the hylups were distracted by the sight of the blood and fell to tearing up their own injured. The rest concentrated on the hog's neck, leaping up from behind the shoulder in order to avoid the lethal tusks.

The black-backed boar swung its head from side to side and, in a frenzied effort to be free of the hylups, smashed itself against the trees to either side. Shrivelled leaves killed

181

by the frost tumbled in showers to the ground. Still the hylups clung on, goading the pig into throwing its weight against the tree in which Leaf and Caspar were taking refuge. Leaf closed her eyes as the shock ran up the trunk and shuddered the branches above. Twigs and leafs cascaded down. Again and again, the hog crashed into the trunk and, with each shock, Leaf's grip failed a little more. Though she scrambled with her fingernails, she was slipping steadily around and, all of a sudden, she was falling.

She never knew when she hit the ground. For a few seconds everything was blackness, and then gradually she became aware of the terrible sound of her own screams as she focused on the open, drooling maw of a hylup. It darted at her, jaws snapping, a run of saliva trailing from its thick tongue.

Leaf pressed herself back into the ground and instinctively raised her arms in a futile attempt to protect herself from the attack. All the same, she could not help but stare at the open mouth. Suddenly, it was swept aside as a hooked tusk pierced the hylup's side and speared straight through its ribcage. Something grabbed her fiercely from behind and was dragging her rapidly through the undergrowth into the thick of the trees. Then she was flung to the earth and her head knocked against a protruding root. She bit her tongue and her mouth flooded with salty blood. The taste triggered her into panic and she began to kick and scream wildly.

It was only Caspar's hand squeezing tightly over her mouth that silenced her and enabled her to get a grip on her emotions. Somehow, despite his injury, he had dragged her here. He must have leaped out of the tree after her. Now he stood over her, flinging his throwing knives in rapid succession as the fiendish hylups came after them.

Two came at them at once. She was certain that Caspar could not possibly slay them both but there were things she didn't not yet know about humans even though she had read five hundred and twenty-six volumes on the subject. Nowhere had it explained that a human could possess such an ability to rise to the occasion. Not only had he leapt before the jaws of death in an attempt to save her but, despite a serious injury to his arm, was now coolly protecting her with his knives and even held one in his left hand. He should have been screaming on the floor in terror or running like a wild man into the forest, yet he stayed to defend her.

The first hylup he brought down, but the second had already leapt through the air before he could pluck out another knife. The dead animal crashed down on top of him, its spread claws raking across his cheek and then shoulder. Leaf, too, was caught by the assault. Crushed beneath the hylup's weight, she struggled for breath. Frantically, she wriggled in an attempt to worm her way out from beneath its body as warm blood trickled down through the coarse hairs and seeped into her clothing.

'Lie still, girl!' Caspar yelled at her, his boot suddenly pressing her down. Already, he had struggled free of the predator.

Again, she heard the whistle of one of his throwing knives and looked up through a bloody mat of hairs to see the man standing tall, his chin set firm and his hand utterly steady. Even in her panic and her distress, she managed to think that it must be wonderful for Rollo to have a father such as this, dependable and determined, looking death in the face and not flinching a muscle. Her own father was confused and forgetful and couldn't be relied upon to find his way to his own breakfast table.

The crushing weight of the dead hylup was stripped from her in a sudden powerful rush. Her eyes wide and black with fear, she looked up to see the animal being dragged away by two of its kind that promptly shredded it, shaking their heads to break the strands of flesh away from the bone. The pigs charged in again, and this time the remaining hylups fled, snapping and snarling at each other as they went.

Leaf let her head flop back against the tree and tried to breathe. They were gone. All she could do was stare up at the interweaving branches of the tree and be thankful that she was still alive. She was aware of Caspar still standing over her, legs spread wide, braced and ready to use his weapons. Her focus sharpened on him as she saw him stiffen.

Following his line of sight, she fixed on the lowered tusk of the black-backed boar.

Chapter 10

'Get up slowly and move very steadily around the tree,' Caspar cajoled in gentle tones.

Leaf stared at the giant boar, its small eyes squeezed by heavy cheek muscles that curled up over fearsome grey tusks. She had seen what they could do to a hylup; it took no imagination to think what they would do to her.

'Get up, Leaf,' Caspar insisted a little more urgently this time.

Bruised and cut, she tried to move just a hand at first but her entire body seemed to have been stripped of bone and her muscles turned to porridge. All she could do was sit and stare at the pig, her rasped breaths silenced in her fright.

Move, she told herself. She must move. Slowly lowering her hand, she grasped at the leafy soil around the roots of the tree as if it might somehow bring her strength. But it was as much as she could do to flex her fingers as the big black-backed boar began to tear up the ground with its cloven hooves, snorting and blowing as if it were a huge bull.

Caspar finally gave Leaf a shove with his foot. She didn't know how she managed it but, somehow, she wriggled along the ground and slunk around the back of the tree just in time to feel the entire trunk shudder under the impact. At first, she feared it had impaled Caspar and that she was now alone in this nightmare, but he must have skipped around the far side of the tree trunk as she crawled around the other. He yanked her up.

'Stay on your feet,' he hissed. 'It's much safer.'

Leaf managed to nod and braced herself with her hand against the tree trunk. She could feel the heavy thump of the hog's trotters as it stalked around the tree. The animal was riled to anger by the sight of its young lying torn and shredded on the ground. One was still squealing with pain, taking its time to die, its distressed cries provoking the parent even more.

It flashed through Leaf's mind why Caspar had not yet hurled one of his lethal throwing knives at the pig. Her eyes flicked over his belt that only had two left and then looked at the broad flat weight of the boar's skull protected by thick hairy hide. It was instantly clear that Caspar doubted he could fell the beast with just two knives. Moreover, if he provoked it further by merely wounding it, they would have nothing at all left with which to defend themselves.

With all the feeble willpower she could muster she kept her legs stiffly braced beneath her. Her heart pounding in her throat, she kept herself as much behind Caspar as was physically possible while he edged steadily to the right, away from the stalking hog.

'What now?' Leaf whispered. 'Should we run?' She didn't know why she asked because she was quite certain that she would not be able to run more than three paces before collapsing.

'You run when I say so,' Caspar told her. 'You're going to run for that hollow oak over there.' He pointed at a cracked and wizened tree whose bark had been stripped from the vast trunk. 'Hide in the crack until I can get to you and help you higher. If I don't make it,' he said matter-of-factly, 'climb up as high as you can. It won't be hard to climb up through the crack in the trunk into the branches above. Can you do that?'

Leaf swallowed and nodded glumly, not really absorbing the full import of his words but simply thinking about the muscles of her legs. She pictured the nerves that ran from her brain to her leg muscles and willed the connections to respond.

Her heart pounded at ten times the rate of the hog's footfall

186

as it plodded around the edge of the tree. Suddenly the world was all a whirl as Caspar leapt forward out into the open, spinning round to face the boar and at the same time yelling at Leaf to run.

It felt like an eternity before her legs responded and it was as if she were watching herself from afar. Putting all her trust in Caspar, she finally leapt away from the sanctuary of the tree and into the open ground. Through the corner of her eye, she caught the outline of the Baron's braced form and the blurred shape as his knife flew from his hand. She had taken only another pace before she heard the squeal followed by a heavy thud as the animal was brought to its knees. The squealing went on and on, enveloping the world in a crescendo of panic. Still running for all she was worth, Leaf heard the hog's laboured grunts and crash of its leg against the hole of a tree as it struggled to right itself. A snort of alarm came from a further pig deeper in the undergrowth that was now roused to defend its own.

Keep going, Leaf urged herself. *Run! Just keep running!*

But she couldn't help but glance over her shoulder to see how Caspar fared. She glimpsed him standing before a charging hog before she sprawled to the ground without even having time to put her arms out to save herself. The shock as her temple whacked onto the frozen ground sent a sickening blackness through her mind and, for a moment, she was disorientated and unable to think of anything apart from the pain. But the desperation to survive forced her body to react before her mind was ready. Spitting out earth from her mouth, she tried to scramble up, only to stumble again. Then something, it had to be Caspar, grabbed her by the collar and she was being dragged up and forward and finally flung towards the blackened oak. Wriggling into the crack, she looked up for a handhold to drag herself up into safety.

At first, Caspar shoved her foot up from below, helping her, but then his hand was suddenly snatched away. Scrabbling frantically, she thought that her handhold would fail and had no spare thought as to what had happened to the Baron since it was all she could do to pull herself up by her arms. All those years of carrying milk pails and her arms hadn't grown a bit; she still looked like she'd done no more than turn the pages of a book all day. At last her toe found a crack in the wood that gave her a good foothold and she was able to push herself up into the tree. Only then was she aware that Caspar was no longer behind her.

'Spar! Spar!' she squealed.

There was no answer and, crammed within the bowels of the split oak, she could see nothing. As a beetle scuttled over her fingers, she stretched up for the next handhold, wondering whether she should go back to try and help him. Deciding that it was more prudent to obey his last order, she heaved herself a little higher, wriggling her shoulders to get through the tight gap. She wondered whether Caspar had known that, with his injured arm and broader frame, he could not follow her up or whether he had simply misjudged the situation and been caught by the hog. It was impossible to tell and so she wasted no more thought on the matter as she struggled upward to a point where she could see and hear what was going on.

There was no sign of Caspar. Frantically, she thrust her head out of the top of the slit in the oak just where the branches spread out from the huge trunk.

I must keep calm, she told herself, flicking back her hair so that she could see more easily. Where was he? The screams, squeal and grunts from below scrambled her thoughts. Her toe was stuck and she was finding it impossible to twist her head round to look in all directions. At last she broke free and, tearing her clothing on the broken wood, she wrenched herself round.

Her breath stopped in her throat. She knew her mouth had fallen open and that her grip on the bark had failed as she simply stared in horror. A vast nose pushed through the trees followed by a broad mouth, the lower lip pushed up in anger. A hand the size of her torso thrust through the trees and snatched her up as if she were no more than a stunned squirrel. It hauled her back out from the safety of the branches and there was nothing she could do to resist. The twigs smacked her face and lashed her back; her breath was snatched away with the speed at which she was whipped through the air. She wanted to scream but found the cold stare of those dark brown eyes froze her voice. Swallowing hard, she stared back into them and watched as they slowly blinked and looked away, down at huge, distant feet.

'Spar!' Leaf exclaimed as she saw that he was being pinned down by the giant's toe, a great big bare toe with huge hairs sprouting either side of the knuckle.

'You owe me a pig!' the giant bellowed, stooping down to pluck up Caspar.

Leaf watched as the Baron's eyes flitted over the giant's fat fingers, his grip on his knife tautening; she could see it was running through his mind whether or not to stab the giant. She hoped not because Caspar could barely inflict any real injury on him and such action would only serve to rouse the Haol-garen even further.

The giant breathed over Caspar, who then gasped and spluttered, his face wrinkling into an expression of acute revulsion. 'You owe me a pig!' the Haol-garen repeated in thunderous tones, stamping his other foot.

It was then that he saw the injured piglet still screaming. Stooping down, he thrust Caspar into the same massive hand in which he held Leaf and used the other to soothe the wounded piglet. Taking his knife from his pocket, he offered mercy by slitting its throat.

The huge man, whom Leaf estimated to be about fifteen feet high with disproportionately large hands, feet and head, slumped back. 'What a waste,' he mumbled. Angrily, he grunted at the two helpless figures crushed in his fist, 'What did you go and kill my pigs for? Why did you go and do such a horrid thing? I was told humans were mean but I didn't truly believe it, and then see how you repay me for giving you the benefit of the doubt.'

Thinking it all a very odd thing to say, Leaf eventually found her voice. 'I'm not a human.'

'Leaf, silence!' Caspar ordered and she was very much taken aback by the sudden authority and command in the man's voice. Up until that second she had considered him to be too gentle a person to speak out like that, especially before a giant.

The Baron raised his chin and fixed the man of Haol-gar in the eye. 'Friend, I am sorry for your loss, truly. The hylups attacked the piglets. We were caught up in the middle of it and, when the hylups were driven off by your pigs, the old boar was still riled and confused. When he heard the piglets still screaming, he blamed us and charged. In order to protect myself –'

'You killed my pig!' the giant exploded in some dismay. 'Stabbed it in the eye! My prize boar. What a thing to do! How could you? How could you?' he repeated dismally.

Leaf felt his grip slacken and, in alarm, found she was suddenly sliding through his hairy fingers. Though a moment beforehand she would have done anything to escape, she now found she was scrabbling to hold on for fear of dropping the dozen feet to the ground. It was only a moment, though, before the great man dropped to his knees and shook Leaf free. She tumbled onto the ground only a few inches from the pool of blood trickling out of the slaughtered piglet. Recoiling, she shrank into a tight ball, not knowing what to do with herself. It was only Caspar dragging at her shoulder that finally brought her to her senses.

'Leaf, come on.' He tugged her hand, heaving her to her feet.

Stumbling, she did her best to run after him as he yanked her into the undergrowth, the back of her hand being torn by a bramble bush. Never to her knowledge had brambles grown in the inner realm in such profusion. They had provided luscious blackberries but had not sprawled like ravenous crocodiles across half the land.

'Just lie still,' Caspar ordered.

Leaf nodded feebly and tried to still her breathing. It had been like this when the dragon had burnt the village in which she had taken refuge with her cousins. The panic had driven out all sensible thought and left her gasping like a stranded fish. If only she could keep calm she might be able to think, but like this her mind was less acute than even a human's. The thought disgusted her. Caspar had been right; they were a fearful people and should never have hidden themselves away from the world as it had only made them more vulnerable when finally their curtain crumbled.

'We'll make a run for open ground and hope the hylups have gone,' Caspar told her.

Leaf was not so keen on the application of hope. She needed rather more certainty in order to make her decision.

'Got your breath?' the Baron asked.

Leaf nodded though she was still panting hard.

Caspar cast his eyes towards the strange Haol-garen, who was stooped over, the piglet cradled in his arms and gasping in sobs. He then turned to Leaf. 'Ready? One, two –'

The count of three was smothered by a bellow of anguish that sent flocks of birds shrieking into the sky. Something was crashing into the trees.

Leaf's legs went to jelly again as she tried to struggle up and follow Caspar. At last, she stumbled to the ground and he fell on top of her, whispering in her ear to keep low and still. 'Hush, Leaf, and lie still, then they might not see us.'

What he said was true but she was having great difficulty listening to reason. She did not think she could bear her fear a moment longer, and a sudden compulsion to rush out screaming into the face of danger overwhelmed her; she thought she would do anything to be rid of the fear. The silent scream in her head that seemed to fill her entire being blocked her thoughts and it was only when Caspar put his arm about her and pulled her close to his body that she managed to calm herself enough to think.

'Breathe,' Caspar murmured in her ear. 'Just breathe.'

Leaf swallowed and managed to force her lungs to work. She took a deep gasp and then found she was panting in shallow, rapid breaths.

'Concentrate on your breathing,' the Baron whispered.

Breathe; the word spun around Leaf's mind. *Breathe*. She remembered the diagrams of the lungs she had read about, of how the air was drawn deep into them and then absorbed by the villi into the blood, the oxygen swept on to feed the muscles. At last, she was able to breathe more steadily and, as she did, she found she could think.

What was that noise? Much calmer now, she asked herself the question and even managed to raise her head to see what was creating that fearsome bellowing. The Haol-garen was still sobbing over the pig but, as the bellowing grew louder, he stiffened up and drew himself up to his full magnificent height. He lowered his head and then slowly raised it as he filled his lungs with air and Leaf wondered how many quarts of air it took to fill such a vast chest. Throwing his head back, the great man erupted with a roar of such violence that Leaf was more amazed than frightened. Even the huge giant did not look big enough to make such a noise.

At least now Leaf knew what was approaching; since the giant's cry had been similar to the first bellow she had heard, it was clearly another Haol-garen. As the second one thumped closer, still blasting out a terrifying roar, Caspar pushed her head down into the undergrowth and put his arm over her shoulder, either to protect her or to keep her still, she could not tell.

The approaching footfall shuddered the earth and Leaf estimated by the strength and frequency of the tremors that the second Haol-garen was about one hundred and forty-two pounds heavier and had a good twelve to sixteen inches in height over the first. Not the tallest of these people by any means, but still a considerable force to be reckoned with.

The rate of his thundering footfalls suddenly accelerated as the approaching Haol-garen gave out a shriek of attack. Leaf wriggled round in order to get a glimpse and was alarmed to see how the attacker was charging in with a great club raised over his head. Before the first great man could raise an arm to defend himself, the club was brought down with bone-splitting force onto the smaller giant's shoulder. But the first Haol-gar managed to duck and dive to the side so that the force of the blow was deflected and the club glanced and skimmed down his arm. A moment later he was on his feet, using his head as a battering ram against his assailant's huge belly.

The attacker stood his ground, absorbed the shock and, far from being winded, raised his club again and, this time, managed to land his blow on the smaller one's head. The ground shook as the giant thudded to the earth. His massive fist reached up and opened imploringly and he tried to pull himself forward.

'Pig!' he groaned pathetically before his face crashed to the earth and he lay still.

Leaf stared at his great hulk, wondering whether or not he was dead. It was a second later before her attention was drawn to the larger Haol-garen. Lowering his club, he began to make clicking noises with his tongue and, in soothing tones, began to cajole his victim's hogs into an orderly herd. He looked at one of the injured pigs for a second then, without further hesitation, raised his club and smote its head, splitting open the skull. Its legs stiffened and juddered before finally falling limp. Vaguely aware that she could still hear squealing coming from somewhere, the sound ringing through her thoughts and shredding her more acute sense of logic, she stared glumly at the smaller Haol-garen lying face-down in the mud. The sounds of his aggressor gradually faded into the distance. A deep tuneful whistle, which he used to soothe the pigs, still wafted to them on the wind.

The force of Caspar's hand pressing down on her shoulder eased and she was able to push herself up to her knees and wipe away the twigs and leaf-mould that had pressed themselves into her skin. Caspar stood up slowly, his eyes focusing on a hazel bush on the far side of the fallen giant. The bush shook and shuddered.

'There's a pig in there still,' he said unnecessarily. 'We have to be careful not to alarm it more. Most probably, it will follow after the others in a moment.'

'What do we do now?' Leaf asked in a hushed voice.

Caspar did not answer. He was staring at the felled giant.

'We should move on and try and find our way,' Leaf continued, rather dismayed that he was moving towards the monstrous man. 'We should move on quickly,' she urged more insistently. 'What if the hylups come back?'

'Precisely,' Caspar continued. 'And what if he's not dead?'

'If he's not dead, it seems most unwise to investigate.'

'You have no sense of adventure,' Caspar told her with a twitch of his crooked nose and a brief grin.

'I can't see what you find amusing in this matter!' Leaf retorted, somewhat affronted that a grown man could take such a flippant attitude while they were in such a deplorable situation.

Caspar's amused grin softened to a sympathetic smile. 'Leaf, it's a way of coping, a way of feeling stronger and braver. It's a way of easing distress. Just laugh a little and you won't feel so scared.'

Leaf snorted at him. 'Laughing cannot possibly change the situation. I know we are in a dangerous place with dangerous creatures all about, and laughing about it isn't going to change my awareness of that.'

'No, but it will help you deal with it and enable you to cope with your fear,' the Baron argued, dismissing the conversation by walking forward towards the great giant. Creeping in close, he dropped his head to one side and watched the Haol-garen's face. He then stopped a little lower and studied his neck, looking for a pulse. After a long minute, he stooped down.

'Man of Haol-gar, can you hear me?'

'Do you think he's alive?' Leaf asked, still very alarmed at the prospect.

'Do you think I'd be talking to him otherwise?' Caspar retorted, nudging the man's shoulder.

There was no response.

'Leaf, help me turn him over. We can't do anything for him while he's face down in the mud.'

'I'm not at all sure that we should be doing anything for him. What if he decides to swat us with his club?'

'Mmm,' Caspar retorted in disapproval. 'He's hardly in a position to grasp his club, let alone wield it. You cannot leave a fellow creature to die in the mud. He needs help.'

Leaf wasn't in the least convinced that they were capable of offering any help to such a vast man, though, with a great deal of effort and application of sticks that they used as fulcrums, they did manage to roll him onto his back. To Leaf's alarm, he groaned.

Caspar knelt by his head. 'We'll do what we can to help you,' he reassured the giant.

Although Leaf experienced no joy in watching any creature suffer, she thought Caspar most unwise. In response to his words, the Haol-garen simply moaned a little louder and so the Baron examined the side of his face, which was beginning to swell and bruise. Fumbling with his one good hand to loosen his shirt, he then examined the giant's shoulder.

'We need hyssop and arnica to reduce the swelling,' Caspar murmured.

Leaf nodded. 'That is probably the best we can do at this stage,' she agreed. 'How are we going to keep him warm though? Our cloaks won't cover half his body.'

'Leaf, you are so sweet sometimes. All those bright ideas buzzing around your head, and you miss the obvious.'

Leaf felt her expression drop as it flashed through her head that she might well be losing her acuteness already. It was too terrible a thought.

Caspar must have caught her crestfallen look because his eyes immediately softened and he reached up to clutch her hand. 'I didn't really mean it, Leaf. It's just the worry of the situation that is making you have trouble thinking. Now gather together some firewood and we'll make a fire.'

Leaf was glad of the activity. Concentrating on gathering twigs and branches helped her feel able to cope. At least she could do something. It played continually on the back of her mind that the crystal shield, which should be cloaking her homeland, had crumbled. Sick with worry, the image of her mother's careworn expression filled her thoughts, soon to be replaced by that of her father's face, which had a distant, glazed expression as his mind wandered through a haze of doubt and confusion. Heavy with her own doubts and concerns for the future, Leaf let her bundle of wood fall to the ground and then began to arrange them for a fire.

Caspar was quick to strike a flame with a flintstone he kept in his pocket, and in a matter of minutes he had a good fire crackling. To Leaf's mind, it was producing too much smoke.

'We'll attract attention,' she warned.

'Yes, but the flames will keep the hylups away,' Caspar reminded her.

Leaf slumped to the floor, wondering how she was ever going to survive. Everything seemed insurmountable and, wherever she turned, another, larger problem thwarted their hopes. 'Poor Isolde,' she murmured. 'I have already failed you.'

'I cannot fail her,' Caspar said with unexpected grit in his voice. 'I promised her mother.'

Leaf nodded as if she knew what he was talking about but at the moment was too exhausted to ask him to expand. Tentatively, she settled by the fire, wearily watching the giant for any signs of movement. He lay still for so long that, when he finally opened one eye, she leapt back in alarm. The eyelid had only slid open a little way and he was looking at her as a cat might watch a mouse with lazy concentration. After a minute or so his other eye opened and his heavy hand slowly moved towards his forehead, which he prodded tentatively, his brow wrinkling. Then he thumped his fist down furiously onto the ground and rolled over onto his knees, attempting to push himself up before he slumped forward, moaning miserably.

'My head,' he moaned and then more bitterly, 'My pigs. My pigs. What am I to do? My pigs!'

Leaf was too alarmed by all the anguished groans and thumping of fists to think clearly. Stepping slowly back, she wanted only to run. What if he suddenly reached for his club? Her foot tripped on a tree root and she stumbled backwards. Caspar caught her before she hit the ground and gently pushed her up to her feet.

'Leaf, steady,' he warned her. 'Just stand your ground and be confident. It's like taming a horse or a bull; you must at least look and sound as if you are in charge.'

'How can I do that?' she demanded helplessly.

'Raise your chin, girl, and breathe deeply. Breathe in life. Be strong.'

Strangely, she noticed that this action deed indeed help her, though she was more reassured by standing close to Caspar who had already regathered all his throwing knives. This confidence did not last long, however, as he proceeded to thrust his last knife back into his belt and stepped forward to the giant. The Haol-garen managed to turn his head and look up at him, half curiously and half angrily, yet at the same time clearly too pained to rouse himself to action.

'Lie still. I have a brew boiling that will ease your pain,' Caspar told him, his voice low and modulated. 'Now, let's get a blanket under your head.'

'You stay back from me, murderer,' the big man rumbled like a brooding volcano. 'You slaughtered my pigs.'

'Just keep steady now,' Caspar said mildly without defending himself against his accuser. 'You're bound to feel pretty bad after that blow.'

The giant seemed to think for a second and then grunted, 'Ogran. He's been following me for weeks and you gave him the opportunity to just go and grab my Truffle. She was my best sow, you know, and Ogran's always wanted her. It's all your fault.'

Caspar didn't answer but sat down beside the big man and began to prod the fire idly with a stick. He then laid it down and tentatively pressed his injured arm, adjusting the bandage to cover the thick scabs. 'Go ahead and try some of my medicine,' the Baron offered calmly. 'Once you are well, things will seem very much easier.'

'How do I know you're not trying to poison me?' the Haol-garen demanded.

'Why would I do that?' Caspar retaliated. 'I could just leave you here to be shredded by hylups.'

The giant's lower lip protruded a little and then he said gruffly, 'I've not yet heard of a hylup that could touch one of my kind even if I were asleep. Give me that brew then,' he demanded, evidently deciding to trust Caspar. 'First you shoot my pigs, encourage Ogran to steal the rest of them and then you try and poison me. How much is Ogran paying you anyway?'

'I don't know Ogran,' Caspar said matter-of-factly. 'And I don't interfere in other people's business.'

'Don't interfere! Ha! Well I never, that's a tall one,' the great man scoffed before taking a long draught of the brew with clearly no thought left at all that it might be poisonous. 'What are you doing now if you're not interfering? And you look like you could do with a bit of this brew yourself,' he said, raising his glass by way of a toast. 'And fine stuff it is too, I might add.'

Leaf thought his tone rather too jovial for his situation. She was, however, persuaded that this giant was not the threat she had at first thought. Perhaps Caspar was right and she was making things worse for herself by always being so fearful.

She was not used to feeling confused and disorientated

and wished with all her heart that these rough times had not been thrust upon her. Generations before her had lived happily without a care in the world; was it fair that her young shoulders should bear this arduous burden?

'What are you feeling so sorry for yourself for?' the giant unexpectedly demanded. 'You haven't just been clubbed over the head.'

Leaf blinked, uncertain how to reply. 'I know, but I have problems of my own.'

The giant chortled and then looked as if he regretted this action as he gripped his sides and winced. 'Now what's a young whippersnapper like you got to complain about yet? You're much too young to have gathered any worries or to have any regrets in life.'

Leaf looked at him in amazement. 'What has age got to do with it?'

'If you were any older, you would know.'

'As a matter of fact, if I were any older my brain would begin to degenerate. For your information, we scholars experience a massive growth in brain development at puberty but we are now suffering from a disease that is triggered by the very process of maturing into adulthood. The moment I come into my full powers of thought, I will start to lose them.' She sighed. 'And you, who have only suffered a blow to the head, dare judge me and my fears?'

Her lips pressed together in an attempt to stop herself thinking what might happen to her in perhaps only one short year, maybe two if she were lucky. As yet she was very much a girl, but the moment her body began to change the disease would be triggered.

The giant looked at her sideways. 'You worry too much; do not ruin the present by worrying about the future.' His brow, however, was beginning to wrinkle up in concern as his eyes looked about him and Leaf assessed that he did not hold entirely with his own philosophy.

'My pigs are gone,' he wailed in a deep rumbling voice. 'And you,' he glared at Caspar, 'will have to get them back for me. I cannot have Ogran taking my pigs. It's not right and not fair and I will have my pigs.' He thumped the ground with his great fist and then winced again, lifting his hand to his temple.

'You just sit there a while and let the medicine take a hold,' Caspar soothed, offering a further cupful of steaming brew to the great man. The giant eyed it suspiciously, which seemed to Leaf to be somewhat absurd since he had already drunk much of the medicine earlier.

'How do you know . . . ?' the giant suddenly blurted and then began to stutter. He frowned as if becoming confused. 'How do . . . How do I –' he mumbled uncertainly and suddenly his head slumped forward.

Leaf blinked rapidly, her breath caught in her throat. 'Is he dead? Has he died? What's the matter? Why did he suddenly collapse like that?'

Caspar held out a hand to slow her down. 'Leaf, calm down. It's quite normal, though obviously his condition is serious. What's happened is that he's more injured than he realized. The adrenaline and anger at his situation kept him going and now that he's relaxed just a little those mechanisms ceased to sustain him, and so he collapsed.'

Leaf nodded. She knew that! Of course she knew that. Why was she asking?

'Keep him warm,' she instructed. 'And it's best if he lies down so that the blood can more easily reach his head,' she advised, suddenly regaining her composure. Crawling forward, she reached out and pulled back the giant's eyelids to peer into the whites of his eyes. Then she listened to his heart and decided the rhythm was firm and strong though a little slow for one of such a size.

Leaf and Caspar busied themselves for some while, trying to make the great Haol-garen comfortable. Leaf spent a great deal of effort scooping together leaves and trying to push them under the giant's body to raise him off the frosted ground and so reduce the rate at which he was losing heat. Meanwhile,

Caspar drank much of the brew himself and rubbed a paste into his wound, which looked a little less angry, a thick knotted scar knitting the gash together. How he had managed with an injury like that, Leaf could not imagine. Again, she put it down to the extraordinary human characteristic of being able to rise to the occasion. Still, she was a little dubious about the manner in which Caspar had prepared the medicines since, in her opinion, medicines from herbs needed distilling to remove the more dangerous alkaloids. She hoped he hadn't overdone it.

Closing her eyes for one minute, she felt for the giant's pulse, counting the slow beats and focusing only on the sense of his life and the strength of his will to live as the energy was pumped through his body. It was a soothing sensation and, just for that short while, she forgot the outside world. But it was into this moment of peace, this oasis in time, that the sound of a low grumbling breath being drawn in penetrated her deeper consciousness. The sound could have been no more than a whisper and yet, because of her concentration, Leaf heard it as loud as if it had been a roar. Dropping the giant's wrist, she snapped her head round and stared into the bushes.

Caspar must have noted her sudden look of alarm because he leapt up from where he had been kneeling on the ground, plucking out one of his throwing knives in one swift movement. In a single bound, he covered the distance separating himself from Leaf and was at her side.

'What is it?' he hissed.

'Did you not hear it?'

'Hear what?'

Leaf wasn't sure and did not answer but instead stared on into the bushes. Perhaps it had only been her imagination. Slowly, she let her muscles relax. Yes, it must simply have been her imagination. Just as she let her gaze slide away from the thicket of undergrowth and she began to chide herself for being so alarmist, Caspar roughly shoved her back towards the giant.

She sprawled onto the earth, grazing her cheek against a broken twig. Her mouth was filled with dirt and her head was dazed. Nevertheless she was instantly aware that Caspar was trying to protect her. She could hear the whistle of his knives somersaulting through the air and the sudden charge of an animal tearing through the undergrowth, the air thrumming with growls.

Whimpering, she crawled under the giant's arm and pressed herself as close to his warm body as she could, hoping that the hylups would be afraid of the great man even though he was unconscious. Closing her eyes, she buried her head into the dark of the crisp leaves beneath the giant, waiting for that crushing pain that was bound to come when one of the hylups inevitably grabbed her. Terrified, she wondered how long it would take before the beast tore her apart.

The giant stirred and gripped hold of her shoulder. Leaf feared she might be crushed and so jerked away in pain but was not able to shake herself loose from his grasp. Frantically twisting round, she saw Caspar standing just in front of her, hurling knife after knife. But he had already hurled more than half his knives and only one or two of the beasts were maimed. Caspar hurled his next knife and a hylup gave out a terrible scream as it was pierced in the rump. But it still managed to keep on coming and, a second later, was tearing at the giant's leg, its teeth deeply embedded in its thigh.

Leaf screamed to Caspar to do something but instantly realized he couldn't as another pair of hylups came galloping out from the thick of the woods.

'Club,' Leaf said stupidly to herself, aware only of the savage noise, flailing limbs and blobs of bloody saliva that were being shaken from the hylup's lips. Somehow, she got herself to her feet and tried to heave up the giant's club. Instantly realizing that was impossible, she reached for a length of wood that had been snapped from the lightning-struck oak, hefted it up and smashed it down on the hylup's head.

It was not actually enough force to do any harm but it was

enough to draw the animal's attention away from the giant's leg and onto Leaf. The hylup looked her straight in the eye; she dropped the club and screamed. Standing rigidly on the spot, her scream grew louder and louder as the hylup leapt through the air, claws spread wide as it aimed for her belly.

For a second, everything was black and Leaf felt no pain. Then the ringing began in her head and the sickness welled up from her stomach, prodding at her throat. She couldn't see properly as she was lying face down in the earth. She wasn't aware of any pain until she began to move and then realized her head felt as though it would explode and that her back was a scream of raw nerves. Someone was pulling her upright and she complained angrily, furious that anyone would try to move her when she was in such agony. There was blood everywhere, rich dark blood.

'Get up!' Caspar snarled at her. 'Get up and work out what we can do for this great man. He's bleeding from cuts to his leg and the smell will bring more hylups or even worse.'

Leaf couldn't imagine that anything could possibly be worse than hylups.

Chapter 11

Rollo watched his father disappear into the distance, Leaf's little figure close at his side. The Baron was swinging his injured arm as if to prove that it was now much better, though Rollo hoped it still hurt him. How dare he abandon him! How dare he leave to look after that strange child! He stared on angrily while bands of pain tightened around his heart.

How dare he choose to go with Leaf into a haven of safety while the rest of them faced unknown perils? He stamped back within the confines of Baron Oxgard's castle and found himself heading towards Isolde's chamber without really realizing why he chose to go there. She was curled up asleep though she moaned and jerked as if battling with a nightmare, sweat dampening her golden red hair.

He sat in a chair beside her, too absorbed in his own distress to worry deeply about Isolde's pain. He was, however, aware that her company gave him a degree of ease. His head was throbbing and lights danced before his eyes so he knew that, if he didn't manage to calm himself, he would suffer one of his fits.

The shrivelled brownish-black skin on her left hand was poking out of the covers and he stared at it as if it were a snake about to strike him. It was vile to look at. Already, the discolouration and leatheriness to the skin was beginning to creep towards her shoulder. He closed his eyes for a moment, trying to suppress the thick jagged blackness that was eating away at the corner of his vision.

But he couldn't suppress his desire to dwell on the events

leading to his father's decision to leave him and go off with Leaf. He had been made to sit outside Baron Oxgard's chambers for hours while the adults discussed their best strategy. Rollo was deeply offended at not being invited into the debate, and this appeared to be the one thing he had in common with Fanchon. Huffily, she had strutted off, casting a hasty look at Baron Wiglaf, who was still fussing over Dominica or moaning about the state of his quarters and appeared to be utterly disinterested in the Torra Altans' plight.

Fanchon had looked from Wiglaf to Guthrey and, not surprisingly, chose Hal's son to prey on. Wiglaf was undoubtedly wealthy but Guthrey was also of noble birth, and Rollo decided that if he were a woman seeking fortune he would take Guthrey's lesser wealth over Wiglaf's any day. Guthrey undoubtedly had charm and Fanchon and Dominica clearly enjoyed his company. It wouldn't have been so bad if Guthrey didn't gloat over his ability to attract the women. It angered Rollo deeply since he couldn't fathom why he lacked such an art. After all, he was of considerable standing – though no one here seemed to care two hoots about that.

His father had come out of the meeting with a quick step ready for action and had barely given him a thought, packing together all the necessary supplies and equipment that he and Leaf might need.

Rollo had felt the tears pricking at his eyes and his head begin to pound as he thought how his father had been ready to abandon him without a second thought – and to look after a stranger at that. It had been only when Caspar was completely prepared to leave that he had sought out his son, and by that time Rollo was too furious to listen to any excuses.

'I think it's best if you stay with Brid,' Caspar had told him.

'Evidently,' Rollo had retorted, hurt by the entire situation. 'I suppose I am not reliable enough to accompany you?'

'No, not at all! I didn't say that. It's just that only a very few can penetrate Leaf's city without attracting attention and,

205

since we know how strong Silas's influence is there, we must not do that. If you are with Brid, there will be more able people around to protect you.'

'Oh, yes, I'm sure. I am sure all you are thinking about is my well-being,' Rollo had said with deliberate sarcasm. 'You're just running away to where it's safe,' he had accused, trying to hurt his father as much as he possibly could though he could see from his father's eyes that the words had not troubled him.

'One day, Rollo, you will understand that is not true,' Caspar had told him with infuriating self-control.

'Huh!' Rollo had snorted, standing to his feet very hastily. 'Or is it because you don't trust yourself in Brid's company a moment longer?' To Rollo's amazement, he had watched his father blink and his mouth open fractionally as if he were about to speak but was evidently lost for words. Rollo was astounded; he had merely said the first thing that had popped into his head without having the faintest inkling that he would touch on a sore point.

He had stared blankly at his father. 'So is that why you never loved me? You never loved me because you never loved my mother. All along you were in love with Brid. Is that why you ran away in the first place?'

Caspar's composure had returned. 'Rollo,' he had said, reaching out a hand to squeeze his son's shoulder, though Rollo jerked back. Caspar wisely had not persisted in an attempt to offer physical comfort. 'Rollo, I love you to the bottom of my heart. I have always loved you and I always will. Your mother meant the world to me and it was cruel for you to say something like that to me.'

Rollo had stared into his father's deep blue eyes, which were blinking at him as if begging for his love and understanding but, unyielding, Rollo simply stared blankly back.

At last, Caspar had given him a pained shrug. 'Rollo, this is simply how it is. Travelling alone, Leaf and I shall make good time. The rest will go after Silas. It is clear that, in the present climate, it would be suicide to travel north and try and return to Torra Alta. Instead, with help from Aisholt, you will travel south-west towards Piscera as all intelligence gleaned from Oxgard's enclosures indicates that Silas has travelled that way. Do you understand?'

Rollo refused to answer but merely grunted.

'Anyhow, I need you to look after Cracker.'

'I can ride him?' Rollo blurted, not meaning to sound so enthusiastic.

'No! Most certainly not. You can lead him or Brid can ride him; he is far too dangerous for you and I don't want to arrive at our rendezvous only to hear that your neck has been broken.'

Rollo scowled at him, brimming with resentment.

His father looked at him sternly. 'You will obey me on this matter, Rollo. Now, in twenty-one days' time we shall meet at the ring of beeches on top of the Pisceran escarpment known as the Fin. It's a remote spot with invaluable view points and, moreover, Leaf has explained that it is easy to reach from her realm. It seems her lands are laid out in the form of a pentacle with one arm pointing due north. That will make navigation much easier. If one arrives there before the other, we are to scribe a cryptic message onto the most northerly beech to say where we are waiting. It's foolproof.'

Rollo had shrugged his shoulders dismissively as if he didn't care. Caspar had looked back at him long and hard, opened his mouth as if to say something but then sighed in that irritating, exasperated manner of his. He had straightened up as if girding in his emotions. 'Well, son, just make sure you behave yourself and put pride into all you do.'

Rollo had refused to nod but just stared at him. After a long minute when neither had seemed to know what to do Caspar turned his back and left without once looking over his shoulder. Biting his lip, Rollo had been possessed by an intense desire to run after his father and cling to him for all he was worth, yet his legs would not allow him. He needed his father to make the first move.

Now, sitting beside Isolde, he sank back, his vision blackening and his head throbbing painfully. Unable to calm his emotions, he sensed the irreversible signs of the beginnings of a fit. He tried to breathe deeply and put his head between his knees to help get the blood to his brain but it was too late and he found himself sinking into a blackout.

He was vaguely aware that someone had scooped him up into strong arms. He sensed a feathery touch on his brow and then a bitter taste on his tongue. The taste overwhelmed all other senses. His world seemed to revolve around his tongue and lips, which felt gigantic and independent of his body. It was as if there were a thousand minute arms on his tongue, embracing the flavours, while his lips, like two blubbery whales, seemed unable to close his mouth firmly.

The distorted sense of proportion gradually receded and his mouth became a part of himself again as the bitter liquid slithered down his throat and hit his stomach. The intense, burning heat spread throughout all his body and, suddenly, he was awake. With a jerk, he sat bolt upright, his head bashing into Brid. She had been leaning over him and staggered back, hand on her brow, cursing as if she were a soldier not a lady.

After a minute, she was able to look at Rollo and grinned at his scowling face. 'Who would ever have known that young girl, Leaf, was right about using a blend of fool's heliotrope and hypericum. It really does work and even better than the valerian. Amazing,' she muttered.

Rollo couldn't help but smile. 'So you are a little put out that someone might know more than you.'

Brid blinked at him. 'My, we are awake and sharp, aren't we? Well, young whippersnapper, you're not as smart as me yet. I know how to learn and whom to learn from. And I can tell you one thing, Rollo, you've an awful lot to learn about life if you're going to survive.'

'Well, that's not a very pleasant thing to say to someone who has only just come round to consciousness.'

Brid sighed and flopped into a chair beside him. 'I know,

Rollo, and I'm sorry. You gave me such a crack on the head. You must have a skull like a boar's.'

Rollo grinned at her, deciding that, even though she was Guthrey's mother and Hal's wife, she wasn't all bad. There was an unconventionality about her that he liked and an inner strength that most other adults lacked. That strength gave him confidence and he felt able to feed and grow off it. Scowling at himself, he wondered if he were not seeking his own mother in her. Perhaps he was already forgetting Ursula, who had been the light of his miserable existence. Perhaps now, like a feeble fledging, he was trying to latch onto the first substitute that crossed his path.

Brid was studying him with her head on one side, those dragon-green eyes piercing his soul. 'Well, now, Caspar's son,' she sighed, as if thinking how things might have been. 'I never knew how to imagine you, but certainly never like this.' She gave him a warm, comforting smile that made him feel as if he were being swaddled in soft blankets. 'You have his colouring, of course, but otherwise you don't look a bit like him and yet not like your mother either.'

'Did you know her?' Rollo sat up smartly, suddenly sober and his mind intense and focused at any mention of Ursula.

Brid smiled again. 'Of course. She was quite magnificent. And so brave. It was no wonder that your father fell madly in love with her.'

Rollo snorted at this and Brid looked at him, her eyes running over the features of his face, studying him closely. She did not pursue the conversation but guided Rollo back to the matters at hand. 'We have a difficult task ahead of us. Oxgard's network of men across his enclosures is breaking down due to the northward migration of hobs. Now that they have destroyed Farona and eaten everything of worth in the midshires, we believe they see Torra Alta as the greatest threat to their occupation of Belbidia. Silas, however, has been sighted on many occasions, unmistakable as he is with his horse and his band of hobs and dwarves. He is heading for Piscera and we must catch up with him.'

Rollo closed his eyes. He didn't feel well enough to travel, didn't like the idea of hobs and was simply exhausted. Perhaps, if he just went back to sleep, the others would go without him?

'What's he doing?' someone was muttering outside the door and Rollo's ears pricked up.

'Well, he has these turns.' It was Quinn's voice. 'He can't help it but it means he's not strong. He really ought to stay behind.'

Rollo felt his pulse suddenly accelerate. How dare Quinn be so magnanimous? It was so infuriatingly superior. And it was so patronizing to believe that he was weak. These fits were in no way a disability. If anything, they made him stronger because he had to endure them and learn to live with them. What difficulties did Quinn have to cope with in comparison? His life was so simple. It would have to be, otherwise he wouldn't have grown to be such a simple, uncomplicated youth always so ready to forgive everyone.

Rollo sat up and stared at the doorway to see Quinn and Guthrey in quiet conversation. Guthrey was staring back, clearly not yet sure of him.

'I was merely resting, waiting for all of you to be ready,' Rollo told them haughtily.

Guthrey snorted disdainfully, which had Rollo on his feet in seconds though, to his mortification, he still felt so dizzy that he immediately had to reach out a hand to steady himself against the head of the couch. He watched the superior look spread across Guthrey's face but was even more shamed by the way Quinn immediately offered his hand to help him.

'Guthrey, you can't sneer at him for his affliction; it's unkind,' Quinn chided his half-brother.

'You think I want your kindness?' Rollo snarled between bared teeth. He shook his head and stood stiffly upright though the room was still rotating around him. He focused on the doorway that stirred and swam before his eyes. Somehow he brought himself to his feet and began to walk stiffly towards it, hoping that he would make the opening rather than hit the door jamb. Quinn stretched out a hand to help him but he refused to look at the youth and strode on stiffly, the echo of his feet unnaturally loud. He drew in a deep breath to steady himself, then paused as Guthrey spoke out.

'I thought we could be friends. When you first arrived at Torra Alta, I was wrong about you and treated you with unbecoming hostility but I was also man enough to admit it. I offered my friendship. What kind of a man are you if you will not accept my apology?'

The hairs on the back of Rollo's neck prickled as he sensed the intense emotion behind Guthrey's words. However, he said nothing but took another step forward, reassured only by the draught through the doorway that he was heading in the right direction. Guthrey's anger had raised his angst and he knew that was always a dangerous sign.

'Don't you dare walk away from me!' Guthrey hissed. 'I offered my apology; you cannot turn your back on that. Are you too much of a coward to admit that you, too, were also in the wrong?'

Rollo growled, no longer able to control his voice, which was now low and bestial. Like a rabid dog, his mouth began to foam. As always, when he lost his temper, he was not truly aware of what he was doing. He knew he must have bit his cheek because he tasted blood that somehow was too sweet. His hands hooked into claws and he raked rather than punched at his opponent, blood spitting from his mouth as he hissed and snarled. He heard nothing but a roar and felt no pain as he locked with his adversary, unaware whether he was mauling Guthrey or Quinn. It was only a thin cry from what seemed to be far away in his head that drew him back from the mad maelstrom world of his temper.

Gasping, he curled his head down and raked on, blood beneath his nails, saliva dribbling from a bloodied mouth.

Then someone punched him hard in the back and whipped him round. Rollo was just able to focus on Guthrey's clenched fist before it smacked into his jaw.

'You vile beast; how dare you attack my brother!' Guthrey snarled. 'You're a madman. You should be chained up with the dogs. If Father were here, he'd have you thrashed.'

'He'd do no such thing,' Brid calmly interrupted as she arrived on the scene, her eyes hastily skimming over Quinn's face then glancing between Guthrey and Rollo. 'Guthrey, you can get outside and help with the horses. Rollo, you can go to the kitchens for some boiling water in a pitcher so that I can see to Quinn's face here. We're riding out in under the hour and I don't have time for this nonsense.'

After glancing at the strips of red on Quinn's face where his nails had sliced the skin, Rollo trotted away, head hung low and deeply contrite. Brid had not been angry with him but her simple, unspoken disapproval wounded him more deeply than if she had been. He felt young and insignificant. He felt ashamed. Angry with himself, he rudely shoved open the doors to the kitchens. Scowling at Oxgard's cook, he demanded hot water and she stared back at him, hands on hips.

'I don't care how fine and mighty your mother and father might be but, to me, you look no more than a skinny whippet and, moreover, a skinny whippet *in my kitchen*. I'll have a word of please from you, young sir, before I lift a finger to help you.'

Rollo's mouth moved up and down in disbelief. No one had ever spoken to him in this manner before. He expected such words from his peers but from a servant . . . It was unbelievable.

'You can stare at me all you want, young knave, but you'll not get what you want till you find a civil tongue,' the cook told him sternly.

Rollo was about to turn on his heel and march out but, on the other hand, he could not face Brid if he returned without water, especially since it was his nails that had made such a mess of her son's face. He hastily capitulated to the cook's demands. 'Please,' he said flatly and without the least indication that he meant it.

The cook's tufted eyebrows rose a little.

'Please,' he said more imploringly this time, forcing a sweet smile onto his face.

'My, my! The boy has a smile for me – and what a winning smile it is! Mabel, Rose, get some water a'boiling for the fine gentleman here, who has graced us with his presence,' she said with a teasing laugh. 'Now, come in, young master, and let's see if we can't feed you a crusty slice of bread that'll fill you out a bit and make you as handsome as that young Master Guthrey now.'

A titter rippled through the scullery maids and Rollo was painfully aware that Guthrey must have been the main topic of their conversation. Two of the girls nudged each other and blushed and Rollo could only assume that Guthrey had spent his time amorously entertaining the young maidens.

He pouted at them, immediately jealous that Hal's son commanded such desire. However, under the cook's authoritative stare, he remembered to say thank you when one provided him with a crust taken off a freshly baked loaf. It tasted good and went a little way to improving his temper.

'Very fine,' he mumbled, one cheek stuffed out with bread. 'It's the finest I've tasted in Belbidia.'

The cook slapped him heartily on the back, which made him choke. 'Well, sir, it's sure that you learn quick, very quick indeed.' She snapped her fingers and one of the maids came forward carefully with a steaming pitcher. 'Now that the young lord has been so kind to us, I think you could carry the pitcher for him.'

'Actually,' Rollo said more for the sake of the truth than to boast, 'I'm not a lord. I'm a prince.'

'A prince in my kitchen, eating my bread! Well, I'm blessed!' the cook said good-naturedly though she didn't actually sound the least bit impressed. 'I won't wash the floor for a week so that I can keep smiling at the muddy footprints you've left.'

'They're not muddy!' Rollo objected in alarm.

The cook winked at him. 'Now, come on, young master, you know I'm teasing. Off you run.'

The scullery maid walked dutifully behind him and it was by chance that they passed Fanchon, who was gliding down the corridor towards them. She beamed at Rollo, eyelashes all a flutter. Respectfully, she stood to one side to let him past, but then stepped into the path of the scullery maid.

'Just watch where you are going, girl!' Fanchon snapped angrily at the servant.

Rollo turned about, suddenly aware that his own behaviour had been much like Fanchon's and how very ugly it was. 'Let her pass, Fanchon,' he ordered stiffly. 'She's with me.' He smiled at the scullery maid. 'Here, let me carry the pitcher. It must be heavy.'

To his satisfaction, the scullery maid blushed and smiled while Fanchon scowled blackly and strutted off. He did not like that woman at all and it angered him that the others tolerated her. The maid tripped along behind, ready to return the pitcher to the kitchens once he had done with it, her mind a whirr at his behaviour towards her.

Pushing open the door to his quarters, he was met with the sight of Quinn's face and almost dropped the pitcher now that he was truly aware of what he had done. Brid had wiped away much of the blood and he saw that what he thought were mere scratches were actually deep gashes. Hastily, he poured the boiling water into a bowl and returned the pitcher to the serving-girl without giving her another glance.

'Quinn . . .' he began, not knowing what he could say. 'I didn't know what I was doing. I'm so sorry. Guthrey was right.' He stared at the lines of blood, which continued to bead up along the gashes the moment Brid wiped them away. The priestess looked suddenly sad and old as she dabbed at the scars and sympathetically kissed the crown of her son's head.

Rollo backed silently from the room, consumed with self-loathing. He didn't know where to put himself, where to hide. His mind was filled with only one thought and that was, if he ran like the wind, he might be able to run away from himself. An instant later, he bolted. Barely knowing his way about the castle, he ran down one row of mews until he found himself in front of the stables. A sea of faces spun round to stare at him. Faceless men with arms spread wide tried to catch him as if he were an escaped piglet. The exit was blocked.

'Steady there now, young man, you don't want to go running about and scaring the animals. We've had enough trouble with that red roan as it is.'

A flash of hope suddenly came to him. Father had left Cracker behind in the stables. Firecracker and his own horse, Chieftain, were the only pieces of home that had come with them all that way across the oceans. The animal Oxgard had provided for him was being prepared at the rear of the stables and looked well enough but, on the other hand, Firecracker was already being led forward though it was taking two grooms to achieve the task. What did he care that his father had ordered him never to ride the animal? If he took Cracker, it would only serve his father right for abandoning him.

Recklessly, Rollo hurled himself into Firecracker's saddle and snatched up the reins. The stallion threw up his head and reared, shrieking out its savage cry. The youth managed to cling onto a handful of mane and only just kept his seat. As Firecracker's hooves struck the cobbles, Rollo just succeeded in finding one stirrup, which helped him keep his balance as they spurted out towards the gate, sparks flying off the horse's hooves.

Only when he reached the castle gate did he finally have his balance and both reins in hand. This enabled him to take one brief glimpse over his shoulder. He must have knocked one of the grooms down as others were rushing to help the man up off the cobbles. Rollo didn't wait to see what more trouble he had caused and fled out into the open.

Hunched up over Firecracker's neck, his face whipped by the stallion's streaming mane, he finally found some sense of release and freedom from his fears and shame. It was as if he were flying. He wanted to be free of the earth, tumbling and twisting through the skies, untethered by the bonds of gravity, and this was as close as he could come to that. He thumped his heels into the stallion's sides. Firecracker threw his head forward, snatched the bit between his teeth and yanked the reins from Rollo's hand in protest.

Before them stretched fields filled with grazing oxen. Winding between the pastures was a narrow lane lined by a huge bank and hedge and it wasn't long before they were clattering along the stony ground. To Rollo's dismay, Firecracker appeared to dislike the tight confines of the lane and veered for the hedge, which was surely too high to leap. Cursing his foolishness in taking the animal, he knew the best thing he could was to balance himself high in the saddle and allow the horse a loose enough rein to do his job. Beyond that, all he could do was cling on for dear life and pray. His heart plunged deep into his stomach as they soared up the nearside of the hedge and then swam up into his throat as they landed. Somehow, they had cleared the obstacle and now Firecracker lowered his head and lengthened his stride, launching into a gallop that snatched Rollo's breath away and swept the water from his eyes back into his temples and hairline.

Nothing could stop them now. Gaining courage from surviving the mighty leap, he leant forward, urging the horse on, not caring which way they galloped, only that they outran any that might pursue them. The effort of remaining squatted and balanced over the saddle to help the horse in his stride was beginning to tax his leg muscles and aggravate his injured ankle. He eased back into the saddle only to find that unbearably uncomfortable as it jarred his spine and so he raised himself up again. They had crossed the open pasture and were now skirting around a peninsula of woodland, leg-ripping saplings all around them. A single ash tree marked the border between pasture and wood.

The breakneck speed had done much to help him forget his shameful deeds and he was beginning to hope that the horse would start to slow. This niggling feeling became a serious concern as the saplings closed about him and he found himself on a muddy track that cut through a wood. It was one thing galloping at pace across open country, something that he very much enjoyed, but quite another to be careering through a wood. He pressed himself low against Firecracker's neck to avoid being stunned by overhanging branches and began to haul on the reins in an effort to steady the horse.

But, like an adolescent, the old horse would not listen but galloped on, weaving along the path that was slowly beginning to narrow, tree trunks flashing past horribly close as they went. Time and again, the dangling branches clawed at Rollo's back. He pressed himself lower.

'Cracker, please,' he wailed helplessly at the horse. 'Please, this is madness.'

Suddenly, they were jolted as the horse misjudged the distance from the solid trunk of an ash. The stallion had made even less allowance for Rollo's knee, which was wrenched backwards. He managed to stay seated but was now in considerable pain from the blow.

'Stop, you vile brute,' he yelled at Firecracker, who simply bucked in protest and crashed on, his shoulder bumping against one tree and then the next. It was almost as if he were deliberately trying to scrape his rider off. 'You're an evil beast,' Rollo yelled. He could not sit back in the saddle to haul effectively on the reins for fear of being knocked off. All he could do was pull as hard as he could from his present position, lying low against the animal's sweating neck. It was as if Firecracker knew he had no ability to control him. Why his father prized this devil, he could not think.

The path forked and forked again and they galloped deeper into the wood. Rollo hated the woods. He imagined that the vegetation was alive and was trying to reach up and grapple him before entangling him in its multi-armed grip. An inexplicable fear of entrapment hung darkly over his spirit. Branches cracked him on the head and he slumped giddily forward. By the time he could focus, they had taken more twists and turns along the path and he was thoroughly disorientated. How was he going to stop this animal before they were both killed?

Naturally, he knew that the easiest way to stop a bolting horse was to pull it in ever tightening circles. Caspar would have challenged the animal in some way. He would have ridden it on, demanding continual changes in gait to make the animal aware that the rider was still its master. But this situation was now way beyond Rollo's abilities and he knew it. He suspected that Firecracker knew it as well.

'How dare you do this to me!' he shouted fruitlessly at the horse, flinging himself to the left to avoid another overhanging bush. A holly tree scratched at his hands and face but at least he made it through without smacking into another branch. He could see daylight streaming into a wide opening and hoped that, any second, he might find some way to halt the brute. The horse pecked at the ground, sending Rollo onto his withers and his hands up to the animal's ears.

Aware of harsh shouts about him, he began pushing himself back but was still too far forward to save himself as the stallion suddenly dug in his heels, dipped his hindquarters and drew to an abrupt halt. Rollo was catapulted over the horse's ears and landed heavily to the ground, his face thumping into the mud.

With the wind knocked from him, it was a moment before he could breathe. Even the angry shouts all about him and the bull-like bellows of rage from the horse did nothing to speed his recovery. Sharp hands were clawing at him, pulling him over. He stared up into thin, dark green faces with long noses. Pixie-like ears pushed up through a creature's spiky hair that was adorned with a holly wreath. Others pressed

218

around the first face. Their limbs were smooth and thin like the fresh holly shoots and they screamed and barked at each other, heads snapping out to bite at any of their fellows that annoyed them.

Rollo could not understand what they said. He knew they must be hollines and that, possibly, they spoke in the old tongue of the Caballan but he understood it only a little and certainly not at the speed at which these creatures talked. One pulled him up by his hair and began ranting into his face. Others had snatched up sticks, which they beat together while barking out a vigorous song that must surely have been a war-chant. Rollo began to shriek uncontrollably as one yanked his hair and pressed a glinting knife to his scalp. Chattering and squawking excitedly to his companions, the holline was evidently asking for approval before slicing off Rollo's scalp.

There were shrieks all about him, and Rollo added to them, thrashing and kicking as hard as he could. One of the creatures bit through the leather of his boot to reach his skin but he managed to raise his other boot and smash it into its cheek. The holline gripping his hair yelled all the more, inciting a rush of bloodlust to the rest of its people. Rollo felt his own blood shrink back from his head in anticipation of the dreaded cut. He had no idea whether losing his scalp would kill him or not but he suspected that, even if it didn't, they would chop pieces off him bit by bit until he was dead.

The cut when it came, however, was not to his forehead as he had anticipated but into his ear and sliced downwards into his cheek. A horrible squeal then ripped out from the holline's throat. Suddenly Rollo was free and he instinctively ducked down and rolled away. Nothing was chasing him. Suddenly all the hollines were screaming and running. Rollo didn't wait to see what was happening but scrambled forward on his hands and knees and dragged himself into the undergrowth, not caring that the thorns ripped his face. Only then did he turned to see what had saved him and his scalp.

'Cracker!' he breathed in grateful amazement. The stallion

was on his hind legs, stamping his fore-hooves down on any holline that came within striking distance. Some now brandished sharp sticks, which they jabbed at the horse's hide, but the animal twisted and spun too fast to make a good target whilst pulverizing the creature that had threatened to scalp Rollo.

Now, at last, the youth understood why his father so valued the stallion as a war-horse. He was not heavily built like any respectable war-horse but he had the meanest temper he had ever seen and was gleefully wreaking his revenge on the people of the forest, relishing the thrill of battle. The pale hooves of his forelegs sliced into the flesh of the hollines' pointed heads and his rear hooves snapped their spindly bones and sent the lightweight creatures flying into the air.

Very quickly, the people of Holly had endured enough. They turned and fled in two separate groups. The horse looked from one to the other, pawed the ground and then pranced off after the group that had headed deeper into the woods. Picking his hooves up high and tossing his proud head, Firecracker's teeth snapped together to show that he still had more ire to vent.

It was then that the second group turned and charged after the horse, hurling their stakes. One pierced deep into the stallion's hide. Firecracker squealed and bucked, breaking the spear loose. He managed to trample down one of the belligerent creatures before they all scattered in different directions again. His breathing suppressed, Rollo pressed his head low into the earth and froze so that he would not be noticed as two hollines clambered through the brambles towards him and almost trod on him. Once they had passed, he looked up again to see a last glimpse of Firecracker galloping away with two more of the devilish creatures clinging to his tail.

Not daring to move for several long minutes, he lay in the cold earth, miserable to the bottom of his heart. Only when the birdsong returned to the disturbed part of the wood did he stir. Once he had dragged himself out onto the path, he stared all around him, searching warily for any sight of Holly's people.

There was no evidence of them and, very soon, he concluded he was alone and lost.

He was mad, quite mad. What had possessed him to ride out alone into the woods? What had possessed him to attack Quinn in the first place? He deserved to die, deserved to die an unnoted death out here at the hands of some savage forest peoples. Forlornly, he stared at the mud, and only then noticed the trail of blood staining the tracks left by the stallion.

'Cracker! Oh, Cracker!' Father will kill me, he thought in despair, finding the idea somewhat worse than dying at the hands of the hollines. He limped after the trail, his bruised knee already swollen and his face and hands sore from the lacerations. 'What will Father do?' he repeated over and over. How could he have let his father's most prized possession come to any harm? He had no idea how he was going to catch up with the animal and he had walked on over a mile before he flung himself to the ground in despair.

'Cracker,' he sobbed, wishing he had never thought all those unkind things about the animal since the stallion had proved so noble in defending him. Lost, alone and afraid for the horse, he lay curled up on the ground, too miserable to cry, wishing that the earth would open up and swallow him. Lost out here, he could not last long. He wished that his suffering would simply end here and now. How much more of his wretched existence could he endure?

Grunts followed by heavy footfalls thumping through the forest quickly drove all thought of desiring death from his mind and he scrambled away into the undergrowth. Looking over his shoulder, he caught sight of the hump of a mammoth's domed head pushing its way between the trees. Crawling deeper into the undergrowth, he saw a fallen tree and scrambled to it, hoping to hide in the protection of its upturned roots. Slithering down into the pit left when the roots had been wrenched from the soil, he gave out a suppressed scream as he thought he had immediately come face to face with yet another holline. However, this creature appeared equally frightened of him. Obviously only a youngster, it was shrieking in alarm, trying to scrabble backwards to flee him. Only when it saw that he was doing the same did it begin to calm itself and relax, putting a finger over its mouth. Rollo assumed it was requesting silence and, judging by the way it then began waving its arm, thought it was trying to express that there were probably dangers lurking in the woods about.

The fragile juvenile creature looked very much like one of the peoples of Holly though, on closer inspection, the skin was browner rather than greenish and it was even thinner in the limb and body. It also lacked any holly wreath.

With enormous round eyes and a nervous smile, the little being looked at Rollo. 'Holly!' it whispered fearfully in the old tongue of the Caballan. Its voice was soft and smooth and so, concentrating hard, Rollo was able to understand. 'Be warned. Hush now. Be hushed.' Its hair was long and curling, tumbling down a naked body that was almost skeletally thin. Coming to the natural conclusion that this was a female of the people of Hazel, Rollo thought that, if the child had been human, she would be no more than nine and a very small nine year old at that.

'No harm!' the hazeline whimpered. 'Do no harm. And what kind of being are you, creature that is not of the forest?' Her big eyes widened in curiosity.

He didn't answer but just looked at her, feeling as naked and as vulnerable as the child looked. 'I'm lost!' he croaked. 'Please, help me.' It was the first time in his life he had ever asked for help and somehow the creature seemed to know that and reached out her little hand in friendship.

'Mamma says there is always help if you ask the right people,' she said very softly, head still on one side as she studied him curiously. 'You have been alone a very long time.'

Rollo wondered what she meant but the thought was soon gone as he heard hound-like yelps from approaching hollines. The little girl immediately curled up into a ball and lay still, pressed against the earth. Her mottled greenish-brown skin

222

blended into the leaf-mould so that even this close she was very difficult to see. Rollo tucked his head down to hide his white face and lay rigidly still, praying that the hollines would not find him. He couldn't, however, keep himself from shaking. The skin on his forehead crept at the thought that, if the hollines found him again, they would certainly scalp him this time.

The yelps receded into the distance and he was finally able to breathe again. In a moment of panic, he thought he had lost his new-found companion and the horror of loneliness overwhelmed him. He was deeply relieved when she stirred at his feet. Automatically, he began to brush the leaves from his clothing and was surprised to see that the girl did precisely the opposite, pressing muddy leaves against her skin to further disguise her form. He wondered what such a young child was doing all alone and was about to ask her when a high-pitched squeal right behind his ear made him fling himself forward back onto the earth.

Nimble hands worked fast around him and, though he struggled and thrashed, he was soon hobbled. He looked up into the face of an adult hazeline, an angry male with a thick beard, which grew half way down his naked chest.

The male hazeline nodded to his companions and Rollo was dragged away, while a distraught mother scooped up the little child who had befriended him. The mother hazeline scolded her daughter profusely whilst hugging her close enough to squeeze the breath from her.

'What are you doing to me?' Rollo protested. 'I meant no harm. Let me go. Please!' he begged. How could he have escaped the people of Holly only to be captured by the hazelines? His only consolation was that no one had threatened to scalp him yet.

Earth filled his mouth and he spluttered and spat in an attempt to breathe. The creatures dragged him over tree roots and through puddles but his spirits were encouraged when he heard a female voices say, 'Mind his head on the stones. Oh, do be careful! That will hurt him.'

'He doesn't deserve our concern,' one of the males grumbled. 'What's he doing in our part of the wood anyhow?'

'Flax, you are too harsh,' a female hazeline protested. 'Shouldn't we just take him to the edge and set him free?'

This time it was another female and not the gruffer male that took up the opposite viewpoint. 'But what was he doing with Lilly? Are they after our young now? We must find out what he is doing here, why he brought the hollines on us and what damage he means to do to us.'

Rollo was too weak and bruised to protest. He merely closed his eyes and wished he could crawl into his mother's arms.

Chapter 12

Leaf thought she would be sick. Hanging upside down, she was being bounced along, thumping against something rough as she went. Branches whisked past her. In an attempt to steady herself, she grabbed hold of whatever it was that she was knocking against and found sacking cloth between her fingers. It must be the giant. Somehow, despite his injuries, he was carrying her off at a pace! All thought of the hylups was gone; this murderous giant had stolen her away.

'Spar!' she squeaked. 'Spar!'

In the back of her mind, she wondered how much more terror she could endure before she lost her sanity entirely. But the very fact that she could think such a thing certainly meant that there was a part of her that was still sane. The thought gave her more courage and she was then able to take in her surroundings. Someone was following just behind her; she caught glimpses of booted feet leaping over fallen logs, whipping through the bracken. Caspar was running after her! But then why didn't he use his knives to bring the giant down? Of course! The giant was helping them, not stealing her! He was fleeing the hylups. Leaf stared at the ground streaking by and noted the trail of blood and despaired. The hylups would follow them with enthusiasm.

'I can't . . . I can't go on for much longer,' the giant panted.

Leaf groaned. Clearly, it was no good running like this. The hylups would skirt round ahead of them in no time. If only the giant would stand still and stop jiggling her brain about.

'Get onto high ground,' she croaked. 'I may recognize something. We must use the topography of the land to our advantage.'

'What?' the Haol-garen grunted.

'Just head for high ground!' she yelled, wondering if these other two species of speaking people ever understood her words.

Evidently, they understood a straight order since the great man of Haol-garen lurched to the right, scraping her against the branch of a birch tree, her hair snagging in the twigs. They were climbing fast, the great man's breathing becoming laboured and loud, his grunts of effort more like those from a pig than a man. Suddenly, he swung her up and she felt giddy as the blood drained from her head. With his head and shoulders poking above the small birch trees, enabling him to see for some distance, the giant spun slowly round.

'Stop! Stop! There, look!' In the distance, Leaf had spied a long thin strip of flat white ice through the frosted branches. 'That must be Grebe Waters. It's an expansive lake. If we get our backs to water, we can use fires to keep the hylups at bay and at least then we can't be attacked from all sides. That way!' She pointed.

Ducking down, the Haol-garen lurched into a run again. This time Leaf had a chance to steady herself by grabbing hold of his large fleshy ears, which pushed out through his straggling hair. She gripped tightly as he hurtled down the hill, slithering on the frost and cutting across at an angle that would bring them dangerously close to the pursuing hylups. One was bounding lengths ahead of the pack. Leaf squealed as the giant man raised his club and swung it into the air just as the beast leapt out from the closely packed trees. The hylup rolled in the air and thudded to the ground. Leaf never saw whether it got up or not as the giant hurtled on, leaping out into a winter-white glade and sprinting across it.

For a split second he faltered in his stride, and Leaf strained to look over his head and see what had distracted him. For the merest second she noted a huddle of dwarves. It was as if the scene had been entirely frozen in time. Stooped over a map, the dwarves were arguing, their faces red with anger and their fists clenched. They had looked up as one and, in a single movement, their mouths had dropped open in astonishment and their hands had reached for their axes. Steam billowed from their mouths as their breath filtered into the crisp air. Leaf saw no more as the great man of Haol-garen plunged back into the midst of the trees.

She supposed that the presence of the dwarves might at least provide a distraction for the hylups but it troubled her deeply to see so many of them gathered together and clearly in heated spirits. How could the dwarves be in the hidden realm? Dwarves meant trouble.

Her heart in her throat, she realized that they were suddenly falling. She floated up away from the giant's back only to thump down hard again against his shoulder blades. The giant's joints cracked like the timbers of a creaking ship as they landed hard onto solid earth.

Once she had recovered herself, Leaf looked about to see that the Haol-garen had leapt down a steep embankment. There was no sign of Caspar behind them. But she could hear running water and she hoped it was quickly tripping its way towards the expanse of ice she had spied. The giant followed the line of the brook and, to Leaf's relief, a grassy bank shelved down towards a frozen lake. Some distance into the sizeable Grebe Lake humped islands rose out of the icy plain.

'Well, there's your lake,' the giant snorted.

It was only a few seconds before Caspar slithered down the embankment and was beside them. 'Sorry . . . had to avoid . . . dwarves,' he panted, bent over double. 'Hylups won't be long.' Still doubled over, he began scooping together dead leaves and striking at a flint in readiness to build up fires.

Leaf hastily followed suit. 'They won't be long. The blood from the Haol-gar will attract them.'

Caspar grunted in accord. 'Except they'll come across the dwarves first.'

'Let's get a defensive ring of fire going around us quickly,' Leaf urged. 'If they come before we're ready, the Haolgaren will be able to hold them off for a while,' she said optimistically.

'Lug,' the giant told them as his great fists effortlessly snapped off branches from the nearby trees and let them crash down onto the lakeshore. He then scooped up armfuls of crisp leaves with which to start a fire. 'And hurry it up. I can hear them coming.'

Leaf concluded that the great man must have far more acute hearing than either she or Caspar, who immediately began dragging the branches to form a defensive semicircle around them on the ground shelving down towards the lake. Hastily, he struck his flint beneath a crisp leaf and blew at it to encourage a flame. A moment later he had a small bundle of leaves alight. Lug began to blow at them, his lungs like bellows, quickly spreading the flames through the leaves beneath the wood. Crisp beneath the feet from the morning frost, the grass began to soften and darken to a glistening green as the fire took hold.

'We shan't be able to hold them off for long like this,' Lug grumbled, helping to build the barrier higher. Leaf's eyes smarted as the coppery leaves smouldered and hissed, giving off a thick black smoke. The twigs suddenly spat and crackled into life, bright red sparks spitting out either side.

Once the fire was fully alight, the great man looked at it in satisfaction before swaying a little. His face now a greenish-white, he slumped down onto his knees and, with trembling hands, clutched at his thighs, the pain clearly returning with a vengeance. The charge to reach the lake must have been his last burst of effort and now his strength was fading. Leaf was still staring at him when Caspar stumbled and tripped over a branch jutting out from the base of their fire. He sprawled to the ground at her feet but, with remarkably agility, rolled upright. When he brushed the mud from his face, she had the curious impression that, within that careworn body, still throbbed the heart of a very young boy. There was still so much about these humans that she simply could not empathize with.

Somehow he had managed to avoid burning himself on the torch he had been using to encourage the fire; he must be very exhausted, she thought, to have stumbled in the first place.

Secretly, she queried her decision to light a fire at all. Though it might keep animals away, any of the speaking races may be attracted to it. She had lacked forethought. The dwarves would surely be curious when they saw smoke rising above the trees. They couldn't just stand here behind their ring of flames and wait for the hylups to go away because the dwarves, and perhaps other peoples besides, would surely be approaching.

Caspar pushed back his thick auburn hair from his face and wiped his brow with the back of his hand, leaving a black sooty streak on his skin. He looked strangely pensive as he gazed from the semi-circle of fire about them and then behind them to the sparkling sheet of ice where the sunlight skittered and leapt from one frosted ripple to the next.

Lug cupped his hand to his large floppy ear. 'They won't be long now.'

Leaf strained to listen and then realized with horror that, above the crackling of the flames, she too could hear the yelps and barks of the hylups.

'Earth below, air above, fire to one side, ice to the other. Oh Great Mother, to which of the elements should we commit ourselves?' Caspar asked and then looked to Leaf. 'Here we are within the four elements. It is surely a sign. Brid would know what it meant.'

'Perhaps,' Leaf said sceptically, and wondered why humans took so much stock in symbolism as opposed to seeing things for what they really were. 'I am not experienced in these matters since the hidden realm has always been sheltered from the extremes of the weather. In your opinion, Spar, will the ice take our weight?'

The man shrugged. 'Probably.'

'What kind of an answer is that?' Leaf complained.

'It's the best I can give. Even here, near the running water, it looks pretty thick, but ice is always variable.'

Leaf didn't want to hear the words *variable* or *perhaps*. She either wanted to hear an evaluation of the risk involved, preferably as a mathematical ratio or, failing that, she wanted to hear a certain yes. On the other hand, it was quite clear that the hylups were hungry and aroused. Already their dark shapes were taking form on the other side of the flames.

Clearly, there was not enough fact to make an informed decision on how best to proceed and Leaf didn't really know how to make any other form of decision. How easy it must be to be a human. Caspar looked at her and snorted, presumably in some form of exasperation at her attitude.

'Arrogance!' he muttered, though he also appeared to be laughing at her.

But his expression changed acutely as the first hylup slithered down the steep embankment and slunk towards the lake and then another appeared. Soon, three of the ugly beasts were pacing back and forth beyond the heat of the fire. One gave out a roar and lashed at the ground, sending a spray of grit and leaves into the fire that sparkled as white dots of flame in the red sheet of fire. Leaf glanced up at the overhanging trees where coils of black smoke caught in the branches before curling up to darken the greying sky.

'It won't take them long to realize that they can climb the tree and then leap over the flames,' she warned.

'Whose idea was this?' grumbled the giant, who pressed his palm against the ragged wounds to his leg. Fortunately, the cuts looked superficial. His thighs were so thick and round that the hylups' teeth had only managed to break through the outer layers of the skin. It was messy and undoubtedly painful but, so long as it didn't become infected, it wasn't debilitating.

Leaf turned towards the ice. 'There is no alternative. We don't know whether the hylups will follow us onto the ice but I can think of no other plan.'

Caspar nodded. 'I would rather give myself a chance and run than just stand still and wait to be eaten.'

Lug looked glumly at the ice. 'First you kill my pigs, and now this.'

Leaf shrugged apologetically and gave him a sheepish grin. 'I'm sorry, Lug. But what can we do?'

The giant scowled and then began stamping his way towards the ice. Caspar leapt up to snatch at his dangling hand. 'Steady there. Let's take your shirt and see what we can do with it.'

'Why not your shirt?' the giant protested. 'First my pigs and then you want the shirt from my very back. Locusts, that's what you are.'

Although the giant man complained bitterly, Leaf could see that he would rather throw his lot in with them than the hylups. By the look on his face, his wound was beginning to stiffen and pain him more and more by the minute.

'All right then, my shirt,' Caspar conceded, throwing off his cloak and his jacket before pulling his shirt off, wincing as he raised his injured arm.

Leaf stared at his lean body; his agility and speed had always spoken of a body that would be well-muscled for his slight frame and she was not in the least surprised by his sinewy muscles rippling beneath his skin. But she was horrified to see the number of purple and white scars that striated his body, not to mention the bloodied bandage that was still wrapped about his left arm. He had led an arduous life, there was no doubt, but also it made her realize that she had led a very sheltered one. Her years hiding in the village, earning her living by milking cows and scrubbing floors, had callused her hands and split her nails. It had been a very big shock to her after leaving the classroom of her scholars, but still there was not a mark on her young body.

The giant removed his belt. 'Will this help?' he asked Caspar.

The Baron nodded as he stuffed his hands back into the sleeves of his jacket. 'Now, I'll hold Lug's belt and, Leaf, you hold my shirt so we have something to grip on to if one of us goes through. Now spread out,' he commanded.

Leaf nodded at this advice though she thought it not necessarily the best thing to be linked to Lug. If Caspar went through the ice, Lug would be able to pull him out, but if Lug went through he would drag both of them with him. Still, after a brief evaluation of her companions, scanning them both down to their boots or bare feet, she thought it unlikely that Lug would break the ice first. Lug was, of course, very much heavier than her or Caspar but his hairy feet were disproportionately broad. She judged that he would probably put less pressure on the ice than the Baron. However, it was Caspar who stepped onto the frozen lake first. It creaked and groaned. Carefully, he slid his boot forward and then stamped down hard before making a low jump to test the ice.

He nodded grimly at Leaf. 'We should go.' He glanced at the ring of flames protecting them from the hylups. 'We should go now before they realize what's happening.'

While Caspar gripped one sleeve of his shirt, Leaf gripped the other and stepped tentatively onto the ice. It sank a little under her weight and creaked ominously but, as she slid her foot forward and moved further away from the edge where the stream kept the ice thinner, it felt more solid under foot. Caspar visibly tensed as Lug stepped onto the ice but, as Leaf had already predicted, he was no more a hazard to the integrity of the frozen structure than she was since the size of his feet spread his weight over a larger area.

Lug, however, looked unconvinced. 'Strange folk, indeed, that listen to the ramblings of a child,' he muttered. 'What do you know, girl, about the world at your age?'

Leaf couldn't think of a sensible retort that this great man might understand. It was irritating that she possessed such superior intelligence and yet those of lesser intellect were not astute enough to recognize the fact. Her mind stayed on the thought only a split second before she was grappling with the next problem of how to stay on her feet. After taking no more than three steps forward, she slipped and crashed down hard onto her knees despite Caspar's efforts to catch her. The pain took her breath away and she gasped. Ice was as hard as rock and she had fallen faster than she would on firm ground since her feet had slid away from her. Caspar pulled her up to her feet and smiled sympathetically into her wincing eyes.

'You'll get the hang of it very soon,' he reassured her, forsaking the shirt as a means of linking them and slinging it round his neck. Firmly, he gripped her hand to help her. Leaf slipped several times more but Caspar now had a tight grip on her wrist and pulled her up before she hit the ice. Her arm socket was jolted and sore but at least that hurt less than crashing down onto the ice.

Limping heavily, Lug continually cast back over his shoulder but, since he appeared to be grunting in satisfaction, Leaf concluded that the hylups had not followed.

Concentrating on keeping upright, she gripped on hard to Caspar though her fingers were already becoming numb. The wind whipped across the open expanse of ice and Leaf despaired at how her world had changed.

'It's not fair,' she muttered.

'What's not fair?' Caspar asked through tight lips that seemed to have shrivelled against the cold.

'Why in my lifetime? Why did all this have to happen to me?'

Caspar laughed at this. 'Do you think there is a generation before you that hasn't said such a thing?'

Leaf snorted at him, frustrated that he didn't understand. 'I know that all new generations believe they are the only ones that see the world as it is, but in my case that's true. Not since my ancestors first built the crystal curtain about our lands have my forebears been subject to the reality of

233

the world about them. They have lived at peace, in glorious isolation, untroubled until now. Worse, the affliction that affects my parents' generation is of such a nature that they cannot be the ones to rise up and overcome it; that task has fallen to me. I do not think it unreasonable to ask of the world "Why me?" in such circumstances.'

'Well, I know why this has happened to me,' Lug grumbled. He fell silent and didn't offer more.

Caspar's curiosity was clearly piqued, though Leaf merely found the notion irritating.

'Why, indeed, has this happened to you?' the Baron asked.

'Because you killed my pigs.'

'Actually, Lug, I killed only one and that was to save my own life. Believe me, I am not in the habit of killing pigs for no reason.'

'One pig would have been bearable,' Lug continued. 'But then what you did meant that Ogran took the rest of them – stole them right out from under my nose. Now what shall I do? Have you any idea how long it took me to acquire that many pigs?'

'Obviously not,' Leaf told him, pulling her jacket up in an attempt to keep her ears warm.

'Two years and three months, that's how long. And Ogran, all that while, had not bothered one jot to better his herd and, now, not more than a week before the appointed day, he just takes them right off me.'

'What appointed day?' Caspar asked.

'The day we put our bids in for our chosen wives. Now someone else will have Grunda. I don't know if I can bear to live.'

Leaf pouted at this silliness. 'People fall in and out of love the entire time. You'll find someone else presently.'

'Oh indeed!'

'Statistically speaking, within the year you will be in love again,' Leaf reassured him through chattering teeth.

'You cannot define love by statistics,' Caspar unexpectedly

scoffed at her. 'Can Grunda only be bought?' he asked the giant.

Lug nodded. 'Ever since we were boys, my brother Ogran and I have fought for her attentions. He is more forward and has more style and found it much easier than me to win her attention, but that is all nothing in the end. What matters is how we impress her father. My only chance to win her is to prove my skill at raising pigs and so demonstrate my worth and therefore how well I might provide for her children.' He sighed piteously. 'But now the great chief will almost certainly choose Ogran. There are others, I know, who wish to bid for Grunda, but now Ogran not only has my pigs but also the precious gems.'

'I did not know that the Haol-garen mined for precious gems,' Leaf commented.

'We don't. We are pig farmers, not miners. But Ogran has been dealing with the dwarves. They have given him crystals in return for his far-sighted vision. Great big hunks of turquoise crystals.'

Leaf was silent for a moment and decided that the dwarves would have instantly recognized the Haol-garen's lack of knowledge of the gemstone's worth. Far from rewarding him with lapis lazuli, no doubt he had been given copper sulphate crystals that were worthless. However, she considered, if they were enough to secure the coveted Grunda, their true value in this case was very high indeed. Value, therefore, was more a matter of perspective and circumstances than a fixed and certain standard.

The giant stamped on gloomily, looking down at the ice. 'I think, by rights, you should help me to win her. It's you who's spoiled my chances and you should make amends.'

'Cannot the poor girl choose for herself whom she wishes to marry?' Caspar suggested.

Lug gave a hollow laugh. 'What an absurd idea! You'll be saying next that children should choose their parents.'

Leaf frowned, wondering how Lug could make such a

ridiculous comparison. She couldn't herself imagine what it must be like to fall in love and so had little sympathy for the great man. Caspar, however, seemed to understand Lug's plight.

'I'm sorry about your brother. But it's not over yet. If your chief values stones from the dwarves, who knows what you might earn today that might overcome the bid from your brother?'

Lug laughed. 'Those fine pigs have taken me half my adult lifetime to breed and they prove my reliability and determination. Ogran earned his stones in a day and stole my pigs in a matter of minutes. That is the difference between us. I have no hope of winning her now.' The big man sniffed. With his shoulders hunched and his head tucked down, he limped and slithered on over the ice.

Leaf did not understand his argument but did not trouble herself with it. Instead, she concentrated again on keeping upright. They were now beyond the islands, where the grebes nested in spring, and more than three-quarters of the way across to the far bank, when Caspar halted. The other two stopped smartly beside him and stared in dismay and horror at what lay before them. Out here on the broad expanse of the frozen lake, the white covering of frost had been swept away by the wind. The ice lay at their feet as a clear sheet, the blue-black water below giving it colour. Lying just below the surface of the ice were a large number of furry bodies.

'They're deer of some sort,' Leaf concluded, staring at them glumly. One humped shape protruded through the ice to her left and an antler poked out to her right. Something had driven them out into the lake where they had drowned, buffeted and exhausted in the battle for survival as chunks of ice had formed around them, their strength already depleted by the cold.

'Careful,' Caspar warned.

Leaf did not need telling that the presence of bobbing bodies in the ice would have prevented the ice from forming as quickly and so all about them the ice would be very much thinner.

'I'll go first,' the Baron immediately offered and Leaf smiled inwardly, so glad that luck had caused her to cross paths with this particular human rather than a lesser male of his kind. Rollo was indeed lucky to have such a father.

'Lug, have you got a firm hold of the belt?' Caspar asked, knotting his shirt to the other end in order to give him more length. Slowly, he eased forward, sliding his foot across the thinning ice.

Leaf watched, her mouth and eyes wide open, her nerves tingling with anticipation as she waited for that first crack to appear on the ice. After that would come the sudden formation of ice splinters bursting out in all directions from his feet before the frozen lake swallowed the Baron. Her heart in her mouth, she watched as he slowly transferred his weight onto his leading foot and stood over the very line where the deer were trapped under the ice. The ice did, in fact, creak but there was no sudden or violent cracking. Caspar slid his other foot forward but, all the while, keeping his feet spread to avoid concentrating his weight on a single weakened area of ice. At last, he had inched across the line of drowned animals.

He looked up and nodded at Leaf. 'You next,' he told her, tossing her one arm of his shirt while gripping the other.

Her face white with cold and bloodless with fear, she gripped the makeshift rope and slid out over the stream of carcasses.

Lug wailed. 'But they are not deer. They are reindeer. They are the Haol-garen's reindeer!'

When it was the giant's turn to step across, he was still moaning miserably. As he slid forward, Leaf wondered why on earth Caspar was holding onto the belt that stretched between him and Lug so firmly. There was absolutely no way he would be able to help the great man if the ice gave beneath him and the likelihood was that he would be pulled into the ice as well.

'Easy does it,' Caspar encouraged. 'Now, just keep on sliding forward.'

Lug, however, didn't appear to be listening but was staring down at his feet. To Leaf's horror he suddenly stamped the point of his heel into the ice and, when it did not give, repeated the movement even harder until cracks radiated out from the point of impact.

'Lug, what are you doing?' Caspar protested in horror, tugging at the end of the belt in his hand to encourage the giant forward.

Lug merely knelt down and plunged his hand into the hole he had made. He gave a curious squeal, triggered, Leaf presumed, by the temperature of the water. A second later, he dragged up one of the beasts by its neck.

'What are you doing? Get out of there!' Caspar yelled.

The dead animal Lug had plucked form the water was very small and pale in colour compared to the rest and also very slippery; Lug's now blue hands had trouble holding onto it. With one last burst of effort, he heaved its rear legs up and laid the creature out on the ice. Only a second later, the section beneath him gave way.

Leaf screamed as Caspar was jerked towards the hole. Lug vanished entirely, water slopping out over the hole he had made. Caspar was somehow still gripping the belt, his heels skittering on the ice before him as he leant hard back, doing everything he could to act as an anchor. Leaf had thought it highly unlikely that the giant would survive the shock of the cold and extremely likely that Caspar would be pulled in after him. She thought it wisest that the Baron let go but she knew enough of him already to be certain that he wouldn't. From the edge of the lake, she could hear the chilling howls of the hylups that must have been excited by their sudden yells though, thankfully, none of them ventured onto the ice.

Seeing there was nothing else to do, she grabbed hold of the back of Caspar's jacket and began to pull, knowing that, although she was small, light and not in the least strong, what she could offer might be just enough to tip the balance.

Clearly, Caspar was not going to be able to haul the giant out though he was trying with all his might, the muscles on his neck proud like taut cords. What he may be able to do, however, was help Lug to help himself.

'He's holding on so there's hope,' Caspar grunted through his gritted teeth. 'If we can at least pull his hand up towards the surface, he may be able to find the hole he fell through. That's the worst of falling through ice; it's very hard to find one's way out again.'

Though Leaf had no particular attachment towards the giant, she was distressed to see anyone suffer. Digging in her heels as best she could into the slippery surface, she did all she could to help. But it was with immense trepidation that she saw they were now being pulled across the slippery surface. Lug must be sinking. The only thing they could do to stop this progress was to let go and allow Lug to fall back into the freezing water. But, at last, her grip on the ice held and, as the belt slackened a little, they pulled back until a hand appeared on the ice, followed by Lug's bruised head as he thrust it up out of the water. Opening his mouth, he sucked in massive gulps of air. Caspar heaved again, holding the belt taught and urging the giant on with enthusiastic shouts.

'Get your other hand out! That's it! You can do it. Just keep going a little while longer.'

With a huge effort, Lug threw his shoulders onto the ice and Caspar heaved for all he was worth in order to help the big man up out of the hole. Lug kicked his legs out and then just lay there, his face blue as he stared at the limp fawn that lay dead beside him.

'I don't know what the point of saving you from drowning was since you're now going to die of cold here,' Caspar berated him, looking down helplessly at the great man of Haol-garen and then across the rest of the lake to the far shore with its wood that was offering their only means of getting warm and dry. 'What fool thing did you do that for?'

Caspar ripped away at Lug's shirt and then threw his bearskin over his back.

'I can do nothing more. You'll have to move yourself. Do you understand?'

The clothes around Lug's legs were already beginning to freeze and they crackled as he tried to move them. Long icicles hung in his ragged hair. Leaf looked at him forlornly. He was too cold to stand, and surely he had only minutes left before he died of cold. It was not that far to the opposite shore. If Lug couldn't walk, they would have to think of another way.

'We'll drag him,' Leaf told Caspar. 'It should be an easy enough task on this ice.'

Caspar nodded and wasted no time in getting on with the act. In fact, Leaf only had to tug hard for the first few moments it took to break Lug's inertia. Lying on Caspar's bearskin, he slid relatively easily once they had got him moving, and Caspar managed the task alone. The hardest bit proved to be getting him off the ice and onto the distant shore, which Leaf and Caspar managed by moving him limb by limb. From that second on, they wasted no time. Leaf scurried about gathering firewood and dry leaves for a fire while Caspar struggled to pull the clothes from the giant's back.

At least the trees all around had given protection from the frost and broke the wind. It took a matter of valuable minutes to get the fire going while Caspar took off Lug's jacket and began to rub the great man all over to get him dry. All the while, he kept the bearskin over Lug's shoulders. For many minutes Lug was silent, his lips blue and his hands curled into feeble hooks, the ends a sick pinky white.

Though Caspar had managed to get the top half of Lug's clothing off, it was much more difficult to remove his trousers and so, finally, he resorted to cutting them away with a knife. Removing the last of the wet clothes helped Lug enormously and he gave out a long low moan much like the eerie wail from a rutting stag, Leaf thought.

'Get some water boiling and we'll get some warm liquid inside him,' Caspar told Leaf.

She rummaged through Caspar's pack and finally found the small iron pot he carried. Hastily, she constructed two tripods from twigs and strung a pole between them on which she could hang the pot once it had been filled with water from the lake. It was a long while waiting for the pot to boil but Leaf had hope that Lug would make it. Clearly, he was in considerable pain but he was a very big man and so it was easier for him to conserve heat, his internal organs being more deeply buried in a larger body.

'You will live,' she reassured him. 'I know it hurts but you will live and very, very soon you will start to feel a great deal better.' Dipping her finger into the pot, she decided it was still too cold.

'As soon as the water is warm, it will help you a lot,' she reassured him. 'Now don't worry about a thing.'

Caspar smiled at her. 'Well done, Leaf. You're a very good girl.'

Leaf found she was much more affected by his praise than she thought she would be. Although she could have felt patronized by his remark she was, in fact, deeply encouraged. She even felt strong enough to cope when Caspar informed her that he would have to go in search of food.

'Can't you stay here and fish it from the lake?' she asked, knowing it was a ridiculous thing to suggest. The lake was frozen solid and the fish would have sunk deep down to the bottom of the waters to conserve their energy.

'No, I'm going to kill a deer,' he told her. 'Lug could do with the warm blood and I'd need to catch a whole shoal of fish before they were of much use to a huge thing like him.'

Caspar's cheeks were pimply with goose flesh as he set off, his blue hands gripping a knife. He stopped and looked back.

'Whatever you do,' he warned, 'you must stay with Lug, here by the fire.'

Leaf nodded. 'I think it very unlikely that we would choose to do anything else.'

The Baron smiled at her. 'You are a very, very brave girl.'

'I don't feel very brave.'

'That's why you are. It's much harder to be brave when you are so aware of all the dangers. It's very much easier for an idiot to be brave.'

Leaf laughed. 'Just hurry, will you?'

He nodded and, as light as a stag, Caspar sprang away into the woods. Leaf watched his back and suddenly felt far colder and weaker than she had done moments before. Her knowledge and intelligence did not give her the solace and security she felt in the presence of the Baron. Sighing deeply, she pressed herself up close against Lug and, in a trembling voice, urged him to drink some of the warmed water.

His bruised eyes looked at her without sparkle and that low moan droned on and on. Leaf began to cry. For a minute or two she had thought that she was going to be able to cope, but now she was sobbing and unable to hold the cup steady for Lug. She didn't really know which particular thing had made her break down. It was not just that she was cold, exhausted and felt desperately vulnerable without Caspar; it was more the years of fretting over the fate of her people and of struggling to grow up as her parents lost their wits. She had grown up alone and it had not made her stronger. Far from it, she was certain that the experience had weakened her nerve.

Choking back on the tears, she did her best to suppress her despair and turn her thoughts to practicalities. How was she going to cope with a giant that was now shaking vigorously as he spontaneously began to shiver?

But, as she expected, the great man was soon much better. His extremities had been dangerously chilled but were now bright red as the blood returned to them, bringing with it needles of pain. His inner body, however, had retained its heat. The cup jerked in his hand and the water sloshed but, once he had it to his mouth, he was able to drink and the warm fluids inside his body helped considerably. His hands closed around the warmth of the metal cup and he gritted his teeth against the pain, his fingers swelling up like turnips.

The bearskin did little to cover his body but must have helped a little and at least his hair was now drying. It was quite to Leaf's amazement, however, when the man suddenly stood up with nothing more than the damp ragged underpants left to cover him. He was extremely long-legged, his lower legs unnaturally long compared to Leaf's kind and hugely hairy, which probably did something to help keep him warm. He stamped his blue feet and reached out over the fire, absorbing the heat.

Wiping her tears away, Leaf stood up and cried up to Lug, 'Now rest and get your strength back.'

The man looked down at her. His large blue nose pushed up tight against hers and her heart missed a beat. 'You little thief. You left it out there on the ice. You go and fetch it for me now or I'll kill you.'

'I've stolen nothing! I've done everything I could to help you. I've tried to keep you warm and I dragged you back here across the ice.'

'You thief, you took the sacred white fawn from me,' the big man snarled. 'First of all you killed my pigs and then, when I find the fawn, sacred to all my kind and source of our great power, you leave her on the ice out there. You just went and left her. I must have her, otherwise all will be lost. How did this happen? How could this happen?' He was trembling with rage and, in his anger, kicked the fire with his bare feet, sending up a shower of white sparks. The next moment, he had Leaf by the neck and was holding her up, his great hand clasped about her windpipe. 'You go and fetch me that fawn otherwise I'll kill you now.'

She almost thought to say go and fetch it yourself but she

243

didn't have the strength. She was fast becoming light-headed and she thought that at any moment she would blackout. Already, the world seemed to be pulsating and darkness claimed the periphery of her vision.

'I'm too weak,' the giant snarled. 'And too heavy for the ice. You go and fetch that fawn otherwise I'll bite your head off. That'll teach you and you'd know to respect me from then on.' Leaf did not think that now was the time to point out how ridiculous his words were. In fact, she was entirely lost for words as he picked her up by the collar and shook her. At last, he dropped her to the floor, her legs jarring on the hard ground. He prodded her with a finger. 'Get up and fetch it. Now!'

Leaf was quite amazed at how quickly her strength and self-control returned. She scrambled to her feet and, though she knew it was probably safer to run after Caspar, she was too scared to do anything but obey Lug.

Slipping and slithering, she half ran, half skated onto the ice, falling repeatedly, the pain sharp as it jarred her bones. But it wasn't far, she told herself, only then remembering her promise to Caspar not to move from the fire. But what could she do? Surely, this was better than being devoured by Lug?

Miserably cold from the wind that whipped across the smooth surface of Grebe Water, she at last reached the fawn. It lay stiffly on the ice, a blue leather collar securing a little sack tied about its long neck. Her fingers stiff and curled with cold, she stooped down to reach for one of its legs. The animal would be easy enough to drag back. For a split second she looked across at where their first fire still burnt jauntily on the opposite banks. The hylups appeared to have scattered, perhaps in eager pursuit of Lug's stolen pigs or because of the dwarves, she could not tell. She looked down again at the fawn and leapt back in horror as, at that precise moment, a huge snake-like head spat out from the hole Lug had made in the ice. It lunged for the fawn and clamped its teeth about one rear leg, jerking it from her grasp.

But having struggled thus far, Leaf was determined not to be defeated. Squealing to reinforce her courage, she lunged forward for the fawn and heaved it back, dragging the snake-like creature half way out of the lake. The creature wasn't a snake; she could see that now. It was only an eel like the ones they had encountered on the beach, but much smaller. And although she knew they could inflict a nasty bite, it was not a sea serpent so she was not afraid any more.

However, the eel was far stronger than she anticipated and it had the advantage of being in its own element while she could not get a grip on the ice. She tried jerking the fawn from side to side but simply did not possess sufficient strength to do more than shake it, which was not enough to break the eel's grip. Rather than attempting to heave the carcass away from the eel, she used the fawn's leg to club the eel over the head. Standing precariously and with such a limited weapon, she could not inflict a substantial injury to the eel but it eventually tired of this abuse and, after giving one last jerk at the fawn's leg, slithered away.

But that last jerk was enough to unbalance Leaf. Her back muscles spasmed in an effort to hold herself upright. Dropping down to lower her centre of gravity helped her to regain her balance but not before she had put undue pressure on the ice at her feet, which was already weakened by the reindeer trapped beneath it.

Still holding onto the fawn, she stood up very slowly. Someone was shouting behind her and she heard Caspar's voice berating her for her idiocy. 'Stand still!' he was yelling at her.

Of course she was going to stand still. She looked down at her feet, her eyes bulging at the sight of a black jagged crack running through the ice no more than a foot away from her. Very, very slowly she turned towards Caspar, her eyes black with fear. She did not want to fall into the ice; she had seen what had happened to Lug. Her own small body would last the barest of moments and she would not have the strength to pull herself out. Even if Caspar got to her in time, she would be chilled so quickly that she doubted very much that she would survive.

'Don't move,' Caspar hissed at her. 'Don't move a muscle. Don't even drop that carcass,' he warned, inching closer. In his hand he held out a long stiff branch, which he was reaching out towards her.

Breathe, Leaf told herself. *I must breathe*. She lent forward, her legs already spread for balance and to distribute her weight.

'That's enough!' Caspar hissed. 'Keep still and let me do the rest.'

'I don't want to fall in,' Leaf whimpered.

'I know you don't,' Caspar said in that calm soothing voice of his, and Leaf immediately felt better. He had a way of taking responsibility for the situation. She had expected him to berate her for her disobedience and foolishness but he didn't trouble himself with such obvious remarks and only concentrated on trying to help her. The scholars would have spent a great deal of time telling her that they knew this would happen.

Gratefully, she stretched out her hand, and just as her fingers touched the tip of the branch the ice beneath her shuddered. With a sudden snap, a large portion of the sheet of ice beneath her broke away from the main body of the frozen lake. Since her legs were spread wide, she managed to keep her balance as the platform of ice supporting her rocked and sank beneath her weight. The water rushed up to her ankles, icy cold as it seeped in through her boots.

The tip of the branch, which she had managed to grab with her outstretched hand, simply broke off and she was left bobbing in the water, buoyed up by the island of ice. Fearfully, she looked down as her frozen island was shaken from below. Through the haze of ice and the cracks about it, she saw the murky shapes of many dozens of eels writhing below, some rising to thud at the ice as they began to feed on the carcasses trapped in the frozen water. Leaf gave out a pathetic whimper.

Caspar lay down on his belly, this time trying to reach further forward, his eyes flitting across the ice as more cracks began to appear.

'You'll have to make a dive for me,' he told Leaf.

'What if it snaps?' she protested.

Caspar didn't reply; obviously he could not give a reassuring answer.

'Just jump!' he ordered.

Her footing wobbled again and, still with one hand on the white fawn, Leaf crouched low to keep her balance. At least she wouldn't have to worry about drowning or dying of cold; she would be eaten alive in seconds. Caspar was still inching closer though he was now perilously close to two dark lines in the ice that ran a jagged course towards him. Leaf, however, lacked the courage to move. She wanted only to cry, wanted her mother to appear magically before her and scoop her up. Instead, it was Lug who reached for her and he wasn't trying to rescue her but recover the stiff carcass of the fawn.

At the back of her mind, she registered how ridiculous he looked without anything on his legs and a cloak that barely covered his shoulders. Driven on by his mysterious desire for the fawn he had found the strength and willpower to skid out onto the ice and follow Caspar. Bending down, he didn't reach for Leaf but for the little fawn, which she was still clutching. Instinct enabled her hand to close tight about the animal's spindly leg and she was suddenly lifted up and swung towards Lug.

He shook her free and clasped the reindeer to his chest, moaning and hugging it as if it were a murdered child.

The jolting shock of hitting the hard ice made Leaf's brain reel. She tasted blood where she bit the inside of her cheek. Her head spinning with pain, it was several seconds before she knew she was safe again. Someone snatched her up off the ice. A second later, she realized that Caspar had picked her up and, flinging her over his back, he skated back towards the fire they had built to revive Lug.

Before either of them had caught their breath, Caspar heaved off her boots and then her leggings so that he could dry her feet. Only then did she realize that her feet and ankles were a horrible purple colour and the source of intense pain.

Chapter 13

'I can't walk!' Leaf protested as Caspar tugged her to her feet. The ground was soaking all about her and the fire had fizzled to a feeble glow. It had rained hard all night.

'You certainly can't just sit here. There may be dwarves in the wood or savage creatures anywhere.' As if to emphasize his point, a buzzard gave out a hungry cry, plaintive and mournful. 'You've had a good night's sleep and we must move. Just think yourself lucky that Lug was able to shelter you from the downpours.'

Lug instinctively shielded the dead fawn cradled in his arms and Leaf blinked at him, wondering what significance the creature held for him. They had all eaten fresh deer that Caspar had slain prior to rescuing her from the ice, and Lug had shown no particular reverence towards that animal. This white reindeer fawn, however, he cradled as if it were a child.

'I can't walk. I really can't,' Leaf continued to moan, but found herself dragged to her feet all the same. To make maters worse, it was beginning to rain again. The sun had barely made any impression on the morning as it had to fight its way through black clouds brooding overhead.

'I know your feet hurt but you haven't got frostbite and the walk will do you good. You've been warmed by the fire, slept and eaten and there's nothing more for it but to move,' Caspar told her briskly, tugging her along.

'I simply can't do it,' Leaf whimpered, feeling the tears pricking at her eyes and thinking that Caspar was most unfeeling.

'Once you get going, you'll feel better,' the man assured her heartlessly. 'Now listen,' he said, gentling gripping her shoulders and turning her towards him so that he could look deep into her eyes. For the first time, Leaf realized that he had the most unusually deep blue eyes and, despite his crooked nose and constant careworn frown, he was quite pleasant to look at. 'We've got to get going. I've been hearing strange cries all through the night and I don't want to be left behind by Lug. He's our passport through this island.'

'He's angry with us,' Leaf reminded him. 'Why should he help us?'

'It wasn't our fault.'

'He doesn't believe that.' She did not, however, agree that it would significantly increase their chances of survival if they kept company with the strange giant.

'What do you think he wants with that fawn?' Caspar asked once Leaf began to trot more willingly alongside.

The Baron had been right. It didn't hurt so much to walk once she had got going and it actually enabled her to think more clearly since she ceased to concentrate so much on the throbbing pain in her feet. She looked quizzically at the strange sight of the Haol-garen before her. The dead deer he had impaled onto a stake and carried it aloft, as if it were a battle standard. Now re-clothed in his ragged garments, his torn trousers flapping around his scarred legs, he used a stick in his left hand to hack his way through the undergrowth.

'But it's so odd!' he persisted, his mind obviously insatiably curious. 'Why would he risk his life for a dead fawn? Why? As I understood it, the Haol-garen were hog farmers only; so why this intense interest in a reindeer? And why, oh why, would he impale it on a stake?'

Leaf shrugged, not troubling herself to think through the possibilities when she knew there simply wasn't enough information to hand. 'There's no way of knowing,' she told Caspar. 'Don't pucker you brow so with trying to figure out the impossible.'

Caspar turned to look at her. 'Are you mocking me?' he queried, somewhat perplexed as to why she might be doing such a thing.

'Oh, no! I was just thinking how differently your mind works to mine. I had noted all those things as strange, obviously, but since there is no way of knowing what motivated him, there seemed no gain in pondering on it.'

'But you must at least have a theory.'

Leaf shrugged. 'I have a number. The cold affected his mind; he was deranged in the first place; he's trying to conceal something from us and is diverting our attention by behaving so curiously.'

Caspar's frown deepened.

'Ah! I see, you had not thought of that one,' Leaf surmised. 'The other reason I can think of is that the fawn is, indeed, very important to him. This impaling and the manner in which he bears it suggests to me some sort of religious symbolism.'

'You see! You do have a theory,' Caspar challenged her.

'I would hardly bestow it with such a strong definition as a theory, merely a few guesses which are tantamount to meaningless.'

Shielding their eyes against stinging rain, which turned the ground to a slurry at their feet, they began to wend their way downwards into darker shade beneath coniferous trees. The beaten-earth track, now slick with rain, was lined with grass that had been cropped close by hungry, grazing animals. Ghosts of mist caught the grey sunlight as it pierced the close canopy of trees.

Leaf knew they were on the north-east limb of what should be the hidden realm. This particular sector was a region with which her people rarely troubled themselves. This was not only because of the lakes, islands and marshy meadows but also because of the infamous nature of the people that inhabited the farthest tip of this sector. She felt uncomfortable because she did not recognize any landmark but became even more uncomfortable when she did recognize large footprints of predatory cats and bears, and the small footprints of Holly's and Hazel's people.

Their path dipped down into a hollow, following the course of a frozen stream, which was rapidly beginning to melt as the warmer rainwater was washed into it. Many paths joined theirs, hastening them on as their own path widened. Leaf looked from left to right, observing and noting all about her.

'I wonder if this is wise?' she asked Caspar.

'We're safest following Lug,' he insisted and hurried on, tugging her by the hand.

Leaf was not sure enough of herself to protest and yet felt increasingly uncomfortable with the landscape about them. The smaller streams from either side converged on the little brook they were following, which, now in the shelter of the trees, trickled under a thin layer of ice. Although it was difficult to see the terrain, she was certain that they had entered the head of an ever-deepening valley. The fact that the paths converged made her suspicious that there was only one route through the valley because its sides steepened dramatically. It wasn't very long before she was proved right. Caspar halted and looked around him as, through the trees to left and right, they glimpsed bare, red sandstone cliffs.

'This isn't too clever,' he muttered under his breath, and Leaf bit back on her desire to say that she had told him so. After all, he had not scolded her for going back out onto the lake.

It was all too quiet in the gorge and Leaf became acutely aware of her own light footfall. Lug still stamped ahead. Now that the undergrowth had been thinned out by the grazing animals, the giant had been making far better time and so it was becoming increasingly hard for Caspar and Leaf to keep up with him. Out of breath, Leaf had no time to express her concerns but kept on hurrying along the path. More than anything else, she was terrified of being separated from Caspar. He would do all he could to protect her; that much, at least, she had learned about this man, though she

252

could not reason why he possessed such a loyal sense of duty to others.

Lug continued to march ahead even when they heard the distinctive cry of a wolf somewhere behind them. Leaf shuddered. Being so numerous across all Belbidia, they had been one of the few animals that had managed to penetrate the hidden realm a short time before all the other strange creatures returned to man's temperate lands.

She began to run harder as Caspar extended his pace in an urgent effort to keep close to Lug. However, their efforts were in vain until the Haol-garen stopped suddenly and the other two came panting up beside him.

The giant waved his left hand at the scene before him. 'Death! All is death. Her mask is bare before us and all oracles cry death!' he wailed.

Leaf's blood ran cold. A phalanx of stakes barricaded the gorge before them. Impaled on each were thin ragged bodies. Two huge jet-black ravens were perched on the heads of two bodies. Hunched over, they were dragging out eyes and brains where the skulls had been split open.

Lug cradled the little fawn to his chest. 'Already it has started. Death follows. Look! A pair of ravens, harbingers of death, stand before us, halting our journey through life.' The great giant took several steps back and slumped down beside Caspar. 'All because you killed my hogs. I can't have Grunda, and Ogran has my animals. Worse, the running herd that leads our way is drowned, all drowned. And now this.'

Now, at least, Leaf had an understanding of the fawn's symbolic meaning to Lug. His people had survived the rigours of the frozen tundra by following the reindeer herds and so learned to depend on them for survival. Naturally, that led to the reindeer becoming deified by the Haol-garen. The pigs they ate, but the reindeer they worshipped.

What a simple people, she thought, trying not to look too hard at the impaled bodies before her, which were strangely bleached and bloated. They were not her own people, which

253

did at least make it a little easier for her. Though mutilated and gored by the great ravens' beaks, she had seen at once that they were hollines and hazelines, being light, long and thin but lacking the stature and musculature of the hobs.

Feeling the sweat break out over her skin, she swallowed, determined to control her rising nausea. She was going to faint or vomit but, she told herself firmly, she was not going to scream. Screaming would alert whoever had gruesomely displayed these wretched people. Instead, she gave out only a low whimper and was consequently most surprised when the great man of Haol-gar squealed, much like one of his pigs may have done.

'It has started already! Chaos is on us.'

Caspar reached for his hand and tugged at it hard. 'This is merely a warning. Someone is declaring loudly that this is their territory and that they will tolerate no trouble from trespassers. After all, Holly's people can cause a great deal of trouble.'

'But not all are hollines.' Leaf felt some sympathy for the gentle hazelines and wondered at the cruelty. 'Hazel's people are deeply considerate, intuitive souls,' she murmured. 'Who could do such a dreadful thing?'

'Someone trying to protect themselves,' Caspar stated the obvious.

Leaf nodded and then, looking at Lug, nudged the Baron. 'What should we do about him?'

The great man had thrown himself on the ground and was now pummelling the earth with his fists. 'Woe and doom! Doom and ruin! We shall die, all of us die, even my sweet Grunda.' He scrambled onto his feet and, before the Baron could stop him, was running off back the way they had come.

Caspar sighed. 'Oh well, there goes our bodyguard.'

'Don't you think we should follow him?' Leaf asked doubtfully. The persistent rain had soaked her through to the skin; she was cold and miserable and her feet were very sore as the wrinkled flesh began to chafe.

'Do you?'

Leaf shook her head. 'No, of course not. The bodies are gruesome but they are not dangerous and are simply designed to deter intruders. The way forward will be relatively safe for us since beasts and peoples alike will have been turned way.'

Caspar smiled. 'I hadn't thought of it like that. I was merely thinking that we can't go back as there is nowhere to go back to other than the treacherous lake, the hylups and dwarves. I suspect Lug will eventually come to the same conclusion and follow us. Nevertheless,' he nodded grimly to the two ravens, 'I do not wish to stare the harbingers of death clean in the beak.' He laughed lightly and Leaf wondered why he did that. It was so strange to laugh at the thought of doom and destruction, but it seemed to be the way he coped with his troubles.

'They are not harbingers of death,' she protested.

'Of course they are. The ravens are always the first to the battlefield and they circle above the gibbet even before there's a body swaying in the breeze.'

'That is superstitious nonsense,' Leaf told him haughtily. 'Indeed, the raven is symbolic of death but he is symbolic of many other things as well. Two ravens like these before us also represent thought and memory.' She tilted her head to one side. 'You see, in ancient times, when many peoples sought to foresee the future, they believed that, once in a trancelike state, their spirit could join with that of a bird and soar into the heavens to look down onto the land. From there, they could perceive things as they truly were and so better choose a path forward. But there were dangers involved. If their spirit joined with a bird that was then killed, the person's spirit would be lost and unable to return to its rightful body. So always a bird of great strength would be chosen as their medium. It would be either an eagle or a hawk or most commonly a raven because, not only does it soar high and with little fear from other birds, but also it possesses great intelligence – for a bird, that is.'

Indeed, the two great black birds stared at her with their

shiny black eyes, giving her the most scrutinizing look. One of them ruffled its feathers and, stretching out its neck long and low, gave out a deep croak.

Leaf noted that Caspar wasn't repulsed by the mutilated bodies whereas they made her feel quite ill. Conversely, she was untroubled by the ravens and yet he seemed to be extremely wary of them simply because of their symbolic power.

She snorted at him. 'I bet you the hair on my head that they are quite tame.' Fetching inside her pack, she drew out a piece of dried crust from her depleted rations bag and bravely held it out towards the ravens. One of them glared at her hand, cocked its head from side to side and then hopped down from its gory perch. It strutted brazenly towards her. Stopping just out of reach, it again fixed her with one eye and then stabbed its beak forward to take the crust.

'You see!' Leaf triumphantly declared. 'They are tame.' She twitched a smile at Caspar. 'Come on then. We must hurry!'

He smiled back at her. 'Well, I'm glad to see you brave for once, little trembling Leaf.'

She was not very amused at being teased. 'I was afraid when there was reason to be afraid. It seems foolish to be frightened by superstition.'

The Baron conceded her point with a nod of the head, rainwater dripping off his fringe. He nevertheless patted his array of throwing knives as if limbering up for action.

'Since you are so brave, why don't you lead the way?' he asked in a mock chivalrous tone.

Leaf marched forward, not really sure whether he was laughing at her or not but, then he caught her shoulder and pulled her back. 'Don't be so silly, young lady; we still don't know what lies ahead. It seems you are as reckless as my son, after all. Let's be sensible about this; I think it is better that I go first, don't you?

'Hmm,' Leaf begrudgingly answered but was nonetheless

happy to comply and even more relieved when Lug came lumbering up behind.

'Dwarves,' he grunted. 'All around the edge of the lake. There's no way forward from here save past these deathly buzzards.'

'Ravens,' Leaf corrected him, though Lug didn't seem to care what they were called. Instead, he flung a stick at them and hurried past, the ground shaking beneath his legs.

'None of this would have happened and I would still be able to buy my Grunda if it hadn't been for you,' he continued to grumble at Caspar and Leaf before drawing to a sudden halt and taking in a snatched breath. 'Look at those giant toadstools! More death and disease!'

Leaf gazed ahead, wondering why all these symbols had been placed in the entrance to the gorge. The dried toadstools had been prominently laid out on a low flat rock. Though they were, indeed, deadly poisonous it was most unlikely that an intruder would not know that. A trespasser would simply avoid the toadstools.

'They are merely more symbols. After all, the hover fly with its array of yellow and black bears the symbol of danger, yet is harmless and not at all like the wasp it resembles,' she said, trying her best to ease Lug's fears though he didn't appear to understand one word of what she said.

They marched on, Caspar muttering at her back that the toadstools were placed there to ward off trespassers and, whatever she thought, sooner or later someone was likely to ambush them in vengeance for this act of intrusion.

'Nonsense!' Leaf refuted. 'The only reason someone might go to such pains to ward away intruders is that they have no real means to deter attack. We are safe here.'

Again, Caspar shrugged his shoulders as if he still thought that he knew better but, all the same, marched on past the toadstools. At regular intervals on this increasingly dark and gloomy track, where dense holly trees bore cascades of old man's beard, there were symbols of disease and death. Leaf wrinkled her nose at the stench from poisoned entrails and felt sickened at the sight of a shrunken head, speared toads, bundles of hemlock, yew and foxgloves. There was even a coffin half buried in the earth alongside their path. Leaf stopped by a little wren that was hopping about frantically, trying to escape the leash about its leg that fixed it to its post.

'Why a wren?' Caspar asked, puzzled.

'Many believe that the wren communes with the dead because it hops about tombs.'

'Is there nothing you don't know?' Caspar asked lightly, while at the same time glancing at Lug, who still had the dead reindeer cradled to his chest and was gibbering nervously. The Baron shrugged and turned his attention back to the distressed bird. Deftly, he caught the little wren and cut it free, allowing it to flutter away into the undergrowth.

Judging by the Haol-garen's state, Leaf could see that he understood the symbolic meaning of much around him. She was astonished to see what a powerful effect the symbolism had on the unlearned.

'Why the horseshoes?' Caspar asked as the way grew narrow and the holly trees crowded about them, forcing Lug to stoop. Their path was crossed by a line of horseshoes.

'It is the iron that the fairy folk fear. It is poisonous to them in its raw form.'

'Ah,' the Baron replied, himself avoiding a bulbous vial from which a smoky vapour rose. The holly-lined path became no more than a low tunnel and even Leaf was beginning to wonder what it represented as, surely, this path in itself was some form of symbol.

But it meant nothing to her until Caspar murmured, 'A trap.'

'A real trap or representation of one?' Leaf queried, for the first time concerned. Lug was the one who protested most loudly about the notion of a trap. He would become snared more easily than any of the others because of his size, and

Leaf felt a degree of concern replace her feelings of annoyance towards the lumbering fellow.

'You would move more easily if you left the fawn behind,' Caspar told the big man.

'Never!' Lug grunted. 'My people cannot survive without the fawn and the precious stone it carries.' A sparkle returned to his eye. 'And though I have lost my pigs, if I am the one to return with the Stone of Clarity, won't I be the one most likely to be chosen by our chief to win his daughter?'

'We should hurry,' Leaf coaxed, not troubling herself to give an answer when there was nothing meaningful she could contribute. 'It'll be dark soon and it's hard enough to make our way though these holly bushes.'

Lug moaned. 'I can't abide them. I can't abide hollines.'

'At least they keep themselves to themselves,' Caspar said, trying to ease the Haol-garen's fears. 'They're better than hobs.'

'Hobs and dwarves, I agree, are more troublesome, but at least you see them coming. Holly's people fall silently out of the dark and, in their hundreds, will club a great man to death with their holly staves. It's a horrible sight and they are so unreasonable.'

Caspar shrugged. 'I have always made a careful point of keeping out of their way. You wouldn't walk into a tiger's den, now would you? It's all a matter of not trespassing.'

'And what do you suppose we are doing now?' Lug grunted.

'Hmm.' Caspar didn't answer directly. 'We have no choice. We are doing no harm and must hurry on as fast as possible.'

'I would say that there are no hollines here,' Leaf assured Lug. 'Don't you remember the first line of impaled bodies? That was a gesture to warn away any holline.'

'That hardly makes it a symbolic threat. It is an outright demonstration of what these people are capable of,' Caspar argued. 'If they can kill Holly's people, they can kill us.'

'They probably didn't kill any of Holly's people. Didn't you see their bloated skin, which almost looked pickled? They were drowned and had spent a long time in the water.'

'Ah,' Caspar sounded reassured.

'You are like an eagle, the way you see everything, and you sound like a book!' Lug told her, his eyes now a little less wild.

Leaf wondered what it must be like to be so lacking in perception and knowledge, whether it was dull or whether it was blissful. It was too difficult for her to imagine and so she turned her thoughts back to the situation at hand. As she pondered, she noted that the rain was worsening again and was so heavy that it easily cut through the branches overhead. They ran on to where the holly trees were more closely packed. They gave better shelter but made Lug curse profusely as he caught his clothing in the prickles and was forced to break his way through. At last, the tunnel of trees came to a halt, the way ahead blocked by a solid dark green wall of vegetation standing thirty feet high. They now looked out on closely cropped grass footing a very tall yew hedge, which was being lashed by the relentless rain.

The downpour was so heavy that they had to shout above the noise as it ripped through the leaves. The sky above looked black so they decided to stay where they were until the worst of the storm had passed. After nearly an hour of the heaviest rain Leaf had ever seen, they were still waiting, her ears numbed by the noise. At last, it eased to gentler drops and they braved the open sky.

'How very curious,' Caspar said, smoothing back his heavy mop of damp hair and plucking out a number of holly leaves caught in his bearskin. 'Look at that hedge. This must be the work of your people, Leaf. As I remember, they were very proud of their formal gardens.'

Leaf nodded. 'Undoubtedly. And it must have been here a long time. We must find a way forward.'

To their left the yew hedge was met by a wall of holly, but to their right a way between bushes of early flowering

260

rosemary flattened by the torrential rain opened up. It led into a walk lined with yew on both sides. At the foot of the hedge grew borders of herbs, somewhat withered and dried in the frost, then battered in the rain. The avenue twisted and turned until it joined another similar walk that eventually forked. They turned left and were shortly led to another junction.

The Baron looked a little perplexed. 'A maze. Which way now? The light is failing and we shall find it increasingly hard.'

Leaf stamped her foot in frustration at herself. She should already know the way and must have missed something. 'Wait here,' she ordered before retracing their steps to the point where the way had last divided. Here she stooped to examine the foot of the hedge where the smell of crushed herbs was deliciously intense. Spending time with folk other than her own kind and constantly having to reassure them was obviously dulling her senses. Hastily, she checked each of the routes that led off from that point and then returned.

'This way,' she informed them, pointing to the right.

'Shouldn't we make some mark in the ground just in case we work round in a circle and find ourselves back where we started without knowing it?' Caspar asked. 'I think we ought to be systematic.'

'We don't need to be,' she retorted, tapping her foot on the ground. 'The message is as plain as can be.'

Impressed that the others followed her without wishing to question the route, she led them towards the right. When faced with a crossroads of five exits, she chose the second on the left. But after they had gone some distance along this route and then changed direction, heading back on themselves, Caspar began to protest.

'Leaf, this can't be right and it's getting very dark. It looks like it's going to rain heavily again. Lug, bend down so I can climb up on your shoulders and then perhaps I'll be high enough to see which way we are going.' His arm now considerably better, the Baron was able to climb to the top of the great man's shoulders without too much difficulty. He craned his head up to see, but even then he could not see over the hedge.

'Believe me, this is the way, and I shall be able to follow it even with my eyes shut,' Leaf tried to reassure him, sniffing in the scent of frost-withered angelica, though she was depressed by the rain that was beginning to pelt down again. Her boots splashed through deep puddles on the grassy way.

The Baron groaned. 'You had better give me a good reason to believe you.'

Leaf drew in a deep breath, inhaling the succulent and reviving smell of thyme mixed with the savoury scent of hyssop, indigo and sage, which the rain intensified. 'It's actually extremely simple,' she explained, finding her patience. 'It's all to do with the herbs growing along the way. You must always follow the herbs. The sequence is thyme, hyssop, indigo, sage, wintergreen, angelica, yarrow. Then it starts again.'

'How did you work that out?' Lug sounded amazed. Leaf gave a little laugh of amusement. 'If you take the first letters of each name, they spell out "this way".'

'And how many times have we been through the sequence?' Lug asked.

'Four,' Leaf replied smartly. 'The ravens gave me the clue. Thought and memory and the very first herb we came upon at the entrance to the maze was rosemary for remembrance so, looking at that herb, I knew I should note and memorize them.'

'How did you know to start with thyme?' Caspar asked.

Leaf shrugged. 'Because in the beginning that's all there was: time.'

'If you ask me, all things start with food,' Lug complained. 'It all sounds like nonsense to me, but if you think you have found a way then can you please hurry up and get us out of here.'

It was fully dark before Leaf eventually led them to a

steadily widening path. Her wet hair was plastered to her skin, which was wrinkled and sore from the constant rain. Her eyes stung and the only release from the torment was that, at last, the rain had eased. Never in her life had she experienced such weather. Of course it had rained in her realm, but the curtain had always filtered it, providing a soft mist. She had not enjoyed this experience.

The scent of herbs was now overpowered by the scent of wood-smoke, joined by the smell of roasting meat. Lug smacked his lips and Caspar quickened his pace. Leaf trotted after them, splashing through the endless puddles, mindful that neither of them had thanked her for her guidance through the maze. She didn't, however, dwell on that for long because she, too, was hungry and that was why she was not thinking clearly enough to be prepared for what she saw.

Lug stopped dead. Before them stood an ancient, crumbling temple. The roof, however, was still intact, providing welcome shelter from the rain. Dancing around a bubbling black pot on the steps of the temple were half-naked, bone-thin people covered in head-dresses and skirts of black feathers. Around them strutted a number of tame ravens. They were anxiously waiting to feed on a watery stew, which was being doled out by a scantily clad crone. Small wooden bowls were laid out in a row, and into each bowl she ladled the steaming brew until it overflowed the vessel. The birds went one each to a bowl and stood, waiting patiently as if they knew the stew was too hot but would cool in time. One or two ravens were offered larger bowls. Leaf wondered if this was a gesture of reverence or one of sympathy, the larger meal being a means to compensate the birds for the treatment they had received. Many were bald in places and their feathers had been pulled out by the strange people, who, much to her alarm, were of her own race.

She wasn't so much disturbed by their behaviour and attire but that they were perilously thin. The moment the three travellers stepped forward, the bedraggled and be-feathered people stood stiffly still and stared before slowly withdrawing into the temple and about a tight knot of young, wary-looking children. At their centre was an older boy enthroned on a lone chair. He was more warmly clad than his elders and had in his hand a piece of crust, which he dipped into his broth. The soup dripped from the crust onto his knee as he held it away from his mouth and stared at the intruders. Though the children remained calm, the old folk hissed fearfully and one ran about wildly wafting hemlock before them.

'Hush, you need not fear them,' the boy said confidently. 'If they made it through the maze, they must either be friends or able to listen to good reason and so will do us no harm. Offer them food at once. Sit them by the fire so they can dry.'

Leaf was vastly relived when a young boy, his eyes large in his head and his skin tight about prominent bones, offered her some of the insubstantial broth. She was able to relax for only a moment though because Lug showed none of the same courtesy towards these people as they had shown him; he raised his club and threatened them with it if they dared come close.

'How do I know that you haven't filled your stew with hemlock? You are dealers in death. All I want is to pass and be on my way.'

'You cannot,' the enthroned youth contradicted. 'Not this way anyway. A simple swineherd like you won't get beyond the river.'

'Please, please be patient with him,' Leaf begged, though she was already wondering what they were going to do if they couldn't approach the city this way. 'We have been through a great deal and are most grateful for the food, which I see you can barely spare. He does not mean to offend.' She turned and looked up at Lug. 'It is quite safe, I assure you. The scholars never hurt anyone; it is simply not in our nature. We are either intelligentsia or herdsmen like yourselves.'

Lug was only content if Leaf took a mouthful of stew from his bowl first but, after that, he ate his within seconds and then looked ravenously around for more. 'I'm hungry,' he complained.

Nervously, one of the children offered him another bowl but all could see it would be impossible to satiate such a huge man on the meagre supplies available. Clearly, Lug came to the same conclusion since he stamped off to break a branch of a hazel sapling and began to gnaw at the green wood.

'Why don't you eat the reindeer fawn?' one of the younger children asked him.

Lug lunged at the child and the boy was only saved by Caspar's timely intervention.

'Lug, sit down. He doesn't know how important the fawn is to you.'

Grinding his teeth, the great Haol-garen returned to his hazel branch while Caspar sat back against a pillar and watched his hosts thoughtfully. Leaf decided that she should not judge this man in the same way that she would judge other humans. He may not have the retentive powers of a scholar but he possessed a natural cunning, which she freely admitted she lacked. Whether that was because she was young or because the lacking was inherent in her race, she did not know.

After eating her fill, she sat back to study her hosts and was soon overwhelmed with sadness. Dismayed and bewildered, the younger children clung about the enthroned youth whom they addressed as Paris. The older people of the community practised croaking like the ravens, strutting up and down and displaying the black feathers that they had glued to their bare arms. The boy sitting on a chair padded in skins looked at them in disgust.

'Where is your parish council?' Leaf asked him.

Paris sniffed and wiped his hand across his nose. 'Here,' he said, wafting his hand at two of the grown-ups who were busily pasting on more feathers as fast as the rain washed them away. 'That's all that's left. The others sent us on ahead when we were attacked. They promised they would follow but none came. Now only the old and the young remain.' He nodded at the wretched folk clad in feathers. 'Although they were forgetful before, they still had some rational thought until the curtain collapsed.'

'The fear and the shock no doubt increased the rate of decline,' Leaf suggested.

Paris nodded. 'So it seems,' he said with sarcasm and Leaf guessed that he was barely coping with his role.

'Where are the other children?' she asked. She had noted the half-dozen who pressed about the youth, scowling at the elders, but that didn't seem to be enough. There were over a score of the demented adults and she felt sure there should be proportionally more children.

'Trying to gather food,' the youth said with some despair.

Leaf nodded. 'You are not the son of a farmer, I perceive.'

He nodded. 'What of it?'

'You seem out of your depth.'

'Of course I'm out of my depth. Wouldn't you be? We fled here as it's remote and can offer us shelter from the diabolical rain. We have barely any food and have nowhere to go. At least up here by the old maze we have been safe from dwarves and other troublesome peoples, but that is all we have achieved. We knew when we came here that there ought to be a plentiful supply of beef above the pastures bordering the upper river. But we underestimated the difficulties in actually getting any animal to the table. We caught one last week and managed the gruesome business of slaying it but the ravens plagued us and have eaten most of it and after that the rain has made everything so difficult. The water meadows have flooded,' he grumbled. 'There has been so much rain and, although it should be a relatively simple manner to ease the flow, it is the problem of mechanical and physical capabilities as well as a result of being preoccupied defending ourselves from raiders.'

'Raiders?' Caspar queried.

Paris nodded at Lug. 'First, several of his kind came stamping up from the valley below, distressed and angered. They killed

266

six of our cattle simply out of spite and took them off without any thought of our suffering. They were angry about the dwarves who have been skulking around the perimeter of our realm as if they are looking for something. But whatever it is they are looking for, dwarves have to eat and they have a penchant for cattle – lots of it. Then finally the outcasts burst out, no doubt intent on one of their evil experiments. They took our grain supplies and routed us from our college. It has always been difficult for us, being so close to them, and we have long expected such an event, though that did nothing to lessen the impact.'

Leaf made a sudden gasp, realizing who these children were amidst the Arcadian landscape. 'You are of the High Order of Mathematical Impossibilities!'

'Indeed,' Paris confirmed proudly, but then his expression sank. 'I have spent all my days at school and, up until now, I didn't realize that animal husbandry was so much more important than logarithms, logistics and lexicons. Can you believe that?'

'Yes! Leaf responded wearily. 'And what news of the city? I must get there; I had hoped that the scholars of the inner circle would be able to help on a most urgent matter.'

The youth shrugged. 'I don't know where they are now. All communication has broken down since the curtain fell.'

Leaf suddenly felt overwhelmed by all these problems. How was she going to cope? She must have looked worried because Caspar reached over and patted her hand.

'Don't worry. Rarely in the history of time has anything ever been achieved by worrying. The key is always action, and if there is nothing to do then you must rest. And I mean rest properly.'

'But what are we to do?' Leaf protested. 'I must find my father and the younger scholars of the inner circle. They will know what to do about the Chalice and, even if they do not, I will find works in the library that will help. It may take a little longer, but I can do it.'

267

'Excuse me,' Lug gruffly interrupted into the midst of this. 'It seems you have forgotten that I must find my people before Grunda goes and marries that numbskull Ogran, and I have to return the stone to our chief. I need help; I demand help,' he added more forcefully.

The croaking elders of the village excitedly flapped about them and began snapping their mouths forward in mimic of pecking birds. Lug growled and raised his club but was not speedy with the weapon and so unable to land a blow. Caspar rushed forward to try and soothe everyone while all Leaf could do was worry about how all around her seemed to be spinning out of control.

Lug shoved Caspar backwards and crouched into a position from which he could move in any direction, ready to attack, his precious reindeer fawn still clutched tight to his chest. 'One of you fools is going to show me a way out of this maze-ridden hell. I have to help my people and, if you don't help me, I'm going to eat you.'

This produced a cacophony of shrieks from the elders and the youth stood up from his chair of office and began shouting, 'This is unreasonable. Outrageous and unreasonable. We protest.'

Lug responded by springing at the boy and lifting him up by the shoulder.

Leaf was horrified. 'Outrageous!' she repeated the futile cry.

Naturally, her objections were to no avail and the giant was now beginning to shake the youth. Certainly, the boy would not survive much of that treatment. However, the Haol-garen gave out a sudden shriek and fell heavily to the ground, clutching his knee. Caspar was standing beside him, holding a long stick in his hand. Without any fear of the consequences, he had whacked the great man of Haol-gar across the kneecap, which had already been severely damaged by the hylups. The Baron then leaped up and sat astride his neck, his club ready to stab him in the eye. Leaf was aghast; she had never witnessed such barbarism.

'Just mind your manners,' the Baron growled at Lug.

'I just need to get the fawn back to my chief,' he grunted. 'Can't you make these people see?'

'Not if you insist on trying to kill them.'

Lug sighed and the aggression seeped out of him. Caspar appeared to recognize this as he stepped down and let the giant rise. Lug looked at the reindeer and then plucked the blue collar from around its neck and undid the small bag that was tied to it.

'The Stone of Clarity,' he said. 'I must take it back to my chief so that he will be able to know how to follow the reindeer.'

'The Stone, the Stone, the Stone!' the elders cried.

Paris was dusting himself down. 'There is no point,' he said sourly, eyeing the great man. 'No point at all.'

'Why not? I must return it so that he can choose a new fawn to carry the Stone. The white reindeer fawn bears one Stone of Clarity and the chief another. Without it, we cannot follow the herd.'

'There is no other stone any more,' the youth told him flatly.

'What do you mean?' Lug growled.

Paris shrugged. 'The dwarves. When your people came and killed the cattle, they were ranting and raving about how the dwarves had stolen their precious stone from the chief. I can only presume it is the partner to the one you carry.'

Lug gave out a moan as if his soul were breaking in two. 'What could they possibly want with our stone? It's ours. We need it. Without it we cannot find the pastures, we do not know the weather, we cannot foresee famine and . . . and we shall die, all of us will die!'

At this, the elders in their sparse cloak of feathers squawked and croaked. It wasn't long before Lug had one by the throat, and again the deranged elder was only saved by Caspar's intervention, bringing the staff smartly up under Lug's chin as he stooped to pick up another.

'You great oaf, these people can help you. Stop attacking them.'

'How can they help?' Lug said feebly, letting the old man slip from his fingers. 'The stone is lost. It is the source of all our power.' He sagged to the ground and kissed the dead fawn's head. 'And now I shall never win Grunda.'

Chapter 14

Rollo blinked, trying to see better in the cramped earthen coffin in which he found himself. His head was splitting and his chin was wet with saliva, the telltale signs that he had suffered a fit.

His muscles aching, he rolled over, trying to ease his discomfort. Unable to straighten out his legs, he felt rising panic. Above him were boards of wood pinning him into a shallow pit in the ground, slits of light filtering down between the cracks so that he could see just a little of his coffin. Turning over, he buried his face into the earth and finally began to cry.

'Is he quiet now?' a male hazeline voice asked.

There was silence above until the boards creaked as someone knelt onto them. 'He's sobbing.'

'Sobbing?' a female echoed in disbelief.

The boards were peeled back and Rollo was lifted from his grave, too confused and distraught to do anything but hang limply in their grip.

He was placed gently on the ground and, at last, found the wherewithal to look about him at the hazelines. Bar a few younger males, they seemed to be almost exclusively females huddled around one larger male. All were very slight, their elbows and knees exaggerated, knobbly lumps jointing their needle-thin limbs.

'What evil do you intend to bring to our woods, destroyer?' the male hazeline, whom the others had addressed as Flax, demanded.

271

'I – I –' Rollo stammered, completely taken aback at this line of questioning. 'I am not a destroyer.'

Flax leant forward and sniffed at him. 'You are not one of the peoples of beech. You are not a wizard, otherwise you would never have been fool enough to end up in this situation. There is no other species that looks like you other than the destroyers. I know I am right.'

Rollo could only shake his head.

'What were you doing with my child?' Lilly's mother demanded. 'Were you trying to steal her?'

'Why would I steal your child?' Rollo asked helplessly. 'This is madness.'

'No one knows why your kind does so many of the things you do! Why does anyone destroy? The hollines are dangerous and attack on sight. They are hostile to all other living creatures that enter their territory but they do not deliberately go out of their way to wantonly destroy others in the way that you do.'

'I do not destroy!' Rollo repeated emphatically, deeply bewildered by this accusation.

'He is lost, Mamma.' The little girl, Lilly, stepped bravely forward. 'Look into his eyes and you will see it.'

'I have never been this close to a human before and I distrust their eyes,' Flax objected to this suggestion. 'Who knows what harm might leap from the windows of his soul. The blackness within might fly out from them.'

'Humans possess no such powers and we are not destroyers,' Rollo emphatically defended himself. 'I am lost and my horse was attacked by hollines.'

'That is sad,' Flax commented, apparently with genuine feeling. 'Very sad for the horse. Though now, at least, its spirit will be free from your tyrannical rule.'

Rollo gave him a hard look, finding it impossible to explain that no one ruled Firecracker and, if anything, it was *he* who had suffered from the *horse's* tyrannical rule.

'The question is, what should be done with you?' the chief hazeline worried.

272

Hastily, Rollo looked about him, glad that most of the creatures about were female and so, he hoped, would be less inclined to inflict some terrible sentence on him.

'He meant me no harm,' Lilly repeated. 'He was simply hiding from the hollines.'

Flax grunted. 'I need food to help me think on the matter.' He promptly sat down and, like most human males Rollo had met, waited for the women to bring him victuals. A rather bland-looking paste and some withered apples were placed in front of Flax and the three younger males in the tribe while the thirty or so women looked at them expectantly. The four males chewed solemnly, asked for more and only when they had finished did the women and children eat.

Much to Rollo's amazement, one of the hazeline girls offered him a plate of food, though she snatched it back when the chief male grunted at her, 'We cannot fairly decide his fate if we have shared food with him. That would be very uncomfortable indeed.'

'He's only a boy,' Lilly's mother said gently. 'He's lost and clearly ill. I didn't see any demons pouring out from his eyes or mouth, did you? It's clearly some kind of illness. We should send for old Grandma Campion.'

There was a muttering of agreement that rippled around the troubled hazelines, though Flax seemed perturbed at the idea.

'Grandma Campion won't like being disturbed over such a trivial matter.'

'Is the life of a fellow creature ever trivial?' Lilly's mother asked.

'All right then.' The chief threw up his hands in defeat; a state he had arrived at very quickly indeed, Rollo thought with some relief. 'We send for old Grandma.'

Lilly's mother snapped her fingers at her child. 'Come, you and I shall go. It is only right since you brought this stranger into our midst.'

It was almost an hour before they returned, by which time Rollo was feeling sick with hunger, the discomfort increased by watching the hazelines scooping up mouthfuls of their paste. When Lilly and her mother returned with an old female hazeline, the rest stood in reverence and bowed their heads.

'Old Grandma, mother of us all!' they welcomed her respectfully.

The ancient hazeline was so stooped over, her flesh so loose and crinkled that Rollo decided she was more likely their great-grandmother.

Patting Lilly's head, she said in a thin wavering voice, 'Child of the child of my granddaughter, is this what has troubled you so?' She pointed at Rollo.

Before Lilly could answer, shouts broke through the trees into the glade.

'Grandma! Grandma! We have found you!' A male very similar to Flax stood outside the natural circle of the glade and, saluting Flax, asked, 'Permission, brother, to enter your home.'

To Rollo's eyes, the two hazelines were virtually identical. The newcomer, however, had a much smaller following of no more than eight females. They jostled each other, anxious to be the one closest to their chief, who appeared to have no males to rival him within his tribe. Rollo barely absorbed these details; he was focusing on something else entirely. What had struck him immediately was that these hazelines held Fanchon. She was firmly tied and gagged, her face puce with the effort of trying to scream through the cloth stuffing her mouth.

'Permission granted, Mistletoe,' Flax said cordially, using the old tongue of the Caballan. 'I see you have another destroyer. Is the wood overrun with them?'

The hazeline shrugged. 'We found this girl beating a poor pony to death after it had stumbled and let her fall. She shrieked that she was intent on finding a young boy and that she meant no harm. It was hard to believe since she had already taken a bite out of Snowbell's arm.'

'Here is the boy,' Flax said calmly, waving his arm to present Rollo.

The bewildered Artoran youth looked at Flax and then Fanchon, wondering how it was that she had come to find him. It seemed impossible that she would have reached him before any of the Torra Altans or Oxgard's soldiers. She was surely not one born and bred to the saddle and he would have thought that she knew nothing about tracking. It was just not what he would have expected for one that was so preoccupied with seducing men.

'Untie her and seat her by the boy,' Flax ordered, remaining in charge, as the senior male on his own territory. 'Grandma, what is to be done?' he asked.

Rollo thought it strange that, though the males dominated the females within the tribes, the ultimate authority lay with this wrinkled old crone. She sucked at her gums and then shuffled forward to sit on a log. The hazelines immediately sat down at her feet and watched patiently, awaiting her words of wisdom. The males, however, strutted up and down.

'We simply need a decision,' Flax grumbled. 'Do we take them to the edge of the wood and set them free or do we take them deep into the trees and let the laws of the forest decide their fate?'

The old woman waved him down with his hand. 'It is not a matter for decision. I need silence so that the answer can flow to me.' She drew from the leather belt about her sagging waist a forked stick, no doubt a hazel branch, Rollo guessed. As she rose, her joints cracked and she muttered crossly to herself about the burdens of being old. Moving to Rollo, she held the forked branch above his head much as if she were divining for water. The branch reared upwards sharply and her eyebrows rose accordingly. She then moved to Fanchon and did the same, but this time the tip of the branch dived downwards towards her head.

Without any discussion on the matter, the ancient hazeline pronounced her judgement. 'Take her to the depths of the wood and set him on one of the paths to man.'

'But they are surely together,' Flax protested. 'Shouldn't we treat them in the same way?'

'I do not know for what purpose the destroyers entered the wood. I only know that her intentions were for harm and he was driven here out of fear. We must help those who, like ourselves, fear the dangers of the world. There is no evil in the boy.'

Rollo stared in wonderment at the old woman. Whenever he had allowed himself to dwell on such thoughts, he had secretly always considered himself to be essentially corrupt. So often he had heard people whispering that his fits were an affliction sent to punish him for his evil soul and he had believed it must be so. Clearly, the aura of mystery was a ruse to maintain her authority over Flax and Mistletoe. He wondered how the males could be so gullible but, once again, considered that human males were very much the same in that respect.

Still, he was very grateful for her counsel, in regard to himself at any rate, and even more grateful that the hazelines immediately acted upon it.

Fanchon screamed. 'No! No, you can't do this to me. Rollo, Rollo save me!' Her eyes were wide and imploring.

He would have said anything he could to try and help her, if it hadn't been for that look she had given the scullery maid. He had instinctively distrusted it and, clearly, the hazelines had sensed ill-intent in her already. She was dragged away, screaming, and all he could do was stare on.

'How could you do this to a fellow human being, Rollo?' she cried bitterly. 'I have influence. Believe me, I'll find my way out of here and I'll see to it that you pay for this. There are powerful men who listen to me!'

Rollo felt cold and empty inside. He knew Fanchon was right; he should not abandon a fellow human being. Yet he was glad to be free of her. Closing his eyes for a moment, he tried to blot all thought of her from his mind. When he opened them again, the hazelines were gesturing him towards a narrow badger track leading out from their glade, which was

276

pocketed with swirls of leaves that looked like giant nests. It appeared these people had no dwellings but simply slept in the undergrowth, naked as they were. He shuddered at the thought.

'I can't go back,' he stuttered. 'I can't! Not without the horse.'

The hazelines looked at him blankly.

'It's my father's horse,' he tried to explain. 'Don't you see? The hollines were after him. He may be injured. I have to help him.'

'No,' Flax said firmly. 'No!'

They bound him tightly, blindfolded him and tugged him through the woods, this time being careful not to bump his head. He felt giddy with being turned this way and that but was, at last, aware of a stiff breeze on his face and guessed that they had reached the edge of the woods. Hastily they untied him, finally stripping away the blindfold. But by the time he had blinked in the sunlight and turned around to protest at his treatment, they were gone. It was as if they had melted into the trees.

Rollo stared about him and, seeing the single ash tree with the broken branch, noted that he was back near the point where he had entered the wood. He wondered how the creatures had known. The ground at his feet was churned by many more hoof-prints and there was no doubt that a number of riders had headed this way and most probably in pursuit of him. Again, he reflected how curious it was that Fanchon had been amongst their number, let alone the first to discover him. Looking back towards Oxgard's castle, he saw a man standing beside a pine. Rollo ducked down low, guessing that the man was acting as a rendezvous for the search.

Rollo was not about to be found. He knew in his heart that he would eventually have to go back to them and face the music. He had made a bad situation into a humiliatingly awful situation by running away like that and causing them all so much trouble, but he was not going back without Firecracker; that was unthinkable.

He turned and trotted until he was out of sight of the sentry and then stopped to take stock of his surrounds. He was standing at the edge of the wood that blended gradually into the pastoral landscape. There was no sense of how large or small the wood was, only that he could not see its limits. He had no idea where to begin looking for Firecracker and wondered which was worse: explaining to his father how he had caused his horse to be eaten by Holly's people or to end up in the clutches of the hollines himself. He drifted into the wood, wondering whether to call the horse's name, and tentatively experimented with this idea only to alarm the birds and set his heart a flutter as the forest screamed at his intrusion.

He hurried on in silence, trying to find his way back to the point he had last seen Firecracker, but it was only a matter of minutes before he realized he was lost again. Cursing himself for his folly, he sagged onto the lichen-covered trunk of a fallen tree and dropped his head into his hands, breathing deeply in an effort to gather some self-control. What was he going to do? It would be better if he had been taken with Fanchon to the heart of the wood. Curling up against the tree and thinking himself quite alone, he allowed the tears to fall.

'Be hushed. Do not cry so!' a little voice crooned in his ear.

He leapt up in fright. 'I wasn't crying,' he protested angrily, seeing it was only the little hazeline child, Lilly.

She reached up with a long finger, very tenderly wiped his cheek with it and licked the end of her finger. 'You were crying. Tears of anguish, age-old anguish. It is the little things that break us but the tears we cry are for the deeper, older pain. That is what Grandma always says,' she hastened to add, evidently not wanting to take false credit for words that were not hers.

'You'll just get me into trouble again,' Rollo protested bitterly at her presence. 'Flax will think I've kidnapped you.'

'Let him think what he will think. He is only a male,' Lilly said flippantly.

Rollo raised an eyebrow at this. 'It seems to me that he was very much in charge.'

'Oh, that's just what Mamma and her sisters want him to think. They prefer it that way. It frees them from responsibility, she tells me. He has no true power. Only Grandma has power. But that doesn't matter right now. You need help and I owe it to you.'

'You do?' Rollo asked doubtfully, thinking that there was very little help this young child could give.

'I do. If I had run away from you as my mother had always told me to do, the clan would have not treated you so ill.'

'Oh . . .' Rollo said feebly. 'But how can you help me? I need to find my horse.'

She nodded. 'He will be at the rutting pit.'

'How do you know?' he asked her sceptically.

She shrugged. 'I just think he is.'

Rollo nodded gloomily. There was no point chasing after this child's whim. She had no idea what she was talking about.

She looked at him hard and seemed to read his expression because she sniffed. 'You don't believe me. You're just like Flax! Humph! Well, I shall just show you and that will be an end of it,' she said petulantly. 'You forget I am a hazeline.'

Without once looking back at him, Lilly picked herself up and marched off, her slight form slipping between the narrow gaps of the trees with ease. Immediately, Rollo regretted his surliness as he felt a wash of loneliness sweep over him. He didn't want to be abandoned in this wood again. Lilly was only a strange little creature but she was company and he had felt little need to excuse his foolish actions to her. But now that she was gone, he was deeply disturbed by the silence in the woodland for fear of what might suddenly burst out of it. Hastening to his feet, he did his best to trot after the little hazeline but was quickly dismayed to find that he did not know which way she had gone. Could he get nothing right?

He was about to fling himself to the floor in despair when he heard a snatch of song winding through the branches towards him.

'Sing, sing the hazel-o,
Drinking from the river-o.
Listen to the music there,
Feel the magic in the air.
Hazel whisper of the world;
All its mysteries here unfold.
Sing, sing the river-o.
Whisper to my hazel-o.'

It was Lilly's voice! Rollo danced after the sound though he had difficulty keeping up as he had to wriggle low beneath the branches and squeeze between boughs that presented no obstacle to the hazeline.

'Wait!' he called. 'Wait, please wait!'

But she skipped on ahead, keeping just a tantalizing distance beyond him, always the sound of her bright little voice ringing merrily through the trees. They were dipping down fast towards the dark depths of the forest, where lichen and moss thickly clad the boughs of the trees. His breath began to steam in the cool atmosphere of the hollow.

Once he had stilled his panted breaths, he was aware of distressed grunts and groans coming from close by. Surely it was too early in the year for the stags to be rutting, he thought to himself. But the scraped earth at the base of the hollow suggested that this was indeed a rutting pit and the grunts and little coughs certainly sounded like those of a wounded stag. He squinted into the hazy gloom lining the bottom of the scrape and glimpsed a large humped shape, reddish in colour, lying at the bottom of the hollow.

'Firecracker!' His voice was thin and strangulated. 'Oh, Cracker, look what they've done to you.'

Not wanting to alarm the animal, he edged forward tentatively until he could see the horse was gravely wounded. His flank was marked by cuts and bites that were ugly and no doubt very uncomfortable, but they were nothing compared to the long rip that ran the length of the stallion's belly. A flap of torn, glistening flesh hung down from the gash and dripped blood. Pinkish-yellow intestine stuck out from the wound. The horse's nostril had also been torn, the flap of skin lifting and falling with each laboured breath.

Rollo staggered forward helplessly. 'Poor, poor Cracker!' Witnessing the animal's deep pain and seeing the wild look of disbelief and bewilderment in the stallion's eyes made him feel sick to the pit of his stomach. He stepped slowly forward, wanting to offer what feeble help he could, but the animal shrieked and struggled to get up as if he were being attacked.

Rollo halted and crept back, biting back the tears. What would Father say? How could he let this happen to so rare and beautiful animal? 'Cracker,' he sobbed. 'Oh, Cracker.'

He tried talking to soothe the animal but his voice was cracking up and he watched on in horror as fresh blood dripped from the horse's nose. What was he going to do? He must find help. But how could he? He couldn't leave the horse for fear that he would be discovered by scavengers and eaten alive. Perhaps he should swiftly and mercifully end the horse's suffering. But he didn't think that he could get close enough to do that and, moreover, his father would never forgive him if he didn't try to do everything possible to save the animal's life.

He couldn't think. The pressure in his brain was building up. How could he have let this happen to his father's most loved possession? It was unforgivable. He sat there, panting heavily, his mouth gaping, his brain grappling with the impossible problem. There seemed to be no way to make a decision and, at any moment, he would simply break down and cry again. It shamed him to be this weak. He was a prince of the mighty county of Artor; his regal mother would never have collapsed and wept. She would have known what to do.

Consoling himself with the thought that he didn't have her special powers, he sucked in breath through his gritted teeth but it did nothing to relieve the squirming sickness that stirred his guts. After turning aside the golden dragon's attack, he had believed that he, too, was special. After a lifetime of believing himself inadequate, he had thought that, like his mother and sister, he too had power over great beasts. But it had been a delusion and he was just as wretched as he had always been. He had not been able to control the red dragons and it had been some weird coincidence that had stopped the great golden dragon's flame.

He felt the tears prick and start to roll down his flushed cheeks. Though he threw back his head and wiped them away, he could still feel the sobs choking his breath, and at any minute they would conquer him and steal away the last of his pride. What finally stopped him breaking down entirely was the sound of Lilly weeping piteously.

'Please, please don't start crying,' she sobbed. 'I can't bear it. And look at the poor horse. He will surely die very soon. What can we do? Should I fetch Grandma to help?'

Rollo raised his sore eyes to the horse. Firecracker was quivering, his breathing laboured. There was nothing he could do for him, but there was something he could do for Lilly. He scooped her up and cradled her in his arms, wanting to do anything to help. He could at least try and comfort her. It wasn't something that came naturally to him but the creature was so helpless that he couldn't stop himself. He curled himself around her, brushing back her hair from her bony skull.

'Poor little Lilly,' he soothed.

'Poor Rollo,' she sobbed back. 'I cannot bear your pain.'

He didn't understand her concern for him but was touched

by it. The hazelines appeared to be profoundly sensitive and caring, totally opposite to the hollines they so resembled.

'I wish there were something I could do to help,' she whispered.

'But there is!' Rollo exclaimed, wondering why he hadn't thought of it. 'Find my people for me. I know they are in the woods looking for me. You must find them and bring them to me.'

Lilly nodded and stood up, head slightly tilted back, but then it drooped and she sagged down again. 'I can't.' She was trembling and her eyes were wide with fear. 'Not all your people are like you. They are the destroyers; I saw it in that woman's eyes. What if the others are like her and not like you? I cannot.' She slumped down onto her knees and sobbed against his chest. 'I cannot.'

He hugged her to him again. 'It's all right, Lilly; I understand. It's not your fault. It really isn't.' Her helplessness strengthened his confidence though he still didn't know how to help Firecracker. His mind, however, was made up for him as he heard rustling in the undergrowth.

He leapt to his feet, sword in one hand and braced ready for action as he scanned the shrubs about him. Three pointed heads jerked into the periphery of his vision and he spun round to see three male hollines brandishing clubs and stalking boldly towards him. Lilly vanished like mist in the wind and he found himself standing alone before Firecracker as the three hollines advanced.

They were small, weedy creatures and he should have been up to the task of fighting off two though he was not so confident about defeating three, especially after having experienced their ferocity.

'Trespassers,' they hissed low and slowly. They cackled and chortled away to one another as two advanced on the horse, licking their lips. The third eyed Rollo but then began to stab vigorously at the undergrowth about him while excitedly sniffing the air. Rollo looked on in horror. Judging by his behaviour, he guessed the holline must have seen or smelt Lilly and was now seeking the little hazeline, his eyes wide with excitement at the thought of the sport.

Rollo did not have to think to make a decision as to whether to protect the horse or the hazeline; Firecracker was all but dead anyway. Setting his thoughts on saving the little child, he ran at the holline, which was stabbing the crisp bracken leaves and stirring the brambles. With sword held high and forgetting all his training, which had warned him always to attack without leaving himself vulnerable to his opponent, he screamed savagely at the holline, enraged that it might want to hurt a helpless little creature.

To his amazement, all three hollines, even the ones that had been crawling forward to reach Firecracker, suddenly upped and ran, melting into the trees as quickly as the hazeline had done. For a number of seconds, Rollo thought that they must have run from him. He was still thinking that when Lilly rushed up out of the undergrowth and threw herself into his arms, burying her head against her chest.

'It's all right,' he murmured softly. 'They've gone. You're safe.' As he said that he looked up and found himself staring at Brid, who was suddenly before him; she must have approached as silently as one of Lilly's kind. The two dogs which Oxgard had given them came rushing up behind her and pressed close to the woman adoringly.

The priestess was staring at Rollo, conflicting emotions toying with her expression. She was so beautiful with gloriously thick hair and an elfin body, neat and shapely. Her startlingly green eyes flashed at Rollo and then at the horse lying bleeding on the ground. For just a moment she looked fearsome, a latent rage welling up from within her and flooding out from those intense eyes. In fear of her wrath, Rollo took a step back, watching the priestess apprehensively. But when Brid's gaze fell on Lilly, her eyes softened and she looked at Rollo as if she were seeing a stranger for the first time.

'Rollo,' she whispered in a dulcet lilt. 'Oh, Rollo.'

He no longer knew if she were angry, disappointed or surprised by him but stared back, his mouth dropping as he helplessly struggled to find words to excuse his behaviour.

Lilly sat up and blinked at Brid. Suddenly as brave as a puppy, she wriggled from Rollo's arms and ran to the priestess. 'You are she!' the girl exclaimed. 'You are One of the Three. You are the Mother! Blessed be!'

Brid reached out to caress the girl's head, but at that second the sound of hooves came thundering towards them followed by shouts of, 'Brid! Brid! We can't have lost her too!'

So that was why the hollines had run. Their hearing must be much more acute than a human's; they must have heard the sound of mounted soldiers. Lilly was gone before Rollo even realized it. Strangely, she had not been in the least afraid of Brid but, clearly, she did not trust the other humans who noisily broke into the glade.

'Lady Brid! Thank the blessed stars you're safe!' Aisholt exclaimed as he led four men towards the hollow. 'The others are just coming. They've found Fanchon in a very . . .' The soldier paused as his eyes ran over Rollo and then Firecracker. '. . . in a very sorry state.' He finished his sentence in no more than a whisper. 'And I see you've found Rollo. What a mess!' he said flatly, staring at the horse. 'What a bloody mess!' Already he was reaching for his knife, but Brid stepped into his path and put her hand on his.

'I know it would be a kindness but you cannot do that to this horse. If it is to be done, Baron Caspar must do it himself.'

'Madam, I have no wish to contradict you but that horse will not last the day and we shall not be able to move him. Perhaps you do not understand . . .' Aisholt politely attempted to dissuade her.

'Of course I understand!' Brid's voice was suddenly terrible and Rollo found that he was actually afraid of her. 'But you, sir, do not know this horse. He will not give up! He will fight for his life however painful the battle.' She stared Aisholt down, and he nodded respectfully at her.

'My Lady, as you wish.'

Brid pressed her lips together and stared long and hard at Firecracker, drawing in a deep breath as if preparing herself for the ordeal ahead. She didn't even look round as Guthrey and several of Oxgard's men broke into the clearing. Dishevelled and bruised, Fanchon was riding behind Guthrey, her arms tight about his waist. Rollo met her gaze for a brief second and shuddered at the cold look of resentment that she stabbed at him. He had no doubt that she sought revenge.

Guthrey rode right up to Rollo and glared haughtily down at him. 'So there you are, you wretch, you slimy snake. Is there no end to the trouble you can bring on us? Have you any idea what you've done to my brother's face and the trouble you've caused, running away like a coward?' He snorted as he finally caught sight of Firecracker. 'Not to mention what you've done to that horse. And on top of all that, you, like a wretched traitor, left Fanchon at the mercy of hazelines.'

'Shut up!' Brid ordered quietly but authoritatively and without troubling herself to look round. 'No one is at the mercy of hazelines. Guthrey, I do not want to hear another word from you right now. We shall sort this out when we get back to the castle.'

'But, Mother, can't you see what trouble Rollo –'

'Silence,' Brid ordered very softly so as not to alarm the injured horse. She finally looked round and fixed Guthrey hard in the eye and raised her finger to her lips. It was neither her words nor her gesture that quelled her headstrong son; it was simply the look in her eye. She was strong, profoundly strong, her spiritual presence so much larger than her physical stature. Guthrey clearly knew it was best to remain silent, though Fanchon immediately began to complain. 'That boy must be –'

'Shut up!' Guthrey growled. 'Don't ever countermand my mother.'

All eyes were now on Brid and the injured stallion.

'Please, my lady, be careful,' Aisholt begged. 'He could still have a very nasty kick on him. An injured animal like that can be very dangerous.'

Brid stepped very calmly towards Firecracker. 'There now, boy,' she soothed, reaching for the leather pouch of herbs that she always kept tied about her neck. With nimble fingers, she loosened its ties and, after a moment, she drew out a dried sprig of herb, which still had dark withered berries clinging to it, and sniffed at it. 'You and I are old friends, remember?'

Rollo had a strange feeling that the high priestess was talking to the horse as if he were Caspar. 'There, there now. It's not so bad. I know it hurts but you trust me, don't you?'

All stood with bated breath as the priestess eased steadily forward. The horse kicked and snorted, half-rising onto trembling forelegs and sending out a spray of blood from its nostrils. Brid paid no attention to the stallion's warning but held out her outstretched palm.

'There, Cracker, lie easy for me and I will make things right.' It took her a full minute to actually reach the horse's head and Rollo found he could not breathe in that time. It was bad enough that the stallion was hurt but if Brid were injured too, and all on his account, the others would slit his throat here and now, he felt sure of it. Giddy and weak with trepidation, he stared on with unblinking eyes.

At last, Brid had her hand to the horse's bridle and he hoped that now everything would be all right. He could see Brid relax just fractionally and it was then that the animal suddenly lunged and bit her. She snatched her hand away and sucked at her thumb.

'Mother, come away. I won't let you do this,' Guthrey told her. 'He'll hurt you.'

'Don't you dare speak out,' Brid scolded but in the sweetest tone as if she were speaking to the horse. 'You won't hurt me, will you now, Cracker?' Very slowly, she slid her hand up the stallion's cheek and gently tugged his ears while the fingers of her other hand held her chosen herb pressed up towards the horse's mouth. The stallion flinched, guarding the gruesome injury to its nose, but Brid persisted and, eventually, the animal took the berries.

'Aisholt, I need you and three others to stand either side of the horse. He'll be down in a moment.'

Brid was right. A moment later, they were supporting the animal as it was lowered to the ground. Rollo found that he could breathe now that Firecracker was no longer in pain. He tentatively stepped forward and watched Brid push the sticky entrails back into the horse's stomach and suture the wound. She took from her pack a small bag from which she withdrew the thick paste of white honey that Oxgard's physician had given her and set a pot over a small fire to warm. She then returned to her bag and produced a small pot of white, waxy-looking beads, which, she explained, were beads of paraffin wax. She placed them into the pot to warm.

Once melted, she pasted the concoction over the wounds and finally made a mash of herbs that she slid into the horse's mouth. Bloodwort, melilot and other herbs that Rollo didn't recognize were crumbled together and warmed over the fire. All the while, he stared at the horse and wondered whether the animal would ever get up again. He wished Lilly had not fled from him. Now, he felt more alone than ever without her as no one else here would comfort him. The angry silence that hung over everyone pained him as, with trepidation, he awaited the wrath that must surely be coming his way.

After nearly an hour's hard labour, Brid appeared satisfied with her handiwork, which Aisholt admired loudly. By this time, only a few men remained. Brid had ordered that she and her companions would rest here with the horse and a few guards while the others returned to bring Isolde and Quinn to them. Then they would move out from here as soon as they were able.

'But will Cracker be able to walk?' Rollo asked, his voice cracking nervously.

'That remains to be seen, but I think he will. He's a very

strong beast and, like any other herd animal, will instinctively want to stand and move on rather than lie waiting to be devoured by scavengers. He will walk very shortly after coming round.'

They sat and waited, Rollo feeling very uncomfortable as he sensed the disappointed and angry stares of the others lingering on him. What could he say? What could he do to make things right?

Guthrey was sitting squarely opposite him, deliberately staring at him. After a long while the Torra Altan demanded, 'What's wrong with you, cousin? Don't you know what harm you've done? Didn't you realize that we had to move out quickly? Isolde is getting worse by the hour.'

Isolde, poor Isolde, Rollo thought remorsefully. He felt sick with himself and wanted to murder Guthrey for so cruelly pointing out his errors to him. It wasn't as if he didn't realize what he had done.

But Guthrey wasn't the only one to glare at him critically. Fanchon's sharp eyes were on him all the time. Pointing at Rollo, she burst out, 'He told the people of the forest that I was evil and they dragged me deep into the woods and left me for Holly's people to find. It was only luck that brought you to me just in time. But he wanted me dead,' she accused.

'The hazelines dragged you into the woods?' Brid asked.

Fanchon nodded. 'And Rollo did nothing to stop them. I found him with them and he set them against me.'

Brid nodded sagely. 'Indeed.' She tilted her head onto one side and looked long and hard at Rollo in that inscrutable way of hers. 'Indeed,' she echoed.

Chapter 15

'Help us, Paris,' Leaf begged. 'We have little time to lose and must get to the city. Silas has done much damage.'

The youth shrugged. 'No one has heard of Silas for days, not since the curtain fell. All is in chaos.'

'Why did the curtain fall?' Leaf questioned fearfully, but didn't wait for a reply. 'You must help us.' She looked to Caspar. 'Help us. I do not know what to do.'

'It is a wise person indeed who admits when they need help,' the Baron remarked, rising and pulling his heavy bearskin cloak straight. His eyes, Leaf noted, looked steadily about him, absorbing detail. 'We must get to the city but we must take time to consider how. There is no point rushing headlong into a land in chaos; there will be no food and none of us will get anywhere without food. First, we must help these people get their cattle in.'

'But!' Leaf protested in frustration. 'We have no time.' They had spent a long night in the shelter of the temple while torrential rain quenched the fire and formed rivulets all around them.

The Baron shrugged. 'No cattle, no food. How far is it to the city from here?' he asked Paris.

The youth rubbed his nose. 'Forty-three and a quarter miles. Not far, but the weather has caused much damage and the ways are closed. Even yesterday I thought it foolish to cross the arched bridge, but by now I should think it's impossible.'

Caspar nodded coolly. 'We will find a way somehow. Lug, you come with me and we'll get these cattle in. We all need food. It's no good cowering here. You'll be eating the ravens next.'

'I'm not getting cattle. I must have the Stone of Clarity,' Lug protested.

Caspar reached up and patted his hand. 'Lug, listen to me. It's simple. Leaf and I must get to the city. Once we are there, I'm sure we can find news of what the dwarves are up to and what they have done with your precious stone. But it's going to be a long journey and we can't make it without supplies. If we help these people, they can help us.'

Lug frowned and then smiled brightly. 'You are right!'

Paris was organizing the two score children that looked to him for leadership. Already, at first light, he had sent a dozen off to do what they could to guide the cows they so sorely needed onto higher ground. He sent others with a handcart laden with the sodden hay they had managed to glean from a ransacked farmstead. They hoped that the hay might entice the cows in the right direction. Leaf, however, looked to Caspar for instructions. Already she had learned to trust this man. She sighed heavily; hadn't her mother made exactly the same mistake placing all her trust in Silas? Wasn't she just doing the same thing? Yet she knew she couldn't cope and he did seem to have the answers.

'Paris, lead me to the cattle,' Caspar instructed. He turned and looked at Leaf. 'You stay here where it's safe.'

She looked around at the croaking elders, who were busy smearing themselves in paste and feathers, and decided she could not bear to watch the slow death of their minds and would rather act. She pitied the children whom Paris had instructed to guard them. It seemed to her to be an impossible task.

'I may be of help,' she said haughtily to disguise her fears.

Caspar smiled warmly. 'That you may.'

She trotted fast behind them, falling in step with Paris, who was perhaps only two years her senior and already growing long in the leg. Though very thin, he was a fine-looking youth, showing much promise, and yet they all knew that it could be no more than weeks now before he crossed the watershed into adulthood and the brain disease would grip his mind.

He looked at her with that same fear behind his eyes. 'It is up to us,' he told her sadly. 'We have so little time and, if we cannot do it, then we shall be lost. I do not want to spend the rest of my days croaking like a raven.'

Leaf smiled back. 'The fear of it cramps my mind.'

He nodded at her and they were suddenly aware of a sense of comradeship through shared calamity. She and he understood each other. To them had fallen the burden of responsibility because they were the oldest with lucid thought, yet both also knew that their own days of sanity were numbered. Leaf wondered, when the day finally came, whether it would be a release from this panic of always fearing when it was going to strike or whether the disease itself was so terrifying that it compounded the madness.

Paris twitched a nervous smile back at her and then drew in a deep breath, preparing himself. Raising his collar against the drizzle, he looked about the gathered company before leading them away. 'We must not dwell on what may be; we must do simply what we can. Look at that human there. He doesn't have the intellect to be aware of all the horrors that will befall him; think of the bliss. He does not think on the perils and so he acts; we could learn things from him.'

'I have already learned much from him,' Leaf said, indignantly defending Caspar's intellect. 'And not least of it is that I have learned never to underestimate him. Man is not like the Haol-garen or the simple warriors of Ash; he is complex and knows many fears. Some crumble beneath them and turn to cruel and deceitful ways of securing themselves a more promising future, and others bear the pain and struggle more nobly to better the lot of all. Such is that man.' She nodded at Caspar.

'The one thing we should all have learnt from recent events,' Paris told her, 'is that man is dangerous. He is knowledgeable and clever enough to devise ways of causing great harm but not clever enough to create the infrastructure and the laws to govern the safe use of such knowledge. They are like children.'

'And what are we?' Leaf retorted. 'Helpless, needy children. You talk of things you do not understand.'

'And I suppose in your short years you have learned so much more?'

Leaf shook her head. 'No, I doubt it. In all my lifetime up until the last month, I doubt I learned anything significant beyond your own knowledge, but in the last few weeks I have learned more than in all the rest of my life put together. I have learned of the other peoples of the earth and how they communicate, react and survive; how they are all surviving better than we are. It's humbling. One learns fast from being humbled.'

The ground was very wet underfoot and lay in deep puddles. The track they splashed along looked more like a muddy stream rushing along on its urgent journey to the sea. Leaf decided she preferred the icy frosts to this relentless rain. It was warmer but made the going so difficult. A distant roar wafted to her ears and she was certain that they were gradually moving towards fast-running water.

Soon they were tramping through deep mud that smothered the banked-up road and lay in black slicks to the left and right of it. The muddy track led them around the edge of a wind-ravaged wood; the crisp leaves that had clung to the upper branches were gone though the lower skirts were still clad in autumnal gold. The roar from a mud-charged river was suddenly alarmingly loud. A few paces more and Leaf was looking out over a flooded plain.

She had never seen anything like it before in her life. Of course she had read about the thousands of people and animals that had been drowned in spated rivers, but that had not prepared her for the actual sight; she was awe-struck. A huge sheet of water spread out over the valley, engulfing trees and forming little islands around the higher ground. The roads

293

approaching an isolated bridge were already submerged in the flood but the bridge itself arced out of the water, clearing the main channel of the river where the waters raced and churned at an alarming speed, cutting through the centre of the flood.

Leaf took one look at the bridge and realized instantly that, as soon as the river rose just a little more, the bridge would act as a dam and send water gushing sideways. Already much water had spilled out into the meadows, where it was far more sluggish and a dark black rather than the red-brown where the bucking river water tore up its bed. The cows could be seen about half a mile away, standing huddled on a low mound completely surrounded by water, watching as it slowly crept higher. They lowed and blared with hunger and fear.

'They will be drowned,' Paris said regretfully. 'See, the water is still rising, and when it reaches the bottom of the bridge arch the main body of the river will be virtually dammed and it will rapidly flood sideways, filling this plain.' He spread his arms wide to indicate the dale. 'And there's not a thing we can do about it. If only we had foreseen this calamity.'

Caspar looked at the river, the hills above and the long thin valley. 'I would have thought it obvious that it would flood in such a spot.'

'We don't normally get rain like this. It was filtered by the curtain.' Paris sounded near despair.

'That's what happens when systems break down,' Caspar said fatalistically.

Lug, Caspar and Leaf stood back by the handcart of hay for a moment while Paris did his best to organize his fellows. Those he had sent ahead were already knee-deep in the still floodwater, but still some fifty yards away from the huddle of marooned cattle. Paris was gesticulating wildly in an attempt to direct them and Leaf looked doubtful as they battled to build a dam upstream of the cows in an attempt to divert the water away from their island. It was a brave plan to create a spit of dry land that the cows could use as a causeway, but the young children were simply not physically strong enough to complete the work.

'It's very simple,' Caspar said, marching authoritatively forward to Paris's side. 'Someone's got to get wet.'

'But the risk . . .' Paris protested. 'The risk is very high, and look at the speed of the water. If someone fell in there, they would simply be swept away and lost.'

'It's very admirable, I am sure, to be so sensible in youth, but sometimes one has to enjoy a little danger simply to survive. You have to take the risk and get wet. You've done a good job slowing the water down, now surely one of you youths has a big enough sense of adventure to wade in and get to the cows.'

'But what can we do when we get there?' Paris objected.

'You can make them move. The cows will swim.'

'It would not take much for one of them to be swept away.' Paris sounded most unreassured.

Leaf agreed with this and thought Caspar foolhardy. 'Wouldn't it be better to reinforce the dam and slow the water more?'

Caspar shrugged. 'Cows are daft creatures. They might see the dam as solid ground and try and clamber onto it only to become entangled or to tear apart the structure. I say we get them off that island and swimming before the water rises any more.'

'They'll drown,' Paris predicted gloomily.

'Trust me,' Caspar assured him. 'Expect to lose one or two that might stumble, but we'll get the majority across.'

Paris looked at Leaf. 'Is it acceptable to lose one or two?'

Leaf felt as perplexed as Paris looked. They were only children; how were they supposed to be capable of sorting such difficulties? She didn't know what was an acceptable risk and what wasn't; her world had always been organized so that there were no risks, but clearly that had been an illusion. All along they had been at risk of their defences collapsing but simply had never been aware of it. She didn't know what to do and therefore concluded that the most obvious thing was to trust Caspar.

'Let him do it,' she told Paris.

Paris nodded at the Baron. 'All right then, sir. What do we do?'

'The food there in the cart, have some of it tossed down just at the shore. Cattle are greedy beasts. Then have two lines of children at the ready to guide the cattle in the right direction.'

Caspar's plan seemed to Leaf to be appropriate since, as soon as the fodder was forked out, the cattle doubled their bellowing and one or two began to stamp and paw at the water's edge.

The Baron cast his eye over the small children and looked at them in despair until his eye fell on Lug. 'It's you and me, great man of Haol-gar.'

'Why should I get wet for them?' the great man protested.

'Because you want your stone back. Now come on.'

Leaving his heavy cloak on the cart, Caspar marched to the water's edge. 'Paris, get all of these children out of the water. It's very dangerous. You must get them well back and onto higher land.'

'But we can still help if we keep building up the dam,' the boy argued.

'Just get them back!' Caspar insisted, and this time Paris reacted.

Once the children were away from the threat of the rising flood, Caspar headed downstream where tufted bushes were still pushing up through the flood. It was a longer route to the island but Leaf presumed it was shallower. Nevertheless, Caspar was quickly up to his chest, pulling himself from one shrub to the next, heading for the cows. He didn't look back at Lug, and Leaf noted his cunning. If he had turned round to encourage the man, it would have given Lug the excuse to refuse him. Instead Lug was left dithering on the brink and then finally, with a grunt of frustration, waded in, creating a bulging bow wave before his powerful legs.

Caspar and Lug made their way around the back of the cattle and gave out whoops and cries to encourage the beasts into the water. The animals did not of course choose the longer, shallower route but plunged into the deeper flood, heading directly for dry land. Lowing and grunting, their necks strained up to help them breathe as they worked hard to keep afloat in the flood. In the excitement of success, the children all forgot Caspar's order to stay back from the flood and came down to the water's edge to guide the cattle. Leaf joined them.

She looked on anxiously as one or two of the smaller beasts were submerged and then came up again. The cattle were swimming hard and half were now reaching firm footing and charging up the slope towards the trail of fodder.

'Get them right up onto the banked road,' Caspar was crying from the island, his eye constantly flicking towards the bridge. A bow of water curled either side of it, indicating that the channel was blocked. Water flooded sideways and more piled up behind the bridge, climbing its walls. 'All of you get onto high ground!'

'Get back over here now,' Leaf yelled at him. 'Before it's too late.'

She didn't know if he heard her words or whether his own judgement urged him back onto the rickety dam. Leaf was only half-aware that she was already standing in water and that the flood was rising fast. She couldn't hear Caspar above the roar from the river but she could see the Baron was waving her back, urging her to run onto higher ground. Unaware of the cold and forgetful of her own danger, she just knew she could not lose this man. They were children, nothing but helpless children, and, though he was only a man, he was an adult and knew how to take command of a situation.

Why couldn't that wretched Haol-garen take him on his shoulders and get him to safety? The great man had two calves by the neck and was heaving them through the water as he hurried forward with the bulk of the herd. Leaf barely flinched as she watched an old heifer being sucked under by the current and suddenly rushed away; she cared only about Caspar.

Suddenly, there was a tremendous groan and roar from

behind her. She didn't have to look to know that the river had broken over the bridge and that a wall of water two feet high was racing over the flood. He won't make it, was all she thought as the water struck her, sweeping her off her feet and dragging her into its hungry grasp.

It was hopeless. She knew that before the current dragged her under. Overwhelmed by its elemental force, there was nothing she could do in the murky blackness, which churned her around and around, but hope she would be tossed upwards into the air. It was a long time coming. She was weak and disorientated by the dark and the cold and the lack of air. How long she could hold her breath she did not know. In terrified panic, she was dragged along the bottom and then entangled amidst something. It rolled beneath her and, for a second, she was out in the air.

Gasping in air, she flailed her arms in an effort to keep upright, only then realizing that she was entangled in the legs of a dead heifer. She had to get free and, somehow, she had to find the strength to swim and drag herself into shallower, calmer water. At last, she managed to tear herself free of the heifer. Now she was floating with three other carcasses swirling around her. Her long hair swept over her face, blinding her, adding to her panic, but she had no strength to wipe it away and barely strength to keep her arms and legs kicking. Straining back her neck, she sucked in air and spray.

Conserve energy, she thought. Rest and float, spread out your arms and legs and wait for an opportunity.

A wave of water washed over her head but at least it swept her hair back. She looked at grey skies boiling overhead. More rain was coming, she thought, amazed at herself for considering such a thing at a time like this. She spun on and on, the roar from the central river channel horrifyingly loud. She must try and swim away from it into the shallows, she told herself, but soon realized she made no progress whatsoever and so simply resorted to trying to keep herself afloat.

Her legs felt like lead. The revolving water, her exhaustion and the cold disoriented space and time. She could have been here hours but that was unlikely since she estimated her survival time in these conditions was restricted to about half an hour at the most. She would soon be perilously exhausted and then the cold would claim her even if she did manage to keep her head above water. Lights began to dance about her and all she could think was what a waste it all was. She had achieved nothing in her lifetime. She had barely begun to matter in this world and soon all would be over and she would be like the floating cows that had been swept into the water, their once creamy white coats a reddish mud brown in the mud-choked flood.

And then she saw it; downstream and to the left of her was a tree root overhanging a bank. It was her chance; she must take it. Her arms barely made a splash as she flung them forward, one after another, in an attempt to drag herself through the water. Her soaked breeches dragged at her thighs and made movement difficult, but her legs had more strength and she made some progress.

But she had seen the root too late. Already it was obvious that she would be swept past it. In despair, she wished she had faith to pray. If the Great Mother loved her, why wasn't she reaching out to help her now? She was too young to die like this. One last burst of effort and perhaps then she would make it. Fighting off her growing lethargy, she kicked hard, water splashing up over her face, and she swallowed more of the foul stuff. A lucky eddy in the current swept her towards the root and suddenly it was close enough. Stretching forward, she was ready to grab it. She had it now in her fingertips but her grasp was not firm enough as another carcass was swept towards her, buffeting her in the face and drawing her under.

It seemed to take forever for the slow-moving bulk to pass over her and, already exhausted, she was barely conscious when she bobbed to the surface again. Unaware that she now had in her hand a log providing buoyancy, she floated on and away from the salvation of the tree root. The coldness cramped her legs. Hazily, she thought only that the clouds looked strangely nearer than they ought to. Mournfully, she thought of her mother and her father. She missed them horribly and was deeply saddened that now she would never see them again.

Caught in the same current as the dead steer, she was buffeted back and forth between their great flanks. They seemed strangely sympathetic to her, though, nudging her only gently. She knew it was ridiculous to think that of a carcass; no doubt, the exhaustion was producing delusions in her mind. Her fist closed tightly about one of their horns and, as the last of her strength left her, she closed her eyes and let her mind sink into blackness.

Chapter 16

Caspar cursed as he watched the water rising. These poor children, he thought to himself. Poor, sheltered children, they do not even know how to herd cattle. Look at them standing on the edge of the flood!

He found it curious that, although they seemed happy computing the velocity of the water and the surface area of the flood, none of them seemed to understand what that meant in terms of the ferocious, unstoppable, unpredictable power of the spate. It was so powerful yet they stood in its path, worrying about whether a few cattle would be drowned.

'Get back! Get onto higher land!' he yelled, doing his best to clamber over the rickety heap of branches that the children had tried to make into a dam. It had been a good idea, but why hadn't they thought to move the cattle earlier?

Leaf was standing anxiously close to the water. She must surely see that the river was about to burst over the bridge banks. How was it that these people spent their time measuring and assessing but had no true understanding of their environment? He yelled in vain but she seemed unable to hear him. There was nothing more he could do as the water surged over the bridge and rushed down the valley towards him.

'Leaf, get back! Get back!' he yelled furiously but his voice was swept away as the river roared, an arching wall of black power sweeping all before it.

With horror, he saw Leaf swept under as if she had been no more than parchment. There would be the barest of seconds before the wave was on him. Knowing that his chance of survival depended on making the best use of his strength and energy, he turned to face the wave, determined not to be dragged under by it. His instinct was to make himself shaped like a cormorant so that the water would have less drag on him, so enabling him to push himself up through the wave. Leaf had been taken by surprise and probably hadn't even had time to draw in breath before the mighty force overwhelmed her.

The bore of water slammed into him. Breath held, he did his best to dive into it, aware of the horrifying pace at which he was swept downstream. He never touched the bottom and was never dragged down amongst the rolling rocks that now scoured the meadows beneath the flood. Kicking upwards, he quickly found air. His task now was to stay afloat and, rather than fight the current, look for a stream that would steer him into still waters. Working hard with his arms, he scanned ahead and noted how the water divided around a huge tree that was still standing despite the pressure of water on its trunk.

The river curving to either side of the tree was moving too ferociously to allow him a chance to cling to the trunk but, so long as he could get to the left side of the nearest tree, the current would sweep him into a slower pool beyond. Once there, he might work his way to the inside curve of the river where the current was slowest. Then he might have the strength to swim out.

He battled furiously. Everything depended on crossing to the left before that tree. He had to make it, otherwise he would be swept to the right and sucked into the maelstrom.

He had to make it! He had to make it for Rollo. His son would never cope without him. However, it was the vision of his daughter willing him on that gave him that last ounce of strength. He imagined her reaching out with pleading arms, calling out to him that she missed him. His heart went out to her; she was such a tiny little thing with the weighty responsibility of an entire realm on her back, and he loved her just as much as he loved Rollo. He felt guilty that he had left Imogen behind, but he could not leave her or Rollo alone in this world.

The water buffeted him. Debris, sticks and dead animals caught up in the path of the swollen river knocked him, draining his strength. He concentrated on his arms, willing them to haul him through the water, willing them forward time and time again. Then there was nothing he could do as the current grabbed him and he was rushed towards the tree, swept under a silver stream of churning water, scraped over the bark of the tree and then hurled beyond. He didn't know which side of the tree he had passed until gentle waves caressed him and he was suddenly lying in still water. With little strength left, he drifted to the edge and crawled onto the bank where he flopped into the mud.

'Sweet Mother Earth, thank you,' he murmured. 'Thank you for not making my children orphans.'

He tried to push from his mind the fear that Rollo may have already run into troubles of his own but consoled himself with the knowledge that, at least, Brid was with him. Thank you, Mother, for Brid, he thought, wishing more strongly than ever that he could look up and see her now. He needed her strength and conviction. Somehow he had to find a way to help Isolde and, to do it, he had to bring this infant nation to some state of self-sufficiency just so that they could reach the elite scholars in the city. The task was impossible. Even Leaf had not had the sense to head for high ground. And where was she now?

In the back of his mind, he saw over and over again the image of her being swallowed by the water. He wondered sorrowfully if she had ever risen again. Poor Leaf. He had to find her either way. He was relying on Brid to look after his son and on a seneschal to take care of his daughter; he must be strong enough to take care of Leaf. His sense of fairness told him that, if he could do everything in his power to look after this little girl, perhaps the Great Mother would repay him by keeping his children safe. Besides, he had grown very fond of Leaf.

Staggering to his feet, he looked back at the flood, realizing how very lucky he was to be alive. Leaf was not nearly as strong as he was and had not been prepared for the first impact. He decided, therefore, that it was most likely she had been swept downstream of him. Time was what mattered now. If she were still alive, she needed help fast.

Caspar shook himself. Brid, give me strength, he prayed, realizing instantly that he was praying to the priestess and not the Great Mother herself. Guiltily, he had the horrible notion that Hal might be able to perceive his thoughts. How could he do this to his uncle after he had looked after Torra Alta all these years? Perhaps he deserved to be as despised as his son so obviously felt.

Biting his lip, he heaved himself to his legs only to find they crumpled beneath him. Taking a deep breath, he forced himself up again and staggered on, his need to find Leaf driving out the cold. He could hear cattle lowing upstream of him and hoped that most of the children were safe, busying themselves with the animals.

'Leaf!' he shouted. 'Leaf, where are you?'

She could be on either bank. He needed a vantage point from which to view the flood. She must be somewhere in all this sorry debris. He tried desperately to persuade himself that, although the girl was obviously not as strong as he was, she was very sharp-witted and surely would have clung to a log and stirred herself to more tranquil waters. After all, he had managed to think and work out a way to the edge. Hope spurred him on. He couldn't believe that such an innocent child, who had all her life to live, was dead.

He hurried along the muddy banks, soggy grass dragging at his feet as he went. Breathlessly, he came to a bare tree and scrambled up the boughs. From here he had a better view, but nothing he saw gave him hope. Dead animals lay upturned and bobbing in the shallows. Sheep, pigs, goats and one or two cows clogged the banks. Uprooted trees raced through the central flow or snagged on other branches and grasses, forming a raft for smaller creatures struggling to survive the flood.

But there was no sign of Leaf. He tried to force from his

mind the reality that, even if she were still alive, she would be impossible to find. Perhaps she had been washed even further downstream. He raced on, hurrying past a bullock that was heaving itself onto the bank, slimy mud pouring from its flanks. He raced on to the next tree, which he partially climbed to gain a better view, and on to the next and the next until he was exhausted.

Looking helplessly up and down the river, he realized that he was half-blinded by the rain. Had he missed her or had she been swept on further? He had to make a decision and there was no way of knowing what was the right thing to do. Should he go on or go back and search the banks again? He knew that if she were on the far bank he had very little hope of finding her. There was no way to make the decision and so he decided to let fate make it for him though he knew that Leaf would not approve of such an unscientific method. He reached for a flat pebble at his feet and scratched one surface with the rune ᚱ Rad, the rune of the seeker, which Morrigwen, the crone before Keridwen, had designated as his symbol. He decided that if the rune fell face up it was a sign that he should go on and search further, but if the rune fell facing towards the earth he should return.

He tossed the pebble into the air. It fell rune down. Compliantly, Caspar turned on his heel and began retracing his steps, though at the back of his mind he was terrified that he was now turning his back on Leaf. Hauling himself up a tree he had climbed earlier, he searched the surface of the water again. Oh, Great Mother, please don't let me be wrong, he prayed, looking into the flood for any signs of where a helpless body might float. She could be under any one of those rafts of debris. Staring at the fast flow of the river at the centre of the flood, which was lined by dark, angry whirlpools, he still thought it most likely that she had been pulled under by the current.

He climbed the next tree, this time trusting the higher branches to bear his weight. Again, he could see nothing but more hogs being swept away in the flood. He hoped they weren't Lug's pigs. Then something caught his eye. He could see the back end of a cow drifting in the slow current of the water. The front end was obscured by a bush. It was a section he had not scanned. Hastily, he slithered down the wet bark of the tree and staggered towards the bush to see that it stood over a small pool, which had trapped a number of carcasses.

Hope driving him on, he slithered down towards the water. The pool had been formed by an uprooted tree. The hollow was deep and sheer sided and so it was difficult to approach. However, he could see that three cows, bloated and belly up, had been trapped in the pool along with a mat of straw and twigs. A weasel was swimming like a snake through the water and clambering up onto a cow. Long strands of wispy straw trailed out with the current. Forlornly, Caspar turned to go on with his wretched search. He had hoped she was there, but she was not.

But the moment his back was turned on the pool a thought struck him; it wasn't straw, it was hair, long, brown, mud-clogged hair. Without further hesitation he plunged foot first into the water and found himself submerged up to his chest. With enormous effort, he pushed past the cows and grabbed the hair. As the mud slid off, it revealed an ashen white face, water dribbling from the lips.

'Oh, Leaf,' he moaned. 'Poor, sweet Leaf.' He tried to lift her but saw she was caught with her sleeve hooked over the cow's horn. 'Oh, Leaf, I'm so sorry! I was too slow finding you. I'm so sorry!'

Unhooking her arms, he pulled her to him, wiping the hair back from her face. She felt cold and there were no signs of life coming from her tiny body. He could not climb up the steep bank but was forced to wade out into the shallows again.

At last, the ground shelved gently towards the dry land of the meadow and he dragged her out behind him. With the rain lashing down and in the dimming light, it was impossible to see if she were breathing or not. He tried pumping her arms and pressing on her chest but no water spewed from her mouth.

Still not knowing whether she was alive or not, he hoisted her up onto her back and began to run as best he could upstream, back towards Paris and his followers. He was too weak to do anything more than jog a few paces and then walk and then jog again as he stumbled through the heavy ground. Leaf's arms dangled down behind him and thumped against his legs but he hoped the movement and position might at least help to drain any water from her lungs.

Staggering with exhaustion, he was beginning to doubt whether he would make it when, at last, he saw Lug striding towards him. The great man stooped down and lifted Leaf from his arms and hurried with her to the ruined temple where Paris and his miserable band of children had retreated. Stiff with cold and weak with exhaustion, Caspar hurried after him, but by the time he got to the huddle of frightened children Leaf was already being tended.

At least these people of the hidden realm needed no help or direction when faced with a drowned body. They stripped off her clothes, got her warm and were busily breathing into her mouth. This they kept up for some time while others prepared potions that they dribbled down her throat.

Caspar felt sick. He couldn't bear to look at her lying there like a rag doll while they pummelled her body in an attempt to make it work. Collapsing by the fire, he could do no more than stare into the flames and was dimly aware that one of the young girls was drying him with a rag and trying to persuade him to get out of his wet clothes.

But it was only when he heard a croaking grown from Leaf that he found the strength to comply and allow his shirt to be pulled off his back. They rubbed him vigorously and wrapped him in blankets while another child pressed a warm cup of broth in his hands. All the while he stared at Leaf's white body, hoping and praying she would make another sound.

In the outside of the circle the elders in their array of black feathers pressed close and cawed, 'Death! Death! It comes. The ravens croak death!'

'No,' Caspar moaned to himself. No, he would not let it happen, not to Leaf, not to Rollo and Imogen, and not to Isolde. They were the children; they were the future. His generation may have made a horrible mess of their lives and the world but they had to make sure the children lived.

Chapter 17

It was good to be on the road again. The cramping despair that had filled Hal's soul was already leaving him as, ahead of the troop of twenty men, he guided his horse down the slippery stretches of the Tor road. Even with studs screwed into the shoes of these sure-footed beasts, the descent was still dangerous; many animals had been known to fall on the steep track. The dogs, however, were untroubled by the ice. The hounds had already run ahead, yelping excitedly, anticipating a hunt. The two Ophidian terriers, however, were trotting smartly beside him, aware of the sense of occasion. It was as if they understood that the foolish hounds had been duped.

He would not look round for fear of catching Brannella's eye. He had not known what to say when he had bidden her farewell but only hugged her close and felt the silent tears roll down his cheek to dampen her soft black hair. Forcing a composed expression to his stubbled face, he had managed to pull back from her, smile and find a few words. 'Be good, my precious daughter, and look after Keridwen; she needs your help.'

He had looked at the old Crone, her eyes meeting his. It was strange to think that it was Caspar's mother who had given him so much support and held him together over the last few months. 'Look after yourself too,' he had said, not able to say more.

She had smiled. 'We've become good friends over the years, Hal. The time I would have spent with my son circumstances have stolen from me, but you have made up for much of that loss.' She had nodded at him, telling him he should go now.

Hal had stabbed his heels into the ribby sides of his horse, desperate not to look back as his daughter wailed for him not to leave her. It was no good looking back, no good telling her that she was safest with Keridwen. Ever since her mother had been stolen away, Brannella had spent the nights sobbing in Hal's arms and, although he knew that now she would cry against Keridwen's bosom, the thought of his child's grief pained him deeply. But he had to go; he had to get food through to them, otherwise they would not live to see the spring.

He looked up into the dark sky that had blown in with the dawn; a ghost of a moon still haunted the heavens and flitted out between threatening clouds. Over the last decade, it had been hard to head out into the Yellow Mountains for fear of the great queen dragon, whose golden wings had too often blotted out the sun as she stooped out of the skies to harry the castle. But he had seen her only inter-mittently over the last couple of months, and lately not at all.

Lieutenant Piperol caught his gaze. 'Do you think she's finally been slain?'

'Pip, the day someone fells the dragon is the day I ask the Captain to hang up his boots and promote you.'

'We all know the Captain will still be running Torra Alta long after we've all gone; besides, an old grouch like you isn't going to promote a woodsman's boy like myself.' The Lieutenant spoke with his usual humour and audacity.

'You know, Pip, every year you've grown bigger and taken on the trappings of a man, your mind has grown smaller. I don't know how I tolerate you.'

'You know,' Pip retorted confidently.

Hal scowled at him but refused to answer. Of course he knew. Pip was the one who took his mind off his troubles; Pip was the one who told him straight how things really were; Pip was the one who judged him as a man and not as the warden of Torra Alta, which was why he, in turn, judged Pip as man and not as an underling.

'Where do you suppose she's gone to, then?' Pip returned their conversation to the dragon.

Hal shrugged. 'It's impossible to say. Perhaps she's found better pickings elsewhere. All I know now is that she wasn't all bad for us. I know she took her fair share of horses, but at least she kept the ravenshrikes away. They are worse.' He sighed deeply, thinking how he was leaving his daughter at the castle to face that nightly attack. 'Perhaps I should have brought her with me,' he said quietly to himself and only realized his words were audible when Pip gave him a hard, thoughtful look.

'It would be easy for me to say you are doing the right thing, that she is safe with Keridwen and that you have no choice, but none of us really knows. What we do know is that all in Torra Alta will starve, including Brannella, unless we get supplies in. All other attempts have failed. It is a difficult task and the men need your leadership; no one else can do it. The Captain, as we all know, is as capable as you are of running Torra Alta, but he lacks your experience in the field. You have to go and you can do that job better without Brannella sitting on your horse's withers.'

Hal nodded. 'You are right, Pip,' he said with a heavy sigh as they began the steep climb up the western wall of the canyon, his horse blowing hard with the effort. He lent forward to help the animal and braced his shoulders as his resolve hardened. He had made a decision and would go forward with it wholeheartedly. It was the right and the best thing to do and he would not give it a further moment's thought. His mind instantly returned to his missing loved ones.

'Brid, my love,' he murmured into the thick ruff of fur pulled tight around his neck. 'Be safe, wherever you are.' He did not share Keridwen's sixth sense on the matter but he did trust her when she said that Brid was alive. Keridwen, however, did not have the same ability to sense the young boys. She had explained that her very close ties with Brid and her blood ties with her son enabled her to sense their vitality in the atmosphere, but she did not possess such skills of divination where everybody was concerned. Hal was reassured by her conviction. Keridwen was convinced of Brid and Caspar's continuing existence and, if they were alive, there was surely hope for the boys.

He turned his attention back to the journey, knowing that the moment they breached the brim of the canyon wall the bitter west wind would be hard in his face. The climb was tough on the horses but they had taken their time to spare the underfed beasts. The sudden chill of the wind was going to be equally hard on all of them. He called a halt just prior to the summit of the zigzagging road, which cut its way back and forth into the hard surface of the rock. Like the road up to the Tor, it was reinforced in places with platforms and buttresses to allow for a little foothold on what was a near precipice.

Carefully dismounting, he moved to his horse's head and pulled a cloth down around its nostrils to shield it from the wind. In this way, he hoped that the animal wouldn't suddenly be sucking freezing air into its lungs. He did the same for himself, tugging a silk scarf up over his mouth and nose and pulling down a heavy bearskin hat over his brow and ears; now all that looked out into the icy winter were his two olive-green eyes.

Even so, as they clambered up over the top of the canyon wall, Hal had to thrust himself forward onto his horse's withers for fear of being swept off the saddle. Once up, he pressed forward, making room for the twenty men behind. The blizzard stung his eyes and pierced his thick cloak so that his old wounds ached. Gritting his teeth, he forced his horse on into the bleak mountain landscape, seeking a sheltered route. They had a very hard ride ahead of them.

The golden brown of the bare rocks pushed up like ribs through the ripples of snow caught in the crevasses between.

'Of course, it's not the best time of year to follow the old miners' roads through to the sulphur mines,' Pip stated the obvious, his eye still casting nervously up into the sky for any sign of the golden queen.

Hal followed his gaze. 'I know. You're remembering the last time you tried to get through: impassable by day because of the dragon and impassable by night because of the ravenshrikes.'

Pip nodded. 'Do you think Ceowulf is still waiting for us on the coast?'

As the wind suddenly swirled and swung up out of the valley ahead, Hal instinctively raised his arm to shield his face. 'Don't ask such damn fool questions,' he snarled. Even his teeth were now stinging in the wind and he was suffering from too much discomfort to be civil. He didn't, of course, know the answer and was therefore extremely irritated to be asked it by the irrepressible lieutenant.

It was a couple of months back that Ceowulf had sent messengers saying he would be bringing supply ships north to them from Caldea via the western coast of Torra Alta. Hal had been grateful for the news but had been thwarted on several occasions in attempts to reach Ceowulf. The winter months had meant that the mountains were impassable and so, for weeks, there had been no hope of getting supplies through. Now was his chance. Hobs, ravenshrikes and the golden dragon had all made it impossible to venture out west. Only a few skilled men at a time, with the ability to travel like ghosts through the dark, had been able to inform him that, two weeks ago, Ceowulf's ships were anchored offshore. The harbour was blocked by ice and so they could not reach land. Now, after a week of warmer weather, the ice should have retreated, the dragon had mysteriously gone and the hobs were concentrating their attack on his southern borders.

How long Ceowulf would wait he did not know, but believed in his heart that his old friend would give him more than a fair chance to reach the ships. The going was slow through the mountains and the enfeebled horses were depleted of stamina. As a result they had spent two miserable nights huddled into disused bear caves, their clothes soaked by the slush and listening to the mountains groan and rumble with avalanches caused by the sudden thaw conditions. Come dawn, the men's eyes dark with lack of sleep, they only marched on because Pip goaded them with taunts of being unable to keep up with him. On the third day, they finally saw the sea.

That day the moist cloud, which had warmed the earth over the last week with a false promise of an early spring, had moved on. Tiny sparkles of snow glistened in an otherwise crystal blue sky. The air Hal breathed in was sharp through his nostrils and cramped the warm depths of his lungs.

'It's peaceful up here,' he told Pip rather than saying exactly what was on his mind. A year ago even, he would have chatted to all the men, trying to learn more about them. He would have been genuinely interested, but he also knew it helped them bond to him so that they would follow him anywhere. Now he could only tolerate Pip's company. Pip was the only one who could possibly understand the depths of his grief.

'Hmm . . .' Pip frowned quizzically at him as if wondering what was really on his mind. 'That's a bit like hearing a battle raging outside your window while crawling down to the bottom of your featherdown bed and sighing, "Ah it's cosy and quiet in here."'

Hal gave him a half-hearted smile. 'You think I'm just pulling the blankets up over my head?' He laughed at the idea. 'No, no, you missed my point, Pip. It is peaceful up here. I know that the world's in turmoil and that we struggle every minute now for our very existence, but do these timeless mountains care? They stretch up to the sky, drinking the heat from the sun, and care nothing of our manic scrabble for survival. They are tranquil, harmonious, timeless.'

'You've been married to Brid too long.' Pip laughed though his voice trailed away as he realized what he had said.

Hal glared at him, his eyes darkening, then he tossed back his head and sniffed. Pip had meant no harm; he knew that. He gritted his teeth hard, struggling to hold down his explosive emotions. Where was she? Where was his Brid and where was his boy? Looking up towards the sun, he wondered whether the great fiery globe was also warming their faces. How was he ever going to live without them? What would he do if he never found them again?

Slowly, it dawned on him that the men were watching him, waiting for his word to move on, their horses taking the opportunity to snatch at the meagre strands of grass struggling to grow in the shelter of the rocks. It was strange, he thought. Before he had lost his family he would have seen every detail of their faces, matched every face to a name, but now they all looked alike. He wondered whether they noted his indifference, but didn't really care any more.

'Onward!' he ordered, his tone grave as he controlled the emotion in his voice.

His horse stepped forward simply at the word of his command, as did the two Ophidian terriers that flanked him. He liked their stolid company and they were excellent guard dogs, but he had brought them along mostly because of their devotion to Brid. They pined for her and he hoped that, if by chance Brid was out this way, they might be able to pick up her scent. It was a forlorn hope, but he thought anything was worth a try. The blunt-nosed terriers had a curious sense of ceremony and marched out with his horse, their company far more bearable than that of any human.

They rode on down into the next valley and up towards the next pass where, suddenly, the sea seemed very much closer, a rippling gust skimming over its oily blue-black surface. The dogs stopped at the rise, each with one foot raised and ears laid flat as they sniffed the air. There was still no sign of Ceowulf's ships nor of anything untoward, and Hal wondered what they had smelt.

'There's a storm coming,' Pip said flatly.

'Are you telling me that being promoted to lieutenant has boosted your sense of divination as well as your pride?'

'Ha, bloody ha!' Pip was not crushed by such taunts. 'I was watching the dogs.'

'Hmm,' Hal said doubtfully though a few minutes later, when the horses began to press their ears back anxiously, he wondered exactly what it was that the animals sensed. He ordered the men forward while he turned off the track and urged his horse up towards a nearby peak to gain a clear vantage point over the land. He slipped from his horse and climbed to the summit of the rocky peak on foot, keeping low so that his outline was not obvious. He looked towards the sea and, at last, glimpsed the tip of three tall masts, the rest of the ship obscured from view by the land. Ceowulf had been true to his word. At least one ship was waiting for them.

Slowly, Hal scanned the landscape. Northwards, he could see across the Boarchase Forest towards Vaalaka. Southwards, he could see only the golden peaks of the Yellow Mountains and the outline of a lone wolf standing on a peak similar to the one he had chosen. The view east was the same though he glimpsed a small herd of deer bounding down the back of one slope, leaping one after another over a stream and then hurrying onwards as if pressed by some predator. Other than that there was nothing of note to see. Hal looked back out towards the sea, scanning the dark waters, wary that he could not actually see the coastline.

Shielding his eyes from the glare of the bright sky, he looked across the sea towards the horizon and blinked. Pip had been right; a dark line of cloud had formed at the edge of the world. He stared at it, watching as it slowly became fractionally bigger. The storm was rolling across the waves towards them.

Hal hurried back to his horse. Bad weather was never a good time to unload cargo from a ship. Bad weather was never a good time to be around ships at all; they had to get to the ships before the storm hit.

Each time they rose up the next fold in the landscape to spy the sea afresh, the dark storm on the horizon had swelled, large billowing clouds hungrily swallowing the sea as they advanced. The ship below them had only just spied the storm, which would not have been visible from their lower line of sight. Sails were being unfurled in haste and Hal guessed they were about to weigh anchor and seek refuge. It was only now, when no further peaks separated them from the sea, that he realized the three-masted ship was not alone but had an entourage of smaller vessels. He had thought the three masts he had seen were those of Ceowulf's supply ship but, in fact, it was a Ceolothian battleship. Smaller traders, bearing Ceowulf's colours, were huddled around her skirts like nervous ducklings. Another warship was scudding in from the south, the topsails catching the higher breeze, whereas the lower sails flapped and billowed where the air was still calm nearer the sea.

Hal sent one of his men to climb the nearest peak to see if he could anticipate where the ships were heading. Out of breath, he soon returned, pointing northward.

'There's a small island with a sheltered beach on its eastern, leeward side. It would give them good shelter and hopefully keep them off the cliffs.'

Hal and his men cut north, skirting the peaks, their horses stumbling on the uneven ground. Immediately, Hal was aware of the eyes of wolves on their backs as they came off the track and was glad that the bears would still be underground, hibernating in their dens.

Although they could see the storm approaching, it still came as a shock to witness how quickly its shadow struck the coastal waters. The placid sea turned black before their eyes as the front crashed across the shallow waters, plucking white demons out of the waves that thrashed at one another. The noise of the wind howling across the sea was suddenly all about them, pounding their ears. Hal tucked his head down into his cloak as the fingers of the gale raked through his hair and pierced his clothing, the biting cold droplets of seawater being swept up in the angry wind. Streaks of rain lashed inland, stinging their faces. The horses curled their heads down low to try and hide from it, and the dogs barked in excited defiance.

'There are devils in the air,' one of the older men grumbled loudly, though his voice was snatched away.

His fingers stiff with cold on the reins, Hal urged his horse down towards the cliffs which protected Belbidia from the

317

pounding onslaught of the sea. They too must find shelter and wait the storm out, he decided. After descending from the bare rocks of the upper mountains, they found themselves in the gentler, coastal foothills, which were clad in trees growing at an angle from the fierce battering of previous gales. They did, however, stifle the wind a little and keep out much of the rain.

Cold and hungry, they ventured into the heart of the woods and found a twisting gully set low that would protect them from the worst of the storm. Hal tried to sleep. He was forced to share his makeshift pillow with one of the incorrigible terriers, which refused to understand that he was only a dog and that the bare ground ought to be good enough for him. With little tolerance left in him nowadays, Hal thought to pay the dog a lesson but then decided he just didn't have the energy. Besides, the arrogant brute was warm and that was at least some comfort.

He closed his eyes, wishing it were Brid's warmth pressed against his cheek. Only utter exhaustion allowed him to sleep and he fell into a deep dreamless slumber from which it is so hard to wake. However, he was awoken abruptly by his canine pillow leaping up and barking furiously. Hal started up, staring into the blackness and blinking hard, his heart in his throat as he struggled to make sense of what had alarmed the dog. The men were stirring around him and he was pleased to see that their training had served them well since they were up and booted, their weapons in hand. In seconds, they had formed a closed ring about the fire.

Both terriers had set up a frantic barking that made it impossible for Hal to think. The hounds were standing dutifully, ears pricked and silent. Just as he had so often desired before, Hal wished the terriers would be a little less raucous. He put a hand on both dogs and called them to heel. Miraculously, they calmed and stood behind his legs. Once the dogs were quiet, it was still very difficult to hear anything beyond the roar and moans of the wind and the rattling branches all about that were taking a thrashing from the storm. Hal strained to listen but it was Pip who heard something first.

'I can hear voices . . . cries,' he announced softly.

Hal strained harder and at last heard very faint snatches of voices on the wind.

'They're cries for help,' Pip said with concern.

'It's impossible to tell.' Hal immediately dismissed the assumption.

Pip gave him one of those cold, disapproving looks that a subordinate had no right to give his lord, though Hal was not angered by Pip but rather admired him for his courage in standing up to him.

'I just know it is,' the young man told him. 'You've been knocked on the head too many times to hear as sharply as you might once have done.'

'And you haven't?' Hal retorted. 'I should have you strung up for your insolence.'

'If you were going to do that you would have done it years ago.'

'Does anyone else hear cries for help?' Hal asked the twenty men in the troop. A number shook their heads but others asserted that they may have done but it was so hard to tell with the wind in their ears. The dogs, however, were alert and nervous and Hal was persuaded that Pip was probably right.

'It's coming from the shore; that I can tell for certain,' Pip told him.

'Right, men; let's pack up and investigate,' Hal ordered.

One of the men looked nervously west in the direction of the sea. 'What if it's sirens luring us into the water?'

'Well, if you are stupid enough to be lured into dangerous water by the sound of someone singing, then you deserve such a fate,' Hal scoffed at the ridiculous idea.

The soldier was now muttering to one of his fellows. 'They could be like those women of Ash. There's men what would give up their lives for one night with one of them women.'

Hal let the men mumble and mutter on; he wasn't in the

319

least interested. He only knew that those supply ships were just offshore and that the cries for help had probably come from them. He knew lives were being lost; he instinctively sensed it from the dogs' reaction, the way the hounds laid back their ears as if pained and the way the terriers were overexcited. They always got that way if murder was in the air, whether it was a hog being hunted or someone trying to swat a fly. Stiff-legged, bristles up along their spines and lips pared back, they were ready to face the harvesters of death.

As they neared the edge of the wood, Hal could feel the wind twisting and spiking through the branches to lift the hair off his face. It was very black within the cover of the trees, so black in fact that they needed torches to light their way. As soon as they broke out into the open, the fierce wind blew out four of their seven torches and Hal immediately buried his head in his sleeve in order to breathe as the wind snatched his breath away. It was now clear that the voices were real and were desperate cries for help. The screams made the hairs on his back prickle with fearful anticipation. It was one thing to die bravely in battle but quite another to be pummelled to death on cliffs by an enraged sea.

The horses squealed and many of the men were having extreme difficulty urging their animals on into the storm.

'I'll go on alone,' Pip volunteered.

Hal shook his head. 'No, we'll leave the horses here with two men and the rest of us will proceed on foot.'

Shoulders into the wind and arms raised to protect their faces from the horizontal rain and salt spray whipped up off the sea, they advanced on the roar of the waves, which was threaded through with the shrill cries. Hal stopped abruptly as he thought he caught sight of a flash in the corner of his eye. He had been looking hard ahead and so couldn't be certain of what he had or hadn't seen. Most probably it was a bolt of lightning, he told himself, though he knew he had not yet heard a clap of thunder.

Days out in brutal weather had depleted his strength. He

wished so much that he could be anywhere but here. His face was stripped bare by the wind, the fingers on his right hand so painfully cold he was beginning to fear he would not be able to draw his sword if he needed it.

On reaching the brink of the cliff, they looked out on the dark swirling mass of the sea below, the sound of the waves deafening as they boomed and smashed against the rocks. Hal could barely see for the stinging rain and had to crouch down and grip hold of the woody heather clinging to the cliff top to prevent himself being swept inland. It was very near dawn now and, even as he thought it, he sensed the grey of the morning sun seeping into the furious black of the storm.

The yells became more distinct, clearly discernible as cries for help from men below. But Hal could not yet see them in the gloom, not until there was another sudden flash of light. He leaped back in sudden alarm. Somewhere, from a point in space out from the cliff, a creature had spat fire.

He blinked, unsure of what to make of it. The brief flash of light had revealed men clinging to the cliffs, screaming in terror as the flames lapped at them. But he had not been looking at the source of the flame and he stared out into space, his hands shielding his stinging eyes.

'What the hell was that?' Pip demanded.

The rest of the men sounded fearful. 'It has to be the dragon. She's returned,' one gasped in horror, though Hal was glad to see that none of them shrank back.

'Silence!' he snarled. 'It's not her.' He did not bother to explain how he knew it was not a dragon. For a dragon to fly through the cool of night was an arduous task since there were no rising heat thermals as there would be during the warmth of the day. Certainly, if they were to fly at night they would not spit fire because their already drained strength would be dangerously depleted. However, knowing it was not the dragon made him feel no more at ease since he still had no idea what creature was out there.

'You there!' He pointed at three of his men. 'The moment that creature lights up the sky, take it out.'

The men readied their bows. They waited perhaps another thirty seconds, listening to the shrieks of terror and cries for help from below. Then the creature roared out flame again and they loosed their arrows into the dark. With such a ferocious wind against them it was difficult to hold a true aim, but at least one of the arrows must have hit the mark because the creature screamed in pain.

The winged beast seemed to be falling away and it was joined by more screams of terror. Both ended in a sudden thud.

Hal breathed deeply. The creature was gone and now all he had to do was worry about rescuing the poor souls on the cliff face beneath him. But there was only a moment's respite before, out of the blackness of the storm, came another high-pitched scream of attack. He knew that sound, as did his men. They reacted instantly. Precarious as they were on the cliff face, they stood boldly upright so that they could properly defend themselves from the ravenshrikes' ear-splitting attack.

But the ravenshrikes did not aim for the Torra Altans. Instead, they swooped downwards to the poor wretches below who must have been washed ashore from a floundering ship. Suddenly silent, their black forms invisible in the inkiness below, Hal could not locate them. He stared into the darkness, hearing only the whoosh and thump of their wing beats. Then suddenly the cliff face below was lit up by three streams of flame.

He started. In the red light he could see the dark outline of bridled ravenshrikes as they screamed and shrieked in terror, forced to hold their positions by men riding on their backs. The burst of flame spat out again, scattering the ravenshrikes, and Hal saw among their number huge leathery-skinned birds with vast beaks. He had no idea what they might be but was even more astounded to see that the fire was not coming from them but from the smaller creatures clinging to harness tied to the creatures' breasts. Fire was spitting from the throats of men. Once the flames abated, the blackness was cut by the bloodcurdling shrieks of attacking ravenshrikes. Men howled in pain and Hal could only imagine that the great birds were plucking them off the cliff face.

It was a long night. Hal was deeply frustrated that he could do little to help since, without two hands, he could not draw a bow. His men slaved tirelessly, sending their arrows into the darkness to pick out the winged beasts; the ravenshrikes mocked them while the winged reptiles carried their flaming burdens towards the cliff face.

Dawn brought some respite as the ravenshrikes retreated, clearly exhausted by the effort of being airborne for so long. Only then was it possible to drive away the fearful reptiles.

As the grey light rippled out across the beach and the rains eased, the Torra Altans were able to see what devastation had been wreaked by the storm. Numb to the whimpering cries for help, Hal looked out at the black rags of men lying washed up on the beach below, their limbs still being tugged to and fro by the waves. A broken ship lay on its side in shallow waters, tattered sails like the ragged standard of a fallen army fluttering in the last gusts of the retreating storm.

But it was not the misery of the ship's crew that so alarmed Hal, nor the sight of three other vessels which appeared to be in trouble. It was the spectacle of another half a dozen smaller, high-prowed vessels, some already wrecked on the cliffs and others scudding southward, that raised his fears. They were not ships from any of the neighbouring countries of the Caballan Sea; they were ships blown here by the storm, ships blown from the west. He stared at the armada of small black-painted ships with red masts and sails. Three of their number lay heaped one up against the other where the storm had thrown them up onto the rocks. Running the length of the entire beach, where one might expect to see a line of seaweed and driftwood, was a line of broken bodies. Hobs, men, giant winged reptiles and a few ravenshrikes lay tangled in their own harnesses.

Hal sat, breathing hard. Belbidia was being attacked from the west.

His mind was still racing over the implications of this as his mouth began to set his men in motion. 'Get these men up off the cliff. They need shelter and warmth. Get them up now!'

He looked down at the cliff and the impossible face of rock that the shipwrecked men were attempting to scale. All of them were in a terrible state and, even as he watched, one slipped and fell to a messy death on the boulders below. There was actually little that could be done to help except offer them encouragement.

Hal sent Pip and half his men to find a safe route down to the shore as it was obvious now in the morning light that the cliffs dipped to their right and they were bound to find a shelving path. 'Gather up any living on the beach and help any lower down on the cliff that you can,' Hal ordered gruffly. 'What a bloody mess!'

He did his best to help but, with only one hand, he was painfully aware that he was not in the best position to haul enfeebled men to safety. 'Hobs on the beach,' he murmured to himself, his lips chapped from the wind and salt spray. Hobs and men, he considered the situation. Hobs and men in the same boats – in foreign boats that had been run ashore by the storm. Men who performed the incredible feat of spitting fire. Perhaps it was only an illusion. Perhaps they had canisters strapped to their backs from which they sprayed out kerosene or paraffin? He had heard of armies that had used flame-throwers though it was a practice not employed in the Caballan because of the high risk to those that deployed them. But he had sworn he had seen with his own eyes the fire spitting from the men's mouths just as if they had been dragons. He had never heard of any other animal besides a dragon that could perform such a thing.

'Brid,' he murmured, 'my sweet Brid. You would know. How am I meant to make sense of this anarchy without you?'

After hauling themselves up the cliff, half a dozen men

324

now lay at his feet, spluttering, gasping and trembling weakly. Several would be dead within hours simply from the burns, though one or two looked like they might survive. Hal looked down at them. Poor wretches. He even considered it would be a kindness to save them from the misery of a slow death, but he knew he could not do that. Even if it were the right thing to do, it would destroy the morale of the rest of the men.

Feeling sick to his stomach, he knelt down to help the man nearest to him and peeled back his jacket only for the flesh to simply come away with the cloth. He pressed it back. A high dose of poppy juice was what was needed. It would at least give the man ease through his last moments.

The saddest thing of all was to watch the very strongest of these men, who had struggled through the fierce storm and climbed highest up the cliff, die from the burns. Hal could almost have wept for them if it weren't for that fact he was still silently weeping for himself. How could he shoulder the burden of others' suffering when he could not even stand the weight of his own? Without Brid, without his family he was a desiccated carcass.

The sun did much to help those who were saved that day. The wretched moaning gradually eased as the worst afflicted finally died and the ones who were going to live found the strength to be silent. Hal organized them into camps and set some of his men to building fires. Others brought fresh water from a stream and Hal now saw that his next task was to feed the two score men whom he had saved. It was a large crew for three ships, and he was puzzled by their number. He could only presume they were sent as reinforcements.

Following Pip, he descended onto the beach. The hobs were all dead – drowned by the sea. He had never seen so many dead hobs at one time and concluded that they were poor swimmers. There were also a huge number of crates floating in the water. Several mules and donkeys lay amongst the hobs and he spied a herd of them still alive, huddled up against the rocks and munching on seaweed.

'Get the mules up onto the grass above,' he ordered one of his men. He then looked at the drowned donkeys. 'But wait. Load a couple with those dead donkeys first.' He clicked his fingers and pointed at the drowned animals. 'Get the beasts gutted and skinned down here to ease the weight, then we'll have them cooked on the fires above.'

No one wrinkled their noses at the thought of donkey meat. They were all too hungry and weary to be offended. When as much order as possible had been brought to ease the chaos, Hal climbed back up the rocky path to the cliff top to learn what he could from the sailors. Grey-faced, shivering and clearly in shock, they sat in isolation, all sense of comradeship gone. For a moment their gloom overcame Hal and he sat, head down, wishing that someone would lift this burden from him. All those years ago, Caspar had simply upped and left with his young wife and left him responsible for something that wasn't his and couldn't even be handed down to his son. He was sick and tired of the responsibility and hated the world for what it had thrust on him. It was he and Brid who should have had the freedom to roam the world in carefree fashion, released from their onerous duties, but life was never that kind.

It was Pip who stirred his spirits. The young lieutenant was tough on the shipwrecked men, ordering them to shape up and to provide representatives who could explain what had happened and where the foreign ships had come from. Hal shook himself. He was not about to be shown up by Pip. He pushed himself to his feet, still clinging to a hunk of half-cooked donkey meat.

'Good man, Lieutenant!' He thumped Pip hard on the back with his stump though Pip's broad shoulders did not flinch. He turned to the bedraggled men. 'Let's hear what you've got to say.'

'The storm . . .' one began.

Hal raised his hand for silence. 'No, from the beginning. Whose men are you? From where have you set sail? Where were you bound and on what mission?'

'Sir!' One of them stood up. He was a small man, less muscled than the rest, and Hal guessed he was used to command rather than labour. 'Ship's mate, William Highwater.' He saluted. 'I'm Pisceran by birth, though at the end of the summer our Baron signed his fleet over to Baron Ceowulf of Caldea. We were bringing supplies north to Torra Alta but saw no means to bring them ashore until recently because of the ice. Along with supplies, we carried extra men to help get the supplies inland. Baron Ceowulf thought it unlikely that Torra Alta had enough spare men to carry the burden.'

Hal nodded at this, thinking how sharp Ceowulf was. He was almost ashamed to contemplate the fact that his friend must have known what a poor shape they were in.

William Highwater continued, 'We were waiting for the right opportunity to come ashore. The worst of the weather was over and we thought that now was a good time to move. We've been exploring the coast, looking for a good harbour and a route inland. But the thaw brought the storms and with the storms came those fiendish ships full of devils.'

'Where have they come from?' Hal demanded. 'Hobs are land-loving creatures. I have never heard of them braving broad reaches of ocean before.'

'We don't know. They appeared to have come straight out of the west with the storm. Yet that seems crazy. It's hundreds of leagues to land that way and those smaller vessels would never make the journey; they would not be able to carry enough food or water and they would certainly be unable to withstand the high seas. See how poorly they weathered the storm. Those small vessels would never make the journey. And yet where else could they have come from? The storm blew so strongly from the west that they could not have approached from any other angle.'

'So, you are telling me that these wretches came out of the depths of the ocean?' Hal raised his black eyebrow as he fixed the man in the eye.

'I didn't say that, sir. All I said was that I couldn't explain it.

I've been at sea all my life and never have small vessels braved the westerly ocean. You need to be as big as a Ceolothian trader if you want to cross the ocean and head out into the Diamond Seas.'

Hal nodded. 'You have delivered your information well, William Highwater.'

The sailor saluted smartly despite the deep gash on his wrist.

'Get rest. Eat and sleep,' Hal ordered the men. 'As soon as you are rested, we'll get these supplies inland and see you to shelter. You are strong, brave men to have survived such an ordeal. I applaud you, fellow Belbidians,' he said solemnly.

One or two raised smiles at this and he sensed that the unity between the men was slowly returning. Comradeship, he told himself, had won more battles than weapons.

They rested, many of the men falling into deep sleep now that the ordeal was over. Even Hal leant back against the wind-blasted bole of a tree and allowed his eyes to close while he waited for the last of his men to return from one last search for survivors. The sound of excited voices brought one eye open and he watched as Lieutenant Piperol jumped to his feet, greeting the men as they hurried forward, dragging between them the limp body of a stumbling man.

William Highwater also leapt to his feet in alarm. 'Kill it! Kill it quick! Kill the fiend!'

Soaked to the skin, the man's face was strangely blackened, his lips red and swollen and his eyes dark with pain. He was babbling and croaking in a foreign language, his eyes rolling.

'Who are you?' Pip demanded in loud Belbidian in an attempt to make himself understood.

Instinctively, Hal leapt forward and yanked Pip back just as the man raised his head and a burst of red smoky flame spat from his mouth, his eyes blackening with the pain. Hal felt the heat on the back of his neck and smelt singeing, but managed to duck away in time. He turned about to see that his men already had the poor wretch on the ground. One had a foot over his throat while a lick of flame flickered in and out of the man's mouth.

'Let him be and give him some space. And some water,' Hal added, now coolly in control. He needed information and so wasn't about to see this poor creature killed. 'He is almost spent. I have fought dragons whose fire could be hurled fifty feet at the beginning of the battle but, by the end, their flames were no more than embers flickering in their nostrils. This man is the same and that will be his last burst of flame. See how he is shivering with cold and looks ravenously towards the campfire as if it were his salvation.'

Though he could hear from the feeble moans about him that the men were horrified, they seemed too exhausted to panic.

'We won't hurt you,' Hal said slowly. 'Try and tell us who you are and where you have come from; then we can help you.'

The man looked at him quizzically as if trying to make sense of his words. At last he croaked, 'Help!' Raising up a shaking hand, he looked imploringly into Hal's eyes. 'Help,' he begged haltingly, the word alien on his tongue.

'Where are you from?' Hal demanded and the man weakly pointed westward out to sea.

'The fire?' Hal interrogated him. 'How do you do it?'

'Help!' was the man's reply. 'Help me. Kill me!' he said with sudden ferocity.

'How do you do it?' Hal repeated. 'What creature are you that you can spit fire?'

The man was breathing heavily, his arms clutched to his chest and his fingers hooked into claws of pain. 'Kill me,' he begged, steaming tears now rolling from his eyes.

'Tell me first,' Hal said calmly, showing neither threat nor mercy.

The man threw out one hand wildly as if trying to express himself, though clearly he didn't have the words. He spread his arms like wings and roared. 'The animal,' he said helplessly.

'The dragon?' Hal offered.

The man nodded weakly. He pressed his hand to his chest

and then swept it up his throat as if expressing words or breath. Of course, that was it – breath. 'The breath of the dragon!' Hal supplied.

The man nodded.

Still none the wiser, Hal looked at him in frustration. 'The breath of the dragon means nothing. What has happened to you?'

The man cupped his hand together, mimicking a goblet and then pretended to sip from it.

'He wants a drink?' Pip suggested tentatively.

'Pip, don't be obtuse,' Hal growled at him, staring down hard at the wretched fire-breathing man, thinking in horror of the implications of what he was trying to tell him. 'Lieutenant Piperol,' Hal order gruffly. 'Take him away and do as he bids. Kill him!'

Chapter 18

Leaf's throat hurt too much to speak. Lying on her side, she stared at the base of a flickering fire, her eyes raw and her limbs too weak to move. Beyond the crackle of the fire, she could hear something louder, a droning roar, and it took her a moment to decide whether it was just a ringing in her ears or whether the sound was real.

It wasn't until she heard a shrill voice shouting, 'It's still coming up fast,' that she knew the noise was real. 'We'll be cut off for days if we don't move now.'

The river! She remembered its churning power as it pulled her under.

People were scurrying back and forth; cattle were lowing anxiously; she could smell meat cooking and the older folk chanting mournfully. She looked out from the open-sided temple to see stars sparkling in velvet-black patches of sky between the black masses of scudding clouds. The heavy clouds drifted over the face of a harassed moon, full and wan, battered by the storms.

The noises faded in and out around her and, although she sensed the urgency and distress, she did not have the energy to stir herself. If she didn't move, it didn't hurt – too much at any rate.

'We've got to move out before it comes any higher,' someone urged.

'It seems to me we are much safer here, keeping still. It's dark and who knows what perils we might be walking into,' came a reply.

'The question is, how much higher can the floods come? Do you think they'll reach this low mound? At the moment we can leave, but how long will the water keep rising? This is a refuge now but we may soon be trapped.'

There was much muttering back and forth and all Leaf could do was think that she did not want to get wet ever again.

'Well, measure it again. That can't be right.' Paris's high voice suddenly intruded on her thoughts. 'It can't have risen six inches in the last quarter of an hour.'

There was much considered mumbling.

'At that rate we have only three hours before it covers us,' someone gloomily announced.

'The moon will have passed on by then and the tide will be ebbing, allowing the water to flow more freely away. It won't continue at that rate,' another argued.

Leaf let them argue. She had read that the best judge of flooding, as with the likelihood of avalanche, was not from calculations and estimates but from the local people who had experienced such things before. There were too many variable factors for calculations to be of any worth and, in this instance, experience was paramount. But of course, no one had experienced flood here before because they had always controlled the rain.

She closed her eyes, no longer caring what they decided so long as she stayed dry. She drifted into a light sleep only to wake suddenly and in alarm from a nightmare in which she was pummelled by the river as the black power of the flood dragged her along the riverbed. She gave out a little scream of horror and sat up, which made her head spin.

An overanxious young girl pressed a cup of steaming broth into her hands. 'Drink! It will make you feel better.'

Leaf could smell sage and bloodwort and thought that the girl was right. But swallowing hurt, as did raising her arm, and she realized that every inch of her body was bruised and sore.

'How did I get here?' she groaned, compliantly lifting her

to allow the girl to help her into her clo
d that her green jacket had been ri
It felt soft and smooth agai
said hoarsely through ... wards a hunched shape crouched. He was swept in after ...d both drown, but he ...an,' Leaf

She couldn't imagine how Caspar had dragged her out of that flood but he had and she was deeply grateful. He must have sensed her eyes because he looked around, pushed himself up to his feet and stumbled towards her. Looking strangely like a huge bear with all his blankets wrapped about him, he smiled down at her. Crouching, he reached out a hand to clutch hers. 'Leaf, you made it. I was so worried for you.'

She could see in his eyes that he was still desperately worried – though probably not for her. 'Thank you,' she mumbled.

He squeezed her hand. 'You and I need each other,' he told her. 'I wasn't going to let you slip away so easily.' He looked anxiously at the glassy blankness that lay in the murk of the valley bottom, the light of the moon reflected in the water as the clouds parted. 'I need to negotiate with Paris for meat. We shall cook it and wrap it and then leave as soon as you are able.'

'Wouldn't we be safest with Paris?'

Caspar smiled. 'I sympathize with your desire to stay with your own kind, but Paris's understanding of his environment is severely handicapped. However much he calculates the rate of rise of the river, he cannot tell whether it will flood or not. He needs to ask an old farmer with long and close association with the land, but all the local farmers have grown wings and are cawing like idiots.' Caspar looked thoughtfully towards the older folks who were hungrily tearing at the raw meat with their teeth or trying to mash it with their gums.

'We cannot go that way!' Paris interrupted, having to speak
over the horrified gasp from the other children.

'Why ever not?' Caspar queried.

'It is forbidden. The Sanctuary sits at the top of this river;
it is the home of the outcasts.'

'Oh,' Caspar said flatly as if this were of no consequence.

'We can't go back there. It would be madness . . . You see,
we fled them with as many of our minders and servants as we
could,' Paris explained. 'The moment the curtain collapsed,
they seized our college and took our livestock.'

Leaf grunted. 'Spar, it is likely that they are right. We
should not go that way.'

'Ah!' Caspar exclaimed with heavy irony. 'I see now! It is
better to be drowned in the flood.'

'We're not going that way,' Paris insisted.

'Can we get from this sanctuary to the High City?' Caspar
asked Leaf.

She nodded. 'As a matter of fact, yes. Due to the location
of the place, special communications were already installed.
It is on the far tip of one of the five High Ways. We would,
however, have to go right into the Sanctuary.'

'Then it is decided. We go. Lug, are you coming with us?'
the Baron asked.

The great man shrugged. 'Do you suppose the dwarves have
drowned, taking my stone down with them?'

Caspar shook his head. 'Dwarves know about floodwater.

Any underground dweller is aware of the ferocio
the water and they will have long since chosen
safety. They, too, will have gone upstream.'

'Then I follow you,' the big man said in his rumbling voice.

Caspar nodded and rose stiffly, pulling around him his cloak which had been saved from the water and dried by the fires. 'Carve the meat up and wrap it in cloths so that everyone can carry a good portion. Take a firebrand each and let us move out now before the water rises further. It won't be long till it's dawn.'

'We won't come with you,' Paris said firmly, 'at least not all the way. We shall work our way into the hills, but we shall not go all the way to the Sanctuary.'

Leaf was relieved that she did not have to walk as Lug lifted her up onto his shoulders. She was even more relieved when he finally placed the impaled fawn reverently on the ground, removed and pocketed the pouch containing the stone and then bowed at the ravens. 'The fawn belongs to you now. I have carried him far enough.'

For the first hour, as the giant splashed through the mud, she could barely see anything but, eventually, as the sun struggled to rise above the cloying mist overlying the floods, she had a good view of the lie of the land.

'I still don't quite understand why it is so much easier to go through the Sanctuary in order to reach your city,' Caspar queried.

'The Sanctuary is one of the outlying focal points,' Leaf explained, trying to disguise her impatience. Hadn't she already explained all this? 'As I explained, the Sanctuary forms part of the venal star in whose image our land is laid out. It is the first point from the north and so, if we face north and then turn clockwise through seven tenths of a circle, we shall head straight to the city.'

'I thought your lands were concentrated in one spot,' Caspar queried her explanation, craning his neck up to look at her.

…hat you say implies that the inner realm is sort of threaded through man's world?'

Leaf nodded. 'The core of it is a single intact unit but we could not achieve a large enough shelter to support ourselves without spreading out from there. So spits projecting from the nucleus were created, interlinked by arced arms that form concentric circles about the nucleus. If we took too much land in one particular spot, man would have eventually done his measurements and realized that there was a hole. However, the populations of Jotunn and Ovissia are not spatially minded, unlike those that have formed the large patterned wheat fields measured bi-annually by the plough. If they had a small field that looked to be twenty chains by a furlong, which they knew they could plough with two teams in a day, but discovered it only took them half the day and their yield was half the anticipated quantity, then they might become suspicious. The livestock farmers are less quantitative in their approach and their fields more irregular in shape. As a result they have less of an instinctive sense that there is something curious about their land.'

Caspar nodded. 'I see. It's alarming to think that mankind has been so easily duped by you for so long a time.'

Leaf laughed. 'You are the easiest of peoples to fool. Those species with perhaps less sophistication and even less intelligence tend to have a sharper awareness of their natural environment. We have to work very much harder to keep out hobs and hollines.'

Caspar grunted in disapproval at her opinion of his people. Trudging on, he kept a good pace or two in front of Lug, but she could see the Baron was tired. Lug was muttering away to himself and sucking at his tongue in a frustrated manner.

'Who would take the Stone of Clarity? Who would do that to us? I don't understand. Never before has anyone interfered with our ways. This isn't right. I just want my pigs back and I want my stone.' He kicked at a pebble on the ground that skittered forward and hit Caspar on the back of the heel. 'This is your fault, little man.'

The Baron didn't even turn but kept on marching towards a low hill, the roar from the river a little more distant now. He didn't speak until they reached the top of the hill, when he turned to Lug and said without emotion, 'Everyone thinks everything is my fault! Why should you be any different and why should it trouble me?'

'If you're going to speak to me like that, I don't see why I should carry your girl for you.'

Leaf winced at these words. She had the greatest respect for Caspar but it still galled her to be mistaken for a human.

Calling to the elders of his sect and coaxing them to stay together, Paris trotted along at the rear of the party while the enfeebled and demented elders skipped along merrily, keeping a wary distance from Lug.

'To the Sanctuary. To the Sanctuary,' one was muttering over again. Another in more panicked gasps proclaimed, 'The river is rising.' It was only after a minute when the lines were repeated that Leaf realized they were chanting in turn.

> 'To the Sanctuary; to the Sanctuary.
> The river is rising; the river is rising.
> Help, help! Help, help!
> We must hurry; we must hurry
> To the Sanctuary; to the Sanctuary.
> All sing!'

Of course! Where else would one retreat in times of danger than to somewhere called the sanctuary; it did indeed make sense, although she knew it was called the sanctuary for other reasons.

'We're not going to the Sanctuary!' Paris told them for the umpteenth time, to which they began their chant all over again.

'Just look at that,' Lug complained, staring ahead. Of course no one else had his advantage of height to see what so perplexed him and he would not explain but merely continued to grumble. 'I should have known this was going to get harder and harder. Nothing in my life is going right now.'

At last, they reached the top of the hill and could see what Lug had already spied in the valley ahead. Until now they had been steadily climbing a slope that had easily shed its water, but now a plateau lay ahead of them. The path had been swallowed by a sheet of grey water that rippled in the steady wind. Up here on the exposed ground, the wind stripped the warmth from Leaf's face and she buried her head in Lug's hair that smelt all too pungent. She scanned the waters until she saw to their right the thin line of an old drove track that cut through the flooded meadows, slightly raised above the surrounding countryside, a small hut marking the way. Caspar waved them forward. 'We must hurry before it rises even more.'

Paris did his best to try and persuade the elders of his order to stop and seek shelter in the hills, but the old folk were enjoying the marching and singing too much and wouldn't listen. As a result, the hungry band of mathematicians continued to trail after Caspar.

Lug wasted no time before lurching down the hill and splashing through the shallows without a care as to how much he soaked the others around. The water flicked up from his heels, splattering Leaf high up on his shoulders. Clutching at his wide leathery ears, she did her best to stay seated and tried not to become irritated by his constant chant. 'Why did they take the stone? Why? They had no right to it, had no use of it.'

'Dwarves are particularly fond of minerals of all sorts. If yours was a rare stone, they would be even keener to possess it,' the young girl impatiently tried to explain for the fourth time. 'There's nothing strange in that.'

'It's of no value to any people but our own.' Lug would not listen. 'You will help me get it back, won't you?' he begged Leaf.

'So long as you don't threaten to bite my head off again,'

she said more lightly, no longer afraid of this simple man. Clearly, he was mostly threats and no action. She didn't care to dwell on his tendency to shake those with whom he became frustrated.

They hurried on through shallows and scrambled up onto the embanked drove track. Here they made better time, Leaf doing her best not to bite her tongue as she bounced along on top of Lug's shoulders. The hut was drawing closer but it wasn't long before the rising flood was lapping at the edges of the road and they were splashing through water again.

Were they never going to escape this water? Was it ever going to stop raining? Leaf scolded herself for asking unanswerable questions but, nevertheless, couldn't stop worrying. The elders flapping along behind were also sounding more and more concerned. They were already weak with hunger and their refusal to dress properly made them vulnerable to the cold. When one fell and sprawled headlong into the water, flapping feebly but failing to rise, none of the others made any attempt to pull him up. It was Caspar who ran back and took the poor old man by the arm and hauled him to his feet.

'You should all go back as Paris advised,' he scolded gently.

Paris himself was wringing his hands in despair but seemed determined to help the old folk as much as he possibly could.

'Death! Death! Death!' the other elderly mathematicians chanted as the youth hauled him to his feet.

'Thank you,' the enfeebled elder murmured at his rescuer, his eyes suddenly lucid for a moment. 'Beware the hut!'

'Why?' Caspar asked. 'It is still high above the flood.'

The old man then staggered and Paris took off his cloak and spread it over his shoulders. 'You are suffering from exposure, you old fool,' he chided him.

The man was now shivering too hard to speak but managed to stagger on. Leaf, however, now focused on the hut. Suddenly it struck her that the old man was right. Any

339

creature sheltering from the flood would cling to it as a place of refuge.

'Spar!' she called and nodded ahead at the little round thatched hut. 'Beware of the hut, like the old man said.'

He didn't question her but, with his hand on one of the knives at his belt, he hurried on ahead. All he did was peek in through the window for a second and suddenly stiffen in revulsion before he turned away and hurried back to Leaf and Lug. 'There's no one there. At least there's no one left alive.'

'Death!' the elders all chorused with increasing vigour.

Leaf scowled at them, wishing that they wouldn't keep saying that; it was so unnerving.

'What did you see?' she demanded.

Caspar gave her an overly bright smile. 'It's nothing. Just the people that must have lived there. I'm afraid they have been slain. Now, we must hurry.'

Leaf, however, could tell from Caspar's forced expression that he was hiding something. 'There's nothing to see?'

'No, nothing,' he insisted. 'They are dead and those who are not are too busy to trouble us.'

'I thought you said they were all slain.' Leaf was immediately suspicious of Caspar's report and, without a moment's thought, slithered down from Lug's back to take a look herself, curiosity driving away all thought of fear. It was uncharacteristic of her but her time spent with Caspar had already had a profound effect on her behaviour. Caspar lunged to catch her but she slipped through his fingers to reach the window. Two red eyes flicked around to glare at her. Long-limbed with sharply pointed heads, two of Holly's people hissed at her, dark red blood drooling from their hands and mouths.

Leaf's eyes bulged in horror. They were sitting on top of a small body, a child of her own race, their hands plunging in and out of the body cavity to pluck out the prized entrails. She thought she would vomit. On the table was another body wrapped in white robes that were splashed with pink where blood had gushed from its chest. A large axe was still embedded in the wound.

'What . . . ? Who . . . ?' Leaf sobbed, stumbling back into Caspar's arms. 'Who would do that? Why would they do that?'

Caspar shrugged. 'I don't know. All I know is that the two hollines are opportunists scavenging an easy meal. Judging by the axe, I would imagine that the poor souls were murdered by a dwarf.'

'What would a dwarf possibly want with one of our kind? It's ridiculous. We do them no harm.' Leaf found that she was speaking through a bluster of tears. She wasn't sorry to hurry on, though the panicked cries from the elders worried her even more as the water continued to rise. 'What would dwarves want with my people?' she repeated. 'We harm no one. We do not use violence. Why would anyone use it against us?'

'You're beginning to sound like Lug,' Caspar complained.

'That's silly,' Lug contradicted him. 'My voice is deep and strong.'

'I didn't mean that,' Caspar said dismissively. 'It seems the dwarves are attacking just about everyone. But why these folk in particular?'

Leaf shrugged. 'They have stolen something very precious to the Haol-garen and have now attacked the Sanctuary's outlying gatehouse, a strategic position.'

Caspar nodded. 'Yes, yes, but why would anyone want to take the Sanctuary?'

Leaf shrugged. 'I don't know. It is very hard to think like a dwarf.'

'Mmm,' Caspar agreed. 'The only thing we do know is that the dwarves have large forces spread throughout the country and seem intent on looting.'

They hurried along the drove track, which was now rising steadily above the plateau, and finally reached the brow of the hill. Ahead lay the square grey walls of a long low building.

A central dome made entirely of glass was flanked by two smaller domes, forming the roof that rose above battlemented walls. Three rows of arched windows of a symmetrical design punctured the walls. Such a fine example of architecture seemed quite out of place set up in the hills. Leaf grunted in disapproval.

'Don't you like it?' Caspar asked her.

'I do not approve of the boldness of it shape. It's too easily identifiable by an outsider intruding into our realm. I disprove even more strongly of its inhabitants.'

'And why is that?' Caspar asked, wiping the rain from his face and pulling at the old man to keep him moving.

'Whereas the scholars sought knowledge and the betterment of their minds, dedicating their lives to wisdom and creating a better environment, they sought a darker knowledge.'

Caspar nodded grimly. 'I see.'

At this point the raven-clad elders looked startled and began muttering anxiously to one another. Much to Paris's relief, they finally conceded to retreat though one stubbornly remained, cawing and croaking, flapping her arms and crying, 'Death!'

The old woman, whom Paris reluctantly abandoned, preferring to look after the majority rather than one lost cause, deeply unnerved Leaf. She felt her breathing quicken and her heart thumped in her chest at the thought that she was actually approaching the Sanctuary.

'Tell me about the Sanctuary,' Caspar instructed.

'The scholars declared many thousands of years ago that knowledge was to be restricted, otherwise greed would force those of a darker nature to seek more and more powerful ways of destroying their competitors. We turned against all kind of violence and all philosophies that claimed it to be acceptable. We did not defend ourselves through violent means but built technologies that promoted peace. But there was a faction that upheld such a belief to be idealistic and unsustainable. Our people voted that all reference to violence and technologies promoting knowledge of how to harm others should be destroyed. But the dissenting faction would not abide by this. Against the vote of our people,' Leaf emphasized the phrase, finding it incredible that anyone of her kind could have gone against a vote, 'they stole the books and retreated to the Sanctuary.'

'Well, why didn't you try to get the books back?'

'That would have taken force. We couldn't do that without betraying our principles,' Leaf explained, peering to the left. She could just make out a line of something running high above the land.

'Oh, I see.' Caspar raised his eyebrows at the statement.

'Well, don't you have principles?' Leaf demanded defensively.

'Everyone has principles; it's just a matter of deciding at what point it makes sense to alter them,' Caspar said practically.

'If you alter them they are not principles,' Leaf argued.

'Does that truly matter when survival is at stake?'

Leaf had no answer to that.

The road became more like a gutter; a steady stream of slippery mud gushed down the hillside. Continuing to look left, Leaf could now make out the flimsy structure she had seen earlier: a long high bridge was suspended from great beech trees. Silver threads hung from the highest branches, supporting a long broad platform, which overflowed with cascading plants to disguise its form. She could see the silhouettes of distant figures hurrying along it.

'What is that?' Caspar asked.

'It's the road to the city,' Leaf told her. 'The High Way. Or it least I assume it must be. Before it was camouflaged by the effect of the crystals in the atmosphere, but now it's plainly visible above the Jotunn fields.'

Caspar nodded. 'I don't suppose it will be long before someone knocks it down.'

Leaf swallowed. Her world was being destroyed.

At last they came to the Sanctuary walls and Leaf slithered

down from Lug's back. She took one brief look at the iron gates and knew that all was not well. A long chain dangled loose from the centre of the gates, a smashed lock lying on the ground. The gates creaked as Lug shouldered them open. Even the raving elder, who had stubbornly followed them, had the sense to cease her maddening croaks.

Within, the Sanctuary was bathed in an unnatural silence and their footfalls echoed on the cold stone. Cloistered aisles spread out in a quadrangle from the gate, surrounding a square lawn with a central statue in the middle. The statue had been decapitated and the head lay in the turf. Leaf felt for Caspar's hand and gripped tight. Naturally she was fearful of this forbidden place, but the fear was compounded by the obvious evidence that something was wrong.

'Where is everybody?' Lug blurted loudly.

'Hush,' Caspar warned him.

The giant grunted in dissatisfaction at the Baron's tone. 'There's nothing here to be afraid of.'

Caspar tapped the ground at this feet. 'Rats,' he whispered, indicating the stream of wet footprint that emerged from a low round building to their right.

'Plague and death,' the old woman prattled. 'I said there would be death.'

A door banged in the stiff breeze.

'Not at all,' Caspar contradicted the woman. 'That must be the grain store. Unchecked, the rats will have poured in, but they must now be fleeing the rising waters.'

Glad to be out of the rain, they took the cloister to the left and followed it round to the double doors at the far end. The doors were thrown wide. Leaf gulped in dismay, her knees buckling beneath her. Caspar caught her before she hit the ground. Swinging her up into his arms, he pressed her head against his shoulder and stroked the back of her head.

'I'm so sorry, Leaf. You shouldn't have had to see such a sight.'

The elder's screeching became louder and more insistent

and Leaf wanted to scream too but she couldn't. She could barely breathe. Only rapid, shallow breaths panted in and out of her exhausted body.

'But why?' she wailed, hot dry tears making her eyes ache, her throat strangled with distress.

'It's hobs,' the giant mumbled. 'Only hobs would wreak such carnage.'

Somehow, Leaf found the courage to look. Still clinging tight to Caspar, she glanced round, feeling her stomach turn at the sight. Thirty bodies lay scattered about the hall, heads and limbs severed. One sat at the throne of a long table, his lungs pulled from his ribcage, his ears sliced off and his eyes staring wide in an expression of excruciating pain.

'Not hobs,' Caspar said hoarsely. 'They mutilate in a less considered way. This is deliberate and controlled work.'

The elder spun and whirled through the carnage, flapping her imaginary wings.

Lug's nose wrinkled up in silent contempt. 'Why can't people simply raise pigs? We never had all this fighting. You raise your pigs and buy your wife and raise your children and raise more pigs. It's so satisfying. At least it would have been.'

Leaf was not listening. What did she care about pigs? Her people, be they heretics or outlaws, had been brutally murdered. 'Get me out of here,' she begged weakly. 'Spar, please. I can't bear the smell and the death.'

Caspar pressed her close and carried her over the gory remains to the far door. Opening it, he hurried through to an airy courtyard that was the antithesis to the scene they had just witnessed. Ornamental trees, leafless at this time of year, were planted about a central fountain, which sputtered from a statue of a young girl in flowing robes, her head wistfully downcast as she viewed her hands. The water spilled from her clutched hand. She should have been holding something but the object was gone.

At the base of the fountain was a brass plaque that had

been smeared with blood though it was still possible to read the inscription:

Though our brethren looked to the skies for their answers, we looked below to the Earth and Her tears welling up to feed us with Her love and bounty. Here, at the sacred source of the river, we drink from the pitcher, which imbues in us Her spirit and Her glory. To drink from the sacred pitcher is to drink enlightenment. Blessed be the Great Mother.

'That doesn't sound like the words of a wicked people,' Caspar remarked.

'Ah, but they were. They had passion. Their obsession with poetry and beauty led to deeper, more traumatized emotions. It led to heated emotions and so to the will to make war. It is not at all healthy, this obsessive study of poetry and arts.'

Caspar twitched his eyebrows at the statement. 'Poetry is not renowned as a fearsome weapon of war.'

Leaf snorted at him, thinking him obtuse for not understanding how words incited and directed people.

'The pitcher, however, is not here,' Caspar continued. He stepped closer to the statue, which was covered in lichen and a green coat of slime. 'But it looks like one of the fingers has been recently snapped off. The stone is still clean and grey. What would anyone want with the pitcher?'

'Power,' the elder who had stubbornly insisted on following them muttered. She was suddenly standing right behind Leaf, her craggy fingers gripping her shoulder. 'All is power. Love and war and war and love; all is power. All is a greedy scramble for power.'

'The pitcher is hardly a symbol of power,' Caspar contradicted.

'Read the inscription,' Leaf contradicted him. 'To drink from the sacred pitcher is to drink enlightenment. Someone has taken the pitcher because it imparts knowledge or inspiration.'

346

'It's an awful lot of people to kill just to get inspiration,' Caspar said doubtfully.

'Let's get out of here,' Leaf urged. 'We have to get to the west gate so that we can hurry towards the High Way and the city. It must be through that door.'

Perplexed and sickened by the sights she had just witnessed, Leaf hurried towards the arched door but recoiled from the door knocker. It was in the shape of two hands protruding from the wood and holding between them a decapitated shrunken head. The handle itself was a skull.

'Stop!' Lug warned her, pulling her back with such force that she tumbled to the ground. No one picked her up but all had moved forward to the door and pressed their ears to the wood. The sound of sobbing was faintly audible and Leaf hastily scrambled to her feet. Yes, definitely there was the sound of sobbing, but it became harder to hear as the elder began to shriek.

'Do not open it! You will let the evil out on all the world.'

'Looking upon evil will not make us evil,' Leaf said firmly. 'We must see!'

Caspar grasped the hideous doorknob. He shoved the great doors outward and they swung in a slow arc, their hinges so well oiled that they made not the slightest sound. It was dark within the hall beyond and Leaf could see nothing for a few seconds as she stood there, eyes wide, blinking in the gloom. Her ears were aware of the sobbing and gasps of pain but she shrieked as a ferocious cry bellowed out of the dark.

She leapt back in alarm at the glint of metal to her left. The bellowing cry was followed by the sound of something running hard at them. Again, she was shoved back, this time by Caspar, and had barely righted herself in time to see the Baron twist and duck and then lunge upward into the dark with his knife. A heavy thud and the clang of metal followed.

It was a moment before Caspar's laboured pants were audible and he reassured them that he was safe and that his

347

opponent was down. Leaf stepped cautiously into the room and, gradually, her eyes adjusted enough to see a solid shape heaped on the floor. Caspar struck a flint and, in the brief flash of light, Leaf looked down at the body and saw it was a dwarf. Blood was oozing from a neck wound onto his thick, heavy beard. The dwarf's square, thickset face was turned up, his eyes blinking rapidly and his mouth gasping for air as if he were a landed fish.

Leaf stared at him for a long cold second of horror. 'This death; this violence,' she croaked. It horrified her to the depths of her soul, yet she was ashamed to admit that she was glad the dwarf was dying. If it hadn't been the dwarf, it would have been Caspar or perhaps even herself. She put her hand to her chest; feeling the inexorable rhythm of her heart confirmed her vitality. Caspar was right; they were cowards. None of her kind would have been brave enough to stand up to the ferocious attack of the dwarf.

'Light! More light!' Lug demanded. 'We need light.' He stamped back out into the courtyard and, moments later, returned with a brazier that he had ripped from one of the walls. Stooping under the door, he carried the smouldering torch into the room, revealing a high vaulted chamber. At first, Leaf thought that the floor was alive but, as her senses adapted and she was able to decipher her surroundings, she saw that there were black cats everywhere. They were crawling over hunched people who were writhing and wriggling on the ground. Other cats weaved through row upon row of shelves that reached high into the chamber.

Leaf's eyes flitted to the ground again and she scarcely knew what to think. Some of the people were severely injured, having suffered deep axe wounds, no doubt inflicted by the dwarf. Others, however, appeared to be writhing in some form of trance while more were staring at the empty shelves and pawing at the books that were heaped on the ground. They moaned with a sense of deep loss that clearly overrode their distress over their slaughtered fellows.

Caspar was looking all about him. 'We must help them. Lug, get them out into the forecourt where we can at least give them water and wash their wounds and perhaps save one or two. And look out for more dwarves.'

Leaf was too frightened to move. She felt just as she had done when the dragon had come to the village and burned them all. She had hidden and cried beneath the heap of bodies, almost wishing she would die simply to save herself from the pain of her fright. Huddled in a corner, she screamed into her hands and didn't look up until she was scooped up by Lug. To her amazement, he gave her a firm hot kiss on the top of her head and stroked back her hair with a large but remarkably gentle finger.

'Come, little piglet,' he crooned as if that were a term of endearment. 'It's never as bad as all that.'

'How can you possible say that? How could anything possibly be worse? The dwarves have slaughtered them!'

'The man doesn't think so,' Lug contradicted. 'He thinks they were dying anyway.'

'Poisoned, I would say,' Caspar expanded. 'There's a great many that are retching and screaming and clutching at their stomachs. It looks like they poisoned themselves rather than let the dwarves take them.'

Leaf blinked, thinking such a thing impossible; it was unheard of for one of her kind to take their own life though, of course, these were the outcasts from the Sanctuary and so, naturally, might behave in a divergent fashion. She looked at their contorted faces, morbidly fixated by the brief moments when they teetered on the knife-edge between life and death. Then, as they slipped away, released from their torture, peace inhabited their expressions.

Leaf was still surprised to find that these outcasts did not look like fiends or hobs but instead ordinary, exactly as all the other people of the inner realm. Caspar was looking from one to another as if deciding which to help and then finally shrugged his shoulders and went to the fountain where he let the water rinse away the blood and spits of vomit from his hands. He looked suddenly very old and tired.

'Help them!' the old elder shrieked at him, dragging one of the smaller bodies to its feet and commanding it to stand, though the moment she let go it simply crumpled heavily to the ground.

The Baron shrugged. 'Those that are not dead yet will be dead in less than a few minutes. There is nothing I can do.'

Leaf buried her head against Lug's hairy hand and sobbed.

When she finally found the composure to look round again, she saw the Baron was stooped over a girl in the corner, who was the only one left muttering as, one by one, the rest fell silent.

It struck Leaf that the dwarves, who had run amok through this library, could only have done so a short while before they arrived. The thought chilled her blood. They might be very close at hand and could return any minute.

Caspar dragged a girl, who looked to be about the same age as Paris, out from the corner and into the light of the courtyard. She was jerking her body about and dribbling as if she too were poisoned but, though her eyes rolled, they continually refocused on Caspar's knife; the girl was pretending, Leaf was certain of it.

Caspar caught the girl's chin in his hand and looked her in the eye. 'Stop it, child. You have long outlived the rest and have not fooled me.'

She gave up her pretence instantly and suddenly stood stiffly in his grasp. 'I didn't want to die. They said we must to protect the secret, which the dwarves were threatening to torture out of us. We are not a strong people and it would not have taken long, so they said we had to kill ourselves. But I did not want to die.'

'So what did you tell the dwarves?' Leaf demanded. It was quite obvious to her that, since the girl had refused to take the drug, she may have told the dwarves what they wanted in an effort to preserve her life.

'I told them ... I told them where it is kept,' she stammered.

'Where what is kept?' Caspar asked.

The girl looked down at her feet. 'The book, the great book.'

'Is a book so important?' Caspar asked, looking around.

Leaf nodded at him, her eyes filled with a look of doom.

'Oh!' the Baron said heavily. 'We had better see whether they found it. Lead the way, young woman.'

'Aconite,' she told him. 'My name is Aconite.'

Pressing an overly rounded belly with one hand, she staggered ahead, while Leaf looked on in disgust. So this was one of the outcasts, a traitor to her own kind, a truly wretched individual. Why wasn't her skin green? she thought whimsically. Her hands trembling, Leaf picked her way through the intertwined bodies now limp on the floor, following the girl who was dressed in a white fur coat, over a white fur dress, both of winter hare. On her head she wore a cap made from a black cat, the mask still attached and the tail hanging down behind. Barefoot, like Isolde, she padded along the stone floor though the blood oozed up between her toes. About her neck hung seven black tails from a stoat and she bore a satchel of white fur matching her attire. Every once in a while it chinked as if there were bottles within. She was not in the least pretty, with a heavy jaw and small eyes, though she held her head high with pride.

'I do not want to die,' Aconite continued to mutter savagely to herself.

No, Leaf thought; it is the endless struggle of all the earth's creatures. The will to live overrides all but the will of one's offspring to live, so she had been tutored.

They entered an atrium where the black walls were painted with images of stars and constellations with interlinking arcs to show the relation between the celestial bodies. Lower down were the names of rare plants and their alkaloids. Beautiful illustrations of each plant were annotated by elaborate

351

formulae of the medicinal chemicals. Leaf acknowledged that she knew all these plants to be poisonous but was not aware of the individual chemical toxins or how to extract them.

Lug snapped his teeth together, his lips slapping loudly. 'Hogbane! What would anyone be doing messing about with hogbane? This is an unclean place, Leaf. Not the place for the likes of good husbanding folk like you or I.'

Leaf somehow managed to give him a lop-sided smile.

They came at last to a grid that was hung like a door. A series of padlocks secured the grid, though these had been burst open. Though the way ahead was clear, none moved for a moment as they listened to the drum of feet running through the chambers above them.

'What if the dwarves return?' Leaf worried.

'Then we lie down and pretend to be dead,' the girl from the Sanctuary said flippantly.

They crept on to the next door, which was of solid metal, built purely for security with no aesthetic appearance. It was also smashed open; scorch lines from the use of explosives had left jagged lines across the surface of the metal.

'Dwarves are very knowledgeable not only about the properties of metals but also about explosives as they use them in their mining activities. We had been doing our best to research their methods but it has always been very difficult to obtain knowledge from them in that area,' Aconite told them.

'Hmmph,' Leaf retorted in disgust.

'You idealists have no idea what you have done to us all,' the girl snapped vehemently. 'Your weak-minded philosophies have welcomed all manner of beasts into our realm.'

'Stop arguing!' Caspar commanded in a steady, firm timbre, which made Leaf listen.

He held up the torch and shards of bright light were reflected back at them from the floor, which danced like a carpet of twinkling rubies and sapphires. Viscous liquids seeped through the shards of glass, giving off pungent fumes. Leaf covered her mouth.

'Be careful,' Aconite warned. She nodded at the glass. 'Many of the gases will be highly toxic. It seems my people have thrown vials of poison at the dwarves,' she added. Her words were given emphasis by the number of dwarves lying on the floor, their faces purple and bloated. 'A haemolytic poison; very efficacious,' she said succinctly, her hand again moving to cradle her belly.

Leaf frowned. The gesture was that of one with child, but surely this girl was too young. Had she really made the transformation into adulthood and attained the great revelation?

Suddenly, Aconite gave out a low moan and staggered backwards, her hand pointed to a dais at the far end of the desecrated hall. Vials, cauldrons and curious implements of all sorts had been smashed to the ground as tables and shelves had been upturned. Beyond them and the heaped bodies was a golden lectern from which hung three broken chains. Two severed arms were still manacled to the last link. A collar dangled from the last chain and below it lay the body of a black dog, its severed head lying several feet away. Two men, each with an arm missing, were writhing beside the lectern, blood spurting from their mutilated torsos. Clearly, the men and the dog had been chained to the book for its security. In order to take the book, the dwarves, Leaf reasoned, had found it quicker to butcher the guardians rather than to break the chains.

Caspar moved forward but Lug caught his arm. 'You owe me a pig, remember. I can't let you go in there and get yourself killed.'

The girl they had rescued ran forward. 'You let them take it!' she accused.

One looked at her in disbelief. Blood dribbling from his mouth, he gasped, 'Aconite! They have it!'

Lying between the dying men was the decapitated body of a huge mastiff, its head now sizzling in a puddle of spilt chemicals.

'They have the Directory!' the man spluttered.

The girl began to quiver and again clutched at her stomach. 'Upwards! We've got to get out onto the citadel roof where we can breathe,' she urged the others.

'But what does it all mean?' Caspar protested.

'Move! Move as fast as you can and try not to breathe. I'll explain when we are in the fresh air.'

The way up was littered with the fallen bodies of dwarves and they were forced to clamber over them and, in places, use them as stepping stones to avoid the toxic puddles. Fortunately for Lug, the halls and staircases were spacious, but he crushed many bodies and was forced to smash through walls when the doorways proved too small. His feet were blotched and irritated by the chemicals but his skin was just thick enough to tolerate such liquids. Leaf was beginning to cough and choke as the vapour from the vials attacked her lungs. This place would not tolerate life for very much longer.

At last, thanks to Lug's efforts to break open the trap door that sealed their way forward, they made it into the open air. Bursting forward as one mass, they gasped and spluttered. Bright stars poked out between the heavy clouds. Far away, the deep boom of thunder rolled across the horizon.

'The night embraces the mad and the wicked,' the elder shrieked out. 'Hark to the sounds of death and fear.'

'I do wish you would stop that,' Caspar snapped in frustration. 'Old woman, think happy thoughts; it will ease your troubles.'

The Baron was staring into the distance and Leaf followed his gaze, aware of how much louder the thunder sounded now that the protective curtain was down. She wanted to curl up and hide like a dog in a cave, but there was nowhere to run to.

Lights were swaying towards them and Leaf now remembered the procession they had earlier spied on the High Way as they had struggled to fight their way through the floods to the Sanctuary. 'They can't be more dwarves!'

Aconite shook her head. 'No, they have what they came for; they have taken the Directory and fled. No, that is the floodwaters sending the rats out from their hiding. The idealists are coming.'

Leaf clutched at her breast and gasped, 'Mother!'

Chapter 19

'Seal the doors to the levels below!' the High Lady Zophia ordered hoarsely, her eyes blinking in bewilderment.

She was trembling and needed two strong youths to support her as she walked. Biting her lip, she looked to one of these youths and shrugged as if she had suddenly completely forgotten what she was talking about. He whispered to her and she nodded gravely.

'We cannot enter these desecrated chambers but must climb to the airiness of the high temple.' She nodded at the pillared structure that stood between the two domes topping the Sanctuary.

Leaf stared on in relief and sorrow at the wretched sight of her mother. Clicking her fingers, Zophia sent ten of her men to search for food and, picking up the hem of her dress that dripped a stream of muddy floodwater, she stumbled into the Sanctuary. Her wet hair clung to her cheeks. Her fingers, red and swollen with cold, clutched at her chest and her eyes flitted wildly about her. Behind her was a grinning old woman who stamped joyously in the puddles. Leaf immediately recognized her grandmother and hoped that her poor afflicted father was also somewhere in the throng. Other men and women in the prime of their years were huddled together, muttering in terrified voices. Many repeatedly staggered and fell and others seemed unaware of their plight as they floundered in the mud. Young children stood by, staring in disgust, while others wept forlornly.

One of the youths, dressed in the grey robes of the Inner

Circle of high scholars, urged the High Lady forward and murmured in her ear. She nodded and commanded in a wavering voice, 'Get to shelter. Mount the steps to the temple and when we are warm and dry we shall take counsel.'

'Oh, Mother!' Leaf breathed through her lips. 'Has it come to this?' She was gravely saddened that her mother was sinking deeper into the dementia that afflicted the adults over the years but was also heartily relieved that she had made it through the treacherous journey to the Sanctuary. Rushing forward, she ran to the bedraggled woman and reached out for her hands.

'Mother! I am overjoyed to see you.' Leaf could not stop the tears that were rolling down her cheeks. 'Mother!'

Lady Zophia took a step back in alarm and grabbed the sleeve of her young advisor. 'I am having another one of those delusions!'

The youth shook his head. 'No, My Lady, it is indeed your daughter, Leaf.'

'Ridiculous name, that! What was my husband thinking of when he called her that? If we had had more children would they have been called Twig or Bark?'

'My Lady, I do not know,' the youth said patiently and gave Leaf a weak smile. 'She ails. The journey was very arduous; we have lost many to the floods.'

Leaf nodded. 'I understand.' She turned to her mother. 'You are here now. You can rest.'

Realizing that it was hopeless to talk more, Leaf took hold of her mother's arm. Supporting her firmly, she drew her towards the temple where Baron Casper had already built a warming fire. Enclosed on three sides, the stone edifice at least provided good shelter from the wind. At the very rear of the temple was a set of doors leading to an inner sanctum, which would have offered better shelter but was not big enough to house so many refugees.

Zophia blinked in disbelief at her daughter. 'So this was where you ran to. You went to join the degenerates here in the Sanctuary.'

Leaf shook her head. 'No, it was not at all like that, Mother,' she protested. But it was at least a half-hour before she could make herself understood and explain that she had tried to seek help in the outside world, only to discover that they were also beleaguered with difficulties. It took her just as long to explain that dwarves had pillaged the Sanctuary and that, beneath them, a hundred souls were poisoned, dead and dying. At last, the surviving renegade in her white hare skin dress, who was being stared at by all the city scholars, was able to explain that the dwarves had taken the Directory.

There were many mouths to feed but, fortunately, those of the Sanctuary had possessed the wits to keep their cattle safely penned on high ground. The only difficulty remained in getting the cattle to the table so those that had worked the land and were familiar with animal husbandry could set about the task of slaughtering and butchering enough animals to feed the refugees. Soon beef was hissing in the smoke rising off the fires and, while Leaf imparted her tale, a sweet aroma of juices gradually filled the temple.

When, at last, a hunk of meat wrapped in a strip of cloth was brought to her, she looked at it for a brief second and then sunk her teeth in. She had forgotten how weak and hungry she was. The food was tasteless and tough but, if only for a while, it soothed the worry that gnawed at her brain. If she allowed herself to dwell on the catastrophe that beset her people, the panic welled up within her and, like the older ones of her race, she just wanted to rave and shriek.

Caspar sat down beside her and chewed silently at his own knuckle of beef. His eyes were fixed on a spot in the earth a yard in front of him but it was as if he were staring into the far distance; his thoughts were ever with his children. At last, Aconite stood tall in the middle of the temple and raised one hand, summoning all the younger people to silence. The afflicted, however, continued to rant or thump their heads into their hands. There was nothing she could do to silence them and so had to speak loudly above the distracting noise.

'We have suffered a terrible loss. What has befallen the idealistic scholars in the city, I do not know. What is certain is that you have been unable to maintain the protective curtain our ancestors devised all those years ago. Equal to that catastrophe is another. The Directory has been brutally ripped from our care by dwarves.'

Leaf looked from her mother to Caspar, then Lug and finally to Aconite. Suddenly the pieces of the puzzle in her mind fell into place.

'Hear me all!' she cried. As she spoke, she noticed amongst the rear of the crowd an old man, who suddenly looked up at the sound of her voice. Anxiously, he began to push his way forward through the crowd. His long hair was draped with weeds and he had small twigs interwoven through his clothes but, for a second, a sharpness came to his eye. Leaf recognized him at once; her pulse racing in exaltation though she made no move to greet her father for fear of upsetting him. She held his gaze as she began to speak. 'I must know what caused the curtain to be destroyed.' She already knew in her heart the answer, but she needed to be sure.

Her mother spoke. 'It was my fault. I trusted Silas because he helped protect us from the dragons.'

'You should have killed the dragons,' the girl from the sanctuary said reproachfully.

'You know that is not our way, and the dragons were not fooled by any of our illusions.'

'Dragons are very powerful creatures,' Aconite said heavily.

'He won my trust because I am weak and my faculties are failing me. I thought he was helping us. I thought he enjoyed the praise and esteem in which our people held him, but then he marched straight into our inner circle and, having learned what enables us to make the curtain, he took away the mercury-oxide ores and stole the Book of Characters.'

Leaf pushed back her bedraggled brown hair from her face. 'I had guessed as much. But hear this. In the outside world beyond, he has stolen a Chalice from the humans. This Chalice

359

has great power, being the catalyst for the transference of essential energy from one medium to the next. Though the Chalice is broken, it can be mended by those that have the technology.'

'By dwarves,' Caspar said flatly.

Leaf nodded. 'Indeed. And, as we know, Silas was using dwarves to help him.'

Zophia began to tug at her hair and tap her foot in a distracted manner. 'Go on!' she said weakly. 'I can see you have more to tell us.'

'I do,' Leaf said smartly. 'On my return here I found this Haol-garen.' She nodded towards Lug who sat hunched low to fit beneath the ceiling of the temple. 'The sacred stone that enables his people to thrive has also been stolen away by the dwarves. Then, when I arrived at the Sanctuary, I discovered that the Directory, which lists a thousand and one ways to cause death, be it of a young child or mass destruction, is missing too.'

There was a heavy silence that clamped its cold hand around the throats of all those present.

'You see,' Leaf continued, 'Silas's intention may be twofold. First, he may be seeking to disable other peoples, sending them into disarray so that they are unable to fend for themselves. Second, he may be gathering to himself things of power in order to increase his own strength.'

A general excited hum rippled through the temple. It was pierced by a shriek from the old woman dressed in the raven feathers. 'Death is here; death is on us. The end looms before us like a great maw ready to swallow us into eternal oblivion.'

Leaf was aware of her mother sobbing beside her and then of ripples of dissent running through the crowd as scholars murmured that Silas was a human and wasn't that being with Leaf also a human? Why did the high family choose to consort with humans?

Leaf sensed that, at any moment, there would be outrage in the crowd and she feared what these madmen would do to Caspar. However, it was her grandmother, Xanthia, who stilled the irate voices.

'The trouble with all of you is that you have no sense of adventure,' she berated them. 'A few puddles here and there and you all fall apart. For most of you, this is simply the first time you have ever valued your life, ever realized that you are truly alive. Where has all the laughter gone? What we need is a song, a rousing song to make us feel brave.'

No, thought Leaf, we cannot hide any longer, not even in song. We must face up to the realities all about us and seek a solution. She withdrew into thoughtful silence as Xanthia began to dance and leap, further exciting the old woman in her tattered raven feathers. Aconite looked on in disgust whilst Caspar was still gazing at the stone paving on which he sat, drawing circles with his finger, clearly deep in thought.

'Don't you see?' The old woman spread her feathered arms wide as if they were wings. 'We are all dying, eaten up by our own arrogance and stupidity, destroyed by our own powers that others have turned against us. We must cleanse ourselves of our folly and rise reborn like the phoenix, young and vibrant, from the ashes.'

At this, she pressed back her wings like a bird diving from the sky and ran towards the fire, staggering into the flames. For a moment, she stood and shrieked, her hair alight and crackling. Then she was engulfed in flames. All stared, some glumly, others shrieking in horror. But Leaf turned her back, trying to breathe, trying to fight away the pitiful image. Was this the fate of her people? She didn't know how to help them, didn't know how to govern; she was only a child. Someone had to do something, but her mother was only staring on in amazement, dumbfounded as her tears rolled down her cheeks. The elders were becoming more and more excited, pushing each other towards the flames.

'Leaf, do something,' Caspar told her. 'Do something before the situation gets out of control.'

'But what can I do?'

Caspar cast his eyes about the rabble, his frown deepening. He shrugged in despair. 'We retreat into the inner sanctum with the few who are fit to understand what is happening,' he told her. 'I am afraid there is little you can do to save most of these people. Your thoughts must be for the future. They are already the past.'

He nodded at her to come with him to the rear of the temple. Lug pricked up his floppy ears and shoved his way through the rabble to follow them. 'Don't think you can get away from me that fast. I shall see to it that you pay your debts.'

Caspar sighed. 'Poor troubled man, do you think a few pigs are on my mind right now? I am sorry for your loss but it wasn't my fault.'

The great man was slowly turning purple. 'I will have my pigs and the stone! It's all your fault and you will get them back for me.'

Leaf reached up to one of his vast hands and tried to soothe it. She knew Lug was unpredictable and barely had the wit to know what was going on about them, but he had proved extremely useful.

While the older scholars raved and the younger ones wept and despaired, huddling together in little knots, wringing their hands at the glinting flood sweeping out below them, Leaf gathered a council together. Her mother, grandmother and the young advisors sat on the floor as there was nowhere else to sit. They were joined by Caspar, with Lug at his back, and Aconite. They were but a sad few of the sharpest minds of her people. Leaf had to admit that Aconite was easily to be counted the sharpest of them all. She was still young, with no sign of the forgetfulness that came with maturity, yet must have, of necessity, undergone the enlightenment in order to be with child.

It was a most curious and unaccountable situation. Puberty in their species, after all, was not a gradual physical change, as was the case with humans, but was marked by a momentous mental change, which occurred in a single week. A surge of hormones swept through the brain, triggering the sudden connection of synapses and dendrites that had been gradually forming their pathways through childhood, doubling the ganglionic mass of the central nervous system. The result was an extreme surge in mental capacity – one which the children longed to experience since the adults described it as a moment of blissful enlightenment.

'We are out of our depth,' Aconite began solemnly and, for the first time, Leaf noted that her cheeks were streaked with tears.

Although Aconite dealt in evil, she appeared deeply emotional and must have suffered immensely with the loss of her kin. Leaf chastised herself for assuming that she would be devoid of feeling. Staring at the pink bloody patch on her white hare skin dress, she was silent for a minute. Leaf was acutely aware of how Caspar watched the girl, how his eyes slid from her rounded bosom down towards her curved belly and then back up to her black hair. Clearly, she did not naturally possess black hair since all the people of the hidden realm had plain mousy brown hair. No doubt she had dyed it to give the vivid contrast with her white attire. Her lips were also artificially coloured and pouted back at Caspar, who shamelessly stared on. Men were weak, Leaf concluded, feeling jealously possessive over the Baron. Aconite may not be beautiful but Caspar was only a human and would be all too easily manipulated by her superior intellect.

'Don't look at her so,' Leaf whispered in Caspar's ear.

The man patted her hand. 'As my uncle Hal would say, a man is always entitled to look. But I was merely intrigued about her condition; she is very young. Don't fret, Leaf, she cannot poison me.'

'High Lady,' Aconite addressed Zophia, 'I am the only one left now of my sect and so must defer to you as I am no more than a probationer.' Leaf was very glad to hear that she had some sense of protocol left. Without hierarchy and protocol, there could be no order. Chaos was unpredictable, unsafe.

'We have all failed,' Aconite continued. 'Like us, your protection has been stolen along with your source of power. We have to get it back, and this man Silas must be stopped, otherwise the hobs will overwhelm us.' Her lips tightened over the word *hobs*. 'Disease-ridden corrupters of the Earth,' she spat savagely. 'We must turn to those more experienced than ourselves in hunting down an enemy.' She pointed at Caspar. 'He may be no more than a man but he is of the outside world and will give us insight into Silas's manner of thinking.'

Caspar bowed. 'I shall do all I can to help in return for help from you. I came here in the hope that you may know a means to mend a child ruined by the Chalice. The essence of a hob was transferred into her body.'

Aconite looked at him grimly. 'There is nothing you can do but kill her. Look at us. How do you think we could help you?'

'But there must be a way,' Leaf objected, seeing the grief contort Caspar's face. 'I will go to the great library and find a solution.'

Zophia shook her head. 'The floodwaters swept through it. The books are ruined. Our knowledge is lost.'

Leaf gasped and Caspar stood up and moved towards the wall of the temple and let his head rest against it in silent despair. Leaf looked at his back, wishing there were something she could do.

'There is only one means to save her and that is to mend the Chalice,' Aconite said, offering hope. 'You must steal the technology from the dwarves.'

Guiltily, Leaf remembered how she had so vehemently opposed the very same plan mooted by Brid.

Caspar turned back to face the wall, determination quickly overriding despair. 'Brid was right. I should have known. We must go after Silas and the dwarves. And not just for Isolde's sake but for the sake of us all.'

The High Lady nodded. 'Someone must. Look at us. We shall starve before the week is out. The flood will soon subside but now any creature can wander into our lands and we shall not be able to defend ourselves. Someone must bring back our mercury oxides and Book of Characters.'

'We could lay poison traps all about the perimeter to protect ourselves,' Aconite suggested.

'And have it leak into the groundwater and our own water supply?' Zophia objected.

'There are many sophisticated traps –'

'And have every migrant peoples angered against us? No!' Zophia was firm. 'Let the rabbit hide in the brambles. Let the mouse hide with the thistle.'

Everyone looked at her for a moment, fearful that little of her mind was functioning properly. Then Caspar snapped his fingers.

'Holly's people! Their drowned bodies were washed downstream to Paris and his tribe. There must surely be more of them. You must go and live amongst them.'

Lug laughed. 'Nobody lives amongst the hollines. Even I know that.'

'Precisely my point. Find a way to live with them and they will protect you from all others.'

'That's impossible.' Leaf rejected the idea.

'There has to be a way, and surely one of your people can think of it?' Caspar reasoned.

Aconite laughed. 'Of course there is a way. We must give them poppy juice.' She patted her satchel as if to imply that she possessed such a potion within it. 'Once they are addicted to it, they will do anything for more, including letting us shelter amongst them.'

'You can't poison them like that!' Zophia said angrily. 'Think of the harm it will do them.'

'Think of the harm that will come to us if we don't,' Aconite argued.

Zophia looked to her advisor, who shrugged. 'We cannot suffer any more than we have. For the survival of our species, we must do this. Perhaps the wise ones amongst our forefathers decided not to exile the renegades entirely from the inner realm simply because, at the back of their minds, they thought they might be essential to ensure our continuing existence.'

Caspar nodded. 'In times of war the hardened criminal can often be your best man.'

'It's no good muttering about criminals to Zophia, my boy,' Xanthia told him. 'She doesn't know the meaning of the word; they had them bred out hundreds of years ago. It's only the children who still have the understanding of the word rebellion.'

Caspar laughed. 'That I can understand. We, too, certainly have more trouble controlling our children than anything else.'

'Except Silas of course.'

Caspar sighed. 'I admit we are not the most blameless of races.'

No one made any comment at this and so, after a few moments, the Baron stood up, sweeping back his thick tousled hair from his forehead. 'However you decide to protect yourselves, we must move and go after Silas.' He looked up at the position of the sun, obscured by grey clouds, and then back at Aconite. 'I assume you are no longer able to distort the orientation of the compass?'

'You are correct,' she told him.

'In that case, we must head west and try and pick up word from my fellows. The dwarves travel fast and will already be a long way ahead of us. But they will be following Silas and I am certain Brid will have picked up his trail. If we head straight for the Fin in Piscera, we shall gain time,' Caspar told them.

Aconite sighed. 'It is a long way to Piscera but we still have our High Ways linking the outlying points of the Haven; they will be very much faster.' She looked towards the High Lady Zophia. 'With your consent, we should leave in the morning.'

'We?' Zophia asked uncertainly.

'I meant the outsiders, along with Leaf and myself. The man will not be able to cope alone.'

Zophia hastily consulted with her advisors and then nodded, though tears sprung to her eyes and she reached out her hands to embrace her daughter. 'I do not want to lose you again, but I fear you are one of the only ones resourceful enough for the task.'

They rested the night and Leaf was vastly relieved to find that her clothes were dry by morning. Already, the younger ones were grouping into work bands in an attempt to rebuild structure and order in their lives. She could see that Caspar was still pensive. The one blessing was that the sun was now bright in a clear sky. There had been a mild frost overnight but at least the rains had abated for the time being.

'We had best be on our way,' she said solemnly, turning to look at her mother, who was bowed over, rocking herself in her arms and looking deeply distressed. Zophia kept looking towards Leaf's father, who looked through the woman as if she simply didn't exist. Leaf ran to him, hoping he would show even the smallest glimmer of sanity.

'Father . . .' she said, holding out her hand, wishing that he would take it.

He stared at her. 'There are no flowers up here,' the old man moaned. 'No gardens. If there were, the water would help them grow.'

Tears choked Leaf's throat. With arms outstretched she moved towards him, but this action only made him look alarmed. He turned towards the wretched body of the charred elder, who had been dragged from the fire.

'Now she looks happy. I could fly up there in the clouds and see the way, see the path for us all.' He lunged out and snatched one of the crisp raven's feathers, which had miraculously escaped the fire, and threaded it into his hair.

'Father,' Leaf implored him. 'Is there no part of your mind that remembers me?'

'Little girl, you are not who you are. You are lost. I am the raven; I see, I can remember. I remember what all have forgotten in their arrogance, hiding from life and the world and the Great Mother. I remember a time of life and brightness when the numbers cascaded out of the sky like rain. I remember the earth's spectrums reflected in the water and how we learnt to read the properties of light and forgot to read the properties of ourselves.'

He reached inside his pockets and brought out a fistful of scraps : a piece of string, a coin, a scrunched up piece of paper, a small pocket knife, a daisy chain, now dried and withered, a conker shell and a golden brown leaf. This last he gave to his daughter.

'Remember! You must try to remember for the sake of us all.'

Trembling, she reached out her hand, grasped her father's arm and took the crisp, fragile offering in his hand. Sadly, she wondered at herself for ever believing that he may have been able to help Isolde; she was indeed lost and forlorn.

For a second, his hazy grey eyes focused on hers. 'It is everything I have of you, all I remember of us. You must remember and find the path.'

Leaf gulped back the tears, deeply shocked and perturbed by her father's dementia. 'I will come back,' she told him. 'I will come back with the answer.'

'The answer is already here,' he retorted. 'But the clear rain has fallen upon the mud and the waters are cloudy. We cannot read the patterns.'

'I love you, Father.' Leaf sniffed back her tears, hoping that at least he might be able to understand that.

He looked at her blankly. 'There are no flowers any more. I miss the flowers.' He reached up a hand and stroked the raven's feather. 'Is it thought and memory or is it death? Is it just death for us all?'

Leaf turned her back on him, barely able to see for the tears brimming over her eyelashes. She clasped the crisp leaf tenderly while she drew out a small calfskin purse and carefully dropped it in, closing and knotting the strings tight and slipping the purse back inside the pocket of her inner shirt.

She must have been longer with her father than she had thought because those chosen to go were ready and waiting. Aconite, in her white hareskin dress, was standing next to Caspar, clearly preferring human company than to fraternize with the idealists of her own race. Lug was tugging at one of his floppy ears, staring down into the flood then anxiously studying the fragile bridge that drifted up and down with the wind. Caspar looked at Leaf, his impatience thinly disguised. His hide trousers disappeared into tan boots at his knee. His cloak, now dry, hung comfortably from his shoulders, giving bulk to his light form. His knives were pocketed about his belt, from which also hung his sword. The bow given to him by Oxgard was slung over his shoulder and he stood stiffly, prepared to move. There was an air of readiness about him absent in the others, who continually checked themselves over as if trying to assess what was missing.

Leaf felt very much the same. Of course there was nothing missing, only a sense of order and confidence, the lack of which didn't seemed to trouble Caspar. She thought it must be wonderful to be so self-reliant.

In silence, they climbed the steps to the bridge and marched onto the wooden slats that were to support their weight. The bridge was surprisingly firm despite the fact that it moved in the wind. Leaf had always been aware of these structures, though the crystal curtain had disguised their outline. From below they had merely looked like an avenue of trees whose interlocking branches had made runs for squirrels high above them. Naturally, she had trod such High Ways before, moving through the trees, but the lands below had been obscured in a haze of leaf and misty sky. That way they had been able to pass through the lands of man, unnoticed and unthreatened. She was pleased to see that, though the mirage created by the curtain had collapsed, at least the solid structures were still in place.

Now, however, the trees were bare and they looked down on the flooded world where the waters lay like sheets of mercury across the land. The visibility was exceptionally good since the heavy rain had been followed by sunshine. Deeply contrasting colours gave the world an intensified, vibrant hue. The grass was bright green beneath streaks of dark blue sky interlaced with black and dun clouds. Shafts of sunlight highlighted patches of hillside and even glinted off the distant towers of Farona far to the south-east. The definite lines of hedges were clearly visible, as were the lines of roads. At intervals crumbling windmills stood, their broken sails creaking and whistling on the wind.

Aconite was following Leaf's gaze. 'What a view!' she murmured. 'To think this has been here all the while though none of us could see it for the curtain.'

Leaf sniffed in reply, not wanting to talk to the renegade.

'What makes you so sure these humans can help us?' Aconite spoke into Leaf's silence.

The younger girl shrugged, giving up her private vow not to speak to the girl. 'I don't know. I only know we have to do something and that the answers lie outside our own lands. We cannot hide any longer.'

'Too true,' Aconite concurred. 'We should have done this many, many years ago when the sickness first revealed itself.'

'Hmm,' Leaf grumpily acknowledged her but did not want to say more. How dare this wretched creature speak to her? And why had Caspar allowed Aconite to come along? She knew nothing useful; she understood only destruction and death.

Aconite sniffed back. 'You don't have to grunt at me like that; I am not so evil as you think.'

'Oh, aren't you?' Leaf blurted. She had intended to keep a dignified silence but found it impossible not to be riled by this girl. 'Your people sought to explore poisons, traps, the darker workings of the mind! How can you not be described as evil?'

'The use of it may well, of course, be evil, but not so the knowledge,' Aconite said authoritatively.

'Ah, but the knowledge allows the use. If you did not study it, such methods of destruction would remain unknown.'

'And leave all such knowledge only in the realms of the dwarves and the hobs? It is you idealists who have been cruel by neglecting the protection of our people. And why don't you despise the Baron there, though he carries a sword? I would say that you admire his spirit, in fact. Why am I hated for having the knowledge in my head whereas you admire him though he carries an article of destruction in his hand?'

'Because we should know better,' Leaf snapped at her, feeling the tears pricking at her cheeks. 'We nearly lost everything all those thousands of years ago because we had the knowledge and the ability to destroy. It took only one deviant mind to use that knowledge, and so many of us perished. We could not let that happen again.'

Aconite sighed. 'The facts are still there whether we know them or not. It would only always take one deviant mind to discover them.'

'It's not natural being up here,' Lug grunted from the rear of the party, interrupting their debate. 'What would my Grunda think if she knew I were gallivanting about amongst the clouds? And her in the way she is too, much like Miss Aconite there.' He rumbled on, talking to cover up for his fear of heights. 'I promised her I had the pigs and would outbid Ogran. I promised her and so she was persuaded and happy to oblige me as it were.' He giggled nervously. 'And now what's going to happen when Ogran wins her only to find out it's my spawn that's in her belly?'

He stamped his foot angrily, which set up a ripple through the structure of the bridge. Everyone turned at once to glare reprovingly at him.

'You'll send us all tumbling out of the sky,' Caspar complained. 'I'm sorry about Grunda. It's wretched when you can't win the girl of your dreams. Life is like that,' he said with some bitterness that Leaf thought could only reflect his own life.

'So, Miss Aconite, how many pigs did it take to buy you?' Lug asked.

'What?' The girl laughed. 'I'm not going to be bought by

pigs.' She looked up at the great man and then smiled more kindly. 'Our ways are different,' she told him and left it at that since, clearly, there was little point explaining all the details to his simple ears.

'No one's ways are different,' the giant contradicted. 'We are born, we fall in love, we have our children, then we die. Where's the difference in that?'

Leaf was about to list the two hundred and three marked differences between her kind and that of the dwarves, for instance, and the seven hundred and sixteen differences between her kind and a hob, but stopped herself when Caspar looked back with a sudden smile on his careworn face. He hadn't smiled in ages and it made Leaf take note of his words.

'You know, Lug,' Caspar said, 'you are right. We are all of the Mother and there is no difference between us.'

What a ridiculous statement, Leaf thought to herself, though she vaguely understood that Caspar must have meant that between them there were no differences that mattered.

Aconite, however, snorted at this. 'Well, one thing's for sure and that is I can't be bought by pigs.'

'No, only the poisonous gall bladder of a pig,' Leaf snapped.

'Will you two stop it?' Caspar barked at them. 'Just stop it! If you've got so much energy to waste on bickering, we can step the pace up.'

However, it soon transpired that it was Lug's weight on the bridge which kept their speed down; the moment he strode out, the whole structure began to shake. The bridge spanned an ice-lined lake, until they were marching above green fields and leafless copses. The oxen below took not the slightest notice of them but warily moved along the bank of a stream, their ears pricked as if listening for a predator that was undoubtedly lurking in the long grass. The yawn of a hylup sent a shiver down Leaf's back and she had to remind herself that they were safe up here in the treetops.

The long, muddy trail of a lake serpent where it had wriggled from the stream and slithered to the lake behind them was

372

remarkably visible from their high vantage point. A herd of goats, busily ripping at the bare birch twigs, bleated nervously to each other as if a predator had just passed by. Leaf hoped that there were no long-necked dragons in these parts or that an overly hungry ravenshrike wouldn't stoop out of the sky come evening.

They had been travelling nigh on three hours with barely a pause and Leaf was beginning to wonder when Caspar might permit them to stop for a meal. She was ravenously hungry and thought she would faint very shortly. He had denied her previous requests for a rest, telling her harshly that she would have to toughen up a little if they were to achieve their quest. However, when Aconite started to complain, Caspar told them they would stop when the bridge lifted them up into the branches of the next large tree.

'Why do you comply with her request and not mine?' Leaf complained.

'Because she hasn't asked thirty-five times and because she is pregnant,' Caspar defended himself.

'Not the most sensible thing to do, bringing along a pregnant girl,' Leaf muttered.

'Perhaps not. I would rather I had young men hardened to marching,' Caspar retorted, 'but I haven't. And since her mind is sharp and her experience undoubtedly broader than yours, I thought she would prove useful.'

Leaf sniffed at this but was somewhat placated when she was able to sink her teeth into a slice of cold beef. Relaxing a little, she noted that, though Caspar ate, he did not sit down on the closely fitted wooden slats, but stood and stared ever westward.

'You should rest,' she told him.

He sighed. 'I cannot. My son, Isolde, Brid, Hal, they are all out there. I cannot stop worrying about them.'

Aconite said smoothly, 'Your worry will not help them.'

'But if I didn't worry, I would not care.'

'Indeed,' she conceded. 'Take some hypericum to ease the stress.'

He shook his head. 'I would never want that. I want to know how much they all mean to me. It somehow diminishes them to hide from the worry.'

He let them rest only five minutes before they set off again, hurrying in pursuit of the setting sun. After passing through the heights of the central city at the heart of the hidden realm, they spent two nights up on the High Way. As they marched on into the afternoon of the third day, both Aconite and Leaf were in agreement that they were above Piscera and that the Fin would soon come into view.

'We've made very good time up here,' Leaf reassured the Baron. 'We're sure to have caught up with the others. They will have had to divert from the straightest course at every river and hill and hylup whereas we have flown straight over the top of them. It won't be long now before we make the rendezvous.'

Caspar, however, didn't answer her. Instead, he urgently twitched his hand at her, gesturing to her to be still and silent. Leaf's breathing stopped in her throat as she saw Caspar's stance tauten in readiness. She had seen nothing herself, but clearly he was aware of danger ahead. The Baron then waved them on again.

'No, it's nothing,' he apologized for alarming them. 'It must just have been the sudden change in wind direction. I just thought I could smell something, but it's gone now.'

They marched on, ears pricked, passing between the dry branches of a huge ash that now supported the bridge. The branches came down low, forcing Lug onto his knees for a while. He was thus a little way behind the rest when they came out into the open again. Caspar momentarily paused to check on Aconite, leaving Leaf to march on alone.

Now, ahead of the others, she looked down to see a number of fires burning brightly below. The smell of incense and thyme wafted up in the smoke. Like the others she gazed down to see who was encamped below and so none were looking ahead when the bridge suddenly shook as if something had thumped down onto it. The air shook with a growling bark.

Leaf flicked her head up, expecting to see a ravenshrike, but was horrified to see it was a half-naked hob that stood before her. Caspar wasted no time and lunged forward with his sword. Leaf clung to the ropes at the edge of the bridge as she was tossed up and down by Caspar and the hob's vigorous movements. Lug was grunting, struggling to pull himself out of the trees. Seeing that his shirt was snagged on a jagged branch, Leaf knew she should run and help him, but she was too scared to move. It was all happening so fast. Leaping down from the branches came another three hobs and she knew that Caspar could not fight them all off though he had managed to smite one hob in the thigh. Dark blood pumped from the wound though it seemed to have done little to deter his attack.

Aconite gave out a shriek of rage as four more hobs leapt out of the shadows. Reaching inside her pockets, she brought forth a vial that she snapped in two and flung as one sprang at her. It squealed in pain as the liquid hissed on its skin.

Lug finally burst forth. Pushing Leaf to the side, he grabbed two hobs by the neck and squeezed so tight that their eyes burst out of their sockets, followed by a pale mash of brains. Leaf felt sick. Caspar had managed to reach for his knives and had impaled a further one through the cheekbone and into the skull, but that still left four hobs. Lug gave out a challenging roar and all four of them responded, springing at the big man who leapt forward to meet them. In an inkling, Leaf knew what was about to happen.

'Spar!' she yelled. 'Hold on! Hold on to the bridge!'

He cast her one look and she fixed him with her eye, trying to impart the urgency and importance of what she said. To her relief, he seemed to understand and twisted his hand through the rope at the edge of the bridge.

Lug's cry drowned out much of the creaking sounds of the ropes as he ran forward but did not mask the sound of splintering timbers and then the sudden twang as the first rope snapped.

Leaf felt her footing go. With all her might, she clung to the rope. The deep, hollow screams of the hobs filled the air as they suddenly fell. Rather than tumble out of the sky with the bridge and the hobs, Lug had reached upwards into the branches above and was kicking for all his worth, his feet entangling in the rope that Leaf was clinging to with fearful determination. Suddenly, the rope snapped and she was swinging downwards, still clutching the rope and squealing as the air rushed into her face. She was falling, falling, falling . . .

Chapter 20

No one spoke to him. He had marched at the back of the party for six days now on the slow journey to Piscera. In the distance, the distinctive ridge, which marked the approach to the western port of Shinglebay, cut into the clouds. Locally the escarpment was known as the Fin.

They had been able to see the purple ridge even yesterday at fifty miles' distance before the weather closed in and drizzle dulled the sky as well as everyone's spirits. Brid had explained that, at the near end of the ridge, there stood a ring of beech trees, highly distinctive for miles about. They had arranged to meet Caspar there and so, even though the trees were no bigger than dark bumps on the skyline, they watched the spot, hoping to see him.

It's all very well, Rollo grumbled silently to himself. It's all such a nice, neat rendezvous point but what if his father had been delayed and missed them? What if Caspar mistook another place as their meeting point? Secretly he hoped so. He felt permanently ill at the thought of what his father might say or do at the sight of his beloved stallion who staggered along lamely, his once sleek hide now matt and dusty and his eye dulled.

As Brid had predicted, the stallion had managed to walk but only with a pronounced limp in his off hind that was uncomfortable to watch. Brid rubbed liniment into the leg morning and night but it made no odds; the limp remained. Rollo dutifully walked alongside the injured red roan, each step, he believed, as painful for him as it was for the horse.

Isolde also walked. She had no trouble keeping up and strode out forcibly on her bare feet without showing any signs of fatigue. The horse shied away from her, as did Quinn and Guthrey.

'It can't be far now to Candlewood Inn,' one of the soldiers called out from the front. 'That'll be nice for you, Miss Fanchon. You'll finally get that bath you've been asking after.'

Rollo made a face. He couldn't understand why Fanchon was still with them. Fortunately, Dominica had so enjoyed Wiglaf's company that she had made no move to leave him, but Fanchon had been entirely different. She had made some ridiculous pretence about needing safe-conduct to the west and would stay with them as long as they went that way. Rollo did not trust her one tiny bit and wondered why Brid tolerated the whore. But then Brid tolerated him, and hadn't he behaved in an even more deplorable manner? Quinn's cuts to his face had begun to heal but he couldn't look him in the eye any more. The only safe place to be was at the back of the procession.

Candlewood Inn finally came into view, a cosy and comfortable thatch set deep into a hollow, its many small windows twinkling in the evening sun. The doors were wide open and from the road it was possible to see inside. It looked warm, the inn crowded, and there seemed to be an air of gaiety that Rollo had not witnessed on their slow march through central Belbidia. The first three nights of their journey had been spent in Oxgard's enclosures and had been rough and cold as well as sparing on food. The territories of Belbidia's heartlands were heavily occupied by the hobs but they had rarely seen them during the day and those that they did ignored them, seeming only intent on hurrying northwards. So long as they were locked tight within the enclosures by nightfall, they were relatively safe. Only the eerie hob barks echoing across the land troubled them and had Isolde sitting bolt upright, eyes staring wildly.

'Hush, Isolde, they cannot harm us here,' Brid had soothed.

'They are heading north. They are mustering and marching on Torra Alta!' the girl uttered, her voice trembling. 'The midshires are already taken. They are focusing their attentions on Torra Alta now.'

Fanchon had remained remarkably calm, even during the one time they came face to face with a small hob gang and a skirmish ensued. Fortunately, there were no more than three hobs that had been sniffing the road, clearly trying to trace a particular scent. The gang had quickly scattered at the sight of Aisholt and his troops charging towards them. One they caught and hacked to pieces, much to the dogs' delight. It was clear that Aisholt and his men knew what they were doing with a sword.

After that, it had been several days before they had spied hobs since the filthy creatures appeared to have relinquished their stranglehold on the Barony of Piscera; and, here at Candlewood, nestled in the shadow of the Fin, there was an air of freedom. Men trotted in and staggered out of the inn at frequent intervals, calling to one another cheerily in an air of celebration, lifting everyone's spirits.

'Fisherman Jerome, how was your catch today?' one called as he departed the inn.

'Indeed, indeed, fellow fisherman Mack, it's been a good three nights and three days on the sea under a favourable moon. Even had me a sea serpent, be it only an infant. Still, I've seen strange goings on out towards the western horizon. Black ships, hundreds of them, so many in fact that I think I must have been dreaming,' he laughed nervously.

'You've been out at sea too long alone. You'll be seeing mermaids next. But I hauled out more mackerel than I've had for three months. Fair times indeed!'

It seemed to Rollo that the troubles still plaguing the rest of Belbidia had swept through Piscera and on to make new victims. There were signs that the hobs had wreaked their havoc, since several dwellings had been torched, their charred roofs having tumbled into the blackened fabric of the house. Carts lay upturned in the ditches at the sides of the road, fences and gates were broken and rubbish was being tumbled about by the breeze. The frequenters of the dozy inn appeared unaware of the ruin about them and acted as if all were perfectly normal.

As they approached the Candlewood Inn, grooms rushed out to take the horses, but Rollo insisted in settling Firecracker into a stall. The animal was no longer the lively, malicious beast he had always been, but crestfallen and slow. He limped after Rollo without even attempting to nip his hand, even when he slipped the bridle off his head. The youth stroked the animal's neck, taking care to touch only an area of skin that remained unscathed after the attack. The roan's coat was dry and dusty, lacking its usual lustre. The jagged wound along his belly was red and angry. The swelling stretched the stitches.

'I'm sorry, Cracker. You could have saved yourself but instead you saved me.' Rollo bit his lip, dreading to think what his father would say when he saw his beloved horse.

With a heavy heart, he went to join the others in the inn. Brid had demanded a quiet table some way from the fire and he could see her and the others, the rain still dripping from their hair and leaving puddles on the flagstones beneath their chairs. The dogs sniffed the ground, snuffling up crumbs left by the previous occupants of the table. The Ophidian terrier had been given the curious name of Walnut because of the hardness of his skull. He had an unfortunate habit of using it as a battering ram against people's shins. While the hound never seemed to question that his rightful place was on the floor, Walnut leapt up onto an empty chair but was promptly tipped out by Guthrey. Brid was clearly irritated by the noise the dogs made and looked around hastily, hoping they hadn't attracted any attention.

'It's no wonder Oxgard was so keen to give them to us. They're uncontrollable,' she complained though no one in the inn had stirred save for a young fellow demanding more ale, which the landlord refused to serve him.

'You've had enough for now, Ned. Go home to Meg, otherwise you'll be regretting it.'

'Listen up, Leof, we've had weeks of it with those sodding hobs camped in our pig pens and killing any who might venture out alone, and now they've suddenly upped and gone. A man's entitled to a drink.'

'Not if he's leaving his wife and young-uns alone all night. Now be off.'

Ned begrudgingly staggered to his feet, only to trip on a man's boots as he stumbled past. Rollo couldn't see the owner of the boots as he was sat within the inglenook, his face and body in shadow while his feet were sticking out ready for anyone to trip over.

'Here, look where you're putting your dirty great boots. Can't you see what you're doing with your own feet?' Ned rudely demanded as he stumbled on.

'Hush, Ned!' the landlord said sternly, obviously embarrassed by the remark. He hurried to the inglenook. 'I'm sorry, sir; he's had a skinful too many and doesn't know what he's about. He didn't realize that you . . . Well, you know what I mean.'

Rollo sat down, grateful of the still ale that was placed in front of him, and waited hungrily for his food. It was no more than boiled fish and he was told cheerily by the innkeeper that there was no choice in the matter.

'Them hobs have eaten everything else we have, which is no doubt why they've moved out now. But they only like freshwater fish and will have none from the ocean and so have left that for us. I would say it was a blessing to have food at all in this day and age,' the landlord told him jovially before rushing off to help another customer.

'Come on, eat up, Issy,' Brid urged.

'It's too busy here,' Isolde objected, her nose wrinkling at the sight of the fish. She looked helplessly at Brid. 'I don't think I can eat that. It looks . . . Well, I just can't eat it. You understand. I just can't.' She shoved the plate away, being careful to keep her sleeve pulled down right over her diseased hand.

Rollo swallowed hard and stared at her gloomily. 'Poor Isolde,' he murmured.

Their eyes met and she blinked. No smile brightened that frightened face any more.

'Oh, come on, Issy, just eat the stuff!' Guthrey snapped at her. 'You'll never get well if you don't eat.'

'Hush.' Brid put her hand firmly over her son's. 'She cannot help it. Isolde, dearest, eat the bread. That is at least something.'

Wide-eyed and with tears trickling from her cheeks, the young priestess snatched up her bread, ate it within seconds and then gobbled up Brid's as soon as it was pushed towards her. Rollo thoughtfully offered her his share and in the end she ate that, Guthrey's and Quinn's and was still looking around for more.

Brid asked Aisholt to call to the landlord for more but he could not make himself heard above the merry hubbub within the inn.

'He can't see or hear us back here,' Brid complained. 'Guthrey, get up and fetch some, will you?'

'I'm still eating. Why can't Rollo go?'

Brid pursed her lips at him. 'Why do you have to turn everything into an argument?'

Rollo stood up. He didn't want an argument. He didn't feel good enough about himself to argue that he should or should not do anything any more. He stumbled through to the main room in the tavern, taking pains not to trip on the stranger's boots that were still visible near the inglenook. Eventually he caught the attention of the busy landlord, asked for another basket of bread and then turned to wind his way back through the tables. He stopped short. The man seated in the inglenook wasn't a stranger at all. It was Arathane; he couldn't believe it! What was the man doing here sitting in an inn rather than racing after Silas? He had left days before the rest of them.

Rollo took a couple of eager paces forward, stopped at the man's boots and smiled up at the hooded face. A big man with long hair, he was quite unmistakable. For once he had removed his horned helmet, which was placed on the table in front of him, and the battle scars to his scalp where he had been sliced with a blade were clearly visible. 'Hello there!' the youth said brightly.

Arathane looked up with a start. He didn't quite look Rollo in the face and his eyes had a strangely faraway look about them. 'Rollo! Rollo, is that you?' he asked.

'Well, yes, of course it's me,' the youth replied uncertainly. 'But, Arathane, you can't see. What's happened to you?'

'Trust a youngster to be so blunt. I've sat in this room three hours now, listening to the comings and goings, and no adult has once mentioned the fact that I am blind. But you come bouncing up and you come straight out with it.'

Rollo was speechless for a second and then stammered, 'But-but what happened? You had better come and join the rest of us. We're at the back.' He offered the man his hand and led him through to the back room, which was very much colder and less welcoming than the main tavern.

Brid stood up immediately. 'Arathane! I don't know if it's good to see you or not. You left long before us. I didn't expect to catch up with you.'

Arathane felt for a chair and sat down heavily, the terrier rushing up to sniff at his hands and explore his unfamiliar smell. 'He got to the port just before me and took a big Nattardan trader that was headed out west into the Diamond Seas. But I couldn't get a passage that way myself. No other vessels were heading that way and, hardly surprisingly, I had nothing like enough money to charter a vessel large enough to make such a journey,' he said flippantly. 'A good ship will cross from here to the Diamond Seas but only the very sturdiest and finest will cross the black waters between there and Athell. I was sitting waiting for the right opportunity and someone who could help me but I didn't expect it to be you.'

'I don't know that we are the right ones either. We certainly don't have that kind of money on us. We need Spar,' Brid said flatly. She carefully explained their decisions that had brought them to this stage, all the while her eyes fixed on Arathane's though she did not ask what had happened to his sight.

Eventually, it was Guthrey who demanded to know what had blinded him, though Brid silenced her son. 'He will tell us in his when he's ready and if he wants to. You must learn patience and a little more tact.'

'Mother, don't be ridiculous. There's no harm in asking.'

Brid snapped her head round at her son and glowered angrily. Guthrey rose in objection to this treatment, letting his chair topple backwards and clatter loudly to the flagstones. Walnut yelped as it caught his tail.

Arathane raised a hand. 'It's too long a tale to tell,' he said gently. 'Please, Guthrey, be seated. We have more worrying things to contend with. Silas has slipped away. If we can find transport quickly, we may catch up with him on the Diamond Seas, but if he gets beyond that it's going to be very much harder to track him.'

'One wonders how you managed to track him at all,' Guthrey said harshly, staring fixedly at Arathane's eyes.

'Please excuse my son,' Brid begged. 'I have failed utterly to raise him in a becoming manner.'

'It would take more than that to offend me,' Arathane assured her. 'But tell me, where is Baron Caspar now?'

'He should have been at the Fin. He should have left his mark to say he had been there, but he has not. It can't have taken him long to get through Leaf's hidden realm and find any answer that there was to be found, and since we have been delayed he should certainly have been here before us.'

Arathane nodded. 'I see. And since we cannot possibly go on without him, we had better set out and find him.'

'I would never go on without Spar,' Brid said flatly and sighed heavily, her whole stature drooping at the thought. She suddenly seemed to remember herself and sat up stiffly as if she had said something improper. 'Naturally, some will have to remain here and regularly check the rendezvous point in case he appears; others must go in search of him.'

Rollo sank into his chair, waiting to have his future decided for him. Though Guthrey eagerly argued about who should remain and who should go, Rollo decided there was no point arguing. He was certain Brid would dictate regardless of what anyone else thought.

'Aisholt, you and Rollo should go,' she said firmly, proving Rollo right – or so he thought at first. 'I must stay with Isolde and it seems best to split the boys up so that we have no more trouble.'

However, Brid did not get the final say. Arathane shook his head at her. 'No, Aisholt must stay with you in case you have need of protection. I shall go with Rollo.'

'But –' all objected in unison.

The blind man smiled at them. 'You think I can't do it! You think I'm a cripple. Well, we shall see about that in the morning! Now, who's going to help me get upstairs and point me in the direction of bed? Ah, a real bed! Now that's a luxury, wouldn't you all agree?'

Come morning, the Torra Altans breakfasted early and were told by the innkeeper that Arathane was already out, preparing the horses.

Rollo looked across at Brid. 'Do you think this is wise? After all, the man can't see.'

She shrugged. 'Your father said there was something strange about Arathane when he first met him. I don't know what to make of it but he seems confident enough and my guess is he's bluffing about his eyesight. I would say he's feigning blindness as it's an excellent disguise and will help him gather information. After all, no one sees a blind man as a threat.

385

We shall see how he manages on a horse, otherwise I shall send Aisholt with you.'

Rollo nodded, much relieved.

After they had breakfasted and Rollo had packed a few essentials, he, Brid and her two boys marched out into the open where the musty smell from the stables flooded out into a cobbled yard. Many armed men stood on duty, keeping an eye out for any stray hobs since horsemeat was widely known as one of their favourites. A clatter of hooves on the cobbles told all that Arathane was ready. The man was obscured by his beautiful mare, Sorrel, who was stamping around excitedly, whinnying at the young gelding Oxgard had lent them, as one of the grooms led it out into the yard. Arathane swung his horse round and raised his head, fixing each of the company of Torra Altans clear in the eye. He smiled broadly and reached out his hand to greet Rollo.

'Make haste, young gallant, the sun is already up and we have no time to lose.'

Rollo looked at him without smiling back. Why had the man deceived them? Brid had been right; it was all a charade. But should he really trust a man who played such games with them?

'Come, we must set out right away and search for your father,' Arathane urged. We cannot delay.'

'But how do we know where to look?' Rollo asked, still fearing what his father would say when he saw Firecracker.

'I've been watching out for three days now and things have changed around here a great deal. Leaf's realm is not so hidden any more, which means something is amiss. I climbed up the Fin only yesterday and saw misty valleys appear in the midst of ploughed fields, and they most certainly had not been there the day before. Anyhow, that is probably why Spar hasn't made it back yet.'

'How is that going to help us find him?'

'Leaf suggested the spot up on the Fin as your meeting point, and there has to be a good reason for it.'

Brid nodded. 'There was indeed. She said it was on the third point of the pentacle from the north, which radiates out from her central city within the hidden realm.' The priestess thought for a minute and then reached inside her pocket for a scrap of paper and a pencil. Hastily, she sketched a diagram and then finally asked Guthrey for some advice. Apparently, Guthrey was particularly adept at the calculation she wished to perform. It took him a minute of scribbling on the paper but soon he handed it back to her triumphantly.

'There you are, Mother.'

'Ah, the wonder of having fine sons.' She beamed at both her boys. 'Let's see. So if you head roughly north-north-east you should be heading pretty much into the centre of the hidden realm.'

Rollo mounted and looked down at the others, wanting to say farewell to Isolde since he was deeply concerned for her. But her face was impossible to see, since she had pulled her hood down low, and refused to look up when he called her name. Rollo shrugged, trying to look as if he didn't care. Brid saved him from embarrassment by reaching up to clasp his hand.

Smiling warmly she said, 'Bring your father back safe and sound, and look after yourself, Rollo.'

Quinn nodded at this. It seemed he had already forgiven him for the scratches to his cheeks. Thankfully, the marks had healed well and, rather than disfiguring the youth, gave him a more imposing look as it marked him out as a man of action. Guthrey, however, shrugged dismissively as if he didn't care whether Rollo came back or not. As a result, Rollo gave him what he hoped to be a bland, superior smile and, on a sudden impulse, rode forward so that he was alongside Isolde. Bending over, he pulled her chin up and kissed her boldly on the lips. Hastily pulling away, the girl gasped in amazement, but Rollo caught the briefest glimpse of her eyes which warmed the depths of his miserable soul. Without looking back, he rode after Arathane, wondering whether he had kissed Isolde merely to rile Guthrey or because he had wanted to please her and make her forget about her ugly, wretched state.

Arathane set a fast pace and the gelding Rollo had been lent was not at all eager to match it. In fact the animal was lazy and spent its time diving for shoots of fresh grass that the warmer weather was beginning to tease from the ground. Forced to constantly drum his heels into the sides of the mulish beast, Rollo was soon fatigued in his attempts to stay with Arathane's high-stepping Tethyan charger. Sorrel was one of the most beautiful horses he had seen, though no doubt his father would still have preferred Firecracker, who was a much longer-legged animal built for speed. Sorrel was heavier but with a little more show, lifting her knees up level with her chest and floating over the ground as she trotted.

Arathane slowed and looked round. 'Come on, Rollo, there's a good lad. Show me what you're made of and get that brute moving.'

'I think the hobs must have eaten all the decent horses,' Rollo grumbled, steadily falling further and further behind as they climbed the steep side of the Fin. The moment he reached the top, the wind, which had been sweeping up from the far side, suddenly rammed into his face and he turned his head to catch his breath. His horse, which was now blowing so hard that it could do no more than walk, lumbered reluctantly up towards the magnificent charger and its rider, who gazed east.

It was wonderfully high on top of the Fin, the wind lifting Rollo's auburn hair from his face. He could taste the wind-borne salt-spray off the sea and felt he could touch the sky. He loved the open and it brought him a momentary sense of peace.

In the foreground, tracks and dusty roads meandered through a patchwork of fields bounded by dry stone walls and populated only by clumps of domed gorse bushes. Beyond that, the roads were swallowed by ancient copses and juvenile woods. A pack of hylups whooped and howled some way to the north while westwards, out towards the sea, a cockatrice lazily circled the sky, looking for young seals that may have been birthed early. The innocent soft-skinned pups would be easy prey as they dragged themselves over the rocks on their first clumsy approach to the sea. Inland there was nothing beyond a pair of honey buzzards to trouble the skies, and the woods were too thick to reveal any predators within. The only thing Rollo could see of note was a curious structure far to the east.

'It looks like some sort of bridge,' he said, squinting into the wind. From here he could just make out dark lines high up in the branches, linking the treetops. The looping structure appeared to be strung out across the treetops for as far as the eyes could see.

'What is it?' he queried.

Arathane shrugged. 'Your guess is as good as mine, but that is surely something made by Leaf's people and should be hidden within their realm,' he guessed. 'Though it's not so hidden any more. Come on.'

Even progressing downhill, Rollo was left far behind, which made him furious with his horse. By the time he eventually reached the foot of the structure they had spied high in the trees, he was red in the face and blowing hard. He looked up to see ropes stringing together slats of wood that formed a broad footbridge high above their heads.

'It must link isolated portions of Leaf's realm,' Arathane suggested.

Rollo nodded. 'If so, we should climb up and use the footbridge.'

Arathane immediately shook his head. 'No, that would mean leaving Sorrel.'

'It would undoubtedly be easier travelling up there rather than working our way through the overgrown woods down here. First, we'd make much better time. Second, we would be able to see far more of the land and so spot my father much more easily. Lastly, if that bridge is a part of the hidden realm, it's more likely to lead us to him.'

'I can't go and that's that, and I would never leave Sorrel unprotected,' Arathane said sternly. 'She would be very vulnerable in these woods alone.'

Rollo frowned at the strange warrior, wondering why he was so heated on the matter. 'Is your horse so important?' he asked curiously.

The warrior nodded. 'Oh yes, more valuable than you can possibly imagine.'

He said no more but pressed on, trying to cut a course as far as possible that kept them beneath the bridge. They rode in silence for two hours or more, working their way back and forth through the thick sections of undergrowth just as Rollo had predicted. He felt uncomfortable in these close woods and longed to be back on top of the Fin with the wind in his hair. He loved the sense of being close to the heavens, imagining that he could taste the sky. Here he felt trapped.

After about an hour, in which Rollo had done his best to ask his companion about his homeland though the warrior had resolutely avoided opening up to him, Arathane abruptly raised his hand for silence. Rollo drew to a halt, listening intently. He heard the sound of growling scavengers snaffling up food and arguing amongst themselves. Immediately, he reached for his knife.

'They're ahead of us,' Arathane whispered. 'Keep your wits about you.' From a sheath buckled to Sorrel's saddle, he drew a short serrated sword with a curved blade. They rode forward warily. 'Stay right behind me, Rollo,' the man hissed.

Rollo swallowed, fearing that the scavengers might be hylups, but as it turned out they were ordinary wolves. Ribs and hip bones pressing through their thin coats, they looked to be near starving and were suffering, no doubt, from the competition of the greater predators. Snatching up remnants of torn flesh, they scattered nervously the moment the two riders approached. Rollo stared down at the messy remains of hobs that had been pulled apart by the wolves.

'How strange to find only dead hobs. If there had been some sort of skirmish, you would expect hobs to have taken one or two victims at least.'

'At least,' Arathane agreed with him.

'So what do you suppose killed them?' the youth asked, looking down in disgust at the purple guts that had been yanked out from the hobs' bellies.

Arathane pointed upwards. 'That's what killed them.' Above their heads, sections of rope were dangling down, broken slats still caught in the tangle. 'They were on the bridge when it broke and they must have fallen to their deaths. Get up there and see if you can see anything while I take a look around here.'

'What? So that I can fall to my death too?' Rollo was not all that keen on heights.

'You'll be careful,' Arathane told him flippantly.

The youth examined the nearest tall tree supporting the bridge. It was impossible to climb since the trunk was smooth with no lower branches to help him up.

'Impossible,' he muttered. At least it was impossible for him. He turned to examine the broken remains of the bridge that dangled down from above. A number of tattered and frayed ropes hung down to within a few feet of the ground and he grabbed one. But he managed to haul himself up no more than half a dozen feet before his arms were exhausted. He was about to give up when he saw a tattered bit of cloth caught in a twist of rope just a little way above him. With one last burst of effort, he hauled himself up the last two yards and grabbed the cloth. His skin burning on the rope, he slithered down and landed heavily alongside his horse.

Arathane, who had been busily examining the ground some distance away, looked up. 'That wasn't much of a look.'

'I found this,' Rollo said, holding up the cloth and forbearing to rise to the taunt. It was a patch of green cloth woven in a distinctive herringbone style, the fabric smooth and oiled on one side and soft and fluffy on the other. 'I'm sure that was Leaf's.'

Arathane nodded. 'I think it's likely. Look what I've found.'

Rollo stared at the footprints in the mud. One imprint was easily recognizable, even down to the crack across the ball of the foot where his father's boots had worn through. He knew that boot, even knew the cobbler who had made it. The other was small and neat and was most probably Leaf's. Rollo bent down and examined the prints more closely. 'There's another pair of boots here not dissimilar to the one I took to be Leaf's, only a little bigger perhaps.'

Arathane nodded. 'Yes, I make four different sets of footprints altogether.'

'Where's the fourth?' Rollo asked doubtfully.

Arathane traced a large area nearly three feet long by a foot across with a stick. 'Do you see it now?'

Even when Arathane pointed it out to him, Rollo saw only a depression in the ground but then began to blink. 'But it's huge!'

'Indeed! Very! And it's unusual to see one. They have large feet for their bodies and so rarely leave an impression in the ground. They are used to walking on snow and so large feet are an advantage.'

'Who are they?'

'Haol-garen,' Arathane informed him succinctly, though the name meant nothing to Rollo.

'Do you think it's hunting my father and Leaf?' he asked in dismay.

Arathane shook his head. 'No. Look. Spar's imprint is superimposed on the Haol-garen's. Mind you, it's also unusual to see a Haol-garen without his giant pigs or reindeer, and there's no sign of either. And it's very strange that he's

392

hooked up with Spar Hmm, Arathane said thoughtfully but, as usual, did not offer Rollo much insight into his thoughts.

Rollo still wondered whether he was to be trusted.

Chapter 21

Leaf's fearful squeal was dragged from her mouth by the air rushing up into her face. She was falling, dropping fast as she swung downwards in an arc.

Her whole being was focused on the whistling speed. Sickness welled up within her as her stomach was left behind. A sharp pain tore at her wrist as the rope twisted round it, biting deeper into her skin. The rope snapped taut, jarring her arm sockets. There was no way that her grip would have held and it was only the loop of rope digging into her skin, stripping off the outer layers of flesh, which stopped her falling.

Lug was now somewhere high above but, as she began to swing upwards again, leaving her stomach behind, she could hear the crack of branches breaking. Like a pendulum, she swung back and forth. Teeth gritted, she concentrated only on the rope, praying the knot around her wrists would hold lest she fall to her death. It seemed to take forever before the violent swings lessened and she was finally left dangling by her arms, feet hanging high in mid-air. She swallowed, struggling for breath, then tried to think and orientate herself.

She had heard screams and cries all about her, mimicking her own, one or two rushing by at tremendous speed and fading as they fell, and she knew those were the cries of those who had been unable to hold on as the bridge broke. Blinking, she managed to nudge her hair out of her eyes with her shoulder. Scrabbling for a foothold amongst the tangle of ropes from the collapsed bridge so that she could take some of the pressure off her arms, she looked downwards. Vastly relieved, she saw that

Caspar was still there, clinging to the debris of the rope bridge just a little way below her.

She looked up to see Aconite just a little to the left and above, but raised her eyes a little more and gasped in horror. A tall bony hob was feeling its way down towards her. The others must have fallen but one had somehow found the strength to hold on. With the ropes tightly twisted about her arms, she was locked in place and had no means of escape.

'Oh Mother, no,' she murmured, imagining how the hob would eat her right where she was, helplessly trussed up like game left to hang. She wriggled frantically, trying to pull herself free as the hob's glinting eyes fixed on her. The two lines of coarse hairs running either side of its protruding spine stood on end with the excitement of attack. It looked down; a thin tongue pushed out between fleshless lips, the nostrils of its nose pared back, revealing the white gristle. It chortled and grunted in its throat, the sinews taut on its legs and arms as it worked down through the interlocking ropes as easily as a spider through its web.

Leaf thrashed back and forth in a desperate effort to free herself. It looked at her and then twisted towards Aconite, its tongue flicking out to taste the air.

'Me smells baby,' it uttered. 'Juicy, wet, moist foetus within the sack. What a morsel! A bloody, tender morsel!' it chortled.

Leaf stared in horror, watching in disbelief as the hob altered its course and slithered away from her towards Aconite. The girl from the Sanctuary gave out a soft moan of fear. Somehow she had already wriggled free from the twist of ropes and was clinging to the dangling slats that had once formed the footbridge but now hung like a stepladder. One arm was hooked around one of the slats. Balancing her feet on the wobbly structure, she looked down at the fifty-foot drop to the ground below as if wondering whether to plunge to her death or allow her belly to be sucked out by the hob. She fixed the hob clear in the eye and slowly moved her free hand to her fur satchel, withdrawing a vial. She bit it and Leaf immediately assumed that she had chosen to poison herself just as her comrades had done in the Sanctuary.

The hob lowered itself further, then, looping its legs through the slats, suddenly swung so that it was upside down, its face right before Aconite's. At that moment, the girl spat out a spray of liquid into the hob's face. The creature screamed, clamping its hands to its eyes, frantically squirming and writhing, trying to rub its eyes to be free of the caustic liquid. A second later it lost its grip and was tumbling down to crash to the earth far below.

Leaf didn't care whether it was dead or just too injured to move; she only knew it could no longer harm her. Her breath came in short gasps; she was beginning to panic. Her hands were going numb from the rope cutting off the blood supply to her fingers and it felt as if her arms would soon come out of their sockets. It was a hand pushing her feet up from below that first gave her hope. Her toes were eased onto a foothold and, a moment later, Caspar clambered up beside her. He nodded at her with a warm smile as if to congratulate her for holding on.

'Good girl,' he praised her for a bravery. 'We'll be all right now. Can you hang on if I cut your hands free?'

Leaf stared back, too frightened to speak; she wasn't really sure.

Caspar again nodded as if he understood. 'Well done, Aconite,' he praised the other girl. 'Bravely done!'

Aconite, however, could not answer because she was busily spitting as if trying to be free of the taste in her mouth. 'Water,' she spluttered. 'I need water.'

Caspar turned back to Leaf. 'I'm going to cut your left hand free now,' he told her. With his knife, he sawed at the bonds until they frayed through. She tried to flex her fingers but they had no grip.

'Spar!' she managed to whimper.

Caspar smiled at her as if this was of no consequence. 'It's no problem, Leaf. I shall simply retie you to myself. We're not going to climb down,' Caspar told her in a reassuring tone as she gaped at him. 'We're going to go up, back onto to the bridge again.'

Leaf nodded. It was of course the most obvious plan and she was just beginning to smile back at Caspar when she remembered Lug. He was still swinging from a creaking branch that all of a sudden gave way, the branch crashing down onto what was left of the bridge above. Leaf cringed as chunks of timber whistled past her. She was expecting Lug's body to follow and crush them all but then she heard the great man's cries above as he thrashed about.

Knotting her to him whilst clinging to the threads of the bridge, Caspar gave out an alarmed grunt and Leaf felt the ropes holding her shake violently. 'Oh no!' he murmured under his breath.

There was a sound of wood tearing.

'The suspension posts!' Leaf cried.

A second later they were falling fast again and were stopped abruptly as the ropes snapped taut. One of the supports must have suddenly given and released a length of rope. Swinging in mid-air, Leaf saw that they were still about thirty feet above the ground. The ropes creaked ominously and the structure juddered as two great feet slowly worked their way downwards, followed by Lug's giant form. He was climbing down what was left of the bridge, ropes twanging free and flying upwards as they gave under the stress. Very soon there would be nothing left of this section of the bridge.

They slipped again and then once more as Lug finally passed them and reached the end of the rope only a few feet below Leaf's toes. He looked up to give them a grin before letting go and thumping to the ground. The bridge sprang up again and they bounced up and down. Leaf was profoundly glad that Caspar had secured her to him, as she would not have had the strength to hold on. At last they came to rest, the ropes above still snapping at irregular intervals.

'Well, we can't very well go up now,' Caspar said with some

regret. 'Lug!' he called out. The great man didn't look up but appeared to be using the heels of his great hairy feet to turn the fallen hobs into pulp. 'Lug, stop that!' Caspar commanded.

Reluctantly the Haol-garen raised his head. 'I don't like heights,' he grunted. 'Don't have wings so I don't like heights.'

'No,' Caspar said patiently. 'But how good are you at catching? We're going to jump down to you one at a time.'

'I'm not!' Leaf contested the idea. 'I can't. He'll miss.'

'He can't possibly miss. You'll only have to drop about twenty-five feet. Lug has big hands.'

'I can't,' Leaf wailed, feeling sick to her stomach and now wishing that the hob had eaten her. She really didn't want to fall.

Without any argument or discussion, Aconite leapt away from the ladder of the bridge and, with arms spread wide, fell towards Lug, who caught her neatly and lowered her safely to the ground. Leaf felt even more panicked, her heart pounding in her throat. If Aconite could do it, so could she, but the height . . . falling like that . . .

'You've got to do it,' Caspar said sternly and took out his knife ready to cut her free.

Leaf couldn't even protest. She just whimpered and closed her eyes, every inch of her body shaking. Oh, if only she could be sitting at her nice cool desk with a newly cut plume in her hand. If only there were a library spreading before her and her task was to correlate the position and progression of the stars with the tilt of the rapidly spinning earth over the next millennium. Then she would be at peace, fulfilled and relaxed. Never again would she be dissatisfied with her lot. She was not an adventurer and it was only her deplorable impulsiveness that had goaded her into helping Caspar, which had led to the horrible trail of events.

'Ready?' Caspar asked as he sawed through the last threads of the rope.

'No!' she shrieked but was unable to resist as he shook her hands free of the rope. He had her fists in his now.

'We go on three,' he told her. 'Lug, are you ready?'

'I guess,' the Haol-garen replied casually, which did little to bolster Leaf's confidence.

'One, two,' Caspar chanted and suddenly Leaf was falling. She had known, of course, that he would predictably try to pre-empt the situation but it had helped a little and though she felt horrible sick as her stomach was left behind she was amazed at how Lug caught her and cradled her to him before lowering her to the ground. A second later, the Baron was placed beside her.

Still shaking with fear, Leaf picked her way through the squashed remains of the hobs to find a bare piece of grass. For a few moments she thought she would be sick, but at last she was able to breathe more easily.

'There, that wasn't so bad,' Caspar said lightly.

'Hmm,' she grunted. 'I am never going to speak to you again.'

'You're beginning to sound like an irrational human,' Aconite teased. 'You know full well that you had to jump.'

Leaf made a face. She did indeed know but it didn't make her feel any better.

'Now what?' Caspar asked, immediately pressing to draw their attention back to their task. 'Can we rejoin the bridge? Or do we have to make it on foot?'

Leaf stared up at the tall trees whose lower branches had all been snedded away in their youth to prevent them from being climbable. She knew that the High Ways were only accessible at a small number of points and it was statistically unlikely that they would be near one of those. There was clearly no alternative but to progress on foot. 'By my reckoning, we have come much of the way towards our rendezvous point already. We shall just have to do the best we can on the ground.'

Leaf ran her trembling fingers through her matted hair. After the trauma of the last few minutes, she found it very difficult to focus and was only able to stagger on after the others. It was only when Aconite halted smartly and she nearly bumped into her that she actually looked up. Hand on her belly, Aconite was looking slowly about her, sniffing the air.

'Blossom,' Leaf confirmed. 'Blossom, honeysuckle and roses and something else; I'm not sure what.'

'Marchpane and sweet wine,' Caspar said with confidence. 'And it's may blossom. Quite a potpourri of intoxicating smells.'

'There is nothing in the least intoxicating about them,' Aconite corrected him. 'They are merely pleasing.'

'Seductively pleasing,' Caspar added.

'Don't be ridiculous,' Leaf chided. 'How can a smell be seductive?'

'You, my dear girl, are simply too young to know,' Caspar commented, looking around him expectantly.

Lug was licking his large soft lips. 'I don't know about seductive. Don't smell like no lass of Haol-gar that I know, though I have to admit there is usually the warm smell of hog about them.'

'I have no doubt,' Aconite agreed with him.

'We should keep moving,' Leaf urged and began to step forward but, to her dismay, Lug had already begun to pace in the opposite direction. 'Lug, come back,' she called. 'We need you.'

'I'm hungry,' he dismissed her. 'I'm very hungry.'

'Lug, you can't leave us. We have food. Besides, you don't know what that smell is,' Caspar warned him. 'And we need you. Don't you understand? Please don't leave us.'

'No, you're right.' Lug stopped and looked back at him. 'No, indeed. I can't leave you otherwise I won't get my pigs back and I need you small, clever folk to track those dwarves and find my stone.' He reached down and snatched Caspar's arm, swinging him forward with ease as if he were only a child.

'Lug, Lug, dear Lug, you are making a grave mistake. Put me down,' the Baron implored him.

But Lug paid no heed and continued striding away over the

brow of the hill, following the sugar-sweet scent that drifted up on a warm breeze.

'No!' Leaf wailed, her voice drifting away in the breeze. Staring after Caspar and Lug, she slumped to the ground, exhausted by the relentless strife. 'No, don't leave us. You can't take Spar from us. Spar!' her voice trailed away and she looked on dejectedly.

After a long minute of empty silence, Aconite and Leaf looked at each other.

'Well, we can't very well stay here,' Aconite said pragmatically.

Leaf was forced to agree with her and, after reluctantly rising to her feet, stepped out alongside the girl.

'You see,' Aconite told her, 'this is what happens when one has dealings with other species; they make irrational decisions and we are forced to follow them.'

'Because we are too weak without them,' Leaf murmured. 'We need them so we can hardly despise them.'

'I never said I despised them. I just said they made dangerous associates.'

'Paradoxically, they are our only chance of safety,' Leaf expanded. 'We tried to make our world so that we did not have to rely on others, but the truth is it was only a sham.'

'All things in this world are interconnected and it was foolish to ignore those bonds,' Aconite agreed thoughtfully.

Though she abhorred everything that Aconite stood for, Leaf was nevertheless glad of the company of another of her own kind. Like herself, Aconite never accepted things as they were but continually re-evaluated the situation.

They reached the brim of the low valley and stared down the far side of the slope. Leaf smiled at the vivid colours below and felt peacefulness unexpectedly infusing her mood. Nostrils flaring, she sniffed in the divine scents and gazed delightedly at the enticing colours below.

'It's beautiful,' Aconite sighed. 'Like iron sulphide crystals.'

'No,' Leaf argued, 'like the dew on holly berries or like the glistening ink on a fresh page before it has yet dried.'

'Hmm.' Aconite pouted at the cupped valley below. Within it was a settlement of sorts, nestled in a gentle dale. Smoke lazily coiled up from dancing fires set in braziers. The trees about dripped sparkling drops of water as the frost melted. Otherwise, they were clad in a fur of hoarfrost that sparkled in the milky sunlight. There were no huts or houses, as might have been expected, but a number of brightly striped tents. Music and laughter filled the air. Distant figures danced around a pole, wrapping it in brightly coloured ribbons. Lug was already striding purposefully down towards the merry gathering.

'Give me wine! Give me song!' he bellowed.

'It doesn't sound like Lug to be so forward,' Leaf commented.

'The smells have clearly over-excited him,' Aconite suggested. 'He has such a simple mind.'

Leaf and Aconite hurried down into the vale and only as they drew nearer to the settlement did Leaf realize that her perspective had been wrong. They were not so far away as she had thought; it was simply that the flamboyant, plumed tents were much smaller than she had reckoned. She had assumed they were occupied by humans but it was clear now that she had been wrong. *Never make an assumption*, her old tutor used to tell her before he too faded into senility. Reflecting that he had been right, she thought it most unlike herself to be so illogical.

The closer they drew to the fires, the more the air sparkled around them and Leaf thought she could actually taste a very sweet wine on her lips. Now the scent of peaches and strawberries filled the air. Leaf couldn't yet quite tell where the music was coming from but she did know that the music was enticing and enchanting; it was therefore quite possible that they were in danger.

She looked anxiously to Aconite for confirmation, who nodded grimly. 'Fairies,' she murmured. 'We should not intrude.'

Though Leaf and Aconite stood still, Lug was clearly obsessed by the idea of tasting their food and wine. He stamped on boldly, stumbling between the tents that barely came up to his ankles. Leaf was vaguely aware of a flash of colour flitting before her eyes and something soft touching her nose but she couldn't actually see anything specific. The music seemed to drift throughout the valley and it was still impossible to locate the source of the sound.

'They must be using some kind of web to deflect the sound,' Aconite suggested.

Leaf nodded, her eyes straining to glimpse one of the ethereal people. Caspar was kicking and struggling to be free of Lug but was unable to make any progress until the great man simply released him and let him fall to the ground. Like a cat, the Baron was on his feet, braced ready for action. His eyes scanned the scene until they alighted on Leaf and then he looked back up at Lug before relaxing from his crouched stance.

How strange, Leaf thought, to be so trained that the first thing on the mind was battle. Still, she conceded, it was probably a more pleasant feeling than the sense of panic that continually swept through her at the slightest unexpected situation. She wasn't used to this chaos and she didn't like it. Although she knew it was drawing her close to possible danger, she hurried forward to clutch onto Caspar, who was the only thing that now offered her any sense of security in this world. Feeling as if she were no more than five years old, just as she had done when the dragon attacked, she grasped onto his hand.

He wrapped his arm around her. 'Don't worry, little Leaf. There can't be anything dangerous in this happy scene.'

'But they are fairies,' Leaf protested. 'I would have thought it was common knowledge that fairies can be dangerous.'

'It's no good trying to comfort you because it always turns out that you know more about the situation than I thought,' Caspar complained.

'I suspect your own children always know more than you give them credit for as well,' Leaf told him.

Caspar laughed. 'Well, that's where I know you are wrong for once, young lady,' he laughed as the more diffident Aconite stepped up alongside them; she was searching pensively through her fur satchel of potions and powders. Lug chose that moment to stumble deeper into the collection of tents. Caspar gave out a moan. 'Lug, no, please come back.'

'Shouldn't we just leave him?' Aconite asked. 'He seems to me to be a liability; he is so unpredictable and has no more sense than a dog and less training.'

'I wouldn't be rid of a single one of my dogs,' Caspar told her. 'They hunt for me and they guard me. Lug is our greatest asset; we're not leaving him behind.'

The great man of Haol-gar was now stooped over a bubbling cauldron and sniffing the air as if he were smelling hot broth or perhaps a brandy butter. His thick tongue lolled out of his slack mouth. A moment later, he was crouched on the ground, the cauldron cupped in his hand as he blew on it ready to drink the steaming brew.

'No, Lug! Just leave that,' Caspar warned, shaking Leaf off him and marching purposefully towards the giant. 'You just put that down right now,' he said to the man firmly as much as if he were chastising a disobedient hound. 'Put it down,' he drawled sternly.

His eyes black and wide, Lug looked at him over the top of the cauldron, defiantly taking one huge gulp, and the brew was gone. Sheepishly, he grinned at Caspar and reached out for another pot. His hand a little more clumsy this time, he lifted it up as if to make a toast. 'To Grunda!' he slurred. 'And my pigs.'

The brew sloshed over the top of the pot and onto Caspar, who shook himself as if dazed. He protested loudly but seemed unable to stop licking his lips. Leaf and Aconite sighed in unison.

Aconite raised her eyebrows at the display. 'It seems there's little difference between a dog and its master after all.'

'It's the fumes,' Leaf concluded.

Aconite nodded. 'The heated liquid gives off vapours, which clearly have a very strong effect.'

Leaf's nose began to twitch; the pleasant smell was tantalizingly and relaxing. When the bright lights came dancing towards her through the growing twilight that had crept up unnoticed, she didn't seem to care. Even Aconite was beginning to smile.

'So peaceful,' Leaf sighed, transfixed by the blue flame of the fire. Somewhere in the back of her mind, she was aware of all the different chemicals that might burn to produce a blue light. But when she tried to concentrate on them, the names seemed to spin in her head. She imagined hands within her mind trying to grasp them but they slipped away from her as if they were wet cakes of soap.

Aconite was on the floor, beginning to hum to herself as she untied her precious fur satchel and revealed twenty-four vials pocketed neatly into separate compartments. She began to tap them lightly with her finger, producing melodious notes.

'It is intoxicating after all. The human was right. There is a smell that we had not identified. One of these,' she studied her vials with a frown, 'I am sure is an antidote to this poison, but you know . . .' She paused and began to bite her lip. 'You know, I really don't know which one it is. And I ought to because I could normally tell you which one it was in my sleep, but nothing seems to be quite keeping still.'

'Fairy magic,' Leaf said, trying to suppress an inexplicable urge to giggle. 'My old nurse used to tease me about it and I always told her – as she wasn't quite as educated as she might be – that magic doesn't exist.'

'Of course magic exists,' Aconite snapped at her. 'Magic is having the knowledge to control one's environment in a way that others cannot understand or detect. I understand this situation perfectly,' she said with an exaggerated slur, 'only I can't quite seem . . .' Again her words trailed off and she began to hum a tune.

Leaf breathed in the sweet smells. 'Ah, but they are so

pleasant.' She understood, of course, that they were breathing in an intoxicating vapour. Lug had even drunk gallons of the pure liquid, but knowing that didn't help them. Her legs and her eyelids were already feeling extremely heavy. Slowly, she sank down onto the damp grass and decided that, just for a moment, she must close her eyes.

She didn't know how long she slept but, as she began to wake up, the one thing she did know was that she was extremely comfortable. Soft black fur covered her naked skin, which was clean for once. Ah the beauty of it! She couldn't believe it since she had been unspeakably filthy for weeks. Someone had even cleaned her fingernails. The marquees and tents were gone and she appeared to be beside a babbling brook, starlight above twinkling in a bright frosty night, the reflection of a fat moon bobbing in the water. She loved the silvery colours and the mystery of night. Sitting up, she realized she was completely naked underneath the furs but that a selection of wispy gowns had been laid out for her use. Hastily, she scrambled into the nearest, noticing with fascination how the moonlight brought out rainbow colours, which twisted and swirled as the feather-light fabric moved.

Her hair, which was normally a plain brown colour, sparkled about her shoulders and she smelt not a bit like herself but as if she had been dunked in a honey-filled vat. For once, she felt no sense of panic but was filled with an inner calm, which she had never before experienced. The feeling was so lovely that she wanted to cling on to it forever.

A glass goblet glinted near at hand and, after sniffing it tentatively and being overwhelmed with the fabulous scent, she drank it eagerly. Though she knew at the back of her mind that she should not and that she ought to be pressing on with their urgent task, she couldn't help herself. Numbly, she drank, revelling in the sensation of physical and mental ease that spread out from the centre of her body. She wanted to dance. Leaf giggled at the idea. Normally, she would not have been interested in such a frivolous activity. She was fascinated to know why other races enjoyed the rhythm and the sense of unity that dancing provided for them but she had no wish to perform such gavottes herself. However, a moment later she was staggering clumsily to her feet, and found herself swaying back and forth to the bass notes of a repetitive rhythm. A sudden flash of light to either side didn't even make her jump as a spray of fireworks flashed into the air and cascaded down as liquid gold and silver.

'It's beautiful,' she murmured. 'Truly beautiful.' Never before had she felt physical pleasure from simply looking at something. It made her head feel warm and fuzzy as if it were floating on a cushion of purple cloud. It was a ridiculous notion but she didn't care. For once, she was not analysing what might be making such fabulous colours but considered only that she loved them. Nothing had ever been beautiful before for its own sake, and it was an enormous release to be able to accept something as it was.

Vaguely, she wondered where Caspar was and momentarily troubled herself with the thought that she should be trying to find him but, at that second, she was simply too fascinated by the colours to care.

She sat by the fire until it was nearly dawn and was unworried that she appeared to be alone. With daybreak came the sound of birdsong intermingled with pipes and harps, which played so softly she wasn't entirely sure that she might not be imagining them. When a dancing light appeared before her, she blinked and tried to focus. Slowly, the morning light gave the insubstantial form structure and she saw a tiny little creature with a pert face and large blinking eyes staring at her quizzically.

'You have not slept long enough, child,' the fairy said in a silken voice. Reaching out a delicate hand, she stroked Leaf's nose. 'You should sleep. You'll feel all the better for more sleep.'

Leaf nodded, agreeing with the sentiment entirely. Without further thought, she curled up in the furs and drifted off into a lulled world of rest. In her dreams, she was aware of the bright sun warming her body. She then felt a chill descend before the warmth eased through her again. Nuzzling into the soft pillows beneath, she guessed she must have slept on through one night and into the next day.

When she finally awoke, she realized that she had been moved and that it was nearing evening once more. She could hear grunts and groans and she presumed they came from Lug. She could hear the sound of light-hearted female voices giggling, the croons of a couple lost in pleasure and the gentle sigh of someone as if they were relaxing in a bath. Again the soft music played, reminiscent of the mellow days in late summer when the entire world seems too hot and lazy to do anything.

She could even taste cider on her lips as if she had slaked a summer thirst with a flagon of the amber brew. It was all very mysterious and confusing. Too confusing. She must try to think, yet she couldn't quite stir herself enough to manage it. She wasn't even afraid any more – and she so enjoyed the release. This was what it must be like to be Lug or Spar, she pondered, without considering all the things that they might be afraid of. 'I want to be like this forever,' she murmured, gradually realizing that she was mimicking the words spoken so softly by a small voice into her ear.

She shook herself violently, trying to thrash her hands as if to swat away a wasp though her limbs would not respond. Suddenly, it dawned on her that this complacency was a result of her susceptibility to suggestion. Something was implanting these thoughts in her head and she was quite happy to absorb them.

A little more insistently now, the hypnotic voice continued in its dulcet tones, 'Dream. Sleep. You never want this to end.'

But why wouldn't I want this to end? she asked herself.

'Dream,' the voice continued its lullaby. 'Dream and rest and all your troubles will go. Everything will soon be righted.' The same voice jarred in her thoughts as it cried out more sharply, 'Where's that vine imp got to? We need more of his brew here. Her mind is still too active. Make haste unless you want to be outside the Haven again. There is no space for mistakes.'

A ladle was pressed to her lips and Leaf squinted at a narrow face that chatted noisily and disturbed her sense of ease. She tried hard to sit up but someone pinched her nose and, seconds later, a warm, alcoholic brew smelling of fermented apples flooded down her throat. She struggled against it for a few more moments and then willingly drank more. It made her feel so good, so untroubled.

The dreamy sleep conquered her again, though she was still vaguely aware of her surroundings as if she were sleepwalking. She had noted varieties of people being brought in to sit by the fire and even oxen that swayed and staggered as if half asleep, tiny little fairies sitting on their back and crooning into their ears. A silvery-skinned woman of Ash appeared in the valley and Leaf's eyes widened in her sleep. Indeed, the creature was as beautiful as the books described her. It was the grace and fluidity of her movements, the perfect oval face and glossy hair and the provocative sway to her hips that would surely attract males of any species.

Leaf could hear Lug smacking his lips together and realized that the woman of Ash must also be drugged as she smiled back and appeared pleased by this attention. Attention from Lug was surely as desirable as attention from a boar. The giant stumbled to his feet and staggered after her as if he were a puppy stumbling devotedly after its mistress.

So that's how they had kept Caspar and Lug quiet, she thought, disappointed in her companions. Males were so easy to manipulate. From whichever race, none of them was any better than the rutting stag that ran around bellowing and drooling until it dropped from exhaustion.

Bow in hand, a centaur staggered onto the scene, looking bewildered and frightened, its speed too great to be stopped at the outer boundaries of the dale. Lights flew up about its face, confusing it. The creature reared up and lashed with its hooves, striking down one of the fairies. This produced a buzz of alarm. The voice in Leaf's ear ceased and, at last, she had the strength to raise her head just a little and tentatively glimpse what was going on. They were in a cosy dell, small cages hanging from sparsely spaced trees in a field of snowdrops. Bells tinkled in the wind. It was beautiful.

'Hasn't one of you found some way to keep that child repressed,' a light voice demanded.

'It's so difficult. The natural curiosity of a child is much more irrepressible and her mind is so sharp. I daren't give her any more of the brew.'

Leaf blinked at the miniature creature with its gossamer wings that fluttered before her.

'How much longer do we have to keep them here?' the fairy continued.

'Until he comes and decides whether they are useful or not. You know that he said to set traps for any of the scholars from the inner realm. He said if he could take one with him that was even half-grown and half-educated it would hold more knowledge in its head than twenty dwarves.'

The voice at Leaf's ear said sweetly, 'If we give her much more of this brew, I doubt that her mind will ever function again.'

It dawned on Leaf that, for the sake of her sanity, she needed to play along. She sighed blissfully and muttered something about the last rays of the day's sun. At the moment, she wasn't strong enough to stand and try and escape, but perhaps she could be, if she avoided more of the tincture.

The moon slipped up into the sky, fat and red, reflecting the sun that had dipped behind the horizon but whose tilted rays still touched the heavenly body. Leaf sensed an abrupt lull in the activities of the fairies. The creatures, which were less than knee-high, were blessed with luxurious long hair if they were females and tight curls if they were male. With large eyes and sharply defined features on their high-cheekboned faces, they were naturally attractive and even more so now that they settled down to rest and stopped their endless flitting about. Each bore a set of filmy wings protruding above the shoulder and, now that they were still, Leaf could see that each wing glistened with a beautiful mix of iridescent blue and green colours.

Feeling the cold of nightfall, she shuddered and gazed into the darkness. Soon she was aware of a figure that had stepped out of the pitch darkness. Manlike in form, he radiated such a powerful life force that all gazes were drawn to his notable presence. The light from a brazier bounced up into his hooded face and Leaf noted his dark warty skin, long narrow nose and skeletal fingers.

'My Lord! Old Man Blackthorn!' The shrieking vine imps threw themselves trembling to the ground, one or two vomiting in their fear. The fairies sprang closer to one another and huddled to form a single united ball of light. For a moment, the hooded being seemed to be stepping through a tunnel where laughter and music flooded out from a point in the air.

Old Man Blackthorn, as the fairies had addressed him, looked around at the scene and then said in a creaking voice, 'The human and the Haol-garen can die but the two girls will be useful. Look at them! You think they are asleep but you do not look into their eyes deeply enough; there is thought there, strong sentient thought.'

'My Lord, do not make a hasty decision on the human.' One of the fairies boldly stepped forward. 'He speaks of the mysteries and the key to man's power being locked within the earth. He is not an ordinary man.'

Old Man Blackthorn nodded and then turned to greet the mesmerizing vision of an old but very beautiful and sweet-smelling woman who had followed him into the fairies' dell. In amazed awe, Leaf stared and realized that she was seeing with her very own eyes two of the ancient guardians of the speaking races. The old man was the ancient guardian of the hobs and the wispy female was the ancient being whose

411

task, set by the primal gods, was to provide help and guidance for the fairies. The little scholar could not believe it. She had been taught that these ancient great ones were the stuff of myth.

'All is well. I shall send the hobs for him. Now,' Old Man Blackthorn turned back towards the flustered fairies, 'what spoke the Haol-garen?'

'He speaks of nothing but pigs,' one managed to tell him.

'Kill him then,' Blackthorn said dismissively. 'Do not waste another drop of your brew on him.' He turned back to his lovely companion. 'We must go, my fairest lady of the honeysuckle; we have much to arrange.'

Chapter 22

Arathane and Rollo wasted no time following the trail of footprints. Rollo was most alarmed to see that, after about a mile, his father's footprints vanished and only the Haol-garen's and two smaller prints remained. They meandered this way and that, working into lusher pastures and warmer dells where ancient hedgerows blocked the wind. Rollo's nose began to wrinkle as he caught scent of a deliciously sweet smell wafting to him in the breeze.

Arathane, too, halted to sniff the air. 'I don't know! It smells like marchpane, honey and sweet apples!' he exclaimed in some amazement and laughed at the idea. His amusement was soon driven away by a deep frown that returned to his careworn face as he pressed on, constantly soothing his horse's neck as he went. 'There, Sorrel, I know it's not easy but we'll be after Silas soon. We can't let him escape with her and at least we know she is still safe.'

'Who is safe?' Rollo demanded, finding it particularly odd that this man should be talking to his horse. Arathane seemed too sane and too practical to do such a quirky thing.

There was no time for the warrior to reply as they broke out into a glade beside a silver stream. Clearly, there had been an encampment here as there were the remains of a smouldering fire. Littered about the place were pots and pans but of ridiculously small proportions. Rollo wanted to laugh. Breathing in deeply, he sensed the sweetness fill his lunges and ease his troubles. A tiny striped tent lay trampled into the mud but it was not big enough to house even a child.

Rollo breathed in a little more deeply and was soon starting to sway in the saddle. Arathane quickly caught him. The knight had already buried his mouth and nose in his sleeve and was warning Rollo to do the same.

'The lingering vapours must be intoxicating,' he warned, retreating to the trees and keeping his nose and mouth covered. 'It looks like your father has become entangled with fairy folk.'

Both dismounted and Rollo followed cautiously as Arathane worked his way around the edge of the glade and picked up the tracks again. 'It seems Father and his motley assortment of friends happily ambled after the fairies.'

'I suspect they were drugged by the vapours,' Arathane suggested.

A faint trickle of music rang through the woods and, as they pressed on faster, the music grew louder and the delightful sound of singing floated to their ears. Rollo sighed deeply, revelling in the music as it caressed his ears and seemed to bathe his entire body in a sense of well-being and peace.

'The pipes of Pan,' Arathane murmured wondrously. 'They speak straight to the soul.'

Rollo longed to hear more. Devoid of all sense of danger, he must have been unwittingly urging his horse forward because Arathane suddenly reached out and snatched at his bridle before Rollo even knew he had moved.

'Don't be a fool, Rollo. We've got to figure out a way of reaching them without falling under the spell ourselves.' He sniffed at the youth, evidently thinking the task was well beyond him.

Rollo sat up stiffly and tried to concentrate. 'I can do it,' he said smartly. 'I won't succumb. Really I . . .' His words trailed off as the music was joined by another set of pipes that seemed to sigh right through the fabric of his body. He had not heard music like that since the women of Ash had played for his mother within the beautiful halls of the palace of Artor. Then, as now, he sat and listened in rapture. His nerves tingling up and down his spine, he slid from his horse and began to walk towards the sound. He had to have more of it. He had to see the beauties that sang like that.

Arathane caught his collar. 'Idiot, boy, think of your father.'

Rollo frowned. He did not want to think of the Baron; it pained him, made him feel unloved and inadequate. He wanted to revel in the beauty.

Arathane stuffed two small pieces of cloth into his hands. 'Plug your ears up with that and then smell this.' He scooped up a steaming wad of horse dung and pressed it into the youth's reluctant hands. It was still warm, obligingly provided by Rollo's horse. 'That will at least counteract the smell from the vapours.'

'Thanks!' Rollo said sarcastically, recoiling at the stinking ball in his hand, but after a moment realized that it did indeed help. 'If we leave the horses here, we can creep in closer and take a look,' he suggested.

Arathane nodded. 'I'll stay with them and you have a look. Can you do that?'

Rollo nodded. 'I think so. But wouldn't it be safer if you went?'

'Safer for whom?' Arathane asked. 'Just go, lad. I can't leave the horses.'

Rollo's forehead scrunched into a deep frown at this strange sentiment. Again, he wondered whether he should trust this stranger. He had too many dark secrets. Stuffing the cloth into his ears, he found that it did dull the thrilling song of the pipes a little and, as a result, he was more able to concentrate. Pulling himself forward on his elbows, he squirmed along the ground but the movement soon dislodged the cloth in his ears. Gritting his teeth, he struggled to muster the willpower to resist the allure of the pipes but, to his relief, discovered that the clear notes had ceased. The song from the luscious voices of the women continued but was not so enthralling. It was beautiful but did not bend his will in the same way.

Again, he wriggled forward on his stomach, being careful

to sniff at the manure every time he was aware of the sweet-smelling vapours wafting towards him. The trick seemed to work and he remained clear-headed as he wormed forward and was, at last, able to see who was dancing in the vale below.

Keeping his head pressed down low amongst the lichen and crisp copper leaves, hoping his red hair would disguise him a little, he peered at the remarkable scene before him. A ring of striped red and white tents was set up around a campfire. Animals and peoples of many descriptions, even centaurs, taurs and a dwarf, lay snoozing by the fire. Many humans were apparently asleep or drugged while others danced maniacally around a young woman of Ash who sang like a lark. Another group of human men, all naked, were chasing after three other women of Ash, who wore insubstantial veils draped over the smooth lines of their silvery bodies.

Rollo blinked, running his tongue over his lips, his eyes following the women. The dance led them round and around the fire, the bluish-skinned women stopping only momentarily to let the men beg for a kiss before they twirled on, their pert breasts bobbing in their gowns. Rollo was so transfixed with the sight that he barely noticed the strange goings on beyond the campfire until the women of Ash danced towards it and suddenly froze before spinning away in fearful awe.

Rollo stared at the two figures which had caught his eye. Taking a deep breath over the foul-smelling manure, he tried to concentrate. From a distance they looked like humans, but he instinctively knew they were not. One was a female, magnetically beautiful with gorgeous wavy hair and slender arms that curled and hugged about her voluptuous body. The other was male, shorter with dark skin and stiff arms. The way they stood reminded him of a tree in the breeze, and the sense of majesty and power emanating from them made him certain that they were two of the great ones. His father had told him about them and, until that moment, Rollo had thought that Caspar had exaggerated their aura of power and presence, but now he could see for himself that it was true.

The hairs on the back of Rollo's neck tingled as the male being spoke, his voice creaking and harsh. 'Those two girls may prove useful. Between them they will possess bountiful amounts of knowledge.' He was gesticulating with a thorny branch towards two girls lying amongst bluebells. One of them was Leaf.

'What do we do with the Haol-garen?' the woman's sweet voice asked though it was a seductive, tantalizing sweetness and did not possess the comforting tone that Rollo had been anticipating.

He stared at them. They had to be two of the great ones, the ancient ones, the guardians of the races of the Earth. The harsh-toned male was surely Blackthorn, guardian of the hobs.

'Leave him for my hobs. We shall have our lands, sweet lady of the honeysuckle,' he addressed his female companion. 'We have been treated cruelly over thousands of years by man and we shall have our revenge.'

'I do not seek revenge, only a haven.'

Old Man Blackthorn shrugged. 'They have cost my people dear and shall repay me. They have turned against the guardians, turned against the ancient laws, and all transgressors must be punished. Punished, you hear? I should tread on the head of that man there with the woman of Ash and watch his brains ooze out.'

Rollo followed Blackthorn's stare and gaped as he saw it was his father who lay wrapped in the naked arms of a woman of Ash. 'Father!' he murmured to himself, his emotions twisting and tumbling within his mind. What was Caspar doing with that woman? How dare he? At the same time he was terrified for him. Father, get out of there, he willed vainly.

Blackthorn grunted in disgust. 'But I have a use for him.' He waved his staff at the myriad of fairies flitting about Lady Honeysuckle. 'Get the man and the two girls. They are the only ones useful here. The rest we can spoon with an extra dose of the fairy potion and that will be the end

417

of it. The Haol-garen will certainly make a good feast for my people.'

Honeysuckle pouted at this command and held out her hand so that one of the fairies was able to alight on her palm. She whispered something and the ethereal creature fluttered away to its fellows, hastily organizing them.

Rollo had seen enough. Wriggling fast through the undergrowth, he was soon back with Arathane. Panting, he tried to explain what he had seen. 'Old Man Blackthorn! It really was him. I can't believe it!' Rollo panted excitedly. 'He's going to have Lug eaten by the hobs but he wants Father and Leaf and another girl alive. He is having them taken away.'

Arathane listened intently, the wind pushing his long hair back over his horned helmet, which served to make him look imposing and fearsome. Like Rollo, he continued to sniff at the fresh dung and his features remained alert. Suddenly, however, he began to blink as if having difficulty focusing. He spun round.

'Sorrel! No! Sorrel!' The animal was swaying and suddenly crashed to the ground. Rollo's horse staggered back in alarm and then trotted off, snorting anxiously. Arathane sank down alongside Sorrel. 'My sweet Lady,' he crooned over her and then suddenly stiffened up. 'Rollo, the wind is changing! I didn't reckon on Sorrel's susceptibility to the vapours. Sorrel,' he murmured, soothing her neck. 'I shall come back for you. We have to move before we also succumb. Rollo, take my hand!' he ordered.

Rollo thought Arathane's request was odd but he did not question it. Already beginning to feel light-headed himself, he gripped his horse's reins in one fist and grabbed the warrior's hand with the other. Dragging him away into the forest, he helped him skirt around the hollow until they were upwind of the camp. Rollo found that, once he could no longer smell the intoxicating vapour, his head cleared immediately though Arathane seemed to be still suffering some of the ill effects since he appeared unable to focus or orientate himself. But, of course, that was how he had been in the inn. The man truly was now blind! Rollo couldn't believe it.

'What's the matter with you? Why can you see one minute and not the next?' the youth demanded, wondering whether Arathane suffered from some fearful paralysing effect on the brain that came and went, similar to his own affliction.

'We don't have time for explanations,' Arathane said sharply. 'I cannot see without Sorrel; it's as simple as that. Now, tell me what's happening. We've got to help them. We're all they've got.'

Rollo swallowed hard. 'The fairies are packing up camp and dousing their fires.' He glared at the pretty little creatures bitterly as, laughing merrily like camp followers who had drunk too much ale, they tightly bound Caspar and the two girls and began pulling them over the dewy grass. 'They've left all manner of animals sleeping in the vale and are beginning to move out, taking only Caspar and the two strange girls.'

Arathane heaved a sigh of relief.

'I don't see that there's anything to be pleased about. They have my father.'

'Indeed, but they have left us the means to rescue him. You said they left the rest behind and I presume that includes the giant.'

Rollo nodded and then, remembering the man couldn't see, said, 'Yes. And Old Woman Honeysuckle must have countermanded Blackthorn's orders because the fairies have not fed any extra elixir to their victims but have just left them to sleep.'

'Well, that is good. I was certain they would never have enough to do any real damage to the Haol-garen, but at least the rest will shortly becoming round now that the vapours are cooling.'

It was in fact ten minutes before Sorrel came round and she was the first since she had inhaled much less of the toxins than the other creatures. Rollo saw her on the far side of the camp. She shook her head, whinnied and was soon heaving herself up onto her feet. It took her no time to come racing around the glade before anxiously strutting towards Arathane, who lifted himself up in happy greeting. A second later, he was in the saddle, immediately competent again. Other animals were gradually beginning to stir but they were clearly more deeply drugged than the sleek black horse.

'Now for the Haol-garen. Keep your wits about you, lad, and be very wary of the centaurs. They're as vicious as cats,' Arathane warned as he urged Sorrel towards the giant sleeping at the bottom of the vale.

Rollo meekly followed. He had no plan of his own and this man appeared so authoritative that he had no wish to countermand him. Carefully avoiding a sleeping centaur, they approached the drugged giant, who was snoring raucously but was beginning to sniff and snuffle as if he were on the verge of waking. Arathane took his spear and prodded the great man's ribs with it.

'Haol-garen, wake up.' He turned to Rollo. 'It would need a vast amount of vapour to keep such a big creature subdued for long; I am sure he'll come round soon.' Rollo tentatively leaned forward to stare into the huge man's face and was very alarmed that Arathane was treating so huge and strong a fellow in such a rough manner.

'Wake up, you brute! You can't let the fairy folk treat you like this.' Arathane turned to Rollo and said under his breath, 'These giants like things simple and, if someone transgresses, they feel the world is out of order until the debt is paid.'

Rollo considered that he felt the same about things. Who was going to pay for the death of his mother? Who was going to pay for forcing him from his home? There could be only one answer, only one culprit. His father was totally to blame and yet, at this moment, he was terrified of losing him.

The giant woke up with a start and even took Arathane by surprise, knocking him from the saddle and sending him rolling into the dirt. But the warrior quickly somersaulted up onto his feet and stood his ground with his spear aimed at the

Haol-garen's left eye. 'Be eased and still, giant. We mean you no harm.'

'With a spear aimed at me like that? Murderers! Destroyers, the lot of you! What more of me do you want? First you are after my pigs and now you want my very eyes.'

'No, sir, I don't,' Arathane said calmly, though he did not lower his spear. 'I want your help.'

'Why should I help you?'

'Aren't you angry with the fairy folk for drugging you?' Arathane goaded.

The giant shrugged. 'I'm more angry with your fellow man who saw to it that I lost my pigs.' The Haol-garen frowned to himself. 'Come to think of it, where is he? Him and his women. I'll have the little wretch. He promised he'd make amends by helping me find my stone. No one breaks a promise to a Haol-garen, least of all to Lug.' He thumped his chest to indicate himself.

'I told you we shouldn't wake him,' Rollo muttered, edging back from the disgruntled giant.

Arathane appeared unruffled. 'Who do you mean?'

'That little man with the red hair and the cut to his arm. Spar, the girls call him. He stole my hogs and had them killed.'

'That sounds most unlikely,' Arathane said smoothly. 'But if you want him, you had better get up and make haste. The fairies have taken him.'

'No one's taking that little thief from me! He knows about the dwarves who took the Stone of Clarity. How else am I going to get it back? How else am I going to get Grunda? He can help me find the dwarves.'

The thought must have driven out the remains of the drug-induced lethargy since the great Haol-garen leapt up onto his huge feet and begin to stride after the fairies, Arathane urging him along.

'I don't see how he can possibly help,' Rollo complained. 'The fairies drugged him last time; they will surely just drug him again.'

'He knows what happened last time; this time he'll be wary. He'll keep a safe distance until we can come up with a suitable plan.'

The Haol-garen, however, didn't appear to be in the least bit cautious but was marching off at a smart pace, forcing the horses into a brisk canter to keep up.

'Your abilities to predict his actions are not quite as sharp as you would like,' Rollo rudely told his companion.

'Certainly not as sharp as your tongue, lad.'

'What gives you the right to call me lad?' Rollo asked petulantly. 'What gives you the right to patronize me? I'm not a lad; I'm a prince.'

'And who says I'm not?' Arathane retorted.

Rollo was taken aback by this. 'You don't look like one.'

'And you, boy, don't behave like one.'

This riposte came back too quickly and unexpectedly for Rollo and he could not think of a smart answer. Instead he was cruel. 'At least I'm not a cripple.'

The warrior didn't answer for a moment and Rollo was suddenly deeply mortified that he had said such a thing. How could he have been so vile? After all he had also suffered all his life on account of his illness, how could he hold the man's blindness against him? He fully expected the man to reach out and punch him, but he didn't. Arathane simply laughed, the sound strange as the wind whipped it from his mouth.

'If you live to be twenty without someone cutting your tongue out for your mean words, I'll be mightily surprised.'

Very relieved that the warrior had a sense of humour and had not taken umbrage, Rollo laughed. 'So why is it that you can see at times but not at others? Is it something like the fits I suffer, some form of epilepsy or seizure?'

Arathane pressed into a harder gallop, determined to keep up with the giant, and Rollo thought he could not have heard his question. Beyond the Haol-garen, he glimpsed a river ahead, and at the sight of it the giant man began to slow, and so too did Arathane.

He looked at the Artoran. 'No, it's nothing like that. It was Silas.' He raised a hand to silence Rollo's flood of questions. 'I don't have time to explain. Look, they're heading for that sail barge on the great Brue River. If they get out onto the open sea, I don't know how we'll catch them.'

Leaf found herself pressed up hard against Aconite, whose eyes were rolled back and white. She was snoring loudly, and to the casual eye she appeared asleep. Certainly, the fairies seemed to believe she was because they nonchalantly clambered over her and three of them were sitting on her ankles as they busily stirred more of their poppy juices into the sweet-smelling pot of brewing honeysuckle.

Aconite was not asleep, however. Leaf knew that because she could see the vein on her neck pulsing. It was not the steady, quiet pulse of someone in deep rest; it was racing. She puzzled over the thought dreamily for minutes that drifted into hours, or perhaps not; she wasn't entirely sure. She knew there was something about Aconite, however, which she should heed. Was it her breathing, her satchel, or the fact that her hand was extended towards her as if seeking comfort?

Leaf puzzled over the thoughts dreamily and, finally, she became aware that Aconite was breathing through her handkerchief. The thought gradually rose into Leaf's consciousness and she struggled to grasp it. There was also a handkerchief in her extended hand. Surreptitiously, Leaf inched her own hand forward towards her companion and touched her hand. Aconite nudged the handkerchief towards her and Leaf calmly covered the cloth with her palm and very slowly drew it back towards her. It felt moist and gritty as if it contained granules. Carefully, she drew it up to cover her mouth and nose.

Keeping her hair flopped over her face and her eyes flickering as if she were dreaming, she breathed in through the kerchief and realized quite suddenly that Aconite had struck on the very simple solution of using crushed charcoal to filter out the vapours. She wondered what other marvels the girl kept in her satchel. Her mind rapidly clearing, Leaf sighed periodically in her best imitation of one contentedly asleep. It took her only a second to work out that she was lying amongst sail bags on the deck of a moving barge. It was rocking beneath her and she knew they were being rushed away. She had seen the ancient guardians and listened to their foul plot. Blackthorn was in league with the fairies; they wanted her lands and they wanted man destroyed. There was no talk of her own people being annihilated, but no doubt they had presumed it unnecessary since they were dying anyway.

She wouldn't have imagined that the fairies could control the vessel if she hadn't seen them with her own eyes. They worked together like a colony of ants and were wondrously successful at achieving heavy and complex tasks. After sectioning a number of fairies into teams, a single chief would select leaders to organize each section. Each leader wore a back pack containing fine ropes which they attached to the barge's halyards, sheets and ropes, enabling the teams of fairies with their delicate hands to control the sails and tiller. In this manner they had no trouble manoeuvring the barge out into the deeper waters and catching the current.

Leaf managed to stir and sigh whilst keeping her eyes slitted open just enough to look back at the quickly disappearing riverbank behind them. In that brief second, she caught a glimpse of Lug charging after them and thought she saw two riders. She didn't dare stare longer but turned over again, trying not to listen to the sounds of a woman of Ash cooing over Caspar. She had grown to depend on the man and she couldn't bear the thought of his attention being absorbed by anyone else, even if he were drugged. She wondered why the fairies didn't just give him more of the potion and make him sleep and considered it must be for the same reason that they hadn't dosed her with more poison either. They wanted them alive and responsive and did not want to risk the possibility of rendering them permanently catatonic.

'Can you swim?' Aconite whispered in her ear when the

fairies began to chant a loud song of work to ease their toil. The sound muffled their voices.

'No,' Leaf whispered back.

'Nor can I. There seems to be nothing we can do but wait for an opportunity.'

The opportunity, however, came sooner than expected though Leaf was not aware of it until the fairies started to panic. After a while, the river passed between high hills to left and right and entered a narrow valley where cliffs rose up sharply from a short footing of gravel banks and a narrow strip of grass and shrubs. The ravine was in deep shadow and stilled the wind. The air thickened about them and soon they were sliding into a dense mist, which rapidly turned to fog. The fairies could no longer see to navigate. Some flew ahead, bearing lanterns, but it was so thick that even their fairy lights barely helped. At last, the chief fairy, an elderly male wearing traditional green leggings and an emerald jacket, called to his fellows to ship oars. Soon, they were drifting and shortly after that they came to a slow, grinding halt as the barge crunched onto a shingle bed. All was quiet. Even Caspar and the woman of Ash had ceased their lovemaking and were now both sound asleep, wrapped tightly in each other's arms.

Leaf wondered whether now was an opportunity for her and Aconite to slip away, but what could she do about Caspar? How was she going to wake him up? Foolish, foolish man, she thought to herself angrily. She glared at them for a second and then turned her attention back to the fairies, and at once noted their fear. The fog had brought about a substantial change in their behaviour. They were now huddled together in the centre of the barge, grasping one another's hands for fear of being swept out into the mist and lost. Clearly, each relied on being a part of the group. At any rate, they were distracted and no longer watched over their captives.

Now was their chance; they should run and leap for the shore. Since the barge had run onto gravel they would not even have to swim. Tentatively, she looked at Aconite, who now had her head raised just a little and looked prepared to act. Then Leaf looked towards Caspar. He was still sound asleep. What could she do? She couldn't leave him. She was about to wriggle towards Aconite so that they might confer, but the young girl from the Sanctuary suddenly leapt up, hurled herself over the edge of the barge and splashed into the shallows below.

The fairies began to chatter excitedly and, forming a long chain, they tried to reach her but, as soon as the fairies farthest from the ship were swallowed by the fog, the rest shrieked in terror and began to haul their fellows back in. Soon they were huddling together again, touching one another to be certain that everyone was all right.

Leaf made to follow Aconite. The girl from the Sanctuary was right; now was their only chance. She must first escape and then formulate a plan to rescue Caspar. Suddenly she was on her feet but it was all too late. The fairies didn't waste time with potions on her. Instead, they wrapped her up in silk threads from their packs as if they were spiders cocooning a fly. At first she thought they were only going to wrap up her hands and feet, but they kept on going until half her body was parcelled into a tight bundle. The wrapping came up higher and higher as the fairies flew about her. Thankfully, they were more gentle as they came to her chest, leaving the cords a little loose.

At least she could breathe. It was not much compensation but it quelled her panic for a few moments as she thought they would surely stop their labour there. But they didn't! Though she begged and wept, they kept on wrapping the silk higher and higher until is was over her neck and then her mouth, and at last she was sealed into darkness, the world now muffled and distant.

For a second all was pitch blackness, and then tiny points of light appeared about her head. With intense relief, she realized that they were piercing the cocoon, making tiny holes to enable her to breathe; but, still, she could not move.

The minute air holes helped only a little and breathing was

extremely difficult as she succumbed to panic. She feared she would go mad in only a matter of seconds, her breath coming in laboured gasps and her heart pounding within the coffin. Tightly bound within her cocoon, she was toppled from her upright position and now was rolling back and forth on the deck, utterly disorientated. She would be sick any minute and then would probably drown in her own vomit.

Be calm; be strong; be detached, she told herself and set her mind to the task of distracting herself from her fear. With a determined effort she concentrated on working out the cubed root of eight thousand and ten, which was the first number that came into her mind.

Chapter 23

Rollo dragged his horse to a halt alongside Arathane. Both horses were blowing hard with the effort of scrambling alongside the riverbank while the barge drifted effortlessly along, assisted by a kindly current. The going had become considerably harder as the valley narrowed and they began to enter a gloomy ravine.

'What now?' Rollo demanded as he watched the barge slide into the heavy fog and vanish rapidly from sight.

Arathane didn't answer but looked up at the giant, who had finally stumbled to a halt and remained still until they caught up with him. His legs were scratched from tearing through the holly tress that raked at his thighs and arms, leaving angry gashes. The great man rubbed at them distractedly.

'However am I going to get Grunda now? If I lose that little man, he'll never help me find the dwarves that took my stone.'

Rollo blinked at this. Dwarves had stolen precious stones from Isolde and Quinn. Now they had taken one from this Haol-garen. It seemed to him that the dwarves were as much of a menace as the hobs were.

'What can you see from up there?' the knight called to the giant.

Rollo looked at Arathane sideways. It still troubled him that this man would not explain anything about why he came to be in this part of the world hunting Silas. And what was wrong with his eyesight? It was most peculiar.

He pointed to the green vegetation, which they brushed

through. 'There's a few bushes around my feet and I think I trod on a beeskep a moment ago but otherwise nothing but mist,' the Haol-garen rumbled back at them. He then sat down heavily on the ground, pulled up one of his huge grubby feet to rub at a callous on the hairy sole and pluck out a dozen holly leaves that were embedded in the flesh along with the broken reminds of a sticky beeskep. 'I haven't run this far in years. This isn't good for me and I don't like the fairy mist. It'll probably devour our minds again. I knew trouble would come the moment my stone was stolen. I knew this was going to happen!'

Rollo sighed and restated his original question. 'So what do we do now?'

'I really don't – What was that?' Arathane asked as a splash interrupted him. He raised a throwing axe and stood stiffly alert, waiting at the edge of the mist to deal with whatever approached. Something was running towards them, breathing hard.

Even though they were expecting someone, Rollo was still surprised when the figure so suddenly emerged from the mist. The figure was not so surprised to see them.

'I hope you are friendly. I've had my share of bad luck today,' a girl dressed in soaking wet fur panted.

Rollo watched as, gasping, the girl slumped down gently, pressing at her softly rounded belly as if it pained her. She breathed heavily for a minute and then looked up at them. 'You stink!' she accused.

'Madam, we have no wish to offend,' Arathane began.

The girl waved aside his words and pointed a slender finger at Rollo.

'You're his son. You have his hair.'

'You were with Father!' Rollo leapt at her words. 'You were one of the ones taken by the fairies.'

The girl, who had a heavy chin and small eyes, looked at him and sighed. 'I got away. Leaf was too frightened to move and your father was too busy sleeping in the arms of a woman of

Ash to know he had even missed an opportunity to escape. Stupid man!' she snapped. 'And I need him.'

'I need him too,' the giant grumbled.

'You do?' the girl queried.

'I wouldn't say so if I didn't,' the Haol-garen told her curtly.

'It seems there's a great many that need him,' the girl said thoughtfully and then looked at Rollo and Arathane again. 'You stink. Go and wash yourselves in the water.'

Arathane laughed. 'Young woman, you are right.'

Longing to be rid of the smell of manure, Rollo gladly dropped from his horse and rinsed his hands and face in the freezing water, his skin instantly tightening as his muscles contracted against the cold.

'You must have been rolling in horse manure,' the girl told them, her eyebrows raised as if they were mad. 'Still, there's no accounting for humans.'

It was only then that Rollo realized she was not human and must, therefore, be one of Leaf's kind.

'You don't need to look at us like that,' Arathane told her. 'It was a perfectly sensible plan. The stench from the dung overpowered the fairies' vapours and so kept our minds alert.'

She nodded. 'Quite a quick-thinking man then, aren't you? I thought men were no better than the Haol-gar here.'

Arathane ignored the remark. 'What's your name, young lady?'

'Aconite.'

'A poisonous name to go with a poisonous tongue.'

She smiled at this as if it were a compliment. 'And yours, sir?'

'Arathane. This is Rollo and that mountain calls himself Lug.'

'I know Lug,' she said curtly before turning her attention to the warrior. 'You look to me as if you should go by more than just one name,' she told Arathane before turning her back on him and glaring into the dense white pall of the fog that

430

clung to the river and surrounding banks. 'I can't believe that between the three of you, with all your weapons and Lug's huge size, you couldn't overcome a few fairies.'

'We couldn't get close for fear of being poisoned ourselves.'

Aconite sniffed at this as if this was barely relevant. 'The fairies are too frightened of the fog to busy themselves with potions at the moment. Far too frightened.' She sniffed again. 'I can smell oleander blossom – so sweet!' She peered into the mist to either side and then smiled at the dark shadows of shrubs that formed a clump nearby.

'How do we get to them?' Rollo asked, finding it infuriating that no one was acting. 'We can't just hang around here waiting for the mist to suddenly vanish. I'm going after them!' He thumped his heels into the horse's side but the animal refused to move and, instead, stood up on its hind legs and reared, thrashing at the mist as if it were some enemy. Rollo reined the gelding back and dismounted. 'I shall go on foot then!' he angrily told the horse.

But he had gone no more than six paces before he was disorientated and lost. Stumbling, he tripped on something and found himself entangled in undergrowth, the sound of the river distant and muffled. He got up and shuffled forward again, hoping that this time he was moving in the right direction. But, only a second later, he was flat on his face again. It was impossible to move through the fog.

Steadying himself, he listened for any sound that might help him find his bearings, but all he could hear was the steady breaths of the giant Haol-garen. Tripping and stumbling, he worked his way back to the others, following that sound, which was so deep that it penetrated the mist where all other sounds were stifled. So this must have been how Aconite had found her way to them. Only when he was very nearly right on them could he hear the strange girl and Arathane talking. Cold from where the fog had condensed on his warm skin, he stumbled the last few paces before reaching them.

Arathane smiled. 'I did not think you would be long. But

you have been long enough for this young lady to think of a plan.'

'At last!' Rollo exclaimed, deeply relieved that someone had thought of something.

Aconite pointed to the oleander bushes. 'Can't you smell them? We must be in some kind of pleasure garden,' she explained.

'What's that got to do with anything?' Rollo rudely asked.

'Well, there's a broken beeskep at Lug's feet. With any luck we might find some honey.'

Rollo scowled. 'How's that going to help?'

'Being so close to the oleanders, I would lay good odds that the honey they make is poisonous. The oleander bush is deadly and the honey made from such nectar is equally poisonous. It's very bitter, of course, but, baked into a honey cake or pancake, the bitterness will be disguised and only the sweet scent of honey will remain.'

'And what good will all these poisonous honey cakes be to us?' Rollo demanded.

'Fairies, dear boy, cannot resist the smell and taste of honey. They do, however, have an extremely high ability to detect most poisons and foreign bodies in substances. I have tried poisoning them before,' she said matter-of-factly as if it were completely acceptable to go around poisoning these peoples as if they were rats. She took from her shoulder a white fur satchel and opened it up to reveal a leather roll, which unwrapped much as if it were a carpenter's wallet. Within were small pockets, each containing a vial of differing coloured potions and powders. 'My supply of my favourite poisons,' she explained and tapped a white powder. 'Arsenic, of course.' She tapped another vial. 'Ground meat riddled with botulism. Then I have oils of belladonna, yew and hemlock; all very useful. And beside many others there is of course monkshood, from which I derive my beloved aconite.' The girl smiled, which did nothing to improve her plain features. 'Strangely, fairies find belladonna and hemlock completely innocuous and the rest they can smell, however much I mix them with spices. You see, they detect most alien substances easily but, since there are no actual impurities in the honey made from oleander but it is the honey itself which is poisonous, they will eat it.'

'And die?' Rollo asked, somewhat alarmed by the idea. He had thought the fairy people so beautifully mysterious and ethereal. It seemed a terrible crime to kill them.

'Yes, of course they will die! The treacherous little beings have been after our lands. They want our haven and, to get it, they have joined with the hobs. It's simple; the hobs have promised them our haven if they will help them to annihilate man.'

Rollo could barely believe it of such beautiful creatures.

'Surely there won't be any honey at this time of year, though,' Arathane queried Aconite's plan.

The girl smiled at him. 'My sweet man, beneath the High Way is a fragment of the hidden realm where there is no winter and the bees will merrily make honey all year. After the collapse of the curtain, which hides the realm, they may well be asleep now in the biting cold, but they will have left some honey for us. I suggest we look and see. Don't you?'

Arathane volunteered to crawl on the floor in search of beeswax and honey that may have fallen from the beeskep after providing Rollo with a pan, some flour and fat from his rations bag and ordering him to make haste with a fire.

Lighting a fire was well within his abilities but he had no idea how to cook any form of cake. Aconite looked at him in despair and pushed him out of the way.

'I should think even the Haol-garen would do better than you,' she told him irritably.

Rollo decided that he didn't like this girl but refrained from arguing with her for fear of looking even more foolish

Arathane soon stood up triumphantly with honey, which he had scooped into a little pot.

'Go and rinse your hands in the river immediately,' Aconite sternly ordered. 'If you have any of it on your hands and you accidentally lick it, you could be dead by nightfall.'

Arathane hastily made his way to the water and spent a long time cleaning his hands in the river. By the time he had finished, Aconite had the pancakes sizzling and Rollo's mouth was watering. He found it impossible to believe that such gorgeous-smelling food could be poisonous.

'So now what?' Rollo demanded, still feeling that the plan was somewhat sketchy. 'And why couldn't Father have escaped with you? I don't understand; if you managed to get away, why couldn't he?'

Aconite laughed. 'Men are very easy to entrap. Don't be so hard on him.' She drew in a deep breath and nodded in satisfaction at her honeyed pancakes. 'All we have to do now is get them to the fairies.' She pouted a little at this problem and stared up at Lug as if thinking that he would be the best qualified to achieve the task.

Arathane seemed to read her thoughts. 'No, I'll go. Haol-garen are not at all predictable. I'll make my way through the fog.'

Rollo laughed derisively. 'It's like porridge. You can barely breathe in it and you can't see more than eight inches.'

'It will make very little difference to me,' Arathane told him flippantly.

After wrapping up his pancakes into a strip of cloth, he gave Sorrel a kiss on her snow-white blaze, nodded politely at Rollo and Aconite before striding boldly into the fog. Rollo watched the man's back, thinking that it would be less than a minute before he returned. Aconite was looking at the warrior with her head on one side, deep in thought. Sorrel threw up her head and whinnied anxiously, stamping her hooves and chomping at the bit. Rollo struggled to hold the animal.

'There, there,' he soothed. 'He'll be back shortly.'

Much to Rollo's surprise the horse looked him clean in the

eye and snorted at him, blowing warm, moist air over his face. Rollo found it most surprising that a horse would look at a man so.

They waited in silence for over a minute, and then another minute passed, in which time Rollo's steamy breath merely added to the fog that still crept towards them.

'We ought to move back a little,' he suggested.

Aconite shook her head. 'No! Whatever happens we must not move, otherwise Arathane will find it very much harder to find his way back to us. He will become disorientated.'

'How can he possibly find his way through the fog? I only found my way back to you by listening for Lug's breaths that were so deep they trembled through the fog. I couldn't hear you and Arathane talking until I was right on top of you. And just how do you think he'll find a silent barge?'

'There's something strange about the man. I can't quite tell what, though,' she said thoughtfully. 'Something in the way he moved when he stepped into the mist.'

Rollo nodded. 'Like he's blind? When he's out and about, riding like a king on his horse, he is fine, but at other times he makes out he can't see at all.'

Aconite looked towards Sorrel, who was pulling at her reins, fighting Rollo for her freedom. 'You had better give her to Lug to hold before she breaks free from your grip.'

Lug held the horse but didn't seem to be concentrating on his allotted task. 'Can't we hurry up? Those treacherous dwarves will be getting farther and farther away. They're probably in another country by now. I must have my stone back. I must. It will be the end of us if I don't.'

Rollo drew a deep breath. 'How can you be so arrogant and self-centred? The people of the inner realm are going mad, my kind are being slaughtered by hobs and all you do is worry about a simple stone. What sort of creature is going to be able to harm a huge mountain like you?'

The Haol-garen didn't reply. Instead, Aconite sniffed at Rollo and laughed disdainfully. 'What a foolish thing to say.

Size has nothing to do with it. After all, think what the tiny fairies have done to us.'

They fell back into silence, waiting glumly as the mist closed about them until all were engulfed and isolated within their own private world. Rollo pulled his thick woollen cloak about him and wished he had the heavy bearskin that his father prized.

'He's lost,' he said flatly. 'Arathane's lost. Probably drowned in the river by now.'

At this, Sorrel began to shriek and rear, but Lug was alert enough to hold the animal.

'We should have built a fire,' Aconite said ruefully, her voice now muffled as it was swallowed by the mist. Rollo breathed deeply in an effort to keep calm and, after a while, realized that apart from Lug's breathing, which seemed distant and unreal, he could hear nothing. All sense of Aconite was gone and he felt alone and cold. Curling up tight, he pulled his cloak over his head and, as the minutes passed into hours, he fell asleep and dreamed he was on his bed at home, his mother rattling at the door and calling to him to wake up but he would not. His bed became harder, the room darker and cool as if he were deep underground. The sound of his mother's agonizing cries, which she had been unable to contain in her last days when the infection tortured her belly, rang through his ears. Her bellowing screams became louder and more panicked. She was shrieking for him but he could not get to her because his limbs were like rags encased in dried mud.

He woke up with a jolt, his arms wrapped around himself and tears running down his cheek. He missed his mother so much that, at times, he found the emotion unbearable and it was as if his grief stuffed his lungs, preventing him from breathing. Hastily wiping his eyes, he sat up and realized at once that Arathane was calling them; the fog was lifting and now, through a veil of mist, they could make out the outline of the barge.

*   *   *

Caspar opened his eyes and smiled. The silvery arms of a woman of Ash were wrapped tightly about his upper torso. Her sleeping lips were still pressed up against his neck and every inch of his body still tingled with the pleasure of her proximity. He was, however, just beginning to realize that there were goose pimples all over his arms and that he was shivering. Frowning to himself, he was quite unable to think what he was doing here and where everyone else was. Slowly, he sat up and looked in amazement around him. Nearby, he saw his clothes tied into a tight bundle and placed neatly on top of his cloak. Wriggling free of his paramour's embrace, he hastily pulled on his clothes and wrapped himself up in his cloak.

Once dressed, he tried to make more sense of his surroundings. A thin mist was lifting from what appeared to be decking at his feet and, at last, he saw that he was standing on some sort of barge. There was no sign of Aconite or Leaf. He prayed nothing terrible had happened to little Leaf; he felt deeply responsible for her.

His hand on the pocket-knife he had plucked from the sheath within his boots, he stepped slowly round to see what else he should note. Someone was watching him, he was certain. He looked round a little further and took a step back in alarm at the sight of a heap of more than sixty fairies lying sprawled, one on top of the other, tongues lolling out, eyes wide and frightened. It had been a savage death. Some clutched something in their hands and, investigating more closely, Caspar saw they were pancakes.

'Don't touch them!' a voice warned.

He spun round and wondered how he had overlooked the man sitting right behind him, slumped against the bulwark, his hand on a staff as he rested, apparently waiting patiently for him to wake.

'Arathane!' Caspar exclaimed. 'Arathane! You cannot imagine how pleased I am to see you.'

The man raised a weak smile, his eyes flitting about and finally resting almost but not quite on Caspar's face. The Baron looked at him and realized instantly that the man couldn't see.

Striding forward, Caspar reached out and clasped his hand, drawing the big man up to his feet. 'I am so very glad to see you! Very, very glad! Now what's happened that brings you to my aid? I thought you were after Silas.'

Succinctly, Arathane explained about meeting up with Brid, Isolde and the others, then about he and Rollo venturing out to find him and then about Aconite and Lug.

'And Leaf,' Caspar prompted, thinking that the man had forgotten her.

'No, we have not found Leaf. She must still be here.'

'We must look for . . .' Caspar began but then stared back at Arathane's face. 'How, in the name of the Mother, did you find your way here and poison the fairies without being able to see?'

Arathane grinned. 'As it happens none of us could see. The fog came down so thickly that we couldn't even see our hands in front of us. So when Aconite came up with the plan to poison the fairies, which worked remarkably well, I must say,' he added, 'I knew I could do it because I have spent many years now stumbling about in darkness.'

Caspar looked at him suspiciously. 'Yet at times you can see clearly, just as well as I can, I am certain of it. No one could handle a sword as you do if they couldn't see. You have to agree that it is most unusual.'

Arathane nodded and felt his way back to the edge of the barge. 'I can feel the mist lifting. We shall see the others soon, I am sure.'

Caspar peered into the white curtain but, as yet, could see nothing. His knuckles tensed on the side of the barge as his tightly curbed emotions rose up from within him; he was desperate to see his boy again.

'Well, I guess there's nothing we can do other than wait,' he said with restraint and then looked towards Arathane. 'Do you not wish to speak of your ailment?'

'It is more than an ailment. It is a curse,' the man told him. 'You see, it was like this . . .' He sighed and almost visibly paled.

He even lifted up his horned helmet and pushed his long hair back, running his fingers across the battle scars that marked his head. 'You see . . .' He paused again. 'It's difficult to know where to start.'

Caspar waited patiently for the man to gather his thoughts as he anxiously cast his eyes over the heap of fairy bodies for fear that any were still alive and might cause mischief. But all looked horribly dead.

'We came from the western shores of the continent of Athell. I was a lowly lord in a powerful and sophisticated country under the leadership of an unremarkable but steady king. He believed in justice, believed in helping his people, but was not all that sure about how to bring such things about. He lacked leadership, but that didn't stop him from being a good man. His name was King Grismark.' Again, Arathane sighed and drew a breath. 'He was wise enough, however, to know the limits of his abilities, and as the threat from the Emperor grew –'

'What threat?' Caspar interrupted.

'The Emperor was a king from the east of the continent. King Argost the Twelfth was of a very long-lived, strong family, which arrogantly believed they were born to rule all Athell. Even before he began conquering his neighbouring kingdoms, he called himself Emperor of Athell.'

'I see,' Caspar acknowledged the information.

'Now where was I?' Arathane looked thoughtful for a moment. 'King Grismark recognized the threat and drew to him counsellors and advisors, eventually forming a synod of learned men whose task it was to help him govern and, most especially, plan how to defend our realm from the Emperor. I was a part of that synod. Being the lesser son of a lesser lord, there was little place else for me.' He laughed. 'You know, I made your son believe I was a prince because I thought it was wrong that he judged everyone by their titles. I do hope you will forgive me.'

'I'm sure Rollo will be none the worse for it,' Caspar replied congenially.

439

'My family still have a fine crest, a serpent wrestling a lion, but in truth that was earned by one of my ancestors more than seven hundred years beforehand when we were a much braver race. Anyhow, I digress. I had spent my youth at a desk, reading and writing and, by the time I was a man, I had specialized in the theory of war tactics. My father wanted me to study something more scholarly like philosophy but I was not interested and I hungered for adventure.'

'Didn't we all in our youth?' Caspar sympathized.

'I told you the king was unremarkable, but that wasn't completely correct. He was remarkable in one way: he possessed two extraordinary daughters, both very beautiful and charming. I fell in love with the older one, who had gorgeous chestnut hair and laughed in a way that reminded you of the summer sun toying with a light shower of rain. She was perfect and I adored her.'

Caspar smiled. 'It is very good to be in love.'

'Indeed,' Arathane agreed. 'Anyhow, as the Emperor grew in strength, we, the synod, were given more power and there was one amongst our number who was remarkably clever and soon was elected chief speaker.'

With a heavy heart, Caspar had already guessed who this was.

'He enjoyed his position and it seemed to me that he obsessively sought praise for his perception, clarity of thought and ability in argument. I never learned what his chosen subject was until I accidentally discovered that he had been tutored by wizards. At the time I found it amusing and didn't realize until far too late that, not only was I foolish, but I had been foolish with the wrong man.'

Caspar looked at him, patiently waiting for him to continue.

Arathane kneaded his thighs, which were cold from sitting so long, and then persisted with his story. 'You see, as I became older and a little more respected in the synod, I found I was eventually brave enough to ask the king for his eldest daughter's hand. I fully expected him to refuse me, wanting perhaps to marry her to a prince from a neighbouring country to strengthen his alliance against the Emperor, but her happiness mattered more to the good-hearted king and so he agreed to our request. We were married very happily for a number of years and, in that time, the speaker of the synod married the king's younger daughter, who was, I have to admit, a little more attractive than my own wife. She had sleek black hair and a vivaciousness unmatched in anyone else I have met. She was not as gentle or as caring as my own wife, but she was impishly charming.'

Caspar smiled. 'I see!' he said, guessing where this tale was leading.

'For a couple of years, we at the synod did nothing but concentrate on sending supplies and arms to reinforce our allies against the advance of the Emperor, and in that time I noticed how my dear wife's sister began to pale and look less bright in the eye. I must confess I felt sorry for her. Then the king's mother fell ill. She lived out of the capital in the summer palace by the warm lakes and my wife went to see what she could do to make her grandmother feel better.' Arathane gulped. 'It was then that her sister came to me sobbing. She was bruised about the neck and back and she was deeply frightened. Though I said I should take her to the king at once, she begged me not to for fear of the revenge her husband might take. I comforted her as best I could and rubbed ointment on her shoulder to help the bruising.'

Caspar's eyebrows rose.

Arathane sighed, his sightless eyes gazing emptily towards his hands resting on his knee. 'She was so pretty. I had always thought her so pretty, and now she was crying. I kissed her head at first, just to try and soothe her, but my hands now touched her bare, oiled shoulders. She fell against me, sobbing, and kissed me back forcibly. I was a fool, an idiot, but I succumbed utterly and a few minutes later we were naked before the fire, making love.' Arathane breathed in deeply through his nose and let his head fall back as if searching for the answer in the haze overhead.

'I can only imagine that it was at precisely that moment that the husband returned,' Caspar said gently, aware that, though the man told the story flippantly, it was a heavy burden on his guilt-laden heart.

'You imagine right, kind sir. The fates were not kind to me, though perhaps I deserved it. You see, I really did love my wife. It was a mistake and I suppose, by rights, we should pay for our mistakes.'

'So what happened? Were you exiled?' Caspar prompted when Arathane fell into a brooding silence. He remembered how Hal had been when Brid had fallen pregnant by another man. Hal was the most jealous and hot-tempered man he knew, but somehow he had coped and resigned himself to the situation. Clearly, however, the cuckolded husband of Arathane's sister-in-law was not so lenient.

'No! The husband did not go to King Grismark. He stormed out and left and we did not see him for three days, leaving me wondering what was afoot. In the meanwhile, my wife returned and, of course, I had to tell her. She was hurt rather than angry.' Arathane bit his lip. 'For a day she shunned me, until her young sister showed her the bruising. My dear wife forgave me and we sobbed and hugged and thought all would be well again. We planned how her sister would divorce her brutal husband, now that she had revealed her dark secret, and all would be mended. But then he came back with three tall men in purple robes.'

Caspar swallowed. 'Wizards?'

'Indeed, wizards; that race of speaking people who understand the power of delusional magic, who can slip between worlds and so call on the power of the earldormen from the Otherworld. The wretch had made a pact. If he were to help them in their aim, the wizards would punish us. So long as he helped them promote the Emperor, who had developed a sinister and mutually beneficial relationship with the wizards, they would see us damned to misery. Even worse, the wretched husband was left with the choice of punishment. First, he turned his wife into a mare.'

Caspar felt the blood drain from his face. 'Raven, that beautiful Tethyan high-stepper, is your wife's sister. So the husband *was* Silas!'

Arathane nodded. 'I'm afraid so. That was her punishment: to dutifully carry him always. He allows her to become a woman for a few hours each night and, for that, she will not leave him, otherwise she is forever a woman trapped in a horse's body. She valued her beauty very highly and will put up with almost anything, it seems, to regain it each night.'

'But surely Silas was not content to punish only his wife?' Caspar asked.

'Of course not. He punished me by punishing my wife. He was so amused at seeing his own wife metamorphosed into a horse that he wished to see the trick repeated. In the same way as he had brought about the mutation of his sister-in-law, he took one of the guard's horses from the stables, a beautiful chestnut with a white blaze on her nose. He slit the animal's throat and caught its blood, which he gave to the wizards who performed their horrible rite on my wife, washing her in the blood. She was not allowed the grace of becoming a woman that he bestowed on his wife for his own pleasure. My dear, sweet Sorrel barely knows she is a woman any more. I sense her mind every day becoming more and more alike with the horse's body she possesses.'

'And he blinded you?'

Arathane nodded. 'It also amused him to take half my hair.' The knight tapped his horned helmet. 'Then he blinded me, yet allowed me sight through a horse's eye. Sorrel sees for me so long as we are close but, if we are separated, I am blind.'

'So that is why you seek Silas – to force him to undo the spell.'

Arathane nodded. 'There is no other alternative,' he said, his eyes brightening as he spoke.

Caspar noted that a slight breeze was beginning to stir the mist and that the sun was now visible as a ghost above. Soon, he hoped, it would burn through the vapour.

Arathane continued, 'He must renew his pledge to help the wizards at each full moon, otherwise they will allow the spell to lapse. Destroy him, and our torment ceases. But he has gathered to him much power. Many of the speaking races have banded against us, each for their own reason, and he immediately saw the advantage of turning traitor. With the help of the wizards, he persuaded the hobs to ally with the Emperor, who consequently swept through our lands and destroyed our kingdom.' He breathed deeply. 'For a time, there was nothing I could do to pursue Silas since we were ravaged by war and I was needed to help beat back the invasion. But in the end the hobs devastated us and it was as if Silas spared us only so that we could suffer the misery of our loss. It was then that he left Sorrel and me wounded and bleeding on the battlefield, our standard trampled and my emblems stripped from my body by the snivelling hobs. After that, Silas fled our shores and I have been hunting him ever since.'

'I am sorry,' Caspar said quietly.

Arathane stood up and smiled. 'Let's talk no more of it. She is coming. The blackness is lifting from my eyes.'

Caspar stood to see that the mist had lifted a little more. The sun was now warm on his skin, its warmth evaporating the clammy mist about them. Peering through the last wisps of mist, he could first see Lug, then Aconite and his son approaching. Sorrel had pulled free from the others and was now galloping towards the barge, stirrups and reins flapping.

The big knight turned to Caspar, his bright eyes focusing intently. 'And so you understand, I can see now. It is just as Silas told me. He said, "I shall teach you a lesson for betraying your wife. I shall show you how precious she is to you. Without her you shall be blind." It is indeed a harsh punishment but, if I could have her back as a woman and free her from the prison of the horse's body, I would do that a thousand times rather than ask for my sight back. And look! After all this, she still loves me and longs to be with me more.' He smiled weakly. 'Or is it just that she believes I will be able to return her back to being a woman? I no longer know whether she understands who or what she is any more.'

Caspar felt his heart leap with joy at the sight of Rollo running beside Lug, who was striding along, his big feet treading lightly on the soft soil. Not far behind him was Aconite, but there was still no sign of Leaf anywhere.

He stared beyond them, looking for her while Arathane struggled to lower planks from the side of the barge to form a gangway. Without any urging, Sorrel trotted aboard and nuzzled her master. Lug looked at the vessel doubtfully and sat stubbornly on the bank while Aconite hurried aboard.

Caspar held out his arms to Rollo, who looked for a moment as if he would finally fall into his embrace, but then the youth pouted and stepped back.

Caspar smiled weakly. 'Rollo, Rollo, my boy, you came for me!'

The youth grunted. 'Brid sent me.'

Caspar nodded, his frown deepening as he still saw no sign of Leaf. 'Where is Leaf? What have you done with her?' he demanded anxiously.

Chapter 24

Rollo scowled at his father. Typical, he thought, typical! Rather than welcoming him properly, he immediately asked after someone else. Caspar no longer had Imogen to worry about and so it had taken him only a matter of weeks to find another young girl to look after and replace his absent daughter.

'What about Leaf?' Rollo answered harshly. 'She must have fled.'

'Leaf wouldn't flee. She is far too brave,' Caspar insisted, looking about him in panic. 'Aconite, when did you last see her? We must look for her.'

'She was right here on the barge, lying next to me. I told her to get up and run, but she didn't. She said she couldn't leave you.'

Rollo snorted at this. Here was proof that everyone bonded with his father better than he did.

'Search the barge!' Caspar ordered. 'Inside and out!'

All immediately began to look about them, opening holds and searching frantically. Arathane was pulling damp-looking sail bags out of a hold and heaping them next to what he took to be a full, smooth, crisp white sail bag already lying on the deck. Rollo began searching in empty barrels but then turned to look at the heap of dead fairies. He reached out a tentative finger to touch a glasslike wing but it shattered under his barest touch. The creatures were so fragile and beautiful in their perfect, miniature formation yet now they were dead and broken. It seemed so sad.

'You're right, lad,' Arathane agreed with his instinct. 'She might well be under those fairies. Let's shift them and see.'

Rollo cringed as he pulled them out of the pile one by one, arms breaking off in his grip since they were so brittle. His flesh crept at the sight and he wanted to weep for them. They were like children, helpless little children. He had seen ugly deaths before and been barely troubled by it but, somehow, these creatures were too beautiful and too defenceless for such an end. It was inexcusable that they had suffered such barbarity. Sickened to his stomach, he knew it had been most ignoble to slay them in this manner. It wasn't as if they were all fairy warriors; many were delicate females so small that he could hold them in one hand. He noted, after one or two moments, that some of them even had babies strapped to their backs and that some of the babies, who were too young to eat pancakes, were, naturally, still alive.

'What have we done! Oh Great Mother, forgive us!'

Deeply shocked and saddened, Arathane looked over his shoulder as Rollo helped one of these infants, who was no bigger than a forefinger, from its papoose.

'It would probably be kindest to poison it too,' Aconite suggested.

Rollo felt sick. He was not about to start poisoning helpless babies.

'Look out!' Aconite cried.

She was clutching her face and had clearly been hit by something. A sound like angry bees came swarming up from out of an unturned barrel and hummed towards Rollo. Blurred shapes swooped up to sting his nose and eyes, wings fluttering against his face, tiny spears jabbing at his cheeks. He guessed they had to be a group of fairies that had escaped the poison. Despite their tiny size, they were extremely difficult to fend off.

'Here! Here! Take the baby!' he screamed at them, holding up his hand, the baby cradled in his palm.

One swept the infant away while others dived at the full

sail bag. Using their spears, they levered it forward and slowly it began to roll towards the rear of the barge. As it picked up momentum, it began to spin faster, rolling under the rail and down with a heavy splash into the river. The fairies shrieked in angry triumph as if glad of some revenge.

'Destroyers! Wreckers! Bringers of doom! It is your turn to suffer now!'

Aconite looked hard at the fairies, then at Caspar and then at the sail bag that was beginning to sink lower into the water. 'It's her! She's in it!' Aconite yelled, pointing at the bobbing blob of white in the water. 'It's Leaf!'

Caspar didn't hesitate but sprinted for the stern of the barge, shed his cloak and dived into the Brue. Rollo and Aconite ran to the bulwark and leaned over. Arathane was already up on Sorrel, clattering down the planking bridge and then wading out towards Caspar, who was thrashing through the water. The white pod, which was being swept away from him by the current, was already sinking. The Baron took a deep breath and dived down into the river. It was a long minute before he resurfaced, gasped in air and then strained to drag up the pod. But, to Rollo's dismay, his father was now being rapidly washed downstream.

'Lug!' Aconite shouted to the big giant, who was still seated cross-legged on the bank, ignoring all their activities. 'Lug, get out there and help them.'

The big giant reluctantly stirred and, muttering away to himself, finally waded out up to his thighs into the fast current that bulged around him. Scooping up the peculiar pod, he brought it back to the shore, leaving Caspar to swim in. Fortunately, Arathane was there to help him up the last few paces onto the shingle bank. Within seconds, all were gathered around the white roll. Arathane and Caspar already had their knives drawn and were working hard to cut open the smooth pod. Caspar was through first.

'It's her feet. Quickly!' he urged as water gushed out of

the opening. 'Cut carefully towards her head. She's probably half-drowned.'

Once they had cut open a crack, Lug used his great hands to split open the pod, which was as stiff as seasoned wood. There was Leaf, white and lifeless, lying in a pool of water. Caspar lifted her out and began rubbing her vigorously all over. It was a moment before she began to cough and splutter. The colour rushed back to her face. Caspar dragged off her wet clothes, revealing slender limbs and a frail body beneath, which he hastily wrapped in his bearskin.

'Let's get her onto the barge,' he said, carrying her in his arms. 'Leaf, speak to us! Answer me! Please speak!'

The little girl merely turned her face towards Caspar's breast and clung tightly to him, sobbing. She cried for at least ten minutes without even trying to stop, and at last fell quiet.

'Leaf, I thought you were going to drown,' Caspar admitted, his teeth now chattering though he refused anyone's request to shed his own wet clothes.

'I could hear you. I could hear you all along but none of you could hear me. I thought I was going to be trapped forever in that cocoon. Then I was falling and the water seeped in. I couldn't move,' she gasped tearfully.

'I know, Leaf, but it's over now. It's over and you're safe,' Caspar reassured her.

The girl sat up, wiped her eyes and looked at the Baron gravely. 'But it isn't over, is it? At every turn we run into hobs or fairies or dwarves and even Silas. All are determined to destroy us. They are winning. We have done nothing to stop them.'

Her words were met by a stony silence. Each and every one of them fell into quiet contemplation and, for the first time in his life, Rollo looked around at his companions and realized that he was not the only one beset with torments. His father and Arathane were struggling to defeat an enemy with apparently no chance of success. Leaf and the girl in the white fur dress feared for their people and their sanity.

There was a hardness to Aconite's spirit that seemed to enable her to overcome her distress. Leaf, on the other hand, was terrified. She had lived a life protected from the outside world but her secluded province had crumbled and her people were going mad. Of all those around him, she was the one he understood most. His world had also crumbled and he, too, was in a strange country, frightened at every turn. Raising his chin, he swallowed hard, suddenly alarmed to discover that he had admitted to himself that he was afraid. He inched a little closer to Caspar, who reached out a hand to squeeze his fingers. Rollo was deeply warmed by the touch but hastily plucked away his hand, still too proud to admit any weakness to his father.

'Lug,' Caspar called, 'can you push us off the shingle here?'

The giant grunted and worked hard for ten minutes or so, eventually resorting to snapping a twenty-foot tree and using the trunk as a lever to lift the boat off the riverbed and ease it into deeper waters.

'Get in,' Caspar urged. 'We'll make good time in the barge.'

Lug waded in up to his thighs and looked doubtfully at the vessel. 'It'll tip.'

Aconite stood up tall. 'Don't be so ridiculous. This is a barge designed for transporting cargo. Your weight is negligible in the scheme of things,' she told him impatiently.

Nervously Lug complied, scrambling aboard and nearly knocking Rollo over the side in his haste to reach the central point of the barge. Showing no inclination to apologize to Rollo, who cursed profusely and was rubbing at his arm where he had been flung against a barrel, he at last settled. Sitting rigidly, Lug's shoulder blocked the movement of a triangular sail, whose very top was just beginning to flutter in the breeze, but no one could persuade him to move to a more sensible spot.

Arathane and Caspar picked up an oar each and did their

best to row and steer, though the current did most of the work. Once they were under way, Caspar shipped his oar and left Arathane to man the tiller while he came and sat with his son and the two girls.

Rollo ground his teeth, fretting over when it was best to break the news about Firecracker. A cold sweat broke out all over his skin; he drew a deep breath in preparation of blurting his admission but hastily closed his mouth again.

The Baron sighed. 'Rollo, I can't say how pleased . . .' He grinned, his sentence unfinished and then, as if embarrassed by his own emotions, hastily nodded at Arathane, who stood at the stern of the barge with the wind now lifting his long hair off his broad shoulders. 'Where would we be without him?' He paused. 'You would not believe the strange tale he had to tell.'

Relieved that he had been granted a moment's reprieve from the torment of admitting his blame, Rollo sat open-mouthed as he learned how Arathane came to be blinded and of the tragedy of Sorrel and Raven. He looked at the chestnut mare, which was contentedly snuffling in her nosebag, and found it impossible to believe that within the brute was trapped the spirit of a woman. Having learned all his father knew about Arathane, Rollo turned his curiosity towards Lug. He was amazed by his size but decided the giant looked too stupid to have a tale to tell. He shifted his focus onto the strange-looking girl in the white fur who looked as if she had far too many tales to tell. She seemed very young but, all the same, was clearly pregnant. Her hands soothed and caressed the curve of her belly protectively.

Her eyes flashed at his. 'What are you staring at?' she demanded.

'You,' he retorted, unapologetic for his behaviour. 'Why shouldn't I stare? How did a girl as young as you manage to fall pregnant?'

'That's an extremely stupid question!' Aconite sneered.

'It's not as stupid as all that,' Leaf quietly defended the

451

youth. 'After all, our kind do not reach physical maturity until we have undergone the transformation into adulthood. The change is distinct; you are still too young and do not have the brightness to the eye that comes with the intense revelation. I was wondering, myself, how you had achieved this.'

'I don't see that it is any of your business,' Aconite said stiffly.

'Indeed not, but I am still curious,' Leaf persisted. 'You must have been given a stimulative herb to provoke ovulation and to make the foetus attach to your womb.'

Aconite nodded. 'Indeed. There were many of us selected for the experiment, and many died or produced deformed monsters, but in the end it worked for just a few of us.'

'Why didn't you just wait until you body developed naturally?' Caspar asked.

Aconite threw her eyes heavenward at his question. 'That was the whole point. We noted in women a very sudden onset of forgetfulness within a year of achieving their full brain development. However, those that fell pregnant showed some reprieve from the symptoms.'

'We had observed much the same thing,' Leaf added, looking at Aconite intently as she drank in her words.

'Clearly pregnancy forms some kind of protection against the illness, and even women who had already had children showed a slower deterioration than the men.'

'Very interesting. So you were an experiment to see whether, if you went through the initiation into adulthood pregnant, you may be protected from the onset of the disease altogether,' Leaf concluded.

'Or at least lessen its effect,' Aconite added. 'We needed to try anything, absolutely anything that offered the merest hope, anything that would lessen the effect, anything that allowed us to have adults as sharp and perceptive as they had been before the onset of the disease. We needed clear minds to solve our problem.'

'Let's hope it works,' Leaf sighed. 'It may be all we have.'

'Silas has taken so much from all of us,' Caspar said heavily. 'We must retrieve all he has stolen.' He looked at Arathane while Rollo looked around at them all again, wondering which one of them suffered the most.

The barge enabled them to make very good time as they were swept along by the current, westwards towards the ocean. Rollo found it an enormous relief to be moving again and escaping the interior of Belbidia where he felt cramped within the endless woods. The sea smelt fresh in his nostrils. Closing his eyes, he breathed in deeply and spread out his arms as if to embrace the open air, wishing that he could simply fly away so he would not have to face his father. He felt sick at the thought of breaking his heavy news and screwed up his eyes in an attempt to blot out the world. Once his eyes were shut, he did indeed have the strangest impression that he was flying. He licked his lips, relishing the sensation of freedom and speed. Feeling empowered, he threw back his head to crow his defiance at the world. He would not be cowed by the disasters that beset them or shackled by his fears; he would soar up into the heavens and dance with the sunbeams as if they were his siblings.

Suddenly aware of how ridiculous his thoughts were, he shook himself and then felt acutely embarrassed as he felt his father's presence close to him. He let his arms drop and looked at the slight man, his heart plunging to his boots. It was as if he had tumbled from the sky and crashed heavily onto hard rock. His heart pounding in his chest, he was intensely aware of his father breathing in the brackish air, sniffing at the scent of mud salts.

He knew he should tell him right away about Firecracker but, instead, found that his tongue seemed to swell until he thought he would choke.

Caspar stood beside his son and smiled kindly at him. 'You looked as if you wanted to fly. Did you know, Rollo, when I was a boy I used to wish I could fly with the hawks?' He smiled at his son and Rollo blinked at him, trying to force words up into his throat, but they would not come.

Caspar continued, 'You see, Rollo, now I no longer wish to escape from it all. I want simply to be as I am and stand tall and one day say proudly, "I was there," when we finally win the day. I want to be able to hold my loved ones in my arms and say, "All is well; fly if you wish because there are no more cares to weigh you down."'

Rollo suddenly found his tongue. 'You are thinking of Imogen,' he barked at him, his sense of guilt making him more angry than usual with his father, 'not me.'

'I was thinking of you both,' Caspar said heavily though Rollo could see from the way his father wrung his hands and gazed out into the distance that this was not so.

'You should never have left,' Rollo told him bluntly. 'You said you were taking me home to my birthright but, instead, you have only brought me to destruction and danger.'

Caspar nodded. 'Do you think I don't know that? I was coming home in the hope of giving you a better future. Instead, I was welcomed by Brid and Keridwen because they thought I was returning to seek the Chalice, which had been stolen from them.' He gave a half laugh. 'And clearly that was the Great Mother's true wish because, although I started out from Torra Alta to retrieve you, I have been forced for Isolde's sake and the good of us all to go on and seek the Chalice. Once I found you, I hoped we could soon return to Torra Alta because there was hope that Isolde could be saved by Leaf's people in the hidden realm, but they are barely surviving themselves. It seems that I must do the Great Mother's bidding after all.'

'Father, there's something I have to tell you,' Rollo finally blurted.

Caspar appeared to be immediately aware of the import in his tone as he fixed him hard in the eye. 'What is it, Rollo?'

The boy took a deep breath, raised his chin and held his father's gaze. 'It's Cracker. He was injured by hollines.'

'Hollines! However did that happen and how badly injured?' the man demanded fearfully, his pupils now black and wide as he pressed for more details.

'He's very badly hurt. His side was ripped open. Brid stitched it up but all the same . . .'

Caspar swallowed and braced himself against the railing. 'Tell me how it happened.'

Rollo shook his head. He was all churned up inside with shame and he couldn't bring himself to admit his stupidity. 'No, I can't.'

'You were riding him!' Caspar guessed. 'How many times have I told you never to ride him? I expressly ordered you not to. The animal is much too vicious and hot-blooded for you to handle. Something was bound to happen. Why won't you ever just listen to me and do as I ask? My horse, Rollo! I've had him over twenty years. He's like my own flesh and blood to me. He knows what I'm thinking. How could you do this to me?'

'I knew you didn't care about me! I knew you only cared about the horse!' Rollo wailed at him, pushing his father away and running back towards the stern of the barge where he watched and waited to see if Caspar would come after him. But he didn't even look around as they swept out from the river into the western ocean. Instead, he went and stood beside Sorrel and stroked her chestnut hide.

With the salt spray in his face, Rollo thumped the railing along the top of the bulwark until his fist hurt. Screaming into the wind to vent his emotions, he struggled to control himself. It was only the action of a wave buffeting against the barge's hull and sending her reeling uncomfortably that allowed Rollo to forget his personal torment. Arathane was struggling with the tiller and shouting to Caspar for help. Clearly, the barge was far more difficult to handle now that they had hit the open seas.

Unnerved by this, Leaf ran to Rollo's side, apparently seeking comfort. 'It's probably a lack of cargo or ballast below which is making her top-heavy,' she suggested, her eyes wide with fear. 'We should keep the sail only partially hoisted so that there isn't too much leverage from the very top of the mast. You must go and tell Spar.'

Steeling himself to face his father, Rollo reluctantly tugged Leaf towards the tiller, where Arathane and his father struggled to control the vessel, and repeated Leaf's words.

Arathane nodded at this. 'Spar, can you do as the girl suggests?' he grunted, struggling with the tiller.

Once the sail was lowered, Arathane's anxious expression eased and he was able to keep a steady heading, mindfully close to shore. Skimming over the choppy waves, they headed south along the coast towards a prominent ridge that rose up from a peninsula. Rollo had no problem identifying the Fin and guessed it would only be a matter of two or three hours before they were back with Brid and Isolde. It would, therefore, be only a similar number of hours before his father saw with his own eyes the terrible wounds inflicted on his prize horse.

His estimate was an hour short, but eventually they sailed into Shinglebay's port where they moored alongside the jetty. Leaving Lug and Arathane to guard the precious barge, the rest disembarked.

Caspar looked at his son without smiling. 'Well, you had better show us the way,' he said flatly.

Immediately Rollo knew he had not been forgiven and that his father's disdain would only intensify when the whole story of how he had so idiotically fled into the wood came out. Scowling blackly, ashamed of himself and angry with his father for making him feel so bad, Rollo led them back towards Candlewood Inn. In silence, they passed through the stable yard where a thin man in a short riding cloak was handing his sweated bay mare to the ostler before hurrying towards the inn.

'Do you want to see Brid and Isolde first . . . or Cracker?' Rollo asked.

'Brid,' Caspar said succinctly, his lips tight over his clenched teeth. '*I* still have my priorities right.'

Chapter 25

Rollo marched on towards the inn, determined to look bold in his actions. But then he faltered as his hand touched the huge metal ring handle on the solid oak door.

'What's the matter?' Caspar asked sharply, immediately noticing his son's hesitation.

Rollo didn't reply but simply turned and looked back at the sweating bay in the stable yard. He focused on the saddlecloth, which was red and gold with a distinctive insignia in the corner.

'Well, now! What's a messenger from Nattarda doing at the other side of the country?' Caspar said quietly under his breath and looked at his son. 'We had better get inside and see how Brid and Isolde are faring.'

The moment they opened the door it was clear that something was seriously amiss. Chairs were scattered everywhere and a huddle of people had fled to the far side of the tavern. The dogs were yelping wildly.

'Go and do something about it, Leof!' a women was shouting at the innkeeper.

Leof, the innkeeper, was standing at the bottom of the stairs and looking up doubtfully. 'It's not my fight, now is it?'

'But they might need help!'

Rollo hastily looked round the room and saw no sign of his companions. Caspar was ahead of him, however, already bounding up the stairs. 'Rollo, look after Leaf and Aconite!' he shouted.

His voice turned into a snarl as he vanished from sight

and, a split second later, the sound of metal against metal rang through the tavern. The others within the inn gave out a yell and shrank into a corner. Rollo pulled Aconite and Leaf towards the innkeeper and thrust them into Leof's arms.

'Look after them!' he ordered and, uncaring that he was disobeying his father's orders, sprang up the stairs after him, sword in hand. His sword was light and well-balanced, specifically designed for him. It was a lengthy and so costly process to create a sword. Twelve pounds of metal had gone into the product that had finally weighed only three pounds as the impurities were beaten away and the metal skilfully twisted and blended together to give it strength. It was craftsmanship at its most expensive but cost never troubled his mother, who had possessed so much money. The sword fitted easily into his hand and he was comforted by its familiarity.

Standing in opposition to his father were two men dressed in red and gold livery, who hacked back and forth with determined efforts, though Caspar was not giving an inch. He blocked and turned one man's strike and then followed through with the pommel of his sword and jabbed it into the chin of the other man, sending him reeling to the floor.

Rollo wanted to help but he could see there was no space for him on the stair and that he would only hamper his father. Once one man was down, the Baron seized his opportunity to turn from the defensive onto the attack and hacked and smote at his opponent with rapid strokes, the air trembling with the clang of steel. The liveried man was retreating, Walnut growling savagely and nipping at his heels while the hound stood guard over Isolde as ordered. Rollo wondered whether he should stab at the man on the ground but he decided he looked sufficiently incapacitated for the time being.

For now, the sight of his father in close combat fixed his gaze. Caspar plunged his sword downwards, slicing through the Nattardan's cheek and then across his neck, the skin opening to let out a spray of blood that coated the walls

459

around them. Caspar turned and pressed the point of his bloodied sword against the injured man's jugular and drew a deep steadying breath, taking stock of his surroundings.

There was a muted thumping and hammering coming from somewhere higher in the inn, but worthy of more immediate attention was the clash of metal ringing out from Isolde's room. A moment later it ceased and Aisholt staggered out, a grin on his face. 'I haven't had such sport with a sword in at least a year. The wretched man just came in through Isolde's window. Still, he won't be climbing any more walls.' He wiped his bloodied sword on a rag from his pocket. 'It's good to see you, sir,' he saluted smartly at Caspar. 'You came in the nick of time.'

The injured man beneath Caspar suddenly began to struggle.

'Move an inch and you're dead,' the Baron threatened menacingly. 'Rollo, what's the matter with you?' he panted. 'It doesn't take you more than five minutes before you've failed to comply with an order. Now go and get some rope: Are you up to that?'

Rollo grunted, aware that, now the yells and crashes of combat had ceased, the hammering and yelling coming from somewhere within the inn was growing louder, but he didn't stop to investigate. Obeying his father, he fled down the stairs and asked the innkeeper for some rope.

'In the stables, young sir!' Leof responded promptly. He was red in the face and puffing with anxiety.

Eager to prove his abilities, Rollo sprinted across the stable yard and spun around the corner of the door, only to be stopped by the point of a sword against his chest. He had forgotten the thin man with the bay horse! How could he have forgotten?

'Well, young man, it looks like I've got one of you. Won't they be jolly pleased with me?'

'You'll get nowhere,' Rollo snarled at him. 'We have the rest of you already. Not much by way of fighting men, are you? I've never seen a man so quickly disarmed.'

'Not as quick as you were, I warrant,' the soldier taunted, though he did look up anxiously towards the inn. 'Now, there's a good boy, just get quietly up onto my horse without too much fuss so things don't have to get messy.'

Rollo couldn't think how he was going to save himself. His only hope was that the man would have to move his sword away from his breast in order to retrieve his horse; that would be his chance. But, before lowering his blade, the soldier grabbed Rollo by the hair and tugged him along to a fresh horse, which he clearly intended to steal.

'Up in the saddle, there's a good boy.'

Rollo obeyed, patiently biding his time. The Nattardan backed the fresh horse out of the stall and deftly lashed Rollo's hands to the pommel of the saddle with a length of leather. Only then did the man lower his sword.

Rollo had missed his opportunity and began to panic. 'You vile bastard!' he shrieked, reaching round to try and kick the man, but found him to be beyond his range. Thwarted, he thought to use the horse beneath him as a weapon. He had been stupid and that knowledge made him even angrier. How could he have forgotten the man in the stable yard? Growling, he jabbed his heels into the horse, which snorted and threw up its head in alarm but did not plunge forward at the Nattardan as he had hoped. Rollo bellowed in rage and then yelled out for help, hoping that the innkeeper might come for him.

Again, he kicked and roared, making the horse squeal. The other horses in the stables became increasingly excited by the commotion and began to kick at their stalls. The rending sound of splintering wood filled the yard. Rollo shrieked savagely, inciting more horses to rear and stamp. Amidst their squeals and panicked whinnies there was one cry that was distinctly savage and ferocious, which stood out from the rest.

'Cracker!' Rollo yelled, recognizing the furious squeal of the beast.

A second later the animal burst out from its stall, a broken headcollar hanging from its ears. Snorting like a bull, the old war-horse charged at the man, who put up his sword to defend himself. Firecracker stood up on his hind legs and furiously lashed out with flailing forelegs, the wound along his belly opening up under the strain. The Nattardan stabbed up at the horse's breast. Rollo jabbed his heels into the mount beneath him and did his best to ride down the man. He succeeded in knocking him to the ground but had been too late to draw his thrust away from the enraged stallion. The Nattardan's blade was stuck in Firecracker's breast.

The liveried man tried to pull his weapon out but was thrown to the ground as Rollo's boot connected firmly with his chin. The man rolled over and leapt up, this time brandishing a pitchfork. The youth instinctively ducked though the Nattardan never got to hurl the weapon. Instead, he fell forward onto the hard cobbles, a strangulated scream bubbling from his throat.

White-faced, Caspar ran into the stalls, leaping over the body of the Nattardan, who had a knife handle sticking out between his shoulder blades. 'Rollo! Rollo, are you hurt?'

'No,' the youth panted. 'No. He took me by surprise. I am so sorry, Father . . . I failed you.'

Caspar did not reply. He simply cut Rollo's hands free, dragged him from the saddle and hugged him close. 'My dear, dear boy.'

'It's Cracker who needs help.' Rollo pushed him off and looked for the noble stallion, which had sagged to his knees but was still trying to rise.

Caspar gave out a pained moan and ran to his horse's side. Horrified, he looked at the sword buried in the animal's breast. 'Oh, Cracker!'

Rollo knelt by his father's side. 'He saved me, Father. Just like he saved me from the hollines.'

Caspar swallowed hard and cupped the animal's head in his arms. Blood dripped from Firecracker's nostrils and his breath crackled and gurgled in his throat.

'Rollo, go and get Brid,' he said slowly and calmly without taking his eyes from his precious horse.

The boy ran across the stable yard and back into the inn, pushing his way past the innkeeper, who was throwing his hands up in alarm at the events of the day. At the top of the stairs, he saw Brid stooped over Aisholt. He raced up and took in the sorry sight. A third man lay heaped over the other injured bodies. Evidently he had been lurking in another chamber and tried to rescue his companion the moment Caspar had left in search of him. Aware of the hammering, which was still echoing through the inn, he looked down in horror at Aisholt. One look at his face told him that Brid could not leave his side. The man's lips were grey, his face a horrible greenish-white. His severed arm lay on the ground beside him. While Isolde was sobbing pitifully in a heap on the floor, Brid was pressing a cloth against Aisholt's belly in an effort to stem the blood, which was bubbling out. Seeing that there was nothing he could do, Rollo leapt back down the stairs to the two girls from the inner realm.

'Leaf, help Brid,' he instructed. 'Aisholt is badly wounded. Aconite, please come with me. My father needs help with his horse.'

'His horse! Why ever is he fussing over his horse at a time like this?' the girl exclaimed in amazement. 'You humans are beyond belief.'

'Firecracker is special to him,' Rollo tried to explain as he tugged the girl towards the door.

'Like Sorrel is to Arathane?'

'No, no. But he loves the beast dearly. Come on, hurry!'

Aconite tossed her hands in the air as if he were quite demented but, nevertheless, hurried after him through the light drizzle that now made the cobbles slippery. Together, they ran into the stable yard.

'I've brought Aconite,' Rollo exclaimed excitedly as he sprinted to Caspar's side and jerked to a halt beside him. Rollo looked down at his father, who was on his knees, the horse's lolling head in his lap. Caspar had thrown his head back in grief. His white lips were pressed together and tears flooded down his cheeks. A bloodied knife had fallen from his grip and blood still oozed from a long, clean slit around the horse's throat.

Rollo didn't know what to say. He didn't dare say anything. He could only stand there and stare, aware of his father's terrible loss.

'Poor beast,' Aconite said gently. 'You did the right thing. He was dying and it was best to end his suffering.'

Caspar managed to nod but did not speak as he feared the torrent of sobs that might erupt from his throat. Suddenly, he turned and savagely grabbed Rollo, pulling him down. At first Rollo thought his father was angry with him for causing the horse's death, but then he realized Caspar was hugging him tightly, squeezing out the breath from his lungs.

'My boy!' he sobbed at last. 'You are safe. Thank the Mother, you are safe. Cracker did what he had to do. He saved you.'

Rollo wriggled free of his father's grip. The man was covered in the horse's blood; the smell stirred his emotions, producing a curiously uncomfortable, hot feeling in his belly and rousing his anger.

'The others need our help,' Aconite said calmly, urging the Baron to his feet. 'You must come now. We shall take care of the horse later.' With jerky movements, Caspar plucked up his knife, wiped the blade and sheathed it before easing the horse's head from his knees. It thudded heavily to the ground and Caspar swallowed hard.

'You old bastard, I loved you,' he told the dead horse.

Once on his feet, he looked at the Nattardan lying in his own bloody nest of straw and, in a sudden burst of emotion, strode over and kicked him hard in the belly, bringing up a gob of congealed blood into the gap between his parted blue lips. Turning his back on the corpse, he looked down at his dead horse and heaved a shuddering sigh before marching stiffly out into the drizzle.

Rollo trotted after the Baron as he barged into the inn and mounted the stairs. His face grey, he looked down at Brid who was thumping Aisholt's chest in an effort to keep his heart going. Leaf was pressing bandages to his gut, but still the blood continued to ooze out. It was quite evident that the women were doing all that could be done, so Caspar looked away, his eyes searching for the sound of relentless banging. The innkeeper also seemed intent on investigating it.

'In the attic up here!' the innkeeper shouted. 'All right! All right! We're coming!'

It was a minute later that Guthrey, Quinn and Fanchon came trotting down the stairs, their hair ruffled and their clothing dishevelled. There was absolutely no question as to what they had been doing up there, but how they had managed to get locked in Rollo couldn't imagine.

'I thought you were looking after your mother!' Caspar bellowed at the two youths, who looked in horror at the scene around them.

'We left her with Aisholt. Surely that was . .' Guthrey faltered and looked down at his mother, who slowly sat back, blood thickly coating her small hands.

She stood up, shaking. Suddenly looking menacingly tall although she was in reality very short, she glared at her two sons, her fierce green eyes darkly intense. 'I couldn't save him. You two were just frolicking about with some whore while Aisholt gave his life to save Isolde and me! You wretches, get out of my sight!'

Guthrey and Quinn retreated sheepishly but would not leave as they stared in disbelief and shock at the sight of the butchered man. There were several stab wounds to his belly, his arm had been hacked off and his face was severely bruised, the cheekbone pushing up towards the eye.

'What's the world coming to when man is set against man whilst we are all threatened by hobs?' the innkeeper said heavily.

'Leave us!' Brid commanded in a terrible voice. 'We must

take care of our dead and be on our way.' Her eyes were searching those about her and she looked suspiciously at Aconite. 'Who is she?' Brid demanded but didn't wait for an answer. 'Spar, you look terrible! What's happened?'

No one was able to reply for the sudden high-pitched and hysterical screaming emanating from the stable yard. The innkeeper, hotly followed by the over-excited dogs, fled to see what now had invaded his inn, and Leaf looked at Caspar.

'I should think one of the women just discovered the horse and the slaughtered man,' Aconite quietly suggested. 'It's a little bloody in the stables.'

Caspar nodded. 'I shall see to it and at least get the blood mopped up,' he said heavily. 'If only I had brought Arathane with me rather than leaving him to guard the barge in the port, none of this would have happened. He would have stood guard and I would have gone for the rope. Aisholt and Cracker would both be still alive. Instead I left him guarding a barge! I can't believe it!'

'It wasn't your fault, Spar,' Brid told him kindly before giving the three youths the task of digging Aisholt's grave.

Though subdued, saddened and shocked by events, the three youths all scowled at one another.

'It's all your fault, Quinn!' Guthrey growled as he stabbed his spade into the stony ground.

'How could it possibly be my fault?' the youth angrily demanded.

'You should have stayed to look after the women.'

'And you shouldn't?' Quinn queried his half-brother's logic. 'Fanchon asked me first, don't forget.'

'She did not! Why would she bother asking you if she meant to ask me?' Guthrey asked arrogantly.

'Clearly she wanted you both,' Rollo wearily intervened as he heaved up a shovelful of soil from the ground. 'Perhaps she could charge more that way.'

'You stay out of this,' Guthrey roared. 'You little snake.

And if you must know, she was not charging us anything at all.'

'Oh, come now, you're not such a big a fool as all that. She's a whore. You may not know it but she was charging you *something*. Anyhow, how on earth were you stupid enough to get yourselves locked in?'

Both youths shrugged and Quinn made a pained face, the first indication that he felt some sense of guilt. 'The door handle just fell away on the inside. Shortly after, we heard screaming and yelling and tried to get out but we just couldn't open it.' He fell silent as the two priestesses, the two girls from the hidden realm, Fanchon and Caspar solemnly approached and gathered around the grave. Servants from the inn bore Aisholt's washed body and laid it in the shallow trench, which was as deep as the boys had managed to dig in the stony ground.

The servants withdrew and Brid moved to stand at Aisholt's head, Walnut standing behind her, his blunt nose bowed down, his expression contrite as if he sensed the solemnity of the occasion. Her face and hair washed in respect of the dead, the priestess looked dignified and calm as befitted the occasion. A white robe hung from her slender shoulders and a garland of mistletoe was strung about her neck. A wreath of yew adorned her head, the dark green leaves intensifying the colour of her eyes.

'Great Mother, lead Aisholt's soul quickly through the Otherworld to your glorious bosom. Give him ease and rest. Let him know our deep gratitude. He sacrificed himself for us, stood nobly before us and fought on even as he was dying. Let him be reborn to a position of grace, for there is none more worthy than he.'

Quinn looked grimly down at Aisholt's broken body as he chucked on the first spadeful of gritty mud that soaked up the damp blood. 'Rollo is right. It was our fault. We shouldn't have been tempted away from our duty.'

'Rollo is never right and knows nothing of duty,' Guthrey

snapped angrily, beginning to shovel faster so that they might cover up the gruesome sight of Aisholt, who still stared up at them accusingly.

Brid looked at her sons coldly and then glared at Fanchon. 'Don't you ever go near my sons again,' she warned. 'You are not welcome with us any longer.'

Rollo watched her return a smile that was confident and gloating. 'Do you think I wish for your company? What good are you to me now? In fact, what good are you to anybody?'

Rollo knew that something was very wrong about Fanchon. Something was very wrong indeed, but he couldn't place precisely what. He looked at her as she turned on her heel and began to walk smartly away, moving too quickly for his liking. Was she fleeing them or was she hurrying to meet someone else? He didn't know the answers; he just sensed something was wrong.

Leaf looked at Caspar, then at Fanchon, who was now running towards the stables. The young scholar bit her lower lip pensively and then exclaimed, 'You told her where the barge is, didn't you? She knew you were looking for a ship to sail out into the ocean and you told her about the barge!'

'What of it?' Caspar asked, looking at Leaf helplessly.

'Fanchon!' Leaf exclaimed in exasperation. 'She's not a whore at all. She's a spy.'

'A spy! A spy for Silas or the hobs?' Caspar asked, bewildered.

'No! No! That would be ridiculous. No, for Baron Wiglaf of Nattarda,' Leaf explained in some exasperation. 'Don't you remember the pirates' cheeses and the notes inside them? They were either meant for or sent by Wiglaf. It's obvious now. Fanchon and Dominica weren't flirting with him; they were reporting to him about you.'

'That's preposterous. Wiglaf is a baron of Belbidia. He would not be plotting against his countrymen.' Even as Caspar protested, his mouth slowed and his eyes suddenly fixed on Leaf. 'Of course! Wiglaf is paying off the hobs with information. His lands are allowed to flourish as a result. He only pretended to need help from Oxgard so that he could learn more about him. He wanted to know all about his comings and goings. I thought it strange at the time when I saw how Wiglaf's farmers were left in peace to work the land even though there were hobs crawling all over it. Wiglaf must have made a pact. And Fanchon's information was a part of that.'

'Wiglaf is helping Silas. I don't believe it!' Brid exclaimed though, in hindsight, Rollo agreed with Leaf that it was clearly true. 'But I'm certain you are right about Fanchon. I should have acted earlier. The hazelines condemned her and since their intuition and insight is so powerful, I should have heeded their instincts rather than waiting for proof. Why didn't I do something?'

'Get her!' Caspar yelled, pointing at Fanchon and launching into a sprint with Quinn and Guthrey close on his heels.

Rollo hesitated, thinking it was not wise to leave the women alone, but that moment the world was shattered by a thunderous roar. Caspar flung himself to the ground as sparks shot up into the air followed by a black pillar of smoke. Guthrey and Quinn staggered to a halt and stared at the horizon.

'It's coming from the harbour,' Aconite pointed out. 'My guess is the barge has just been blown apart, probably by some dwarfish mining device.'

Leaf nodded at her. 'That's my guess too.'

The explosion had allowed Fanchon to flee on one of the innkeeper's horses. Rollo caught a glimpse of her as she sped away, riding most unlike a lady and far more like one accomplished in the hunt. Rollo knew now how she had managed to find him so quickly after he had fallen prey to the hollines. Eager to learn about the son of an eminent noble so that she had more to report to her masters, she had been following him. The flimsy clothes and coquettish smile were all a front; in reality she had been an accomplished woman totally capable of riding hard and fast.

But the black column of smoke pumping into the sky meant that all thought of chasing after Fanchon had to be abandoned. Without consultation, all hurried towards the harbour only to be met by Lug striding towards them. Guthrey and Quinn faltered in their stride at the sight of the mammoth man.

'Come on!' Caspar urged.

Since the Baron was clearly untroubled by the sight of this monster, whose head was level with the squat huts of the fishing village, the Torra Altan youths followed on though they stared warily at the giant. He was trembling all over and staggering after Arathane, who was mounted on his horse. As he drew close, Rollo could see that he looked angry rather than troubled.

'I left Lug to watch it. I just took Sorrel ashore to stretch her legs for a moment and I told him to watch the barge,' the warrior complained angrily.

'I was watching it!' the giant protested. 'I sat on the quay and I watched it. Then it exploded.'

'You fell asleep; that's what happened. And now we have no way of getting out of here. You're a thundering great oaf!' Arathane accused.

Lug stamped his foot; Sorrel snorted and danced up high on her toes, bucking with indignation as the ground shook beneath her feet. Arathane stroked her neck in an attempt to soothe her.

'Something must have got to the barge while this idiot fell asleep,' he explained as Aconite and Leaf arrived a moment after Brid and Isolde.

'It was only a barge,' Caspar gently assured the warrior. 'We can find something better. The important thing is that you're safe. Are you hurt at all?'

'No, we're both fine,' Arathane told him while still glaring angrily at the giant. 'And I'm not at all sure that the barge wasn't important to us. I've spent days trying to obtain a vessel

470

and as soon as I have one this lumbering idiot allows it to be blown out of the water.'

Rollo thought it most unwise to treat such a huge and powerful-looking fellow with such disdain.

'You might be fine, but what about me?' Lug complained. 'I'm covered in cuts and bruises all over.'

'Let's just get back to the inn,' Caspar said heavily.

Lug's arrival brought a further round of shrieks from all at Candlewood Inn. Doors were slammed shut instantly. Brid angrily rapped at the solid oak front door until the innkeeper's nose poked out through a shutter in the wood.

'We don't serve giants!' he snapped.

'It's of no matter, coward,' the high priestess scolded him. 'But you will serve us. Now open the door; he will not harm you.'

'You've brought destruction and murder to this inn, madam,' Leof complained. 'I'm not sure that you are welcome either.'

'I'll bring a bit more if you don't co-operate. We want to be on our way as fast as possible, but we need supplies,' the priestess told him flatly. 'Now open up!'

'So long as it is as fast as possible,' the innkeeper grumbled. 'And what about the mess in my stables? There's still a dead horse in there.'

'I am just about to take care of that,' Caspar said gravely, and Rollo could feel the aura of black grief clinging to his father. The Baron stepped forward and pressed three gold coins into Leof's hands. 'Now see about those supplies,' he insisted. 'And we want good flour and as many hogs and cows as you can lay your hands on. Failing that we'll take barrels of fish.' Caspar glanced at the Haol-garen and said to Brid, 'How much do you suppose he can eat?'

The priestess shrugged and reached out a hand to grasp Caspar's, squeezing it tightly. The Baron met her sympathetic eyes with a weak smile.

'Come,' she said. 'We had best see to Cracker. You boys go

471

and pack. And look after Isolde. Spar and I have something to take care of. Lug, you can help.'

Rollo was hurt that his presence wasn't requested; after all, he had grown up with the horse, in awe of its brutish behaviour. Surely, his father needed his comfort more than Brid's. However, he moved to obey Brid's order but, in the end, rather than help prepare their things, he merely stared out of the window. His gaze had fallen upon Lug, who hugged in his vast arms the body of the red roan, which he held much as a man might hold a large hound. Walking stiffly under the weight, the giant solemnly followed Caspar and Brid as they marched to a pile of faggots the far side of a large bare ash. The bonfire had been built up a little distance from the inn so that the sparks from the funeral pyre would not spray up and set the thatch alight.

'So the horse gets all the pomp and ceremony whereas Aisholt received only a common burial,' Guthrey commented over his shoulder.

Rollo wasn't interested. He felt excluded and, at last, resolved to stamp out of the inn and march after his father. Already, Firecracker's sleek body was stiff and charred and the air was filled with thick black smuts that floated up on the rising heat before spiralling back down to earth. Indignantly, the boy strode towards his father. Far from being intent on comforting him, his thoughts were only on why he had been excluded. But his resentment crumbled as he looked into his father's face to see it streaked with tears. Rollo stood beside him and slipped his hand into Caspar's.

'Father, he saved me.'

Caspar hugged his boy to him. 'I know! And for that I am grateful, eternally grateful.' Fiercely, he kissed his son's hair. 'You know I was going to skin you alive because you had allowed him to be injured, but now I am grateful that he is dead because you are alive.' He sniffed and managed to smile. 'But you know what, lad, that horse probably had no thought of saving you. He had the most vicious temper any horse ever possessed and he probably thought nothing of you but was simply so angered by the Nattardan's intrusion that he struck the man out of defiant rage. Though the finest in all the world, he was only a horse and he always hated man for stealing his freedom. I think he even hated me.' Caspar sniffed. 'But for all that I loved him.'

Chapter 26

Rollo felt sick. He wanted to get into the fresh air but Captain Milo had sent them all into the hold for fear of the squall they were about to hit. The hold still reeked of rotten fish, which intensified his nausea, and, as the ship tossed and groaned, all he could do was lie on the floor and cover his head, wishing that he were anywhere but here.

The others were not as sick. Lug was singing in his very deep voice about reindeer and the sparkling snow, which was keeping Guthrey and Quinn amused. The adults were deep in conversation with Leaf and Aconite, though Isolde, like him, was lying on the deck mewing softly. There was no escape from the seasickness. All Rollo could do was bear it but he doubted he would manage it for much longer. He wished Isolde would be quiet, as it seemed to make his interminable sickness worse. It felt as if he had been lying on the rolling floor of the hold for hours when Brid came to check Isolde over.

'Poor little thing,' she murmured. Sitting beside her, Brid scooped Isolde into her arms and cradled her close.

Rollo wished someone would hold him. Was there no one in this world who would comfort him? He had offered Caspar solace after Firecracker's death, and now where was his father to offer him comfort? Rollo wanted to turn his head to look for him but didn't dare in case he was sick.

They had been at sea for three weeks and he had been sick for two of them. He felt far better when he was on deck with the salt spray stinging his skin and the fresh air filling his lungs, but in the stale stuffiness of the hold he felt violently ill. It was a fine ship, a three-masted trader, and he had noted with some amazement that Arathane had been impressed at the speed with which Caspar had procured such a vessel.

After the unfortunate demise of the barge, Caspar had gone at once to the Baron of Piscera, who was castled not more than twenty miles from Candlewood Inn, and demanded an audience. The Baron of Piscera had come running and embraced his father with open arms, so Guthrey had told Rollo. He had not been present since he had been ordered to remain and protect Isolde. However, he suspected that the main reason he had been kept away was because his father feared he might cause embarrassment. Guthrey had further reported that the Piscerans, having just been freed from a plague of occupying hobs, were determined to fight off any further attack at any cost.

So, when Caspar had asked for a ship, the Piscerans had offered their fastest deep-water vessel and ordered wagon loads of supplies to fill the hold, which had previously carried crates of prized smoked salmon and sea-trout to the countries of the Caballan. On the return journey, *The Pisceran Porpoise* had proudly carried home fine gold and silver trinkets from Camaalia and beyond. Evidence of these treasures was still to be seen on the Captain's table, which bore lavish plates and goblets that seemed very out of place in the man's sea-hardened hands.

Though he complained that the ship looked undersized for the voyage, Arathane had been pleased with her fine lines and narrow hull, which would cut through the waves at speed and, hopefully, ride the savage storms which ravaged the black waters between the Diamond Seas and Athell.

After promising to return his ship to the Pisceran nobleman at the first opportunity, Caspar had asked after the where-abouts of the King, but none had known. Rollo wondered in his seasick misery what dreadful fate King Rewik had suffered.

At last, he must have fallen asleep because it was now

morning and the ship was finally still. The stinking hold in which he lay had been deserted by all but Arathane and Isolde. Arathane lay beside his horse, which he would not leave, and slept while Isolde sat hunched in a far corner, her hood pulled down to cover her face. Rollo wanted to go up on deck to get some fresh air but he could sense the girl's eyes on him and wondered what she was thinking. He staggered over to her and sank down beside her.

'How are you feeling?' he croaked.

'Go away!' she growled, pulling her cloak down a little lower.

Annoyed by her attitude, he snatched her hood and ripped it back off her head. His hand fell away in shock and he stared, open-mouthed, at the transformation. The skin over all her body had darkened to a greenish mud-brown and was dry and leathery. Her eyes, which were once a glorious green with speckles of gold, were now brown with a rim of red about them. Her nostrils were flared, the skin peeled back to reveal the gristle, and her lips were thin, covering jagged teeth. Even her fingers had grown long and skeletal. She looked at him defiantly and smiled a caustic smile.

'See! Now you can run from me just as Guthrey and Quinn did when they saw me. They mutter behind their backs, "Oh poor, Isolde," but they will not sit and comfort me.'

Rollo thought he would be sick at the sight of her but, at the same time, he knew how others had beheld him when he suffered one of his fits. They had gawped at him and retreated in revulsion when he writhed on the floor, his muscles in spasm, and he would not treat her the same. She was the same Isolde underneath, just as he was no less himself. Steeling himself against the bile rising in his stomach, he pushed back the ragged slime of her hair, which felt like wet seaweed, and ran his creeping fingers down her back, which was bumpy with enlarged bony nodules jutting from her spine through the flesh. He pulled her close.

'Sweet Isolde,' he murmured. 'Sweet, sweet Isolde. You

are the bravest girl that ever lived.' He kissed the top of her head and felt her shudder from the touch. A moment later, she began to shake and her voice cracked as she broke into sobs.

'I am not brave at all. I am so scared, so miserably scared, and the worst of it is that I hunger for fresh meat. I can smell Sorrel over there. I can smell her fear; she senses me as a predator. Rollo, I want to eat her! It is driving me mad.' She clutched him close. 'I am not just changing in my looks. Soon I shall be a hob through and through.'

'I do not believe it. These changes are physical character-istics only. You will always be Isolde.' He kissed her again and, to his astonishment, she began to laugh.

'You are very brave, Rollo. Braver than Guthrey and Quinn who have pretended to be kind to me though they cannot bring themselves to touch me.' She prodded her own flesh. 'Can you imagine what it is like to be repulsed by the feel of one's own skin, by one's own smell even?'

Rollo thought that he could. He had long wished to be other than he was. He was fair to look at, he had to agree. Not as fair as Guthrey, admittedly, whose dark hair and defined features turned every maiden's eye, but he was well built with a straight nose and clear grey-blue eyes. He was particularly proud of his straight nose since his father's was crooked and he had dreaded that his might one day end up like that. Still, he found his own skin somewhat soft, his muscles slow and his body cold. He had never quite felt comfortable with himself. However, he did not say this out loud; instead he said very softly, 'Poor, Isolde, you do not deserve this.'

'Ah, but I do, Rollo, I do. After everything I have done, it is all my fault. Don't you see? I have caused this to happen. It is my recompense.'

Rollo snapped his head up, suddenly aware that someone was standing over him. It was Brid, looking deeply pained.

'You may go now,' she imperiously dismissed Rollo and crouched down beside Isolde. 'Do not talk like that, child.

You are a fine and wonderful girl. If only you would believe in yourself . . .'

'How can you possibly begin to understand? Quinn is the only one who can understand, and even he won't talk to me any more.' Isolde curled up into a ball and began to sob.

Rollo stood there, wanting to comfort her, but, having been dismissed by Brid, he didn't dare put himself in a position where he risked rejection or further rebuff. To his amazement, Brid did not comfort Isolde but scolded her harshly for her self-pity.

'We have all had to make sacrifices. It is your role and lot in life and you must endure this transformation bravely. It is after all a testament to your own courageous act. It shows little depth of character if you cannot endure what you brought on yourself. Now grit your teeth, girl, and believe in your strength.'

Rollo stamped angrily away as he listened to the sound of Isolde sucking in her sobs. 'Brid, I am sorry; I have failed you.'

The high priestess softened her tone towards Isolde. 'No, sweet girl. If you fail anyone, you fail yourself. Be proud of who you are because the Great Mother has made you that way and all things she touches are perfect.'

'*She* may have made me perfect, but *life* has spoiled me. This transformation merely shows me for what I am. You cannot understand, Brid.'

The older priestess forbore to argue but merely placed a platter of food emphatically before her charge. 'Eat!' she ordered.

After climbing up out of the forward hatch and onto the deck, Rollo was glad of the fresh air, but it did not ease his anger. It was early morning and, though the sky overhead was blue, a chill mist still clung to the sea. The air was still and the sails drooped impotently. Someone at the prow of the trader was sounding out the depth. 'Three fathoms and rising!'

Guthrey and Quinn were busying themselves with a game

of Dead Man's Truce and were already arguing about the rules. Rollo was livid with them, particularly Quinn, for ignoring Isolde when she so needed support and sympathy. He strode up to Quinn and looked him hard in the eye.

'I thought you and Isolde had a special bond, a special friendship.'

'We do!' Quinn insisted.

'Well, why aren't you down with her now, playing Dead Man's Truce with her to take her mind off things? Instead, you shun her.'

'She told me to go away,' Quinn defended himself.

'So! She's lonely and afraid. You could have tried a little harder to help her.'

'What business is this of yours anyhow, foreigner?' Guthrey broke in. 'How dare you attack my brother like this!'

Rollo didn't know whom to hit first. The way Quinn and Guthrey had shunned Isolde for her looks reminded him of how he had been shunned all his life for his fits. Spitting with rage, he roared and flew at Guthrey, simply because he was the closest. He hated him now even more than when he had first met him. He hated him for looking like Hal and for even smelling of him. He hated him for his magnanimous apology after their earlier quarrel and the condescending way in which he had offered his friendship.

But he didn't think of that right now; he thought only of the moment and how best to hurt the youth. Rollo already knew that Guthrey was quick-fisted so he kept his head tucked down low, his fists in tight, and rammed his head up against Guthrey's chin, sending the youth rolling backwards. The Artoran launched himself into the air and landed heavily on his rival's chest. Having the advantage, he thumped Guthrey in the ear and raised his fist to thump again, only to find it caught in the jaws of the Ophidian terrier. Walnut clamped his teeth tight, though he refrained from breaking the skin. A second later the boy was hauled to his feet by a rough hand and the dog transferred its grip to his ankle. Rollo spat and snarled almost as much as Walnut, who was finally silenced when a bucket of water was sloshed into his face.

Captain Milo stood before him, his eyes stern and his frown deep, though nothing else of his expression was visible for the coiling beard that masked his chin.

'What are you thinking, lad?' he growled. 'If you were one of my regular crew, I'd have you flung overboard for this behaviour.' He turned to his first mate at his side. 'Here, Salty, isn't that so?'

The very little man, who was never more than a couple of paces behind the ship's master, nodded grimly. Unlike Captain Milo, this short man was dark and clean-shaven, which showed his scowl off to best effect. 'In these waters we don't have time to waste on misdemeanours. We should be watching the bottom at all times. On a still morning like today, the mist squats over these sandbanks and, in places, the seabed nearly rises to the surface. We have but feet in hand. I don't like any behaviour that takes our minds off the ship, and I don't like this lad, Captain. I don't like him at all. You can trust a dog's instincts if you ask me. Got a nasty streak to him, he has. You should put him in the hold. Lock him in with the horse where he can't do no harm. Can't have lads attacking one another. It's not safe, not safe at all while we're navigating the sandbanks – and in the mist at that.'

'I agree with that, Salty, I do. Wise, wise words. Let's have you back in the hold, lad. I don't want to see your face atop deck no more on this passage.'

Caspar was striding hastily across the deck as the sailor at the stern cried out, 'We have three foot of clearance, Captain Milo!'

'Captain Milo, let me answer for my son,' the Baron said hastily. 'On my word, he'll cause no more trouble or I'll put him in the hold myself. But it's stuffy down there, and no doubt that's what's caused his temper to flare.'

Rollo squinted and glared at his father. He was not about to be rescued in such a patronizing manner. 'I'm not having you answering for me,' he muttered and began stamping towards the hatchway to the hold. 'I'll take myself below.'

He had not taken more than four paces, however, before he was stopped in his tracks. 'Hard to port! Hard to port!' a sailor was yelling, and the ship reacted as if it were a nervous colt shying away from danger. As the sailor's cries still rang through the air, the ship lurched to the left and Rollo staggered to find his balance.

Another sailor was yelling, 'Ship ahoy! Ship to starboard!'

Disorientated by the motion of the ship and unused to the seafaring language, it was a moment before Rollo raised his eyes in the right direction. A black ship was looming out of the mist; angry blasts on a horn blared across the calm surface. It was running before a gentle breeze and heading straight towards them. Along with a square sail, it bore a single tier of oars that splashed and caught the water with a surprising lack of rhythm and precision. Whether it was through incompetence or a deliberate will, the black ship still made straight for them, though surely its crew must have spied them.

Caspar had Rollo by the shoulder and flung him down on the deck alongside the hatch cover. 'Stay low, keep out of the sailors' way and hold on fast in case we're rammed.'

Rollo nodded, his eyes fixed on the ghastly shape of the approaching ship. Their own vessel was alive with the sounds of ropes hurtling through pulleys. A confusion of whirring, clanking and shouts filled the air. 'Dear Mother, don't let me drown out here in the vast expanse of the ocean,' he murmured, and then forgot himself as he remembered Isolde. 'Father, Isolde's down below! What if we're rammed and water fills the hold?'

'I know!' Caspar cried, firmly placing his son's hand onto one of the ship's many ropes fastened to a cleat on the deck. 'Hold on tight and don't move from this spot. I'm going below for her!'

Rollo clung to the cleat, feeling alone and inadequate. The

sailors were frantically hauling on ropes to which they gave unlikely names. The ship rocked and reeled but finally the very highest sail, the royal, filled and caught a breeze, be it only a very gentle one. Apparently there was nothing more the sailors could do but wait for nature to assist them. All eyes stared at the oncoming craft, which was still skimming through the water towards them.

'Why aren't we moving? Why doesn't someone do something?' Rollo despaired, his teeth tightly clenched.

Dragging his eyes away from the oncoming ship, he stared at the hold, waiting for his father to reappear. But the threat of the oncoming vessel compelled his eyes back to the high-prowed black ship, its oars angrily thrashing the water. His heart pounded. Already he could make out the shapes of white letters written on its side, though he could make no sense of them. As the mist rolled back from the deck of the ship, he saw a figure at the prow, a horn at its mouth, blaring out the eerie sound. But he knew already it was not a blast of warning but a war-horn rousing the spirits of those on board the black ship to prepare themselves for attack.

One by one, other black shapes loomed out of the mist, flanking the figure with the horn. They were tall and thin, their limbs long; there was no mistaking the angular, spare form of a hob. They were stamping in unison, and thumping short spears to the ground, waiting until they were in range before they hurled them. Or perhaps they were simply waiting for their vessel to do the work for them. Rollo swallowed, thinking about the sharks that must prowl these crystal blue waters.

'Come on, come on!' old Salty yelled at the sails. 'We're not going to make it!'

The black vessel looked suddenly huge, the sound of its bow cutting through the water like the hiss from a giant sea serpent.

Rollo stared on. 'Please, Great Mother, please,' he begged.

Caspar staggered up out of the hatch, hauling Isolde after him. The girl was struggling ferociously and lashing out in an attempt to break free from him. In a croaky voice, she implored him not to drag her up on deck.

'If we go under, you'll drown in seconds down there. Arathane cannot leave Sorrel; we understand that, but at least, up in the open, *you* stand a chance.'

'Does it matter? Wouldn't it be better . . . ?'

Brute force alone enabled Caspar to pull her up through the hold. He kicked the hatch shut and stood on it in an attempt to prevent her fleeing below again. Rollo was no longer watching. Clinging to the cleat, he was staring at the fast-approaching vessel. He could make out the hobs' shrieking faces, their wide gaping mouths and their frenzied movements. He could smell the stench from their overcrowded ship. His body tensed as he sniffed in the air and he had an unnerving sense that there were ravenshrikes within the belly of the enemy ship. The hairs on his spine prickled and he had an inexplicable desire to throw back his head and roar out his defiance at their intrusion.

'Look!' one of the Pisceran sailors yelled. 'Behind the hobs!'

'Men!' Brid exclaimed in alarm.

For a split second Rollo assumed they were slaves or prisoners, but then he saw that they too bore spears and were chanting out the same ferocious battle cry. His eye, however, was focused on the prow of the black ship, which he now predicted would hit just forward of their stern. They were no more than twenty yards away now; it was only a matter of seconds.

All were still and silent, braced for the shock. It was unbearable. The wind was so still; Rollo could crawl faster than this and yet it was all they could do to escape. The Belbidians stared, all frozen to the spot as the ships inched towards one another.

483

Suddenly someone was running across the deck of *The Pisceran Porpoise*, light feet pattering on the boards. It was Leaf sprinting towards Caspar and Isolde.

'Get up there!' the curious little girl from the hidden realm was squealing.

Isolde was backing away from her in alarm but Leaf flung herself at the afflicted priestess, ripped her cloak from her shoulders and began scrabbling at her dress. Isolde howled in protest, the cry deep and bestial.

'No, no! Stand up there, by the edge of the ship!' Leaf was frantically tugging at Isolde. 'Show yourself to them!'

Isolde suddenly seemed to grasp Leaf's plan and ran towards the edge of the ship, where the great black prow of the hob-filled vessel hung over their own. She flung off her cloak, ripped away her dress and stood tall, arms spread wide. Throwing back her head she barked out angry words that had an unmistakably imperious ring to them. Rollo blinked as he stared at her scrawny naked outline; she was a hob. Every inch of her had completed the fearful metamorphosis. Frozen to the spot, he stared on in horror, expecting the huge prow of the black ship to spear right into her and crush her into the decking of their own vessel, but already the hobs' chant had altered and they were barking and squabbling, gesticulating wildly and frantically pulling on ropes. Isolde's harsh voice whipped out again and a single hob barked back at her. Oars crabbed and splashed in the water or banged against one another as the oarsmen sought to reverse their strokes on one side and so turn their vessel away.

Caspar ran forward and lunged for Isolde as the starboard side of the hobs' ship nudged their own craft. The vessel shuddered and timbers squeaked and rendered under the pressure. Oars snapped. Then, with a judder and lurch, they broke free of one another. The crew and passengers of each vessel stared at one another in curious disbelief. Isolde shrieked out her command again and then fell back against Caspar, as it seemed the danger had passed. The crew from the other vessel were running to the stern of their ship, staring on in confusion and shouting at each other as if uncertain what to do.

Captain Milo took the helm. 'I see ripples on the water ahead. We'll catch a useful breeze in a moment and be clear of them. Luck and the mist was all they had on their side. They're not accomplished seafarers, and the moment we have the wind we'll be out of sight. See, look! The wind is already clearing the mist!' Cheerfully he looked around at his passengers, who were still clinging to anything tied down to the deck. Then his eye fell on Isolde. 'You never told me we had a hob on board. I've been paid handsomely for this voyage, but it's not enough to be transporting hobs!'

Isolde was hurriedly pulling on her clothes and furling her cloak about her when a cross-breeze skimming across the sea finally filled the sails. The wind then scurried on to sweep over the black ship, which was rocking in the water and appeared to be manoeuvring round in pursuit. Clearly they were still uncertain as to whether they were friend or foe. Rollo was about to look away when the sight of something large and dark was revealed by the retreating mist. His mouth dropped and his hands went limp as he stared. Leaf was suddenly at his side and slipped her cold little hand into his.

'They were so close and we never knew they were there!' she breathed in horror.

Rollo swallowed. It was horrifying, horrendous. They could have sailed right into their midst. At first, one ship was revealed and then another three and another eight and quickly they were beyond counting. Some had their oars in the water and were underway; others were chained together, moored alongside one another. Horns blasted and shouts, now loud, no longer muffled by the mist, rang back and forth. It was an entire armada of ships of different shapes and colours; frigates, fishing vessels, warships and schooners, but all were black, bearing the distinctive angular figures of hobs on their decks.

The Torra Altans drew together in a tight knot about Isolde and Leaf tugged Rollo to join them. Aconite wearily slumped onto the deck, clutching her belly and shaking her head in disbelief at what had just happened. In silence, all stared at the scene that had been lurking, hidden in the ocean mist. The ship which had so nearly rammed them was still trying to catch up but was now being left far behind. With the wind in the sails, the Pisceran trader had no trouble skipping over the water and racing away; the hobs were clearly not a seafaring race.

The crew grunted orders and heaved and hauled on the ship though always with half an eye on the armada mustered over the sandbanks. The Torra Altans stared on in silence. As they raced away, the wind stiffened, driving away the last of the mist and their view of the ships became clearer. Rollo squinted as the sun glinted down on strange shapes now revealed in the water. A tangle of broken ships jutted out of the water. Hundreds of wrecked ships formed an island in the midst of the vast ocean. There were shapes crawling all over them.

Captain Milo paced towards Caspar and handed him a long thin cylinder. 'Here, take a look with my telescope.'

The Baron looked at the instrument uncertainly before putting it to his eye. He pulled it away and blinked at the contraption before raising it again and staring at the island. 'I can't see anything. It's just a blur.'

'I see you've never used one of these before,' the Captain remarked. 'Here, twist this.' He put Caspar's hand on the end of the telescope.

The Baron gasped. 'I can see everything! There are hobs and men crawling all over the wrecks. They are making something. It looks like a giant platform of some sort, and I can see huts. They're turning the sandbanks into an island.' He lowered the telescope and returned it to Captain Milo.

'But why?' The Baron dropped his gaze to look at Leaf. 'And don't tell me it's obvious.'

'All right then,' she said smartly. 'So what do you want me to say?'

Caspar shrugged. 'Just tell me your theory. I know you have one.'

Leaf drew in a deep breath. 'The writing on the hobs' black ship is the script used in Athell. It read *The Pride of the Empire*. From that I can think it's reasonable to assume that the hobs and their armada are from Athell.'

The Captain laughed and patted Leaf on the shoulder. 'Child, it's clear you cannot possibly understand such things. Such vessels, such badly handled vessels at that with no draught, could never have crossed from Athell. Only the great ships can make that journey safely. Our own ship is a little undersized but she's built for rough water, and in my hands we'll make it.'

Leaf smiled sweetly back at him. 'Captain Milo, it's clear you do not understand. I do, however, concur entirely that these ships would not generally make the journey from Athell. They have, in my opinion, been sailed at risk with a light crew during the doldrums of the summer when even the Blackwater Deeps are relatively tranquil.'

Aconite nodded at this hypothesis.

Leaf continued, 'Those damaged on the way have been scuttled over the sandbanks, while the rest sat and waited in the quiet waters of the Diamond Seas, biding their time. The vast traders have continued to brave the Blackwater Deeps, bearing supplies and reinforcing troops, both hobs and men, for the smaller vessels to ferry across the more tranquil waters from the sandbanks to mainland Belbidia on their many raids.'

'But why?' Guthrey asked curiously. 'Why would anyone go to such lengths? Why not just go the whole way in the huge vessels?'

'The answer to that, lad, is obvious!' Captain Milo told

him. 'A large ship cannot stealthily approach and sail in close to the Belbidian shoreline, nor slip in up the rivers as the hobs have been doing. It can mount a single attack at one point, if someone was obliging enough to provide a deep-water harbour, but such harbours tend to be heavily fortified. With their small vessels they can slip inshore and creep up the rivers to strike at the heart of our country.'

Caspar stared in horror at the island of shipwrecks. 'They are on the point of mounting a full-scale invasion. What we have suffered up until now has been nothing compared to what is to come.'

All stared on glumly, their eyes turned towards Belbidia whose shore had slipped beyond the horizon days ago.

'What can we do?' Brid croaked. 'Should we go back and warn everyone?'

Caspar shook his head. 'No, there is no point. They will realize for themselves soon enough, and our warning will not help. We must go after Silas. Not only must we retrieve the Chalice for Isolde's sake but we must do what we can to strike him down. I'll stake my life that he is the mastermind behind this. Imagine that this mass of invading hobs is a dragon; to kill it we must strike at its weak spot and reach the brain. Silas is the brain.'

Brid put her arms around Isolde. 'Come, we'll get you below decks again.'

Isolde nodded weakly though Captain Milo barred the way. 'I don't know that I want a hob on my ship. What's the creature doing here?'

'She isn't a hob,' Brid started to explain.

'She looks like one, she smells like one and she talks like one. That's a hob in anyone's book.'

Brid drew in an exasperated breath. 'It's too complicated to explain. You will just have to trust us that she is on our side.'

'How do you know she wasn't passing on valuable information to the hobs on that ship?'

488

Isolde flung back her hood and angrily glared at the Captain; Rollo fancied that her red eyes would burn through his skin at any moment. 'I told him I had slaves from central Belbidia who had vital news for Silas in Athell. At least for a moment, before they had time to think about it, they must have believed I was a friend because one of them shouted back that Silas hadn't gone straight to the Emperor but was headed first for the Opal Isle. They thought we might just catch him quickly if we caught a good wind.'

'Well, why didn't you say so earlier?' Caspar demanded.

'Nobody asked.' With that Isolde turned her back on them and began that curiously double-jointed walk, striding towards the hold.

'Where's Opal Island?' Caspar asked Captain Milo.

The bearded seafarer shrugged his broad shoulders. 'There's a thousand and one islands dotted across the Diamond Seas and a few ancient volcanoes that rise out of the Blackwater Deeps. And who's to say the hobs' name for it is the same as ours?'

'We'd better ask Arathane,' Aconite calmly suggested. 'Since it's nearer to his homeland than ours, he might know.'

'And that's another queer thing about you folk; why doesn't that man ever leave his horse?' Salty muttered uncomfortably.

Clearly, nobody felt it was their place to explain as all shrugged innocently.

The Captain grunted in a dissatisfied manner. 'I'll consult my charts and see if I can find anything.' He looked up towards the sails that were now filled and stretched, hauling them into choppy waters beneath a cloud-streaked sky. 'We're making good time but that's no use to us unless we are making good time in the right direction.'

One by one, the Torra Altans, Rollo and Leaf slipped into the hold. Sorrel whinnied and snorted anxiously at Isolde's approach, though Arathane's hand on her muzzle soothed her somewhat. For ten minutes or so the air rang with shrill voices as, all at once, they related the scene to Arathane.

The warrior listened patiently and then soothed his long hair back over the scalped patches before lifting his helmet onto his head. 'It's a small island, only about twelve miles long and four miles across, about a hundred miles off the eastern coast of Athell. It's about a week's sail under a favourable wind but takes us through the roughest seas I've ever sailed.'

Rollo thought he would die; the very thought of the Blackwater Deeps turned his skin green and churned his stomach.

Chapter 27

Like little drops of acid, Isolde's tears stung Rollo's skin. Nevertheless, he hugged her to him, pressing her head against his chest. The storm had ceased earlier that morning but he did not feel strong enough to crawl out of the hold. Besides, Isolde needed him.

Arathane was rubbing down Sorrel's coat, trying to bring back some shine. The chestnut mare stamped her feet and tugged at her headcollar nervously. The voyage had been distressing for the animal and Arathane looked very tired. He had not left her side in weeks but sat comforting her and telling her stories as if the mare understood them. Rollo wondered whether any part of the animal still held the sentient thought of the woman she had once been. He doubted it. Only the dogs appeared content. Walnut and the hound had slept through most of the gruelling voyage, and if they had to lie in the foul straw for another month Rollo doubted they would care. The only thing that showed they were awake was their ears following the sounds of the sailors above, who shouted to one another.

He knew the hold must stink but he had become accustomed to it and no longer cared. Many times Brid had suggested to Isolde that she go topside for some air but the girl refused, saying the salt spray irritated her skin and that she would be able to smell herself up there. At least down in the hold the heady stink of dog and horse disguised the fetid smell of hob.

Arathane was tacking up his horse. 'Come on, Rollo, it

won't be long now. You and Isolde had better get yourselves ready. You heard your father; they spotted land hours ago. Don't you want to see for yourself as we approach the shore?'

'Land!' Isolde grunted gratefully. She then clung to Rollo even tighter. 'You must stay close beside me. Guthrey and Quinn are repulsed by my appearance. They are afraid and you are the only one who sees me as I am.'

'I won't leave you,' Rollo promised, though the flesh on his hand cringed as he soothed the slime of tangles sprouting from her wrinkled scalp. Although he did feel intensely sorry for Isolde, he also felt a degree of self-satisfaction that he had stood by her when Guthrey and Quinn had failed her. But it was still another half an hour before he persuaded her just to reach the foot of the ladder rising out of the hold but she would go no further until Brid coaxed her up into the open. The little priestess tugged at Isolde's long fingers and then enfolded her in her own cloak once they were on deck. Caspar and Arathane were hard at work, opening up the large trap door to the hold while a sailor operated a capstan in order to winch out Sorrel.

Rollo blinked in the dazzling daylight and for the first time in months felt pleasurable heat from the sun on his back. Artor was much warmer than Belbidia, and he had missed the sunshine. Here, in the midst of the Blackwater Deep, which was indeed as black and forbidding as its name, a white-hot sun blazed through a brilliant blue sky before it sank into the fathomless depths.

Captain Milo had his telescope trained on the coastline while the rest stared longingly inland, glimpsing a white beach protected by two horns of land, welcoming them like arms towards the mountainous isle. After the weeks in the belly of the rolling ship, where he had felt like curd within a butter churn, Rollo was delighted at the sight of land. Opal Isle reminded him of home. Tall mountains stretched up above dense green forests. Waterfalls tumbled from the peaks, somersaulting down to commune with the thirsty expanse of the brooding ocean. A seal barked to them from a rocky prom-ontory shouldering the beach, whose white sands beckoned them with the promise of being warm and soft under foot.

Rollo itched to run on those sands and climb towards the blue cliffs at the head of the beach, which buried their shoulders in a mass of succulent vegetation. He stared, gazing at the land until they were close to shore and Captain Milo gave the orders to drop anchor. In frustration, Rollo looked at the sailors and thought they were taking far too long to lower the rowing boats.

At last, two twenty-five-foot rowing boats were in the water and the sailors began the difficult process of lowering Sorrel into the middle of one. They were, Rollo guessed, still about a quarter of a mile from the shore and he hoped Arathane would be able to control the mare. If she panicked and leapt overboard it would be a long swim. Lug, who was grumbling bitterly about the heat, was urged towards the second boat. Brid had rubbed ochre onto his skin in an attempt to protect him from the sun's fierceness but he was fair-skinned and also had a low tolerance of strange experiences.

Of their company, Aconite was the only one who remained on board. The seasickness coupled with her pregnancy had taken its toll and no one could persuade her to rise from her bed. Rollo patiently waited his turn to climb down into one of the boats while Captain Milo repeated his warning to Caspar.

The bearded sailor pointed behind him at the two spits of land that protected the beach from the lashing waves of the sea. 'There's a shallow reef across this natural harbour and our keel barely made it. The tide's still coming in at present, sir, but once it turns in about three hours you must be back within another three hours or we won't make it out again and will find ourselves stuck in the sand. For now, this is a safe spot as the two spits of land hide us neatly from any ship, but you have six hours and that's it.'

Caspar nodded solemnly.

As he took his place in the boat and flexed his fingers on an oar, Rollo felt momentarily abandoned as Isolde rejected him in favour of clinging to Brid. However, he was not to be left alone for long since Leaf picked her way towards him, seeking his comfort. 'I hope Arathane is right about this,' she murmured.

'Do you think he is wrong?' Rollo queried, leaping at her words.

'I have no way of knowing. Aconite – when she's been well enough – your father and I have studied the charts with the Captain and all are agreed that Arathane's suggestion is likely. If Silas were still on the island, he would almost certainly have gone ashore on the far side where there is a harbour serving the old mines. It's just a matter of whether he's still there or not.'

His muscles bulging as he effortlessly tugged on his oar, Old Salty grunted, 'If he's there or not all depends on whether that hob creature with you is telling the truth.'

As they hauled on the oars, Rollo found his muscles weak after the long confinement aboard ship. They fell into silence, ears listening intently for any danger as the oars rhythmically pulled through the water, a gentle foam hissing against the bow of both boats. Lug's boat, with Guthrey, Quinn, two sailors and the dogs, pulled ahead, and Rollo watched the sandy bottom of the shelving seabed gradually rise towards them. Tiny fish flitted in and out of the sands, chased by larger ones. He shuddered at the sight of long brown tentacles streaming out behind a jellyfish that was nearly a yard across. He hoped Sorrel would remain calm and not upset the boat.

The boats were heavy and it was a long hard row to the beach. Leaf looked lost in contemplation. They were nearly at the beach before she spoke.

'Arathane, what do you know about this island? Is there anything notable about it?'

'Not especially,' the big warrior replied without taking his eyes off his horse. He still held her bridle firmly in both hands.

'There are many islands off the coast of Athell. Most are flat but some, like this one, are mountainous. They say it's an extinct volcano.'

'Is it inhabited?'

'Not for decades. Not since they finished mining for opals. Hardly any of the islands hereabouts have ever been inhabited,' the knight grunted as he struggled to hold Sorrel. Rollo guessed she had scented fresh grass since she was stamping and tugging at her bridle in eagerness.

There was no time to talk further. As soon as the bottom of the rowing boat brushed against the sand, Sorrel broke free, knocking Caspar off his seat as she leapt for the shore, dragging Arathane with her. Brid anxiously pulled Caspar upright again and asked after his wounded arm while all the others scrabbled out and splashed to the shore. Isolde and Rollo were the last to leave. The priestess looked at the shallow water in dismay and then down at her long, spidery feet.

'Carry me,' she begged hoarsely, her eyes wild with alarm.

Although she was thin, Isolde was remarkably heavy, a hob's bones and muscles being very much denser than a human's. Grunting, Rollo staggered through the shallows and then dropped her onto the firm sand. She sighed as if she had been holding her breath for the last hour. Even Rollo felt his spirits lift and kicked his boots off just to enjoy the feeling of the warm sand on his bare toes. He curled them, digging them into the sand and then spread them wide again; it was a most delicious feeling.

Lug, Quinn and Guthrey were already standing at the head of the beach amongst the tide line. Quinn flashed Rollo a quick smile, his eyes nervously scanning Isolde, who would not look up at him. Guthrey, however, was standing with his hands on his hips and frowning in disapproval.

'What do you think you are doing? We're not here on a picnic. Haven't you any idea how serious this is? Time is of the essence!'

Rollo stared back at him darkly, wishing he could think of

something cutting to say, but failed. Instead, the two youths glared at each other angrily until Brid came between them.

'Now is not the time for your petty quarrel. We have a hard trek ahead of us to the other side of the island. Let's just hope that the information from the hobs was correct and that Silas is here.' She smiled a tired but optimistic smile at Isolde. 'It won't be long now before we have the Chalice back.'

'The broken Chalice,' Guthrey harshly corrected her.

They crunched across fine shingle that grew steadily coarser as they worked their way up the beach. Crisp seaweed left behind by the retreating sand crackled and popped beneath their tread. Walnut joyously nosed beneath every stone, his thick tail wagging furiously, while the hound picked his way more serenely. Caspar reached the high-water mark first and halted, peering down at his feet. Soon all were beside him. Amongst the bleached driftwood, flotsam and jetsam was a line of white objects polished by the abrasive action of the pebbles and tide. Leaf stooped to examine them.

She looked up at Caspar. 'Bones, she informed him succinctly. They are chips of bone.'

'Whale bone?' the Baron asked.

Leaf shrugged and then knelt down to pick up a few more of the white chips. 'No,' she said hesitantly. 'No, look; this is a phalange.'

'A what?' Arathane asked, urging Sorrel on through the pebbles, her big hooves finding the uneven ground extremely difficult to navigate. The horse snorted anxiously and jerked her head, trying to pull away from Arathane's grip as they neared Isolde. The priestess slunk away, creeping to the far side of Brid.

'A joint from a finger,' Leaf expanded.

'A human finger?' Guthrey prompted.

'I would think so. It's not hob, hazeline or holline. It could be a wizard's finger or come from one of my own kind, but statistically it's most likely to be human.'

All looked glumly up and down the high water mark.

'There must be thousands of bones here,' Guthrey commented in disbelief. 'It looks like a slave ship must have been wrecked on the coast.'

Captain Milo's charts had indicated that the main harbour was three miles to the west around a headland but he had pulled into this particular cove for fear of being spotted by the Emperor's ships. All had agreed that it would be safest and more prudent to approach on foot but now, faced with the reality of the terrain, Rollo wished they had dared to sail a little closer.

After leaving the beach, they followed a stream a little way inland so as not to be readily visible from the sea. At first the climb was not too steep, though the rocks here were sharp and did not provide good footing. The ground was still littered with bones though here the segments were very much larger where they had not been broken and ground by the toiling waves. There was no mistaking that they were human.

'But how did they get here?' Quinn asked.

Brid halted and pointed up at the distant waterfall, which tumbled from a sheer-sided peak. 'They must have been washed down by the waterfall.'

All looked glumly at the bones, a sense of increasing alarm tautening their nerves. The further upstream they went, the more intact the partial skeletons became until they were staring at half-chewed limbs and the split half of a head. It was just like a pig's head that had been split with a cleaver in preparation for making brawn, only it was not a pig's head but the head of a middle-aged woman.

It was curiously the two non-humans in the company that were most affected. Leaf doubled over and was sick. Lug sat down heavily and dropped his head into his great hands.

'I can't take any more of this barbarism. Grunda and I were just going to spend our days with our hogs and now, since all your meddling, you've made me lose her and forced me to witness untold atrocities. I just want to go home!'

No one was paying him the slightest heed. Isolde was

breathing heavily, her red, raw eyes bulging at the sight and her thin brown tongue poking out between her fleshless lips. Rollo felt faint and swallowed hard in an effort to keep control of his senses. Guthrey's face was set hard and he drew back his shoulders in a determined effort to remain detached.

Brid raised her head and stared up at the blue rocks of the mountain, which soared above the dense forest just as a sound like distant thunder rolled down at them from the blue peak dominating the isle.

'That wasn't thunder,' Arathane said with certainty.

'It's not a volcano?' Quinn asked in some concern.

No one answered him, though all the rest were surely thinking exactly as Rollo. It was the cry of a dragon.

Brid turned back to looking at the torn limbs and fragments of human carcass that littered the riverbank. 'This island may not have been inhabited for years but, for there to be so many bones here, there has to have been a sizeable population lately.' She looked to Arathane and then Caspar. 'How do you suppose they died?'

Rollo thought he would be sick; the priestess bent down and merely scooped up the split head in her bare hands to examine it more closely. 'It's such a clean cut that I would have guessed it was cleaved with a sword, but not all these remains are the work of steel.'

Rollo looked at the human debris about him that had been torn and crushed and he knew what had caused it all. His head began to spin and he sat down heavily on the ground.

Still covering her mouth and as white as milk, Leaf staggered forward and glimpsed over Brid's shoulder. 'Look at the indentation in the top and base of the skull where it's been compressed. My guess is that it's been split open by the serrated teeth at the side of some huge and powerful mouth.'

'By a dragon,' Rollo said weakly.

'By a dragon,' Leaf agreed. 'Or something like it. But look at that skull there.' She pointed at one which had a huge round hole the size of her fist bored through the temple. 'It's either been punctured by the eye-tooth of a dragon or a giant beak has drilled into it. I would say there are dragons or ravenshrikes or both up in this mountain.'

'So this is where Silas keeps his giant pets. And he uses this island in order to keep them away from the Emperor. This man is no slave to his overlord; he seeks his own ends,' Brid declared. 'We do not need to go around the coast. If we follow the stream, we'll come to him and his creatures. At least we know why he chose this island.'

'We do?' Caspar queried the priestess.

'Because of the mines. They are a perfect place to keep dragons and prisoners. And the cliffs on this mountain are ideal for the ravenshrikes. He will need to keep them apart from the dragons. Dragons cannot abide ravenshrikes.'

Rollo felt extremely uncomfortable. It was daytime, so at least the great black birds were likely to be asleep, but his flesh crept at the thought of their beady eyes glaring down at him. They could stoop out of the sky at any moment and then it would be his skull that would be impaled by one of their ferocious beaks.

Abandoning their original plan, they set off straight towards the peaks, trudging in single file with Caspar at the fore and Arathane at the rear. The knight was finding the going difficult because Sorrel was not built for such mountainous terrain. The dogs were reluctant to follow and squabbled over a crushed arm that had been ripped clean out of a shoulder socket. Walnut, of course, being the far more determined of the two dogs, won the battle and charged off with the arm in his mouth, the hand waggling as he ran. Though the dogs were doing no harm, everyone found the sight so abhorrent that, until Walnut was brought to heel and had the thing removed, no one would move on.

Guthrey and Quinn spent the best part of a valuable five minutes trying to wrest it from him, but when they failed Brid offered the stubborn terrier some of her medicinal honey, which she kept in a jar in order to smooth over wounds. The dog clearly had a sweet tooth and for the promise of honey relinquished his prize. Once his bloody trophy was dropped, the eager, over-excited air about the dog calmed and, head down, he trudged on behind Brid as if in mimicry of her stance. The climb steepened and at regular intervals they paused to draw breath, turning back to look at the seascape below them.

The sea was a greenish black, the brilliant sun barely penetrating the surface, the waves snatching the light and dragging it down into the darkness.

Arathane pointed to what all had plainly seen. 'More ships. We won't be safe here for long, and if they see Captain Milo down below . . .'

'If they destroy our ship, we'll be trapped and turned to stew by the dragons and ravenshrikes,' Lug complained.

'We must hurry,' Caspar urged. 'We have very little time. Besides, if Silas leaves this island we shall have great difficulty sailing on towards Athell as there appears to be a great number of Athellan ships navigating these waters.'

Isolde took the lead, racing past Caspar. She, more than anyone, needed that Chalice and her strong long legs were far better suited than anyone else's to the terrain. A constant drip of recent rain trickled down through the thick canopy, the dampness visible in the steam that rose from the warm forest floor. The smell from the river of the rotting bodies had become unbearable. With the dogs on leads to prevent them from scavenging human remains, they climbed up in silent single file. Rollo could sense the tension all about them. Brid was constantly scanning her two sons and Isolde, then casting her eyes up towards the crags. After doing this four or five times, she halted.

'Spar, can't we send the young ones back to the ship? You, Arathane and I can go on alone.'

'Mother! If anyone is turning back, it's you,' Guthrey protested. 'Do you think I'm such a coward that I would let my mother march into danger while I snivel and whine aboard ship?'

'No, Guthrey, I don't but, as your mother, the very last thing I want is to see you torn apart by a ravenshrike. You should respect my wishes.'

Caspar nodded. 'I think Brid is right. You should all go back – Brid included. Arathane and I will go on alone. In fact, the fewer the better since it will be easier to keep hidden.'

'It'll be just as dangerous on the ship,' Leaf pointed out. 'Any one of those warships might come in close enough to spot *The Pisceran Porpoise*. It makes no difference to me if I'm eaten or drowned,' she added fatalistically.

Brid smiled at her. 'Nothing like that is happening to any one of us today, you hear? We'll stick together,' she said in resignation. 'That way, at least we can look out for one another.'

'I haven't noticed a single one of you looking out for me,' Lug complained, trudging onwards.

Everyone ignored him as they continued the climb into the heat of the day. Despite his freckled skin, Rollo adored the warmth; it reminded him of home. He was not, however, enjoying the climb, which was extremely hard on his thighs. The others, who were accustomed to the mountainous terrain of Torra Alta, seemed untroubled by it but he was very short of breath and was beginning to feel giddy. Relieved that the sensation was not the cramping pain in his head, which usually troubled him prior to one of his fits, he struggled on, watching Isolde clamber speedily ahead.

A narrow goat track, slippery with loose stones, led the way up the lower slopes of the cliffs. Head down, they clambered on, panting. Hot sweat soaked Rollo's shirt and trickled down towards the base of his spine. When he next looked up, Isolde was on the skyline, waving them on. His chest heaving in and out, Quinn was staring at her, his eyes beginning to water.

'Mother,' he panted, turning to Brid to help her up the last rise, 'will the Chalice really save Isolde?'

'Yes!' the priestess replied over-emphatically. 'But, even if we fail, she is still the Isolde you have always loved. You can run ahead far more easily than the rest of us. You should stay with her. She needs your comfort.'

'No!' Quinn said with surprising resolution. 'I can't go near her. I loved her; I would have died for her, but I cannot go near that thing!' he blurted with unexpected bitterness.

'If you cannot then you never really loved her.'

'Mother, you don't understand! How can you understand what it is to be in love with the most beautiful girl in the world and then fate turns her into *that*?' He pointed resentfully at the gaunt female on the skyline. 'Of course *your* love for her hasn't changed. You loved her like a daughter in the same way as you love Guthrey and me. And you would love me come what may, but this is different. She was beautiful, sensuous, mysterious and magical. She stirred me up inside. I would have died for her. I know it's shallow but she's a *hob* now, for goodness sake!'

Arathane looked at him sourly. 'I love Sorrel just as much now . . .'

'No, you don't,' Quinn objected. 'You love the memory of her and you cling to the mare in the hope of winning your wife back. But it's easier for you. Sorrel is a beautiful mare; Isolde is a vile hob! There's a big difference.'

Brid glared reproachfully at her son. 'Hal would love me whatever I looked like. Isolde may look like a hob but she is still Isolde.'

Rollo snorted at Quinn disapprovingly but, as usual, it was Guthrey who came to his brother's defence. 'You think you're so noble, befriending that thing. But you never loved her so all you've had to be is sympathetic and not cope with the pain of seeing your love destroyed. You make yourself look so generous, so noble and grand, but in truth you were only sympathetic because you are both freaks!'

Rollo's jaw wagged up and down as he tried to think of an equally cutting remark but was stopped by Quinn barging in front of him. 'Guthrey, you never loved her either!' Quinn launched an unexpected attack, at his half brother. 'You never cared. You never loved anyone but yourself.'

The two stared at each other, fingers flexing

Suddenly Guthrey relaxed. 'You're right! I didn't. But I would have bedded her!'

'When you knew I loved her?' Quinn almost wailed in his anger and frustration.

Guthrey gave him a smug smile. 'Wouldn't that have been half the fun, half the challenge?'

Rollo was surprised at himself. He wasn't listening to this ridiculous exchange but was fuming over Guthrey calling him a freak. Normally, he would have long since launched himself at Guthrey in violent attack, but he now felt peculiar. The hairs along his spine prickled, warning him that a predator was close. He had seen and heard nothing; it was more a primeval instinct that made him certain of danger. A second later the hackles on Walnut's spine were all abristle. Isolde gave out a chilling bark of warning and then finally Rollo heard it; something was working its way through the trees ahead. It scratched at the ground and then produced a curious clucking sound.

Walnut barked aggressively and the clucking instantly mutated into a wild shriek of attack. High-pitched and shrill, it stabbed at Rollo's eardrums.

Arathane braced himself on his horse and raised his spear.

'Ravenshrike!' the knight bellowed in warning.

Chapter 28

A black beak stabbed through the canopy of trees. Rollo bellowed out in outrage, his cry escaping as a hoarse scream. What was the ravenshrike doing out in the daytime? It had no right to be here! His only thought was to fly at this oversized vulture that dared trespass so close to him.

It was Brid who saved him. Though she lacked the strength to snatch him in her arms, she did not lack the wit to trip him with her foot. As he sprawled to the ground, a throwing axe whistled over his head. The air thrummed with arrows and, finally, a heavy crash shuddered the soft ground. Rollo tried to rise from his undignified position on the floor, but suddenly he was bombarded by black shapes darting in from all sides. Sharp toes scratched at his back and raked his cheek as he lay in the moist earth. He struggled upright to see two-foot-high, furry-looking black creatures racing on bird legs back into the forest. They could only be ravenshrike chicks that were now running wildly about, cheeping in the most raucous tones, utterly bewildered by the death of their mother.

Arathane dropped from his horse to retrieve his weapons. 'We must be more careful. Clearly, when they have young to feed the ravenshrikes are up during the day as well as the night.'

No sooner had he spoken than another shriek cut through the rumbling roar of the nearby river, which had grown louder as they had climbed alongside it. The company huddled together, the youths and men dutifully pressing the womenfolk behind them though Isolde wriggled away and stood her ground on her own. Their first aggressor, a cock ravenshrike with a stiff crest crowning his head, raced out at them, his vicious beak extended and thrust forward in vengeful attack. Walnut, followed by the less courageous hound, spurted up from the humans' feet and leapt at the ravenshrike's neck. A moment later, three more ravenshrikes attacked, cornering them.

Rollo spun round, his reactions slowed and confused in comparison to Quinn and Guthrey, who were stabbing up with spears at the ravenshrikes' breasts above them. Rollo staggered back.

Weapon! Use your weapon! he told himself, struggling to overcome the compulsion to do nothing but bellow at the giant birds.

Walnut growled and snapped somewhere overhead and Rollo looked up to see the fierce terrier with his jaws clamped about a ravenshrike's neck. Blood was gushing over the dog and the great bird staggered on its feet. For a second, Rollo thought that Walnut might even manage to bring the monster down until another ravenshrike strutted forward. It twisted its head to one side and blinked at the dog before snapping its beak out.

The dog gave a blood-chilling howl as the giant bird cut through its spine. Almost in two halves, Walnut fell to the ground, jerking in spasms for a few seconds before a great claw pressed down on the dog's ribcage and a pulp of broken bones and lung squirted out between the toes.

Rollo was somersaulting backwards through the air before he knew what hit him. He landed heavily on his back. Dazed, it was a moment before he realized that the ravenshrike had kicked out backwards and sent him flying. He shook himself and staggered to his feet. Everyone was scattered. Two of the great birds were dead on the floor and Lug was wrestling with a third. The last enraged ravenshrike was stabbing at the ground with its beak; someone gave out a yell that was quickly stifled. Barks, yells and whoops rang down at them from the cliffs above. The two remaining ravenshrikes snapped up their heads and strutted off at pace, beaks open, as if someone had sounded a gong, summoning them to a feast.

The sorry company picked themselves up out of the dirt. Brid was fussing over Guthrey, who was unable to stand. Quinn was panting heavily. Leaf, not unexpectedly, was crying while Arathane and Caspar gathered their axes, knives and arrows from their victims. The hound was looking down at Walnut's body. His head to one side and ears flopped forward, he yipped very softly as if telling his friend to rise.

Caspar strode anxiously towards his son. 'Are you hurt?'

Rollo glumly shook his head but was not looking at his father. He was staring at Guthrey whose back was arched in pain while he gritted his teeth and sucked in shallow gasps in an effort to escape his agony. The ravenshrike had bored a hole, two inches across, into his calf. Brid was doing all she could to stem the blood and comfort him.

The priestess looked up at Caspar. 'You will have to go on without us. Lug will have to come with us. There's no way Guthrey can walk like this so Lug will have to carry him.'

The Haol-garen muttered something about how he would have liked to have been consulted but, again, no one paid him the least heed.

Caspar nodded. 'I would rather the rest went with you too. Arathane and I shall go on alone.'

Surprisingly, despite her shocked and distressed state, it was Leaf who spoke out against this plan. 'Of course this is dangerous. Did any one of us honestly think it wouldn't be? But the more of us who go forward, the more chance of success we have. We have to reach Silas and stop him. We have to!' She wiped her eyes and sniffed. 'He has been gathering powerful artefacts with which he can control all the peoples of this earth. We few are all there is to stop him. A little danger should not deter us.'

'Nor does it!' Isolde croaked hoarsely. 'I am afraid of nothing except failure.'

'Spoken like a true priestess!' Brid applauded her.

Caspar still looked uncertain. 'Brid, I should at least send Quinn and Rollo to guard you.'

Brid shook her head. 'If Lug can't look after us then no one will.'

The arguing was halted by the sound of hobs above them, grunting and barking at one another.

'Quick, go!' Caspar hissed at Brid. 'We'll be back at the ship before three hours after the tide turns.' He glanced up at the sun, checking its height in the deep blue of the southern sky.

'You had better be,' Brid warned him. Her eyes locked onto Caspar's for a very brief moment and it was as if their eyes spoke a thousand words to one another. The next minute, Brid, Lug and Guthrey were gone while the rest clambered higher, nervously veering away from the hobs and heading for a bare point of rock whose jagged sides climbed up above the trees and would, they predicated, afford them an advantageous view.

The hound stood mournfully over Walnut's shredded remains and then loped off after Brid. Rollo was shocked at how the courageous and tough terrier had been so easily massacred. Angrily, he stamped on, his ears pinned back for the cries of the hobs, whom he could hear muttering and barking noisily on the far side of the stream.

The company huddled together below their vantage point and Caspar hissed, 'Isolde, can you understand what they are saying? Any hob I've met can speak the old tongue of the Caballan well enough, but this must be their own language.'

She nodded solemnly. 'They are calling the ravenshrikes. They have human remains for them from the mines.'

Guthrey looked at her sideways and then gradually his eyes began to widen as if a thought had struck him. 'I didn't think of it before, but if you can understand them that must mean your mind is also changing to a hob mind.' He stepped back in revulsion and then looked at Caspar. 'If this is the case, can we trust her?'

Isolde impatiently flicked her hand at him as if telling him to be quiet. 'I'm listening,' she growled, cocking her head to one side and biting her brown pointed tongue in concentration. She sighed with relief. 'Silas *is* here. They complain that he spends his time down in the dungeons, talking to the golden dragon. It seems the great golden queen, who has harried our own mountains for so long, is now with Silas, *talking* to him.'

'Dragons don't talk,' Caspar said emphatically.

'Legend has it that they did once but were so angry with man for betraying them that they refused to use his speech ever again. No one knows if this is true but, if the hobs are correct, it suggest that it is,' Leaf commented.

'Shh! I haven't told you all!' Isolde complained. 'They are wary of the dragon, which has already killed many of their kind along with any captives that Silas has offered her. The flight here, apparently, was arduous for her. Now she is recovering in the belly of the mountain, holed up in the old opal mines. And she's very angry!'

'Why is she angry?' Quinn demanded, looking anxiously towards the blue mountain of rock jutting up above the trees. They all turned and stared, only having to wait a moment before a roar trembled the mountain and a shower of scree tumbled from one of the sheer faces.

'How would I know?' Isolde angrily growled at him. 'I can only tell you what I . . . Hush! Let me listen!' Again, she cocked her head on one side.

'What are they saying?' Quinn nervously repeated when Isolde remained silent for a moment.

'The hobs gossip about Silas and the dragon arguing over the Chalice! The dragon is furious that it is broken and has threatened to kill every one of Silas's hobs if he doesn't get it mended. Apparently, he promised her use of it once her task was done. But the queen is saying that Silas cannot be trusted with it and must give it to her now. Silas is trying to persuade her that she will not achieve her ends with the Chalice alone and he will not help her unless she continues to help him. He has offered her numerous other treasures but it's the Chalice she wants and she's furious that it's broken. The hobs are very worried because they claim the dragon is irrational and merely seeking an excuse to murder them all.'

'Well, at least we know that Silas and the Chalice are here, though hobs are notoriously inaccurate reporters,' Brid said guardedly.

Isolde shrugged as if she didn't care.

Leaf was trembling. 'It seems we must walk into the dragon's lair.'

'That's just suicide,' Arathane objected.

'And standing out here with ravenshrikes and hobs isn't? No one is going to bring the coveted Chalice out into the open; we have to go and get it,' the small girl said courageously.

'We'd be dead within seconds,' Arathane objected.

Isolde squared her bony shoulders. 'They are feeding the dragon human captives. It should be an easy matter to herd you into the mine and then cut you free just as we reach Silas. If we can get close enough, we shall somehow snatch the Chalice.'

'And how do we get out of there? Fly, I suppose,' Leaf objected to this plan.

'Do you have a better suggestion?' Isolde croaked. Her hob-like form had evidently lent much steel to her timid character.

'I can't take Sorrel in. She will be immediately eaten by hobs,' Arathane pointed out.

Caspar took a deep breath. 'Arathane, you must stay here with Leaf, Quinn and Rollo. Isolde and I shall go on alone and, if we fail, you must come up with a better plan.'

A deep moan rumbled through the mountain and Rollo felt an overwhelming desire to cry back, but managed to stifle his tongue.

'I'm coming with you, father,' he said determinedly. He couldn't bear the thought of being out here with the ravenshrikes and was deeply drawn to the bellows within the mountain. It reminded him of the bears of his homeland.

'You will do as I say!' Caspar thrust his weapons into Rollo's hands. 'Look after these for me.'

A moment later, Isolde and Caspar were gone. Rollo stared on for just a minute before dropping his weapons and running after them. There was nothing anyone could do to stop him for fear of drawing attention to themselves. Rollo was careful to stay a little way behind his father to avoid detection and then planned to join him once it was too late for him to turn back.

Soon, they cut towards the corpse-charged river, which spilt out from a mouth in the side of the mountain a short distance above them. Isolde urged Caspar to stay put while she scuttled down towards the fast-flowing current. After taking a brief drink, she plunged her mouth straight into the bloody water and then moved to one of the corpses. She tugged at its arms and, a moment later, returned with a length of rope in her hands, ready to manacle Caspar.

Rollo chose this moment to reveal himself.

Caspar's face reddened in anger. 'How dare you disobey me!'

'You didn't think I'd let you go in there alone,' Rollo replied smoothly, his eyes rising to catch a glimpse of a hob on the far side of the riverbank.

His father followed his gaze. 'Now we've been seen! Act as if you are bound,' Caspar snapped at him.

Rollo gave him a defiant grin and waited patiently while Isolde hurried back for more rope.

'Do we look grubby and bruised enough for prisoners?' Caspar asked the afflicted priestess.

Isolde gave him that disconcertingly thin-lipped smile and it flashed through Rollo's mind that Quinn may have been right about whether she could be wholly trusted any more. 'It won't make any difference. Humans all look alike to hobs.'

Broad-leaved ferns grew alongside the tumbling cascade as it poured out from the rock. Rollo's skin began to itch as he was soaked by the humid atmosphere. His nose twitched.

'Keep your head down,' Isolde growled at him and shoved him hard in the back to keep him moving.

He tripped and thumped into his father. Instinctively, he twisted round in an attempt to strike back at Isolde but she was obviously thinking much more clearly than he was and punched him in the diaphragm.

'Wretched human slaves!' she growled loudly in the old tongue of a Caballan.

Rollo wheezed and finally caught his breath whilst thinking how disturbingly good Isolde was at playing her part. He also thought she was over-acting a little until his nose twitched at the strong scent of male hob and he knew more of the enemy were very close. Soon, hobs were marching in from all sides, hurrying upwards towards the mouth of the waterfall.

As they approached it, the noise from the tumbling water grew so loud that Rollo could barely hear himself think. Isolde urged them onto a tight slippery path that cut into the rock and led towards the lip of the waterfall. Clearly, it was possible to enter the mountain at this point since other hobs were going in and out. A large gangling hob caught them up and snatched Isolde's arm. He sniffed at her while she stared back in wide-eyed horror. Rollo willed her to act appropriately as she was staring at the creature as if it were an alien beast. The hob's long fingers crept up towards her shoulder and then began sliding down her noduly spine, teasing the coarse hairs sprouting from her back. Hissing, Isolde suddenly lashed out and raked her nails across his cheek. Rollo was horrified but the hob withdrew and chortled at her, continuing to stride along behind her, sniffing pleasurably at her scent. It seemed Isolde had behaved exactly as she should.

Once into the cool cavern, the roar from the waterfall was quickly muffled as they paced along a broad smooth ledge that wound beside a sluggish river. Other humans, dejected, bruised and bowed, trudged ahead only to be shoved aside by any hob wishing to pass them. Several hobs called to one another and Isolde even added her own excited bark but Rollo had no idea what they were saying. He marched on, guided by Isolde, who continued to play her part by shoving him hard in the back. Fortunately, the party of captive humans led the way for them. But Rollo was certain that, even if they had not been there, he would have known which way to go; he could hear the dragon's purrs thrumming through the rocks and it set his nerves tingling.

It took about twenty minutes to reach the hollowed chambers of the opal mine. It was a slow, steady climb all the way, following the coarse of the river, which drained the groundwater from the mountain crowning the island. It was pleasantly cool in the mines but the smell of fetid hob and rotting meat was utterly overpowering. They were ushered forward through mining shafts whose walls had recently been hastily shored up. Being the hallmark of a hob craftsman, the poor workmanship was entirely what Rollo had expected.

At last, they came into a wide chamber lit by fires. Even before they turned the corner into the chamber, Rollo knew she was there; the very air seemed to throb with the beat of her double hearts. His mouth became dry with anticipation and he walked on as if in a dream.

When he turned the corner, his own heart missed a beat; the dragon was indeed talking, though it was in the hob tongue and he could not understand it. Though he had seen her before, he was not prepared for how huge she seemed, crammed between the rocks, her claws flexing and stretching over the smooth floor in frustration. The light from the fires reflected off her scales, which gleamed like liquid gold. Her forked tongue flicked in and out as she growled at Silas.

The man looked old and worried. Without his armour he appeared less imposing, his long hair giving him an air of mental eccentricity rather than one of dignified wisdom. The firelight played over the many battle scars which disfigured his face, making them seem redder and altogether more hideous. He was seated opposite the dragon on a simple chair that looked quite out of place in the deep mines. At his feet was a circle, which had been etched into the rock. Across the circle, apple halves and rowan sprigs were methodically arranged just as Brid had previously demonstrated they should be in preparation for invoking the magic within the Chalice. At the centre of the circle was the Chalice itself, trickles of water seeping out through a crack. The great dragon looked down at it in frustration, her tail thrashing the sides of the chamber, and all instinctively ducked as dust and fine sand sifted down from the ceiling.

A man was dragged forward and stood trembling while a hob pressed a knife to his throat. Already, the man dripped blood from many other wounds. Rollo swallowed, somehow certain that this poor captive was not a simple meal for the great queen.

Silas nodded at the dragon and she duly produced a thin jet of fire, which she directed straight at the Chalice, which hissed and steamed, the liquid within instantly heated to boiling point.

Silas barked orders at the hob, speaking in what Rollo guessed to be the tongue of Athell. The hob forced the man to his knees and, using a cloth to pick up the white-hot Chalice, yanked back the man's head and poured the liquid into his mouth.

The man gave out a gurgling scream. He clutched at his throat while his lips blistered and steam belched from his mouth, blood sputtering up with the foam. He staggered and swayed before collapsing to the floor where he writhed and mewed, clawing at his breast. Finally, he jerked weakly and then lay still.

Rollo blinked and stared in abject dismay. He was horrified to have witnessed the man's death but even more distressed that he was in line for the same fate. His father pressed closer to him.

'Perhaps next time you'll do as you're told.'

Rollo could not believe there would be a next time. However, he drew hope from the observation that Silas and the dragon both appeared enraged by the failure of their spell. Silas snatched up the cup with a gloved hand and tilted the crack towards the firelight. Rollo could see it had been mended with a bright white gold but the metal had peeled away from the main fabric of the cup and liquid continued to seep out. The dragon snapped up the dead man at her feet and crunched through his shoulder and neck. She chewed angrily before spitting out the crushed bones. A gang of small female hobs hurried forward, gathered up the bones as if they were gleaning corn and tossed them into the underground river that spewed into the waterfall.

'Too much heat,' Isolde murmured under her breath at Caspar and Rollo as a disgruntled chatter rattled through the mustered hobs. 'Apparently Silas and the dragon had made it work before the Chalice was damaged, but now the spell fails every time even though they have done their best to repair it. They think the broken cup cannot cope with the necessary heat. The resultant spell is imperfect and too violent on its victims. They're looking for stronger people to withstand the pain and they're going to try a different method.'

The dragon bent her long neck round and, with her teeth, brought out a man who had been pinned behind her tail. He hung limply in her jaws and sagged to his knees when she placed him on her feet. A hob who had been standing on the dragon's right strutted forward and pressed a dagger against the man's spine whilst barking at him to stand. Rollo noted how the hob strutted forward with an air of self-importance, his fleshless nose turned up at the hobs to either side. He was small for a male, his limbs short and his head over-large, but he seemed to be enjoying his role.

'Gobel!' Silas shouted the hob's name before launching into a string of angry Athellan words.

The short hob forced the man forward towards the etched circle in the rock before refilling the Chalice with fresh water from the underground stream and placing it at the man's feet. The man looked unbearably tired as if he had not slept in weeks. His eyes were red and rimmed with black bags and his lips were black and blistered as if he suffered from some plague.

514

He moaned, closed his eyes and threw back his head, filling his lungs with air before throwing himself forward towards the Chalice and belching out flame. Rollo and Caspar stepped back in alarm. Many of the other humans captured by the hobs screamed or wailed. One or two crashed to the floor in a dead faint.

Silas snapped his fingers and a short, middle-aged man with a pronounced limp was dragged forward towards the leaking Chalice and forced down onto his knees. This time it took three hobs to hold the victim down and pin back his head. Pinching his nose, they waited the seconds before his mouth opened before sloshing the boiling liquid into his face. The screams were horrible. The hobs helped him upright as he jerked and spasmed, steam gushing from his mouth, his skin red and blistered where the liquid had splashed him.

Silas stamped in anger, his eyes searching the other prisoners. Caspar nudged Isolde.

'He is looking for stronger men to survive the ordeal. Push me forward, then you will be the one who refills the cup. Once it's in your hands.'

The Baron's whisper was cut short as Isolde shoved him and Rollo forward and barked loudly at Silas to catch his attention. Jostled by hobs, they stumbled forward towards the circle. Two huge male hobs grabbed their shoulders with a vice-like grip worthy of a ravenshrike. As calmly as if she were picking up a basket of cakes, she bent down for the Chalice. Rollo stared on in panic. Was she to be trusted? If she spoke the hob's tongue, did she not also think like a hob, as Guthrey had suggested? Perhaps she was on their side after all. Even if she were to escape with the Chalice, there was surely no hope for himself and his father.

He did not want to die. Why, oh, why hadn't he obeyed orders? He looked at Caspar and decided that he could not bear to see his father die either. There had to be something he could do.

Caspar's eyes were working fast, flitting over the dragon and

515

Silas; Rollo was certain that he was trying to think of a plan. But they were trapped. They were trapped with hobs all around them and a huge enraged dragon before them, her body wedged tightly into the back of the cavern. Caspar sank to his knees at the side of the circle before the big hobs could force him down. It was as if he sought dignity in his execution and did not want to die screaming and kicking. Rollo followed suit, brushing away the hobs, which let him kneel and did not bother to restrain him.

Caspar looked at his son through the corner of his eye and, as the noisy hobs began their excited mutterings again, he whispered, 'Run where they least expect you to. When the panic starts, run straight for the dragon.'

Rollo was about to tell his father that he was mad, but there was no time.

Silas barked orders at Isolde and she turned for the stream, striding away in a confident and unhurried manner. At least Rollo hoped it was Isolde; she was in fact almost impossible to tell apart from the other hobs. Her skin was, he thought, a little lighter, but in these dim halls it was difficult to say.

'Ready?' Caspar warned.

Rollo did not reply but merely flexed all his muscles, praying they would work for him when they were most needed.

From somewhere behind him came a distinctive splash followed by silence.

Silas screamed in anguish as if he were being branded by a hot iron. The dragon snapped her head forward, her long jaw hovering above Rollo's head. Suddenly hobs were everywhere, yelling and shouting. Isolde was gone. She had leapt into the river with the Chalice.

'Now!' Caspar screamed.

Rollo reacted instantly and was up on his feet and charging wildly to the dragon's shoulder. He would have to run hard and fast in order to climb it without the use of his hands, though, thankfully, Isolde had tied them in front of him. Caspar was behind him, shouldering him up, and he scrambled over the

516

scales that snagged in his clothing and cut right through to his skin. Once he was up on the shoulder, he hastily sawed the rope bonds back and forth over one of the dragon's spines. Suddenly he was free. He reached back for his father and, grunting with the effort, hauled him up the last few feet to where they were perched amongst the jagged row of spines that armoured the dragon's back. It took Caspar valuable seconds to work through his own bonds and then he nudged his way towards the dragon's golden tail.

'Now what?' Rollo demanded.

The great queen was clearly unaware of them because she was bellowing and roaring at the swarming mass of hobs and people below. Many she incinerated in one breath. Their blackened bodies stood rigid for a moment before crumbling into ashes, leaving a broad gap in the hobs' ranks and so opening up a line of sight through the rabble to the river.

'I'm hoping there's a passageway at the back of this cave. Then we can escape into the mountains,' Caspar shouted over the riotous noise.

Rollo nodded. There was no need to ask why they weren't trying to help Isolde. It was certain that, if he and his father had tried to follow her, they would never have left the chamber alive. She was faster and stronger than them and had possessed the advantage of surprise. The very best they could do was to try and get themselves out.

The dragon's scales were slippery and Rollo clasped hold of each spine as he worked his way back, the razor sharp edges slicing his fingers. He reached the dragon's rump and could feel the powerful thump of her pulse though her scales beneath his feet. Peering into the gloom, he fancied he could see a way out; surely that was light at the end of the tunnel. He blinked and then realized his mistake as the light swelled into a red flickering flame and revealed a nest of small red dragons hiding behind their mother.

They were trapped. Worse, the golden queen beneath them was now slithering forward, swaying from side to side as her powerful legs whipped forward. Her neck scales rasped against the ceiling and Rollo thought that, at any moment, they would be crushed between the dragon and the rock above, his body speared by one of the great spines along her back.

'Forward again and keep down!' Caspar ordered, scurrying nimbly over the dragon's back and then sitting down between two spines just at the base of her neck. Rollo ran forward and sat in the gap between two spines behind his father.

'She can reach round to her tail and rump but I don't think she can reach us here,' Caspar cried optimistically as they lurched forward, crushing hobs that stood in the great queen's path.

She was running furiously and it took all Rollo's strength to hold on. For a moment, he looked down and caught Silas's eye, which looked up at him aghast before screaming furiously at the dragon though she didn't appear to hear him. Rollo stared back at the treacherous man and was sorry that he had not found a way to kill him; they had failed Arathane. But he still had hope that Isolde had made it with the Chalice.

The dragon plunged into the river, which only came half way up her flanks. Wading through the pools and then scrabbling over the shallows, she moved quickly through the mine and soon a circle of daylight was visible ahead where the river cascaded into the open.

'Just before we reach the waterfall, jump into the river,' Caspar urgently ordered.

'But we'll be killed on the rocks below,' Rollo protested.

'It's the best chance we have,' Caspar told him firmly. 'Jump when I say.'

Rollo gritted his teeth. He had just escaped being burnt to death from within; he did not now want to be crushed and splattered over rocks.

Suddenly, they were in the light, the bow of blue water curving away from them and seemingly disappearing into nothing but spray and rainbows.

'Jump!' Caspar screamed, leaping up and launching himself into the silvery bow at the top of the waterfall.

For a split second, Rollo thought he couldn't bring himself to do it and then, when he lurched to get upright, his breeches snagged against the dragon's sharp scales.

The dragon was moving fast, swept on by the accelerating current. Suddenly, she spread wide her magnificent wings. Rollo was too late; they were airborne and if he jumped now he would be jumping into thin air.

Chapter 29

Rollo's bleeding hands clung to the dragon's spine as they soared above the spray from the waterfall and high into the cobalt blue of the cloudless sky. His eyes were clenched tight and his stomach was left far behind him; all he could do was pray.

'Dear Mother, do not forsake me. Remember me,' he feebly murmured through clenched teeth.

He knew he should give the Great Mother a reason why he should be spared, why his life was worth more than others, but, in truth, he could think of none apart from the fact he did not want to die.

The air rushed into his face, tugging at his hair and clothes, and he felt himself being pressed back against the spine behind him. At last, he opened his eyes as he felt the dragon level off, her wing flaps less regular now as she glided on the hot air rising from the dark rocks of the island. Sick to his stomach, he peered over her shoulder and gazed down at the scenery below. He wondered at how ridiculous he and his kind had been, thinking they could hide from the predators of the sky. From up here he could see everything. He could see the huddle of Silas's ships crammed into the harbour on the northern arc of the island. He could see Captain Milo's ship in its haven, the tide now rushing out, rippling over the reef that guarded the natural harbour. If *The Pisceran Porpoise* didn't leave soon, she would be trapped. The rowing boats were on the beach, waiting in readiness to collect any survivors.

Swivelling his head round, he could see hobs gushing out

from the hole in the mountain where the waterfall sprang, but there was still no sign of Silas. He looked ahead, searching the wooded skirts of the island for any sign of his companions, but all he could make out was the vein of the river gushing towards the sea.

A high-pitched scream like that of a giant eagle cut through the air and he turned to see three red dragons burst out from the mouth of the waterfall and soar up towards their mother. Screaming angrily, they swarmed towards her.

Rollo realized that, in comparison to the armoured dragon, he was so small and light that, even now, the old queen still had no notion that he was on her back. But clearly her offspring did and they screeched through the air like three arrows, climbing above her. One then swooped down and stretched out its claws to reach him, but he ducked below the golden dragon's spine and clung on rigidly. The smaller red dragons, however, alerted their mother to his presence. Her wing beats slowed and she stretched round her neck, her eye swivelling until it focused on him. He glared back in open-mouthed panic, unable to think.

It was as if the great she-dragon also needed time to think because, for the next few seconds, she merely flew on and Rollo had time to look down at the ground far below and wonder how long it would take him to fall. Staring down at the river, his eye caught the movement of Arathane on his chestnut mare, galloping for all he was worth along the lower reaches of the river. He caught a glimpse of something gold in the water just ahead of the knight. There was a dark shape clutching it and only then did Rollo realize it was Isolde. She had made it. The rushing water had taken her far ahead of the hobs; Arathane would surely see her to safety. The man was wily enough to save her from the dragon, Rollo determinedly decided.

And if Isolde had made it, surely his father was also in the river being swept out to the safety of the sea and Captain Milo's ship.

Rollo's thoughts were jolted away from him. The dragon

screamed furiously and bucked in an attempt to throw him off. However, his breeches were still snagged into her scales and he was clamped tightly to her body. Another of the younger dragons swooped at him and this time knocked his head with its talon, the shock jarring his brain. Giddy with the pain, he tried to clench his teeth and hold on but he had been knocked sideways and was only just managing to cling on with one hand.

Sensing that he was losing his grip, the dragon dropped one wing, raised the other and flipped over. Suddenly Rollo was upside down. Clinging onto the spine, which was cutting into the flesh of his hand, he dangled in mid-air, too scared to even scream. One of the queen's brood snapped at his feet as it swept up underneath its mother, buffeting the queen's flank. Rollo gritted his teeth and willed his fingers to remain clenched about the long thin spine, but he could feel it slipping through his shredded palm.

The great dragon barrel-rolled in mid-air and Rollo found he was flicked upwards; the spine slipped through his bloody grip. For a second he was weightless, floating in mid-air. Instinctively, he spread his hands wide in a futile effort to slow his fall and, in that one moment, he screamed out in desperate prayer, 'Mother, Great Mother, help me! Help! Mother, do not let me die like this!'

Suddenly, he was plummeting. He screamed on and on as the wind rushed upwards, his clothing flapping and his hair streaming up above him. The scream became a thin shriek dragged out of him by the fearful speed as the ground rushed up towards him.

His cry was answered by a panicked scream from above. His speed accelerating, he plunged down and down, the river now large and turbulent beneath him, the jagged rocks clearly defined, darkened by the shadows of the queen dragon and her brood. His mind raced in horrified panic at the inevitability of his death. Though he knew he had many faults, he had never considered cowardice to be one of them and so was ashamed

522

at his terror. He had always wanted to die bravely but now all that filled his mind was whether the impact when he crashed onto the rock would be painful.

The speed took his breath away and his senses darkened. Perhaps it wouldn't be painful after all. Perhaps he would be unconscious before he hit the ground, he thought in a detached and confused manner, before a tearing pain stabbed through his leg. His arms and head were still falling but his leg had been jerked upwards. He thought his spine would break as it snapped taut. The blood rushed to his head and his entire body flailed and flapped. His senses were overpowered by a raucous scream, deafeningly close.

Perhaps it was his own scream. Perhaps he had actually hit the ground, caught by his leg first in the crevice of a jagged peak, and it was his dying scream that he heard.

Very slowly, he realized he must still be alive. The pain in his leg was too sharp and he felt sick. He was fairly certain that dead people did not feel sick. And he felt sick because he was dangling upside-down in the clutches of the great golden dragon. She had dived for him and snatched him in mid fall. Wings stretched wide, she was straining her long neck out and up to curve her flight upwards.

Too much blood continued to cram itself into Rollo's head and he thought his entire stomach would force itself out through his mouth. His discomfort was only increased as the great lizard began to beat her massive wings, which clapped together on the downward stroke, slapping against him. At last she dropped her tail, spread her wings wide and glided effortlessly down towards cliffs overlooking the sea. She landed high on a cliff overlooking one of the arms of land sheltering the natural harbour that concealed *The Pisceran Porpoise*.

The talon clamping his leg relaxed. Rollo tumbled to the ground and spread his arms wide, clinging to the sparse, crisp grass in an effort to still his spinning senses. The roar from the waves below breaking against the cliffs was barely audible for the pounding in his ears. Groaning, he rolled over, too confused to focus on the huge monster stooped over him, the ruff at her neck spread wide and her wings hunched, tent-like, over his wretched body. He didn't even know what the dragon wanted. Did she think he had the Chalice? Or, dare he believe it, was she responding to his cry? Did he indeed have the power to control the great golden dragon just as his mother had possessed the gift to control the bears?

He changed his mind rapidly as one by one her five remaining offspring thumped to the ground, necks arched aggressively, tails thrashing and the sound of a thousand snakes hissing from their maws.

The queen roared at them and they twitched their heads towards her as if listening to her command. On heavy lumbering legs, they manoeuvred clumsily to form a semi-circle about him, trapping him against the cliff behind him. Their talons lashed back and forth like angry cats. Perhaps he was simply food or, if the queen dragon truly was intelligent, perhaps he was now a hostage in exchange for the golden Chalice. That was it! She hadn't realized he was on her back but, when she did, she shook him off only to realize, seconds later, that he was valuable to her.

The great queen leaped into the air, thrashing her wings vigorously in an attempt to rise into the sky. Rollo had no doubt that she sought Isolde and the Chalice. Rolling over, he stared out over the cliffs, scanning the turquoise for the young priestess. He refused to contemplate that she hadn't survived the ordeal.

Feeling his back burning from the stares of the red dragons, he squinted into the glare. *The Pisceran Porpoise* had weighed anchor. There was still an empty rowing boat on the shore but Captain Milo had unfurled his sails and was now heading for the safety of the open sea.

At first Rollo was appalled and distraught. They had abandoned him, left him here for Silas and the dragon. Then he saw a glint of gold aboard the deck. His human eyes could not discern exactly what it was but someone was frantically waving something gold as if trying to attract attention. Could it be that they were waving the Chalice in an effort to draw the dragon away from him?

The ship accelerated as it caught the rip tide funnelling out through the narrow strait over the reef. The golden dragon circled above it warily, as if wondering how to attack the vessel. She seemed uncertain of the ship. Perhaps she thought it was a sea monster capable of destroying her. Rollo guessed she would not blast fire at the ship for fear of destroying the Chalice. What was certain, however, was that five red dragons were still breathing over him.

He slowly turned his head to look at them. Three were looking up at their mother and crooning as she circled *The Pisceran Porpoise*. The other two were fighting over a human leg, which one must have brought with them from the mines. He moved a hand to test their reaction but the snout of one dragon, which had been gazing at their mother, immediately darted towards him, sniffing at him curiously. They were more alert than he had anticipated. He lay still for what felt like hours, panicking about how he could escape.

The dragons' activity, however, had excited other inhabitants of the island and it was only a short while before a ravenshrike gave out its distinctive shriek, which had a remarkable effect on the red dragons. Immediately, the spines on their backs stiffened as if they were hackles on a hound. Their armoured heads spun about to roar in anger at this intrusion.

Rollo knew this would be his only chance. It would be better to die now in an attempt to escape than lie snivelling, waiting for them to pull him apart and lick out the inside of his skull with their long quivering tongues. He reacted at once and without further thought. There was only one way to go and that was over the cliff.

Dropping to his belly, he wriggled feet first back towards the edge of the cliff. A rush of panicked adrenaline drove out all awareness of his injuries, enabling him to move fast.

Gripping at the sturdier roots of the grasses lining the brink of the cliff, he lowered himself until his legs were dangling off an overhang. Clinging on to the thin layer of turf, which jutted out into mid-air, he swung his legs forward, hoping to find a footing and praying that the turf wouldn't tear away and let him crash onto the rocks below. One foot found a solid toehold. Squinting to protect his eyes from the falling dirt which he had dislodged from beneath the turf, he desperately sought a more secure handhold. Right before his eyes was a small nook used by choughs for nesting. The worst moment was releasing the grip of one hand and flinging it forward into the stony niche before his other hold failed.

Gritting his teeth, he lunged. Though his nails scrabbled and scraped to hook in, he finally had a firm purchase and was able to release the grip of his upper arm on the turf. Now he was below the overhang! Though very steep, the cliff was jagged and notched and so gave him plenty of foot- and handholds. His fingers already cut, he shredded their flesh even further as he used them to break his controlled slide from one desperate handhold to the next. He didn't have time to pick and choose a more careful route. Though he could hear a ravenshrike squawking in panic, he guessed it would only be a matter of minutes before the red dragons, like giant terriers, had torn the creature apart and returned to the task allotted to them by their mother.

Scraping his shins and tearing his fingernails, he dropped from one ledge to the next, his speed increasing as the angle of the cliff lessened until he was no more than twelve feet from the smooth slab of rock footing the cliff. Here, the rocks were polished smooth by the turbulent waters churning over them at high tide and he had no hope of finding any grip to help him down. His heart in his mouth, he leaped, stumbled and rolled onto the smooth rock below. He jarred his ankle but it wasn't enough to stop him crawling back under the belly of the cliff where he would be hidden from the red dragons' eyes.

Bent over double, he allowed himself just seconds to catch

his breath before scurrying along in the shadow of the cliff, amazed with himself for escaping from five dragons. The red dragons, he knew, were reputed to be much stupider than the magnificent golden dragons but, all the same, it was quite a feat. Keeping low to the ground, he splashed through the shallow pools of warm water trapped in the hollows of the rocks and raced along the bottom of the cliff until they dropped towards the gentler rise of land that separated him from the natural harbour. His only thought was to reach the mouth of the river in the hope of finding any of his companions who may not have yet fled to the ship.

Noise bombarded him from all sides. The roars from the red dragons above were mixed with the rumble of the river ahead. The terrain upstream rang with the barks of hobs. Perhaps he should just hide, he told himself. But he had seen the rowing boat and all he wanted to do was to get off this wretched island somehow.

He staggered to a halt; now it was too late to make a decision. Right before him stood a thin little hob, water dripping from its ragged hair. The creature fixed him with its red-raw eyes and peeled back its thin hideous lips as if to bark but instead it calmly croaked his name.

'Isolde!' he gasped.

The hob smiled, ran forward and tugged at him, dragging him away from the river and into the dense cover of green vegetation. She pulled him deeper under the canopy of dripping leaves, which soon soaked through his clothing, making his skin itch. Pushing between vines and giant ferns, she drew him into a dank hollow and halted.

Rollo blinked. There was Arathane, though there was no sign of his horse. He was smeared in wet mud from the waist down and the rest of him was soaking wet. The man was staring in an unseeing manner while his fingers were tightly clutched about the golden Chalice.

'Isolde?' the knight urgently demanded in obvious anxiety.

'Yes!' she hissed. 'And I have him. I have Rollo!'

'Thank the Mother! You have done well.' He sighed and sagged down to his knees. 'Now we rest and wait before making our escape under cover of night.'

'But how? The ship has sailed,' Rollo panted in bewilderment.

'Yes, I know, to draw the dragon away from you. But they left the rowing boat and the plan is to meet up on the Calf of Cannac, a pirate's stronghold on the tip of the peninsula on mainland Athell. As I waded out into the river to pull Isolde and your father out, I saw you up there in the clutches of the dragon. Then you landed on the cliff top. Spar had also seen you from the river and, even before he reached me, he had planned to lure the dragon away from you by using the Chalice.'

'But you have it,' Rollo protested. 'You have it in your hands.'

'It would have been madness to use the real thing!' Arathane laughed at the idea. 'Besides it was an obvious chance to get cleanly away with the real Chalice since the dragon and Silas would be distracted by the decoy.'

'I don't understand!' Rollo complained in frustration.

'They will follow the ship, allowing us to make our own way. I was going to race back to the ship with the plan when I stumbled into heavy clay at the edge of the river.' He tugged at his leather leggings, which clung to his thighs. 'I was making very slow progress whereas your father was already ashore. I told him to take Sorrel and get her away from the hobs. We couldn't hide safely with her because the smell of horse would attract them. He raced away while Isolde and I remained to try and find you. Of course, without Sorrel I wasn't much use, but that barely matters now since we have you.'

Rollo sagged down next to Arathane, and Isolde joined them. The big knight placed the Chalice in his lap and put his arms around the two youngsters, who let their heads flop against his chest. Rollo was beginning to shiver, not with cold but from exhaustion. He realized that he had survived his ordeal.

'You mean, the dragon and Silas are chasing after some trinket from Captain Milo's table?' Rollo asked.

'I do indeed!' the knight said with amusement.

'But what about the others on board ship?' Rollo said in dismay. 'How are they going to escape the dragon?'

'You don't think a dragon, even a golden queen, could outsmart both Leaf and Aconite, do you? They will find a way,' Arathane told him in calm, reassuring tones. 'Now rest.'

Isolde's long bony hand crept out and inched towards the Chalice. Her trembling fingers ran down the crack in the goblet and then closed about the stem of the Chalice. She drew in a deep, satisfied sigh and her eyes raised to meet Rollo's.

He smiled. Despite his exhaustion and worry, he couldn't help but smile. There was no need to declare his joy out loud. He could sense her triumph and relief, which sung out from her eyes in the same way as his own heart cried out in cheer and celebration: 'We did it! We have the Chalice!'